DRAGON
CHOIR

BENJAMIN DESCOVICH

To fathers lost

& fathers found.

For Kristin

Your faith is all I need.

I'm very grateful to

Amy Mildwaters,
Paul Descovich,
& Robert Brown.

Alpha Readers Extraordinaire.

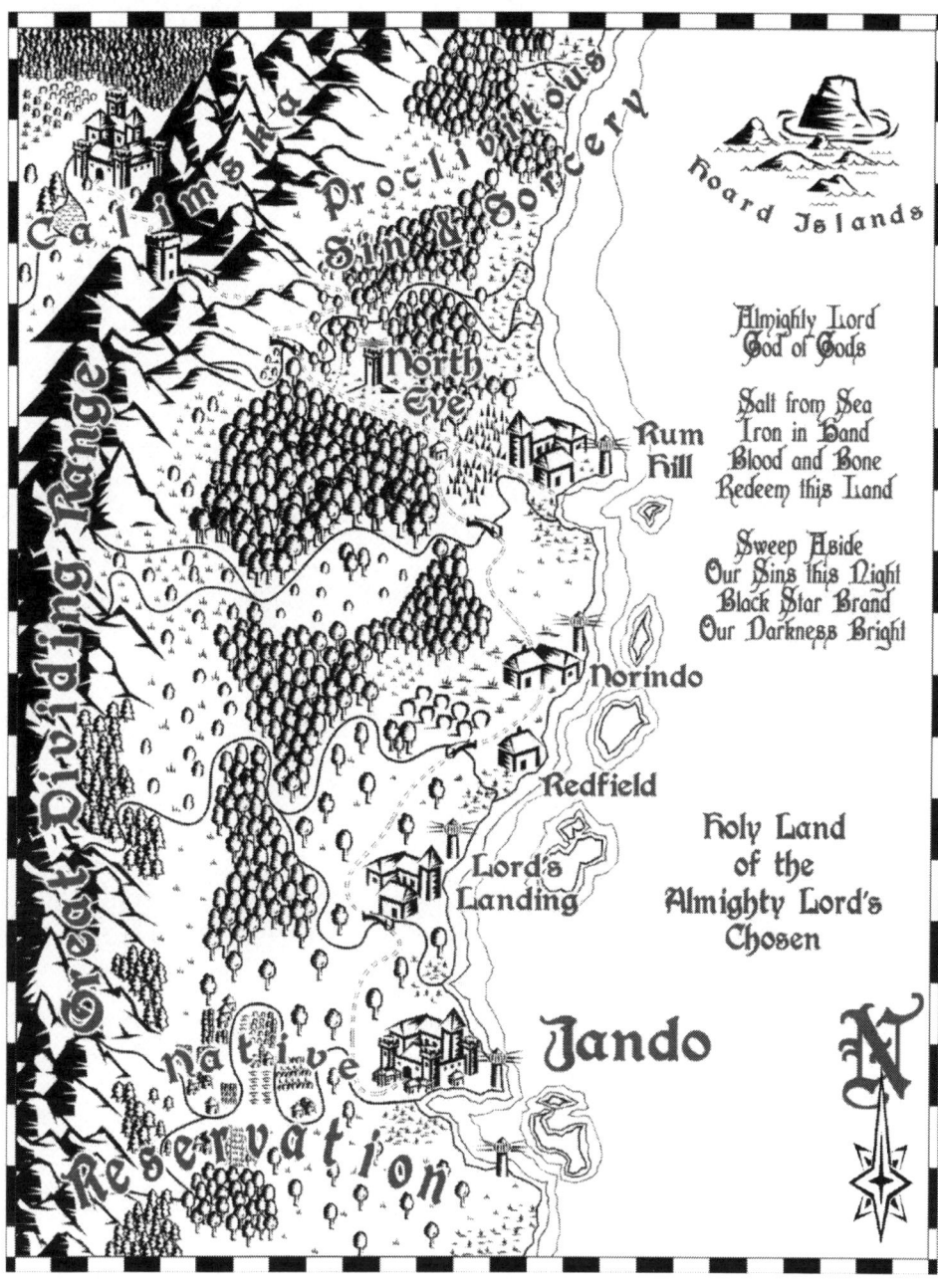

DELIVERY

Had the young man known of what would come, any premonition of the tempest he courted, he would have restrained such curiosity.

He knew it was wrong, but after the footman went upstairs, Elrin crept out of the antechamber and into the drawing room beside the Guildmaster's study. Ancient artefacts and peculiar devices crowded shelves and hung in glass cabinets along every wall. Elrin loved this room. It had the musty scent of knowledge; a sense of condensed thought. Shamanic totems of bone and feathers hung beside unusual metal machines, their springs and cogwheels still and silent. Yellowing maps and detailed charts mixed with rich oil paintings.

Each time he entered the room he was reminded of how little he understood of the world; how much he wanted to learn. The messages he couriered for Herder Kleith to the Guildmaster were another mystery. There were more of them every moon, strung up and sealed with unmarked black wax, different to the others Kleith had him deliver around the city. Without an official guild seal, the contents couldn't be of much consequence. What mattered was that he got paid, though the missive was already absorbing the sweat from his hands. With sensible haste, the young man dabbed the damp spots with his handkerchief and tucked it into his vest pocket, careful not to break the black seal. There'd be no chance of a silver tab if the message was damaged. An ink smudge would have his shine down to half a copper and that wouldn't buy a broken loaf.

Sweat beaded on his face, the stagnant air bestowed no mercy after the long run up the hill from the Hall of the Dead. The Guildmaster neglected making any improvements to the residence; an extra window here and there wouldn't have gone astray, the place was all bottled up.

The Guildmaster's rigid tones complained through the closed double doors of the study. Some poor sod was getting an earful, which was fine by

1

Elrin, it would give him more time to nose around in the drawing room. The Guildmaster had a mind for lengthy lectures and Elrin wasn't going to interrupt.

He inspected the trophies of knowledge, pondering their various uses, moving to each case and cabinet, peeking through the glass displays, taking care not to touch them. Each step gentle, testing the timber for creaks before he applied his weight.

After a circuit of the room he came to his favourite piece, an elegant dagger. Unlike the rest of the artefacts, this weapon was not jailed in glass, pinned to a stand or framed on a wall. It rested on a low table near the door to the Guildmaster's office, as if it too was waiting, forgotten.

Elrin knelt down to admire it; it was beyond him how such exquisite craftsmanship would be left out to gather dust. In sympathy he gathered it up, reverently nursing the antique blade. Its handle welcomed his grip; the balance was perfect. He caressed the foreign symbols etched across the curved blade.

The Guildmaster's voice pressed though the walls, stealing Elrin's attention away from the dagger. The ageing sorcerer was losing his temper; nothing unusual. The other voice yelled something coarse and unintelligible. This promised gossip; and gossip was valuable. One of the tavern lasses would pay well to hear who was brave, or daft enough to yell at the Guildmaster. Elrin pressed his ear to the door.

"No! You listen to m—" the Guildmaster yelled, but was cut off. It was unclear what the other was saying. The guest's voice was audible yet somehow, indistinct, as if the wood from the thick door would not let it pass. Elrin repositioned his ear over the keyhole.

"... increase production. The Council's veiled threats will not persuade me otherwise." The Guildmaster, paced past the door.

Elrin pulled back from the keyhole thinking he was caught, but the door remained closed and the argument continued inside. He considered returning to the seat in the waiting room. If he was found snooping with the Guildmaster in this temper, he risked losing his job—and worse. Mother would be disappointed once more, then she'd cry again. He hated it when she cried.

While turning to leave the drawing room and wait, as he should have to begin with, a single word struck through the door and grabbed Elrin's attention.

Arbajkha.

What had Father to do with the argument? Maybe he wasn't dead. Had he returned after so long? Could it be true? Mother would be happy like before. He'd make everything bright again.

Elrin went back to the keyhole and listened. His heart beat in his ears and he clasped at the dagger's grip, straining to hear. Something shifted.

Elrin's ear heard only stones rubbing and the trampling of sodden earth, but his mind fathomed the meaning; somehow comprehended a language. It was disconcerting. His sense of space twisted, leaving him dizzy. It was as though he were being tugged through the door and down, deep into the darkness of the dirt.

The voice morphed into understanding; slick with confidence. "It will be no more difficult than it was for Arbajkha. That worked out, and he was a surprise."

The Guildmaster's voice cracked in anger. "No, it's not the same and you know it. This is too ambitious; it's not what we agreed on. The forces you toy with can't be trusted. They wield power akin to the gods."

"I assure you, I have everything in hand. The risk is all mine."

"As is the debt."

"What other choice do you have?"

"How soon? I will have to recalibrate the net and increase the dampeners. Do you realise how many complications you've introduced? Have you even considered the draw this will need for the transition?"

"Worry about the transition later, just ready the net."

Elrin didn't know what they spoke of, or if it mattered, he had just one question seared in his mind like a brand.

Where is my father?

Stones collided and soil churned, "Who speaks?"

A ripple of energy washed past him and swept back, probing like a hungry eel.

Elrin pushed away from the door and stumbled backwards. His arm reached for support and found a display case. His momentum was too great and the case tipped over. Elrin fell on his back and the glass case shattered beside him. Fragments scattered across the polished floor.

The door burst open, slamming against the wall, revealing the Guildmaster with a look of supreme irritation across his angular face. Golden robes hung on his thin limbs like linen drying on a line. A moment of calculation pulsed across his tight, even features.

Elrin hurried to his feet, glass biting his knees. He hid his hands behind his back, hoping the Guildmaster hadn't noticed the dagger. He had to run, but there was no window from the drawing room for a quick escape. If he could make it back out the front door and hit the streets fast enough, the old Guildmaster wouldn't catch him.

The Guildmaster's lips curled in a strange guttural incantation and he pulled an embalmed frog from a belt pouch, crushing it in his fist. Magical essence seethed around his robed arm, surged up his neck and erupted from his mouth towards Elrin. The energy encased Elrin in a constricting embrace, folding over him and through him until he was seized in place; paralysed. He had to concentrate just to breathe.

"He is a liability," the disembodied voice of stone and dirt uttered an avalanche. "He must be dealt with."

"He's protected. An investor felt that ..." the Guildmaster hesitated in thought, staring at Elrin.

"Well, now you have an excuse," boulders split and fell into a swamp. "End him!"

The energy warped around him and then evaporated, retracting the presence and leaving the air tight like the skin on a drum.

The Guildmaster opened the back door to his study and rang a bell beside it. Four warriors responded immediately, their scabbards clacked against their armour as they filed through. Their surcoats bore the insignia of the city guard with the golden sun rising over the mountain range, but these were no ordinary city guardsmen. City guards were fitted with short swords and light armour, maybe a spear or pike for sentry duty. These men had their own weapons, broad swords and axes. The leader walked with a mercenary swagger, like the sellswords that loitered around the trading post.

"Get him out of here, Malek," said the Guildmaster.

Malek bowed his head, so as not to look the Guildmaster in the eye. He glanced over the scene, noting Elrin's paralytic state.

"Official business Master?" Malek rubbed his neck and grimaced.

"No." The Guildmaster brushed the frog's powdered remains from his hands into a dustbin. "Take him to the slumper alley."

"Does he need an introduction?"

Malek waited for an instruction, but none came. The Guild Master sat down at his desk and took a sheet of paper from the top drawer. He dipped his quill in ink and scratched away.

"Guildmaster?"

"No!" The Guild Master slammed his hand on the desk, breaking his quill and tipping over the ink well. "A farewell, Malek. This is to be a farewell."

Malek bowed, and motioned his men forward to collect Elrin. Two took his arms and one his legs, lifting him out through the study door.

Elrin struggled to move and panicked; his lungs could not keep pace with the pulsing of his heart. He strained to send a limb into motion, to wiggle a finger, even to blink. Nothing would work. He gave up trying as the guards carried him down winding stairs and through a confusion of dank passages. Breathing became his priority.

They stopped at a dark green door with a torch burning beside it. Malek's keys jingled in the lock and the door opened with a shove. They lifted Elrin outside and rested him against a stone wall in the alley beyond.

A gang of ruffians and delinquents crowded around a game of dice. Seeing the guards emerge from the green door, they gathered up their shine from the cobbles and backed away, pulling their weapons out, ready for an attack. Unstable eyes considered their chances against the city guards. These men were on edge. Their eyes were black wells, unsure whether to run or fight. Others lay beside the wall on piles of hessian and straw, their haphazard positions betraying an unnatural slumber.

One of the guards, the biggest among them, kicked an unconscious addict in the ribs. "Piss off slumper! You lot too. Take ya skagin' arses out of here!"

The slumper stumbled to his feet, half dazed. His remaining wits spurred him to flee down the alley and the dice players followed. The big guard kicked another slumper dozing in a sky dream and moved him on too.

"Get some ink, roach!"

The guards laughed. One hurled a stone after the fleeing man. It missed and skittered across the cobbles.

Elrin assembled his thoughts, searching for an escape.

A meaty hand slapped him across the face then grabbed his chin. "Right then. You're off for the long snooze like a good little slumper."

⬥⬥⬥

The alley was narrow and drenched in cold shadow from the high stone wall behind him. Red brick tenements rose across the other side with willows crowding beside a small courtyard wall, eager to watch his fate. The burly guard tipped Elrin to the ground. He hit the cobbles, stiff like a plank, but felt nothing of the impact.

"You got the blaze?" asked one of the guards.

"No," Malek cut back. "Why would I have it?"

"Well we don't, you know. We didn't ... I mean, we've never ..." The guard looked to the others for help, but none was offered.

"You think I just carry around a kit to get set up on my break?" Malek shoved the guard into the stone wall. "I'm no slumper!"

"You had the blaze with you last time is all. I just thought."

Malek struck his foot against the green door, slamming it shut. "Ash to all of it! How many more of these do we have to do?"

The guards waited in silence as their captain cooled off.

Malek opened the green door. "Right. You pillocks keep an eye on him while I go back and get the kit." He stomped away into the passage under the wall.

"So what did you do, eh?" The mouthy guard stood over Elrin's head. "What's the matter, can't you talk?"

The guards chuckled with the self-congratulating idiocy of practiced thugs.

The mouthy guard leant over Elrin and struck him across the face. "Feel

5

that?"

Elrin's body crumpled over. Blows thumped upon him, brittle brown leaves crackled as his body scuffed the cobbles with every kick. He felt no pain, but his ears were insulted by the stupid, juvenile laughter of the guards having their fun. With no control of where he looked, his vision skipped from stone wall, to red brick; blue sky, to black.

He didn't want to see, but the darkness swallowed his breath and panic clawed at him. Was he dead? No, he still heard the taunts and the scraping of his body against the ground. Not dead yet, but soon he would be. Perhaps he should welcome it. He was tired of his life; almost twenty and not one tattoo to show for it. He knew more than any apprentice his age, but books were as good as dust without a father. No guild apprenticed without a father's approval, so he'd never get his ink; he had nothing.

There was only hope if his father lived. But, where was he? Was he here in Calimska? What did the Guildmaster have to do with his father? So many questions wrenched at him.

He searched for any trace of feeling from the beating, but there was nothing physical, his paralysis was complete. All at once, Elrin's vision rushed back. One of the other men was jumping on his abdomen and laughing at the mouthy guard who had his shoe off, rubbing his foot in pain.

"Ya never learn Ginny. Boot'n 'em hurts like kickin' a rock. Jumpin's more fun. Look at him. Can't even frown!"

Malek came through the green door holding a leather pouch. "Get off him, arseholes!"

"C'mon Captain," whined the guard. "Once the Guildmaster stiffs 'em up, ya can't hurt 'em none."

"You're no good to me with broken bones. Off!"

"Get this Captain," said Ginny. "I reckon I know this poor bastard. His ma's the old Pride of the Bard's guild; that plum who's all mournful these days. What's her name?"

"How would I know his mother's name? He's the errand boy for some priest of Nathis, Herder Kleith or something. Who cares?"

Ginny put his boot back on. "You fellas remember that bird don't cha? I reckon I could make her happy again. Though she'd be crying right after."

They all laughed, stirring Elrin's defeat into burning anger.

"Cor, she's a looker. Big pair a lungs on her, eh. And those outfits make your mind travel." Ginny thrust his hips.

They laughed again and Elrin strained in his petrified state. He was sick of being the bastard son, the relic of celebrity and the arse end of jokes. He was tired of Calimska and all its rules, the damn guilds who wouldn't have him. Everyone had him marked for scorn and it burned in him. An angry heat seethed inside. It raged against the magical bonds cast upon his body.

Malek held a flame to the bottom of a stoppered glass tube. Elrin watched and boiled inside. The powder within turned to vapour and the guard captain knelt beside him, jamming the vessel in Elrin's mouth. He drew it into his lungs and his vision swam. Rage exploded, searing through his body. The fire reignited his senses and energy rushed through his limbs.

Elrin gripped his hands to fists and found the dagger's hilt already upon his palm. He sprang up and slashed out with the mysterious blade, driven by an urgency to cut and kill before the poison shut him down. The first slash tore across Ginny's face and he fell to the ground, struggling to hold his mouth together, blood pouring across his clasping hands. Elrin wheeled around and caught another guard's arm reaching for his sword upon the cobblestones. Blood coursed through the air and splattered on the pavement while the guard shrieked and grasped his wound, falling to his knees.

Captain Malek drew his sword. "How in the five hells did you do that? That lot would've put down an ox."

With his mind aflame, and chest heaving, Elrin boiled with power out of his control. The young man's hands shook and the dagger seemed to pulse in his tight grip, as though it were alive and hungry for more blood.

The remaining two guards drew their swords and edged toward him.

Elrin was no battle hardened warrior, he did what a lowly messenger did best. He ran.

IN A DOOR, OUT A WINDOW

Elrin fled down the alley, feet tingling with every stride. The blaze whipped at his heart and his vessels thrummed with power, pushing thoughts through his mind faster than his legs could travel. Searching for a way to safety, he careened out of the alley onto Merchant Circuit which bustled with trade. He jostled and weaved through the crowd, dodging around an elderly woman and vaulting over a vegetable cart. He leapt further than he expected and ploughed headlong into a rack of colourful silk garments. Scrambling to his feet and trailing green and yellow brocade, he darted down the adjoining alley. Halfway down, he chanced a glimpse over his shoulder. Malek, the guard captain, had caught up after the fall, taking the turn into the alley alone.

With a swing of his arm, Elrin knocked over a stack of crates and sped on, Malek's heavy footfalls still pounding behind him. The guard captain crashed through the hazard like a raging orc, cursing and yelling for blood.

After a dogleg in the alley, Elrin spotted another of the Guildmaster's men at the next street opening, flanked by two city guards. They shouted and drew their swords, muscling down the narrow backstreet, blocking any escape. The only door was without a handle and no amount of shoving would make it budge; there was no way out. He backed up to the door holding his dagger tight, ready for his last stand.

Elrin raised his eyes to the heavens praying to Nathis to take him to paradise. There above him his eyes found the gift of an open window; Nathis must be have been too busy to take his soul. Not one to let an opportunity pass by, Elrin clenched the blade between his teeth and leapt for the sill. His hands found it and he pulled himself through, arms still surging with unnatural strength.

The blaze crashed through his system while the city guards ran off down the alley, one of them ringing a bell. Every clang registered in his ears like a brass cymbal upside the head. They'd be back soon and the whole city would be out for him. Malek ordered one of his men to kick in the door. "You just wait up there, you can't run from me."

Elrin shut the window, squinting in the dim storage room where barrels were mounted on stands and the yeasty whiff of spilled beer fouled the air. There was a door. He took his chances, running out and knocking into a barkeep. The startled man was quick to grab at his collar, but Elrin was faster.

He bounded left and right, dodging tables and pushing past the morning drunks nursing their tankards. As he got to the front door, it burst in and four city guards blocked his escape.

Elrin swung around, chest heaving, eyes wild. He charged up the stairs, taking the full flight in three paces. Dashing down a narrow hall, he tested each door, desperate to put a barrier between him and his pursuers, but none would open. Elrin rushed to the window at the end of the hall which wouldn't open either, so he cracked the hilt of his dagger through the glass and clipped off the remaining shards. He was about to go through when the door beside him opened.

A woman stood in the doorway wearing a short silk nightdress. Her hair fell wild about her shoulders in a tumble of cinnamon and saffron. Dark eyes appraised him.

"Try my window." The woman beckoned him in. "I've a much better view."

Elrin's voice stuck in his dry throat. He entered her room, unable to refuse or think with clarity. The woman winked, closed the door between them and locked it.

Guards, thundered up the stairs and down the hall. The beautiful woman stopped them outside, but Elrin could not make out her words.

What if she trapped him and was after an easy reward for his capture? He moved to her window and tested it. It opened with well-oiled ease. He hesitated a moment, checking for guards down on the street below. It was perfect. The high roofline obstructed most of the street view, concealing his exit.

Once out the window, he padded across the tiled roof to the side of the inn. He jumped across the gaps between the buildings, careful not to be seen and descended to the street, using the down pipe of a nearby building. He began to jog along back streets, heading home, then the futility of the plan struck him.

They knew where he lived. City guards were already being posted to each corner of his block. He would never get past them all. The only option was to return to Herder Kleith. He would help.

Elrin backtracked towards the inn. There were no guards, but some locals gathered near to the front door, gossiping and gawking inside. People would still be on the lookout for him.

A young vendor smiled with a conspiratorial wink. His stall was an upturned crate just inside an alley off Merchant Circuit.

He waved Elrin over. "Fair clip you get on those pins. Faster than most what I've seen."

The vendor was around Elrin's age. Like Elrin, he was a man ready for ink, but had none to show. Messy black hair licked across his brow and his clothes were rough spun. His display of ornaments for sale were precisely ordered, graded by size and colour in three neat rows.

Two city guards came down the main road in their direction. Elrin edged further into the alley, ready to run.

"Easy now," The vendor placed a small statue into Elrin's hand. "Just have a peek at the wares and a natter. They won't notice you here. They're out for a rabbit not a fox."

Elrin pretended to inspect the scrimshaw trinkets and sandalwood beadwork. He made every effort to keep his back to the road, instinct urging him to face the threat. He bottled it all down, forced his feet to stand still. He picked up a statuette.

"Only the finest dragon bone, see."

"Really?" Elrin examined the small figurine of Ona, the Mother. "Looks like horn."

"Of course it is, my mistake. Dragon horn it is. And for three coppers, it's the perfect gift."

"Only three?" Elrin felt awkward. Was this a bribe to keep quiet? There was no chance the statuette was dragon horn at that price.

The scruffy vendor peered over Elrin's shoulder. "They're most past now," he whispered. "Just wait here and mind the merchandise for me."

The vendor walked out of the alley and onto Merchant Circuit proper. He looked up and down the road and returned with a knowing smile. "You're set to go. Want the Good Mother for your travels?"

"Thanks, but no. I don't have anything to give." Elrin shook his empty pouch to prove it.

"If you've pissed off a guilder then you're all right with me. See now, with no ink on you and none on me, we're almost brothers."

"If it's all the same, you keep it." Elrin left the Ona statuette on the table. "Thanks for your help."

Elrin crossed onto Merchant Circuit and walked beside a wagon rolling down the street. An off street took him behind the leatherworkers' guild house. Further along, he ducked down a back alley. It was filthy with refuse. He followed the alley as it slunk left and right, collecting festering waste from the knacker's yard and the tannery vats. The alley became more like a drain than a thoroughfare; slick with green and brown algae. It terminated in a barred sewer entrance. He climbed up the iron grill and onto a small road running behind the Hall of the Dead and Herder Kleith's residence. He knocked on a small rear door and waited.

಼ೲ

After a moment Herder Kleith opened the door. Although he held the highest station as the Hand of Nathis, Herder Kleith dressed simply in robes of grey roughspun. There was no way of telling the rank or station between each herder, they all wore the same. Elrin knew Kleith's kind face though. It was a welcome sight.

"Have they come?" Elrin looked up and down the alley and peered in the room behind the priest. "Are the guards here?"

"Your eyes child. My, what is wrong with them? They're set to burst."

"Please Kleith. Are they in there too? Tell me and I'm gone. I won't bring this on you if they are ... are they?"

"No child. Quickly now, in, in." Kleith coaxed Elrin through the door, shutting and bolted it after him. "Come and sit."

The priest guided Elrin to a plush lounge and let him sit. Elrin's hands shook and his jaw was clenched, grinding his teeth to sand.

Herder Kleith rang a small bell and Elrin jumped. "Easy child, I only call for tea."

"Sorry, Kleith. The Guildmaster rang his bell too and he wanted me dead. He cast a spell on me, I couldn't move and then these guards came. They were dressed like city guards, but they kicked me and jumped on me. The guards, they ..." Elrin traced the sigils on the daggers blade, curious that no blood marred the steel after the fight. "I think I killed one. There was so much blood."

Kleith set his brows together, but his eyes softened. "Firstly, tea. Then we will start from the beginning."

Tea came and Elrin told his story. Herder Kleith listened closely.

"This is indeed serious."

"I have to get back to Mother. They might have her. They might think she knows where I am. What if they kill her?" Elrin's mind raced into a panic and he stood up. "I have to go warn her."

"No. That is not wise. You must escape. I will protect her."

"Then what of Father? Why were they speaking of him? Why would they want to kill me for eavesdropping? I don't even understand what they were on about."

"This dagger you mentioned. The one you used against the guards. Do you have it with you?"

Elrin presented the dagger without hesitation.

Kleith gingerly reached out and touched the blade then winced, recoiling

11

and shaking his hand as though it had bitten him. The hilt grew hot and the sigils glimmered gold.

"Describe it to me Elrin. Is the blade curved? Is there a large black stone at the end of the hilt?"

"It's right here. Can't you see it?"

"It wishes to remain unseen to me. It is wise. You had best follow its good example. Come, we must get some robes. They won't be searching for a herder."

The guilder took the young man upstairs to a dressing room and fitted him in the grey garb. The garments were baggy enough to fit over his clothes, hanging to his knees with long sleeves that covered his hands. A cowl hung low over his face, concealing his features.

Kleith rushed about anxious for him to leave. Elrin knew he was trying to keep him from harm, but all he wanted was an explanation. There was so much unsaid. Kleith knew something. He had to. What was he holding back?

"Why don't you speak of Father when I ask? You were his best friend. He must be alive. He might be here. Don't you want to find him too?" Elrin tried to catch Kleith's eyes, to find some sign of the truth, but the collector averted his gaze and focused on packing a satchel.

"There is much afoot here Elrin. Calimska is folding upon itself and you are not safe here. Your mother will not be safe with you here either. You must leave."

Tears welled in Elrin's eyes. "But, what of Father? What of him?"

Kleith gripped his shoulders, his own eyes moist. "You are Arbajkha's son indeed. He was always at the point of a situation. Always in the wrong place at the wrong time. That dagger followed him around too you know."

Twisting the weapon, Elrin remembered his father's bedtime stories of heroic adventure. The tears took over; it was all too much. Kleith had been there for Elrin and his mother, but he never spoke the name Arbajkha. Not since his father left. Mother was the same. For all Elrin's asking they never spoke of him. His mother would cry and Kleith would comfort. Things were better for his mother without hearing of Arbajkha and now she would not hear of Elrin.

He had to go, or die. He didn't understand why, but knew it was serious. Kleith always looked out for them and knew what was right.

"Easy child, leave these tears." Kleith put his arm around Elrin's shoulders again, his grip firm and comforting. "You must be strong if we are to aid your father."

Elrin's heart leapt. Father is alive! Just as he always believed. He took a deep breath and did his best to stem the tears. He would be strong and listen.

"You must travel to the Hoard Islands. Seek the Dragon Choir."

"Dragon Choir? You mean the Dragon Cord, like in the legends of Drensel Tath?"

"No. You must seek the aid of the Choir."

A loud banging on the door downstairs gave Elrin a start.

"Quickly, there's no time. Take the hall to the resting chambers then leave through the chapel. Make haste!" Herder Kleith rose and left the room.

Elrin grabbed the satchel, stuffing the dagger inside and raced down the hall, careful not to thump his heels on the boards. He passed through an arch and down a spiral staircase that led him below ground to the chambers of respite. Glow pots and candles illuminated scores of dead at rest. It made him uneasy, the mourning silence thickening the chill air where the dead lay to farewell the living.

He hurried through the dank chamber into the chapel's gentle warmth. His unceremonious entrance drew a glare from a priest kneeling in prayer. Elrin slowed to a brisk walk and bowed in apology, keeping his face concealed.

"And don't forget the crook this time prentice, lest it be your last. Plenty more poor boys to replace your forgetful lump of adolescence." The Priest returned to his prayer and Elrin did as he was told, seeking the crook to avoid suspicion.

The crook was a tall wooden staff with a silver incense condenser hanging from a chain. Elrin had witnessed Kleith prepare the crook many times before and repeated the ritual, adding several hot coals to the condenser followed by three squares of resin. He shut the lid and smoke began to rise from the silver lattice of the condenser; a little too much smoke.

"Get out of the chapel with that, you dolt! By Nathis boy; the lost are out there. Out! Out!"

Elrin opened the chapel door and moved into the street. He squinted in the glare and waited for his eyes to adjust. People in the street kept their distance. They covered their noses to avoid the smoke billowing from the crook, as if breathing the incense would call Nathis to take their souls while they still lived. It was a ridiculous notion, but convenient for him nonetheless.

The vapours still pumped in his system. It was an effort not to break into a sprint for the gates and keep on running. Elrin got to the end of the road where a market square began. Four guards were on watch, waiting at the market entrance. Elrin kept a steady walk and held the crook high in front of him. He concentrated on an easy gait, transferring a gentle swing to the condenser with each step. One of the guards looked straight at him for a moment, but did nothing. The others averted their eyes, hoping to avoid the death collector's attention.

Elrin continued through the market square and took Lake Road through to the Silk Gate. Wagons and riders trying to leave the markets were being stopped at the barbican while guards inspected their cargo, searching for a stowaway.

A wave of nausea swept over him. All he wanted to do was turn and run. People on foot were passing in a steady flow through the wicket gate, but a guard stood either side of the passage, eyeing off those leaving the city. Elrin was about to turn around and seek another way out of the city when the guards pulled a young man to the side. People kept moving through the pedestrian access while the poor fellow was searched and questioned.

Elrin's gut squirmed, but he took his chance, pressing ahead to the passage through the city walls. The crowd made way for him and the guards gave him no notice at all. He passed through the pedestrian access without being stopped.

Further down Lake Road he felt his legs growing weak and headed to the shade of a tree. The violent surge of strength had vanished and his vision swam. The blaze vapours were making a rapid retreat, leaving his body empty and the world distorted. Elrin fought to contain his gut and failed, retching beside the tree, spasms contorting his insides. With a throbbing head and trembling limbs, Elrin crawled away from the foul mess and rested against the tree.

He worried over how to reach the Hoard Islands and find the Dragon Choir. Thinking of his mother all alone, staring out the window awaiting his return, clouded his eyes with tears again. Kleith would take care of her; keep her safe. He wiped the tears away; crying would likely attract attention. Not that the vomiting wouldn't. Although, people mightn't think a drunken apprentice was so far out of the ordinary.

Wagons rolled by on their way between the market square; inside the city walls and the trading post; not far from his tree. Most of the wagons were small traders from the local area, their wagons packed solid with produce from the fields and orchards. A few were heading out of town, but the empty wagons that he might fit in were likely headed back to the farms of nearby hamlets. The wagons going through the mountain pass to the east were the only option.

Elrin gathered his strength, pulling himself up to stand with the crook for support and staggered to the trading post, seeking passage to the coast.

TRADING POST

Minni urged her painted mare forward, cutting ahead of the carriages and wagons that were backed up from Calimska's Silk Gate. Merchants and farmers stuck in the queue called to each other, trying to find out what was going on. Just before she got to the portcullis, two guards stepped in her path.

One had his thumbs tucked in his sword belt, splaying his tanned arms out like a roast chicken. "Citizen?"

"Not on your life, the food here's much too salty," Minni smiled, hoping the guard could take a joke.

"Permit?"

"All talk aren't you." Minni leant forward, searching through a saddlebag.

"That's a lovely bodice, Miss. Where do you go to from here, so well equipped?"

Minni lifted her head to speak to the guard, but his eyes strayed to her chest; men were so simple, it made her job all the easier.

"I know I put it in here somewhere," she pouted. "I always lose these things. Perhaps, you would just let me through?"

The guard shook his head and gave his partner a sly grin. "This one'll need a pat down, I reckon. Jandan spy, no doubt."

Minni laughed. "Have you ever seen a Jandan woman? No? That's because they are all house bound sipping tea and praying to their one Lord almighty. What are you going to search me for anyway? Do you want to see the rest of my smalls? Is that it? You dirty little perversion. Save your mitts for the whores you can afford on your fancy streets of gold."

Her vitriol roused a crowd of onlookers. The traders and farmers waited for the guard's response, a few even heckled from the back. The guard was lost for words. Being sliced to ribbons by the sharp tongue of a woman wasn't how he imagined his opportunistic search to turn out.

His commanding officer strode over. "Just let her through Guffer. Does it look like a kid could hide away in those saddlebags?" He clipped the back of Guffer's head. "Hurry it up, twit!"

The crowd laughed and jeered at the guards.

"Thanks. Guffer was it? I'll remember your kindness."

"Right, well bugger off then. Smartarse Reik." Guffer stepped away from the horse and let Minni pass.

Minni galloped to the trading post, hoping she had not missed her target. Under the rising heat of the morning, a collector of Nathis staggered on the side of the road, leaning on a crook. A stain streaked down his robes. Another pissed prentice no doubt, off drinking with the dead.

The trading post was as big as most of the hamlets skirting Calimska, the great City of Gold. It grew like the weeds after dragon season had passed, a sprawling mass of traders, merchants, and opportunists. Minni preferred the chaos of the trading post to the regulation the guilds enforced in Calimska. She guessed it was set up outside the city for that very reason. It kept the rabble outside and the best shine safely inside the gates.

Minni took a side track to bypass the hectic trade yards, riding via the ale tents and food stalls, wary of cutpurses mingling in the traffic. On the eastern side of the makeshift trading town were the loading yards. Wagons and carts lined up on both sides of the road; one side for loading and leaving, the other unloading for trade.

Minni dismounted and tied her horse to a hitching post outside the noisiest ale tent. It sprawled across an empty yard next to the waiting wagons. The sides of the tent were torn and there had been little effort to patch it up, given the patrons wandered through the holes like doors. The roof was intact at least, and the cool breeze that flowed through the ragged holes was a pleasant change in the rising heat.

Porters, roadies and sellswords passed the time with dice and drink. Barrels of cheap ale created a wall behind the bar at the back of the tent. Minni approached the counter, ignoring the whistles and common calls from the roughnecks she passed. She caught the attention of a skinny girl who was listing jobs wanted and vacancies on a chalkboard nailed to the wall of barrels.

"Got one, or you lookin'?" The girl wiped her nose with the back of her hand, rubbing a stripe of chalk on her face.

"Looking." Minni tapped the bar with a tab of gold. "You still taking the shine?"

"Till season's come." The girl stepped away from the board and walked to the bar. "What favour's it for, or are ya givin' it away?"

"What's the latest? Have the Jandan rollers come up?"

The girl slipped the tab off the bar and tucked it into her apron pocket along with the stick of chalk. "Two unloaded the mornin' past with slaves I'd say. This mornin' has barrels goin' on. Don't know what's in em' though. No chalk on the boards for either, there never is. They've always got their own crew; same in, same out."

"Have they left yet?"

"Doubt it. That's some of 'em over there. There was another fella too; all hands and swill."

"No loss then," Minni gave the girl another tab of gold. "Keep them from thirst. And keep it to yourself."

Minni left the bar and found a stool near the Jandans. Their language clashed against the soft notes of the lyrical Calimskan tongue. Though it was harsh, Jandan was easier for Minni than the complex tones of Calimskan. Jandan speech cut with precision and thrust with guttural contempt. It was a language struggling with righteousness and sin.

She listened in to their conversation; their companion was quite late. Minni waited while the Jandan caravan guards plied themselves with her complimentary ale. During the first round they eyed off each of the patrons in the tent and argued over who their benefactor might be. The second round had them toasting all of the patrons in the tent with good cheer. By the third round the conversation increased in candour and volume. Between the odd bad joke and self-aggrandising they debated the whereabouts of their missing comrade, supposing he was their mysterious benefactor supplying the drinks. His failure to show up for duty justified their excuses to remain and drink.

"What if he returns and we're gone?" said one.

"No honour in that!" said another.

"Never leave a man behind!"

They could not reach any sensible consensus on the adventures of their comrade after his last drink with them the afternoon gone. Had he eloped with the girl he spoke of meeting? Or had he fallen to the dice? Perhaps he won so much shine he could stay in Calimska till the season passed?

Minni was quite amused by all of their stories. She knew his fate to be far less glamorous than their elaborate imaginings. The chalk girl was on the mark; the man was all hands and swill. If he had any manners to go with his looks, he could have enjoyed a late night and a longer life. But, as Minni found out many times before, Jandans had great difficulty affording much respect to the finer sex.

It was just past midday when the sergeant strode into the ale tent searching for his men. His face beaded with perspiration and his moustache was slick. The Jandan was a man of distinguished girth and had difficulty allowing for it in the fit of his uniform. His neck and head thrust out like an angry bull, red from the tightness of his collar and the temper of the moment.

"What by the charity of our Lord gives you reason to hold the shipment this long? Tegit? Come on man! Where is your dim wit scout?" The sergeant noted the men were dulled with drink. "Have any of you the ability for your mission?"

"We're not all that drunk, sir. Just a lil jolly is all." Tegit stood and saluted to prove his capability. The salute succeeded well enough, defying his inebriation. Sitting down proved harder than standing and he stumbled backwards over his stool.

"You've had half the morning to find him. Where in all the hells has he got to?"

The men looked to each other for support. None was sure what they thought had happened to him.

"Answer me!"

"Deserted, sir." The guard who spoke did not try to stand, knowing that such an action would lead him to the ground beside Tegit. "We thought to wait a pint longer. In case ..."

"In case what? He came back with a trifle for you all?"

"No, sir."

"Are any of you fit?" The sergeant sat down on a bench, exasperated.

Minni stepped forward and addressed the sergeant before they answered. The men were relieved by her distraction.

"Might I offer my services, sir?"

"You're Jandan? No. Your accent ... Reik is it? What do you have to offer? Tell our fortune? I can guess that, lass."

"Outrider, sir," said Minni, seeking to appease his authority.

"Woman though. I don't think you cou—"

"Better than this lot, sir. I've had an opportunity to overhear some of their talk. It wasn't all that quiet. If you're headed for Rum Hill I can scout for you. I know the trail. I have my own kit and mount."

"You ready to ride?"

"Just have to unhitch my mare from out front."

"What's your price sellsword? Will you take gold?"

"Ash on that. I'm no man's fool. You're headed the wrong way for shine to be any use. Eighty in shell ... plus rations."

"Cowries?" The sergeant raised his hands to the heavens. "Sinner be damned! That's more than this lot twice over."

"And who do you imagine will ride well enough to earn a quarter their keep? You best be sorting your men out should you face a challenge on the trail."

The sergeant's eyes narrowed in frustration as he appraised his inebriated crew. "Right then, I've no shell here. You'll be paid on delivery in Rum Hill. Done?"

"Done."

Minni left the tent, took her horse over to the wagons and introduced herself to the drivers. They were Jandan conscripts near the end of their service. She noticed a cloaked figure in the shadows.

This had better not be another change. Why can't they keep to the damn plan? She kept the figure in her peripheral vision and maintained the conversation, wondering who was thick enough to contact her this late in the operation. The figure crept towards the rear wagon.

The other wagon drivers gathered around Minni, asking inane questions and openly leering. She felt for their poor wives, suffering the mistakes of marrying such base creatures. Her sympathy was short lived; there was work to be done, and these dolts had their uses.

"Damn hot today, don't you think?" Minni opened a button on her blouse and fanned herself. "They got you pushing loads till first shadow like last season? Caught a lot of good men out last year."

The men took in the view and shared their thin wisdom on the difficulties of the job. With the guards distracted, Minni chanced a direct look at the cowled figure skulking closer to the wagons. It was the collector from earlier. He must have lost or traded his crook and was staggering rather than sneaking to the rear wagon. If the contact was injured, Minni would need a bigger distraction than her cleavage.

Minni tested the tension on the ropes of the lead wagon.

"Is this rigging secure enough for the road through the pass? I heard a trader going on about a downpour up there this morning. Might be a touch bumpy."

The drivers bustled around the rigging, checking it over and arguing their opinion on its condition. They were soon split on how it should be altered to accommodate any damage to the road. Some thought it was fine, but others were sure they would need more rope to keep the barrels from jostling out.

Minni stood back, letting them argue while the collector stowed away in the rear wagon. There must be a message for her. She went to the rear canvas and secured it, ensuring no one else noticed. The sergeant emerged from the tent, his men falling in awkward step behind him. Complications of walking straight dissolved the heady residues of their earlier cheer, as did the sergeant's continual reprimands.

"Who's manning the rear wagon? Lord's mercy! Do I have to be all over your tails every bloody time?" The sergeant strode to the milling drivers at the lead wagon. "Get to your damn stations. We're rolling out. I want these wagons through the pass and safe by the North Eye before dark."

The drivers climbed to their seats, cracked their whips and the wagons were away, kicking up dust as they went.

"Reik! Get on your nag and scout no more than one mile ahead. Report anything unusual. You'll camp alone. I'll not let these imbeciles be tempted by another witch."

Minni let him go on, imagining her blade sinking through the sergeant's swollen throat. She would let his words drown in the venom that pulsed in his heart. Jando, the City of Bones, would have no redemption from her.

Flesh to ash.

OUTRIDER

Minni paced her scouting just as the sergeant ordered. Better to keep him happy for the moment. She surveyed the road ahead of the wagons searching for signs of covered tracks or careless prints. Orc raiders would claim unwary caravans travelling through the pass. She doubted a hunting party would take on a heavily guarded convoy though; orcs were not as stupid as men made out.

Humans, on the other hand—they were brazen enough. The real danger were highwaymen. A couple of wagons in a train might be irresistible; the more guards, the more it was worth. Like Minni, they would love to have what the wagons carried.

The Council of Jando rattled sabres and the Guilds of Calimska soured tariffs. Tensions between the two powerful cities were building. Yet something else lurked beneath. Things were going on in the shadows and Minni had not been able to figure it out. Shipments of black powder had increased travelling to Rum Hill since the last moon. They knew the shipments sailed on to Jando. The rebels had eyes and ears all up the coast and nobody could tell Minni what Jando and Calimska were up to.

The road cut around the foothills up into the mountains. The miles peeled away into late afternoon with only a trickle of late season merchants heading for Calimska. In places the surface was washed out and pot holed, making her lie about the rainy weather seem true enough. The drivers were thankful for her earlier advice and encouraged her to ride with the wagons for some conversation—and likely, the fair view.

"Keep your eyes on the road fools," shouted the guard sergeant, riding up from behind. "And you ... do your job, woman. Quit your seductions, get up that range and find out what's ahead."

Minni wished to kill him now. She could do it if she wanted to. Most of the guards were still pickled. The sergeant might be a problem, but if she picked them off from a distance it would not be too difficult. No, that would be foolish. Minni would wait; patience was how they would win this campaign, she would see the plan through.

The collector hiding away in the rear wagon was a concern. If he were a messenger for her, why hadn't he contacted her earlier in Calimska? She was there long enough. She hoped the stowaway was just another youth running from an unsavoury apprenticeship. Whatever the reason, he'd be run through if he was found out; Jandan officers had no compassion. She'd see to him when they made camp. Food and water and some pointed conversation. He might have some useful information and could make an ideal recruit in any case.

They made good time through the pass, only at the cost of their draft horses. The poor animals' condition declined with the increasing grade and the relentless pace set by the guard sergeant. He allowed no breaks to feed or water them, none even to rest their legs and catch a breath. Chilled wind from the northern peaks blew down the old road, sapping the warmth from the sun, dimming her mood even more.

At the head of the pass the road thinned and the mountains rose on either side like a great rocky fence. The Calimskan outpost was wedged in between. It guarded Stoneheart's Bridge, the only safe access from the coast to Calimska and the many lands of the West. The bridge spanned the frigid waters of the ancient River Hiron, which melted off the Ice Peak Mountains far to the north, carving a treacherous course from stone to sea. The outpost tower huddled close to the mountainside as though it were afraid to look up to the peaks or down into the rapids far below. The natural geography of the mountain pass and the river gorge gave the outpost a perfect defensive position.

Minni stopped at the checkpoint with the wagons. Two pillars barred the way to the bridge, each made of interlocking stone blocks. The foundations of both were encircled with magical sigils, carved out of the stone. Calimskan soldiers gathered beside a brazier, playing cards on a small table.

The air around the pillars hardened with the proximity of the wagons and dancing arcs of energy began to play across the sigils. High on the tower battlements, a thick-faced man in brown woollen robes watched them. It was Stoneheart, the guardian of the pass.

The Jandans were tense. The wagon guard near Minni moved his hand to the crossbow slung at his side. Stoneheart paid the Jandans no mind; he was interested only in the wagons and the toll. His eyes tunnelled down, hesitating at the last wagon for just a moment.

The sergeant rode forward holding out a large purse to one of the soldiers by the brazier. The soldier checked its contents and placed the bag on a set of scales. The toll was of sufficient weight and he nodded up to

Stoneheart.

Without a word, the earth mage plunged his arms into the stone battlements. The ground vibrated and the two pillars blocking their way transformed. Each stone block tumbled apart then reassembled into two golems, both larger than a wagon on end. They shifted their immense forms to the side allowing the wagons to pass. The bridge across the river was made of stone like that of the golems. Large and small blocks fused together flawlessly in a complex pattern.

Minni led the wagon train across the span without delay. She hated crossing this damn bridge. Stoneheart's will bore them safely, but at any moment could pummel them with stones, set the giant golems on them or drop them to their deaths. What if the old bastard was having a bad day? Stoneheart's bridge stole all control from her and that was not a feeling she appreciated.

Riding down the range might have improved the horses' spirits had the sergeant not pushed the wagon train so hard. He swore and cursed at his drivers, goading the men to whip their horses bloody to outrun the closing fingers of night. The Great Dividing Range behind them cast an early dusk across the woodland below and long shadows swallowed the road. The silhouette of the mountain peaks cut against the orange and peach sunset like black blades.

After a long scout down into the forest without any sign of bandits, Minni returned to the wagons.

"The bridge across Dayglow Creek is down," she told the sergeant. "Might be best to make camp here and try a different way at first light."

"Hells to that. There must be another way past."

"There's an old track that splits off before it. That'll take us across upstream, but it might be harder for the wagons at night. I think we should stop and camp by the stream. Rest the horses."

"Quit wasting time and earn your keep, witch. Scout upstream."

"You might not make it through," Minni baited.

"Do you want a lash? We'll not stop in these damned dark woods with a witches moon on the rise."

The team of wagons proceeded, and when they reached the fork, Minni guided the lead wagon to the smaller trail off to the side of the main road.

She called to the lead driver. "There are a few dips, but nothing like the range before. Slippery though, so take it easy."

The track was clear and she urged her horse into a trot; she knew this track well by dark or by day. She came to the stream and dismounted, leading her horse to the slow rolling water to drink. Out of sight, Minni pulled a mouthpiece from her saddlebag and blew into it twice, sounding an ibis call into the shadows of the forest. After a short pause a call echoed back from the shadows across the stream. Minni blew again, elaborating a complex series of honks. She paused. The ibis called again followed by the wook wook of two barking owls on one side of the path. Then came the whistle and zip of a bristlebird from the other side.

Minni mounted again and rode back to the wagons making their way down the path to the stream.

"Clear ahead," she called to the first driver. "I'll wait on the other side of the stream to guide you through."

The driver nodded and kept on.

The wagons came down the small slope taking care not to wedge the wheels burdened by the heavy load in the sand. The lead wagon entered the water and the horses pulled it across the creek. Once the wagon's front wheels passed safely out the other side, the sergeant called the rear wagon to proceed down the slope.

Minni made a loud ibis call from her mouthpiece.

A rope sprung out of the sand and stretched tight, trapping the back axle of the lead wagon. The driver cracked his whip across the horses. The wagon lurched forward, but could not pull the wheels clear. Now at the bottom of the slope, the rear wagon was wedged in; neither could manoeuvre their way out.

The guard sergeant began yelling commands to his men, but was silenced by an arrow piercing his throat. Arrows danced from the shadows, taking the life of each man with silent accuracy. There was no opportunity for defence, no possibility of a counterattack. The only sound that remained after the short cries of the fallen was the restless murmur of the creek, playing the blood of the dead away into the darkness.

Shadows in the forest stretched forward, gathering around the wagons. The rising moon revealed men and women of motley height and build camouflaged in mud and ferns. They set to work. Each performed their task in silence, bow and blade slung to their backs. Some dragged bodies to litter bearers who took the dead into forest. Others cleaned the blood spilled on the wagons and steadied the horses.

Men in Jandan uniform emerged from the shadows as if the fresh dead had risen. They took up the positions of the former Jandan guard. A woman draped in an ochre poncho approached the horses. She whispered to each in turn, stroking their damp manes and offering them each a blue fruit. Minni's horse devoured the fruit quickly and nuzzled for more.

Once each horse received her attention she waded into the creek singing, water lapping at her thighs. She knelt down and dipped her body under. The song continued as she raised her head, water cascading over her body. Thin fabric clung to her delicate curves in the light of the lonely moon, her hands raised to the sky gathering light in each palm. Bringing them together in a cup she drew water from the stream and drank deeply. Moonlight rippled across her body, shimmering as though she had become water herself. She spread her arms in the direction of the horses and her song altered. Her voice blended with the murmur of the creek until all became quiet. Moonlight cascaded from her hands and enveloped the horses.

Energy rushed from the forest towards ochre woman. The charged air gathered with the scent of a breaking storm. The water bubbled and whirled, drawing into the wild mage's body until the creek drained to nothing, leaving her kneeling in damp sand. The woman dropped her hands and the magical light faded from around the horses. She slumped and waited in the sand. The water returned, replenished from upstream and she stood slowly, singing softly, returning to the forest.

❧❧

A tall thin man approached Minni after the wagons were pulled to the other side of the creek.

"Only watching this time. Why so?"

"Your crew is too fast, Wendal. I had my eye on sparring with the sweet sergeant. You never leave anything for sport. Never any time for play."

"This is no game."

"And yet you enjoy it so."

"Death is enough for the Jandans. No more."

Minni alighted from her mare with a chuckle. "You are too serious. You won't let me have any fun with you." She rummaged in her saddlebag and pulled out a leather pouch and threw it to Wendal.

He opened it and pulled out a handful of painted figurines. Wendal's face creased with a smile.

"Minella, I thank you."

"I know how much you love moving your pieces about on a map. Though, I can't see how it will improve your work any; this job was perfect. You need another hobby."

"Without Jaspa we must be extra cautious. What if they have him and are keeping it quiet? What if they already know our plans?"

Minni laughed. "The Jandans don't have Jaspa. If they did he'd be dead and they'd be singing in the cathedral so loud we'd hear it from here."

"How are you so sure?" Wendal studied her face. "Have you received word?"

"No. You?"

"Nothing." Wendal shifted his feet. "Is Delik up to this?"

"It's just a little hijack, Wendal."

"Hardly. *This* was a little hijack. That ... That will be a bloody miracle."

"Are you a believer now? Got an angel hiding somewhere?"

"Please, be wary. Kobb has no master except his ego. He'd turn for a

25

title; might have turned already. If they've bagged Jaspa, then you and Delik are next. You're vulnerable together."

"At least if all goes to ash, you've got new figurines. Who better to lead than you?" Minella winked at Wendal and mounted her horse.

Wendal frowned and returned to the wagons to talk to his men. Minni knew he was right. Honest Wendal; he never bothered with sweet lies. A lifetime digesting bitter truth had diminished his humour. He was a good friend, a true friend. It was wicked of her to toy with him. Minni thought of hollering something nice, but it would only embarrass him.

She rode ahead, following the old trail to where it rejoined the main road between Rum Hill and Calimska. North Eye stood alone atop a small hill cleared of trees. Warm light flickered through arrow loops and high windows. A timber stockade encircled the tower with torches lit around the perimeter.

They would have to hurry past the Jandan outpost to avoid detection. A bright flickering light caught her eye, pulsing out a complex series of flashes from somewhere up in the mountains. Had the Jandans spotted the ambush through the canopy of the forest?

The beacon on the North Eye pulsed a quick response then four pigeons were released. They circled around the tower several times before heading east. Two horsemen galloped out of the stockade and down the hill, heading right for her at the junction. They had been discovered. The Jandans knew. There must be a traitor in Wendal's crew.

If anyone had witnessed the ambush and given word, they would have to scrap the entire mission. Without cover from the Jandan caravan and its cargo, they would draw unwanted attention in Rum Hill.

The stowaway. Minni had forgotten all about him.

Wendal was right. Kobb double-crossed them. Mongrel! The Council would have sent a redeemer if they knew. At best the stowaway was just an agent, hitching a ride home. The Jandan guard sergeant must have known about the stowaway all along. She was a fool. She thought to protect him, even feed the little bastard. Perhaps he had escaped after the attack; made a break for North Eye to warn them?

No, Wendal placed lookouts all through the forest, so he would never have made it to the keep. Then again, if he was a redeemer, he might have magicked a message and remained concealed. Ash it all. Wendal's entire crew would be dead before she rode back to warn them.

Even if she dared ride back and check the caravan, the outriders from the Jandan tower would spot her fleeing and become suspicious. If the stowaway was a redeemer, there was little she could do; the dog would have stripped their souls and gnawed their bones; he would be too powerful to overcome.

There was no time to dwell on the worst. Minni calmed her breathing and refocussed. She dismounted, inspecting the foreleg of her horse. With a tap of her mare's caramel shoulder, the horse held its hoof off the ground as though it were injured.

"That's my girl," Minni gave her mare a lump of sugar. "Hold steady."

The two outriders hurtled down the path, hooves beating the ground and throwing up sod. One of the riders thundered past, following the road to Rum Hill without slowing. The other eased up and stopped without moving for his blade.

Thank the Welcome Stranger. Luck was with her still.

"Swap horses?" Minni flashed a tight smile up at the rider. Moonlight glossed across his chainmail, but was swallowed by the black star embroidered on his blue surcoat.

The soldier grinned and slapped his thigh. "I've just seen a bounty that would buy you a paddock full." His breath reeked.

"Why? Someone find a king to kill?" Minni laughed off her nerves with the rum filled Jandan.

"Who cares what he did. The bounty's more than any rebel head will fetch. Lord's truth, it's more than what's on Scrambletoe. Someone's gone and pissed off Calimska's high and mighty Guildmaster. Ha! The famous Golden Shield, imagine that. All that unholy sorcery and he can't even catch a street rat."

"What's this rat look like?"

"Young fella. Dark hair, brown eyes and tall."

"So, like every other Calimskan." Minni shook her head. Some dead letter this will be.

"That's it though, isn't it? How many stray Calimskan's you see this time a year? They all live the good life up in that golden nest. Count their glitter while we all get fried by the dragons. This pup's got no chance."

"How much is the bounty exactly?"

"Chest of gold and rights to land and title by the Guildmaster." The rider leered. "Anything interesting on the way down then? We could share the pot."

"The only shiners I've seen were headed home to their families. I won't keep you from yours."

"Fancy a ride with me before my ship sails? It's sure not safe out here in the night for a pretty lady."

"Tend to your own. I can look after myself." Minni drew her blade from behind her saddle to establish an understanding.

The soldier pulled his horse out of range. "Want to play highwayman? I've shell for whores and steel for thieves. Which is it then?"

Minni was happy for the opportunity to paint his grin red. She was no longer a toy for Jandan pleasure.

The caravan rattled its way up the rise.

27

Minni kept her eyes on the soldier, her hand on her blade.

He turned his horse, checking his chances between Minni and the caravan.

"Take the dead letter home soldier. Give bread to your wife." Minni drew a dagger from under her sleeve. With the comfort of a blade in each hand she relaxed her body, ready to kill.

"Your bones be bagged, witch." The soldier dug in his spurs and galloped his steed down the road following the other rider to Rum Hill.

Minni sheathed her blades. The caravan rolled to a stop at the junction and a rebel disguised as a Jandan guard approached Minni.

"Commander?"

"A dead letter is on the march, something special to get the dogs barking." Minni patted her mare's shoulder again and the mock lame hoof returned to the grass.

"Not for one of us?" The guard's eyes followed the soldier as he rode in the distance. "Is the rider a problem?"

"No, let him go, he's not a threat. Though there may be trouble with our cargo. We have a stowaway." Minni gave another sugar lump to her horse and mounted.

"Ma'am?" The guard drew his sword.

"Stay your blade. I suspect he's another bird, flown the golden nest."

"One for the flock?"

"Maybe so; I want eyes on him and see he doesn't fly off into harms way. With a bounty that big and North Eye quick to take notice, we've landed a prize worth at least double what the golden city has on offer. Continue to the Crab and Petrel, no stopping; the horses are eager. Three of you at point. Report as needed, no more."

The caravan rattled down the road to the coast. Minni rode out ahead of the wagons, tallying her victories for the day and marking the oddities. The more she thought about each happenstance, the more the mysterious stowaway increased in value.

STOWAWAY

Elrin's body was wracked with tremors. He was cold all over, yet his heart seared; cooking him from the inside out. His robes were a false comfort from the chills, only serving to soak up his perspiration. He huddled in a quivering ball. Overcome with exhaustion and lulled by the rocking of the wagon, he drifted into a fitful sleep.

The guard he killed had bled out and the baked earth drank it down. The woman with eyes of spring and hair like autumn pulled him into her chambers, brushing her body close to his. She left him yearning and blocked the exit while men screamed outside and a red slick pooled under the door. Unseen forces closed on him, barricaded him in. He couldn't run. He couldn't breath.

Elrin woke in darkness gasping for air, coaxed from the nightmare by a beautiful song. It sprung deep in his head, his mouth tingled and water beaded on his skin. While he had slept the barrels had slid closer, pressing him in, but now his breath returned and a mysterious energy rippled around his body, washing over his tired muscles. It was a pleasant renewal compared to the wildfire of the vapours. The after effects of the blaze must have been giving him hallucinations, for it was all too strange. No sooner had he begun to grasp what was happening than the song drifted away, as if borne by a river flow.

The canvas opened and Elrin kept still, hidden amongst the crush of barrels. It was secured shut again and all was silent except for the occasional birdcall.

The wagon shook into motion, leaving Elrin wondering if he had slept through his chance to escape. He could have been asleep for an hour, or a day, and had no idea where the wagons were going; the canvas was too thick to see out. He wouldn't risk lifting it open or the guards would spot him. It wasn't worth getting caught just for a peep; that was a lesson he'd not soon forget.

Propping himself up against a barrel, Elrin ruffled through the satchel hopeful that Kleith had sent him away with some decent food. There were several broken biscuits and a hard cheese wrapped in cloth. It wasn't a great deal for a long journey, but he was ravenous and devoured the lot, down to the last crumbled carcass of a biscuit which he scraped up and pinched into his mouth. His appetite petitioned for more so he uncorked the water skin and drank deeply. The cool liquid tasted of home, refreshing his body and fooling his stomach.

After a brief stop the wagon changed direction then jostled along at a fresh pace. Elrin braced against the weight of the barrels, which shuffled across the floor, squashing him in with every bump and divot.

He had no idea how he would escape if the wagon kept on going. It didn't matter so much, as long as it was away from the Guildmaster. He hoped his mother was safe from the trouble he caused. Kleith would look after her, but Elrin craved her comfort for himself. Just a word of reassurance would give him strength. It was a ridiculous fancy. He'd never be able to return home; not until he found his father, or this Dragon Choir; whatever that was.

There were ships at Rum Hill and the traders or fishermen might want extra crew. That would be the best way to begin his quest and work his way down to Jando. They might be overly fanatical about their almighty Lord down south, but they controlled the sea, and Kleith said he had to get to the Hoard Islands. Surely they all weren't so bad, maybe someone there would know of the Dragon Choir too.

He couldn't recall if Kleith mentioned which one came first. Should he look for the Dragon Choir to get to the Hoard Islands or was it the other way around? A local in Rum Hill would know more. Some old salt at the docks would steer him in the right direction for a favour or chore. Elrin was not ashamed of honest work, he'd laboured his body for shine and he'd do so for shell. Whatever happened he had to get to the Hoard Islands before the season broke.

The wagon stopped after several hours had passed. Elrin's muscles ached from holding the barrels back from crushing him. The wagon guards began to chat together. It was the first time he had heard them since he woke up. Their absence had almost convinced Elrin he was aboard a ghost caravan carting the dead to the afterlife. Maybe he had arrived. At least Nathis would recognise him wearing the garb of a humble herder.

Muffled cheerful banter seeped out of a building; a tavern, maybe a roadside inn. A female voice called out and the men beside the wagon trailed off towards the music and laughter. The woman's voice was familiar.

He waited for it again, but there was nothing; she'd gone. Elrin was left with an occasional snort from the horses for company.

Elrin dared to move in the silence. It was difficult; his stiff back and aching joints slowed him down, though he fancied that it improved his stealth. He pressed his ear to the canvas searching for any movement of a guard nearby, then knelt down and peered through the canvas flap.

There was no one guarding the rear of the wagon, so he eased himself out and peered around the corner. Some guards had gathered by the lead wagon and a few others hovered around the door of a busy roadhouse, snug in a clearing beside the forest.

Summoning his courage, he dashed through the moonlight into the shadows of a large tree overhanging the wagon. He waited, stretching his legs and listening to the night, but there was nothing. A quick peek around the tree trunk revealed no one had noticed the escape.

His stomach clenched with joy and adrenaline, imagining himself a hero like his father, vanquishing dragons and taking their treasure. Maybe he wasn't a real hero, but things could be set right again. Finding Father would return everything back to normal, together they would walk through the gates of Calimska and demand justice. Mother would sing again and Father would lead new adventures. Elrin could take a name and get his ink; finally be someone with a guild to call his own, at last he'd be accepted.

The shadows cast by the bright white moon and the warm yellow tavern lamps hid Elrin as he crept towards the roadhouse. The front door hung open, ventilating the well-lubricated banter of men finished a long days labour. Above the group of Jandan soldiers congregating around the entrance hung a sign painted with a seabird making off with a crab in its beak. A gull of some kind, just like the ones around the Lake of Tears back in Calimska.

To get past the guards without being noticed, Elrin needed a distraction. He picked up a pebble and lobbed it into the bushes beside the guards. One guard looked then returned to his ale and conversation. Elrin chose a larger stone and aimed it closer to them. The stone arced high and hit the sign above their heads, bounced off a guard's shoulder then dropped into his tankard.

"Ash it! Not my bloody drink!"

The guards looked straight at the bush, which Elrin hid behind.

"That you Minni?" The struck guard squinted into the shadows, shielding his eyes from the lamp that hung by the door. "Quit pissing around. Come and have an ale with us before you swallow the damn sea!"

After a quick translation, Elrin dashed off behind the roadhouse to avoid any deeper scrutiny. Knowing the Jandan language would serve him well on the coast. His father had taught him many tongues of trade important to Calimska, though Jandan was his boyhood favourite, it was so different from the languages west of the range, flavoured by the exotic empires far across the Salroc Sea. It had come naturally to him under his father's tutelage and while Kleith did his best after his father left, Elrin never trusted the Herder's pronunciation of the clipped toneless language. They couldn't afford a proper tutor, so Elrin practised on Jandan traders whenever they came to market. Amongst folk this side of the range his Calimskan accent would stand out, so he would say as little as possible, have an ale and let his ears adjust to the local cadence.

The back door was left open and a heavy man with a greasy beard and a filthy apron lent against the wall beside it, smoking a pipe. When the cook finished his puff and walked into the darkness to pass water in the bushes, Elrin crept through the open door and into a small kitchen.

It stank of rendered fat and wood smoke hung in the air. A cast iron stove held a lonely skillet frying a joint of lamb. His stomach groaned. The corner of the room was piled with dirty pots, pans and plates. Beside this, great vats of dishes stagnated amongst floating islands of lard in a slosh of dirty water. It was enough to put him off the idea of ordering a meal.

Elrin pushed through a swinging door into the taproom. A short crowded bar was wedged in the near corner and at the far end of the room an impromptu company of local musicians had coalesced. They played a fine tune considering the ragged state of their instruments, singing along in weathered harmony; rough and cheerful. Patrons crowded together sharing bench seats and resting their ale on stained timber. Several tables were occupied by dice games; shine and shell flowed back and forth with good-natured cheering and jeering. Local farmers and labourers, fishermen and traders shared jokes and recounted exaggerations of the day's events.

There was not a Calimskan in sight, no one would recognise him here. He was free to relax and make merry, to celebrate his escape and new beginnings.

As he scanned the room for a place to sit, Elrin's throat clenched. In a dim corner alone at a table a woman sat staring at him with a look of interest akin to a cat examining a sparrow. It was the dark-eyed woman from Calimska. She smiled and he blushed; confused and abashed. She was intoxicating, filling him with equal parts fear and desire. What was she doing here? She helped him once; perhaps she would again.

He made his way to her table through the crowd and took up a seat, removing his cowl.

Elrin whispered in his best Jandan. "Are you following me?"

Minni laughed. "Should I be? Who are you anyway?"

"I'm Elrin."

"That's it? You shiners have longer titles than that." Minni smirked, holding back another laugh. "Oh, I see. Keeping your ink up your sleeve. You must be in trouble."

"I'm just Elrin, my father didn't—" Elrin was annoyed at himself. He was no good at keeping his secrets close. "Why should I say? Who are you?"

"Minella, Minni, Witch, Wench, Reik, Jandan Spy. Your pick is as good as another's."

"Are you really a witch and a spy? I don't want to get mixed up in anything."

"Too late for that; seems you're the politics of the day, Elrin No Name." Minni handed Elrin a notice. "Picked this off the wall on the way in. Know anything about it?"

It was a dead letter, scrawled first in Calimskan then translated into Jandan. Elrin shook his head in disbelief. "Why do I have a dead letter against me? These are lies. I'm not a spy, nor am I a poacher."

"A killer?"

"I suppose I am." Elrin avoided her accusing eyes. "But, he was trying to kill me. A whole bunch of them were."

"So you ran?"

"I had to. No ink, no justice."

"So you're anti-guild then. You wanted the Guildmaster dead."

"No."

"You just happen to quote the anti-guild mantra."

"You've got it all wrong. I was just a messenger. Not officially, I never got a guild tattoo, but that's not the point. Look, I overheard something I shouldn't have, something about my father and something about the power of gods. The Guildmaster had his guards try to kill me. I got away, thanks to you. But, this bounty, I'll have to ... now I don't know what to do. How do I outrun that?"

"How about you start by pulling that cowl over your face." Minni eased her expression. "I tore this from the board out front, doubt any here could read much anyway, but it only takes one and word will spread. I've never seen a bounty so rich, with land and title to boot. It's got the Jandans all flustered, sending riders and birds like it was the return of their Lord. Every bounty hunter in Jando will be out to bag your bones."

Elrin followed her advice, covering his face and sinking down into his seat. The charges on the dead letter were as preposterous as the bounty was exorbitant; the Guildmaster must be desperate to keep his conversation a secret. If only Elrin could understand what they were on about he might find some leverage.

The front door swung open and knocked against the wall. Three hard faced men, heavily slung with weapons, muscled in. They scanned the room. Their leader, a bearded man, spoke to the barkeep while the other two questioned a table of sailors.

Minni knocked Elrin's foot under the table. "The wolves are hungry. It's time to head off, before they catch your scent."

"You go. You're not safe with me." Elrin tapped the dead letter. "Not with this."

The bearded bounty hunter tossed a purse onto the bar. The barman tested the weight and peeked inside before nodding toward Elrin and Minni. The bearded man glared at them, spitting a gob of tobacco onto the floor. A lingering strand of spittle stuck to his wiry red beard. He called to his men and pointed across the room to their table.

"Too late now." Elrin got up from the table, put on his satchel and grabbed Minni's hand. "We've got to leave."

Minni shook free of his grip. "You go. I'll be fine."

"No, I got you into this." Elrin grabbed Minni's hand again and this time she obliged.

They ran out through the kitchen.

"Into the forest, quick!" Elrin urged Minni to run ahead. He knocked the skillet off the stove then ran out behind her.

The bearded man crashed through the door and slipped on the oil. His two companions kept their footing and took chase.

Once outside, the bounty hunters fired their crossbows. A bolt whizzed passed Elrin's ear, spurring his legs to run with everything they had.

Minni was too fast; he couldn't keep up as she dodged through the trees. It wasn't long before he lost her in the shadows. He pressed up against a trunk, silhouettes ran through the bush all around him, making no more than a gentle rustle as they flew past. How many bounty hunters were there? The Jandan soldiers must have joined the hunt. With the size of the bounty, Elrin imagined the whole roadhouse would be after him. Even if the patrons split it, they'd all have more shine than they would ever knew what to do with.

Searching the shadows of the forest for a place to hide, Elrin crept behind the wide trunk of a fallen tree. Guilt crouched down beside him, silent and knowing. He had lost Minni in the chase. She was on her own against all those men. The Reik ran so fast, perhaps she was a local and knew the forest well enough to make her escape. She must have known which way to go; if only he'd managed to keep up with her.

A man's cry for help was cut short and someone ran towards him. Elrin couldn't figure out how far away they were. The forest confused his ears, dampening and spreading sounds around him. He was used to the clatter of the city streets. Men calling their wares, hooves on the cobbles, hammer on nail and anvil. Here it was a cacophony of nature. Crickets played a vigorous melody against the call of night birds and the cool night breeze stirred the trees to rustle and sway. Twigs snapped and cracked in all directions. Were there people in the forest or just forest animals?

Elrin glanced over the log and was shocked to find the bearded bounty hunter standing beside his hiding place. The man had his back to Elrin and was peering into the shadows cast by the moon, hooking his neck left and right at every call of the night birds in the forest. How did he get so close without making a sound? Elrin lowered his head behind the log and waited.

"Minni!" The bearded man's voice boomed into the night.

His voice startled Elrin. It was so close now. Elrin kept still and breathed as little as possible. He didn't dare lift his head to look.

"Let's talk about this. We can make a deal."

The bounty hunter's guile went unanswered. Gentle footsteps pressed the forest floor, disturbing fallen leaves and brittle twigs. Birds called nearby.

"Just a little misunderstanding. A quarter'll do."

There was honking in the distance, accompanied by an owl hooting from further away.

The whiz of a bolt letting fly pierced the night, followed by a cry to arms. Duelling swords clashed. There was a thump on the forest floor.

The bearded man leapt over Elrin's log. The young Calimskan sprang to his feet, drawing the dagger, expecting to face off against the man. Instead, he watched the bounty hunter flee deeper into the forest.

At once relieved and shocked, Elrin kept still; waiting, listening for footfalls. The woodland was quiet except for night birds calling, so he crept back in the direction he imagined the road would be, paranoid about the noise he made. The forest floor made such a racket, no matter the care he took with each slow step. He hadn't gone far when he came across the body of one of the bounty hunters slumped over a log. Elrin spun around, ready for a trap, though nothing sprang from the shadows.

He knelt and touched the patch of darkness around the body; blood, thick and sticky. The bounty hunter must be dead. He threw a stick at the body just in case. The body didn't move, so Elrin took a closer inspection. It was shameful for him to take from the departed, but at least he was dressed for the job in the herder disguise.

With great care Elrin rolled the man off the stump and onto his back. The dead man's clothes were soiled with blood and entrails bulged from his side between a gap in the cuirass. His weapons had already been taken, so Elrin removed his pauldrons, bracers, and greaves. He examined how they were attached before trying them on. He'd never had his own armour, but was taught to assist his father to dress with far more complex pieces than these.

The dim light of the moon and the blood made it difficult to manipulate the buckles and fixings. Most of the armour appeared in good condition. A strap was severed on the cuirass where the fatal blow had fallen, and the bounty hunter's belt hung together by a sliver of leather. Elrin kept his cowl on, but removed his grey robes and laid them beside the dead body using them to wipe the blood off the armour before fitting himself with the serviceable pieces.

He bowed his head.

"Nathis, take this soul to shelter," he said, remembering the simple words recited by herders when they collected the dead. Priest or not, it wouldn't be right to take from the dead and not ask Nathis to herd him to his maker.

The armour was an imperfect fit, though it would suffice. Elrin searched for some money. A loose leather thong held a small pouch around his neck. Inside were small bones; Elrin shivered. Finger bones.

The young man wished for the gold, silver, silk and spice of Calimska; not that he had much of that pass into his own hands. Still, a copper tab or two in your pocket was better than a bag of body parts. He would have to get used to trading in bones and shell on the coast and remember there was no protection from dragons outside Calimska with the season closing in. There were a lot of things to get used to.

The remains of a bandolier lay to the side with a severed strap. Two pouches were empty, but the remaining pouch had an onion and two small rounds of hard cheese. Elrin wiped his hands on his vest and sunk his teeth into one of the rounds. It was salty, but he made short work of it, spitting out the rind as he ate. The remaining cheese and the onion were rationed into his satchel for later. Elrin didn't like the idea of eating a raw onion, though it would be better than starving. It might be of use to a ship's broth if he got passage.

As he covered the dead man with the grey robes a shiver coiled up his spine. All at once he felt as though he was being watched. He stared into the shadows, but saw no one. The feeling remained; eyes were there somewhere, watching. Elrin took off into the forest; he did not want to be dead beside the fallen bounty hunter. He jogged back towards the roadhouse, following the faint roll of distant conversation drifting out into the evening. Once he had the roadhouse in view, he skirted around the edge of the forest, remaining hidden.

It was getting late; the wagons he had arrived in were gone and the roadhouse was quieter than before. Elrin didn't dare go inside to ask for a room. Someone would pick him for the bounty and he'd be hauled back to the Guildmaster before the morning sun rose. The young man had to get to Rum Hill without being discovered.

He pulled on his cowl and walked down the road heading east. It had to take him to the sea eventually, and from there the Hoard Islands awaited.

UIGHARA

The scaphoid on the blackstone rattled and a dim yellow glow radiated around the sacrificial bone. The redeemer placed his hands on the polished jet tablet, knowing who it would be. The fourth time today and less than half the day had past; it was a waste of a good carpal.

A delicate murmur whispered from the ether.

All the bone of Jando and he'll sacrifice a distal phalanx to make reach; parsimonious old dotard. Shuffling in his seat, Uighara removed two metacarpals and sacrificed them on the blackstone, praying for a better connection.

"Almighty Lord, hear my call, take this generous offering and strengthen the reach of your humble servant's devotion."

The glow took to the additional bones and the voice of the High Priest pressed from the ether with a sudden, glaring clarity.

"Brother? Come on then, answer ... Make reach. Is this even working?"

Uighara grinned. The old fool could wait.

"I know you can hear me! I feel you there, damn you! Spit spat, I'll have your head for a hat!"

"Your Grace, I apologise. Your voice was not clear. What say you about a cat?"

"I sense your levity. Mark the distance you travel from the Lord's path, lest you lose your way. He is ever vigilant!"

"Yes, Your Grace, wise words from Oranica's most sage. You will assuredly join Saint Jan and Saint Norin beside the Lord's golden thro—"

"Enough of that now; your platitudes are not easily digested."

"Of course, Your Grace. What do you require of me? I do not wish to waste your time."

"That remains to be seen. Have you caught that sinful little man yet?"

"The pirate ship we have been tracking was not Kobb's ship."

"Don't speak the name of that recalcitrant little whelp."

"Your Grace, surely the greater mission is the capture and redemption of a more potent sinner."

"I've given you everything you need to accomplish that, nothing in my power has been spared."

"The armada, your Grace. How went your discussions with the Lord's high admiral?"

"Very well indeed. Such a shrewd man. You could learn a tot or two from him."

"So he's agreed to send the Armada? Your sainthood is assured."

"Not so."

"That will be a problem. Did you not just order him? You are the Word of the Lord, he must obey."

"There is no problem. I quite agree with him. As does the rest of the Council."

"What? You ... I cannot bring you the greatest sacrifice without the armada. How else will you be blessed a saint! Calimska will forever be a thorn in the heel of the Lord, halting the march of redemption. Precipitous sin and sorcery lurk at our very doorstep. Only one thing can reform this land. We must strike at the heart of the evil. These wyrms behave as gods unto themselves, hoarding his treasure, corrupting his power. They forget the almighty creator!"

"Calm yourself, dear Brother."

Uighara wiped his brow with his white silk sleeve. "My apologies, Your Grace."

"Your fervour will be rewarded, but the Council is in no hurry for my sainthood. Do not fear, Jando will survive another season and I will endure. The Council is less concerned with redemption and more so with pirates and rebels leeching our strength."

"Then I will bring you proof of the pirate lair from the mouth of our new Commodore."

"Yes, that will serve all our interests, Brother. Redemption is but one of the Lord's miracles. We must accommodate compassion for the Lord's faithful with equal measure."

"As you say."

"Lord's blessings go with you, Brother."

"Also with you, Your Grace"

The ether retracted from Uighara's mind. Three neat white piles, tiny dust mountains, were all that remained of his sacrifice, the essence now degraded. He puffed across the blackstone, blowing the dull powder off its mirror surface. A gentle press and shake of a belt pouch was sufficient to reveal about a hand and a half remained. That would serve for the moment. The redeemer pressed another pouch and tucked his fingers in; both treasures were still there. Pulling them out one by one, he felt the energetic potential tingle up his palm. An incisor and a molar; they'd be a godsend if there was an emergency. He'd not waste them on the blackstone. Bones of the faithful just weren't as clear over these distances, though blessed or not, they would have to do for now.

Removing his cowl, Uighara lay back in a hammock, enjoying the gentle lull of the ocean. His shoulders and neck ached from the day's mental exertions, there were so many details to arrange, so many powers to appease; pawns to manipulate.

Considering the logistics of it all, only a few problems had arisen, all solvable of course. The greatest of all the Lord's work would be done; things were falling into place nicely. The young upstart Commodore had a whiff of pirate and wouldn't let up the chase until he knew the location of the lair. He was no different from his nit-picking father, always seeking proof to the detriment of faith. He wouldn't take Uighara's word for it, as obvious as it was.

Uighara's father was the same, so powerful, yet so weak. He couldn't grasp what he had and would surely let another opportunity slip away. The fool had no idea.

The tide of sleep came in and Uighara drifted to the deep rest of the exhausted.

❧⚜

A milk faced undanae with black saucer eyes and a pointed grin stood by the door. He bent sideways like a waning moon, his head tilted, eyes devouring all light.

"How nice to have a nap, yes?"

"Zarkas," announced Uighara with a boy's voice steeped in innocence long faded. He rocked on a wooden painted horse in his childhood home. The walls were decorated with endearing pastel murals, the floor warmed with colourful rugs.

"Why do I always find you as a boy, hmm?"

Uighara grasped his lucidity and refurnished the dream. He weaved his surroundings into a spacious stone walled chamber with blazing hearth, ornate tapestries, redwood furniture and gilded finery.

"More to my taste, certainly," Zarkas enjoyed a wry smile, deepening the dark wells of his dimpled cheeks. "Though, I must say the horse is a little small for you now."

Flustered and ashamed, Uighara dismounted from the wooden horse. He willed it gone, but it would not be undone. Dreaming an axe into his hands, he hacked it to pieces, throwing them to the fire. The angels of the Lord knew his every weakness.

"Why do you call?" Uighara dusted his hands off then warmed them by the fire, watching the lacquer crack and blister the head of the horse. "Everything is in order."

"That perhaps, is your problem. Shall order bring the return of our Lord?"

"It is just an expression, our plans proceed without complication."

"Humans make little sense."

"The barges are built and armed, our net is ready. I have already told you this. What do you want?"

"When, is the question. When do I want?"

"We await our reserve supply of reagent to be loaded. Once it is stockpiled and secure at Lord's Landing we will proceed to engage the pirates."

"Do you have the armada?"

"No, not yet, the Lord's High Admiral will not rally the armada without proof. I will extrac—"

"You dally when you need speed. The Lord will be displeased."

"Everything will be in its place."

"Time is short. If you are incapable, then I will find another. Perhaps the High Priest would have made a better choice."

Uighara sneered. "That old dolt barely understands the process, let alone the ritual. You need me Zarkas. You know you do."

There was no reply. Zarkas was gone and the room had transformed back to that of his childhood; his horse burned in the fire, a crippled mess of charred limbs and broken memories.

RUM HILL

Elrin woke the next morning to the sun rising over the sea. He had walked through the night to get there, trudging on until the moon set and fatigue forced him to rest. In the darkness he hadn't noticed how close he was.

Cane fields filed off beside the worn road, which stretched on to Rum Hill. The port town was a shamble of buildings strewn around a small harbour. The town centre nestled against the foot of a grassy hill that rolled up and out into the ocean, ending in a sheer headland. Elrin drank in the view of the sheltered bay and breathed in the sweet scent of molasses.

At the edge of the town people were busy. Teams of mules turned cane mills and workers hovered over steaming segmented vats, cooking down cane juice into rich brown syrup. In the town centre bunkhouses, storehouses and distilleries lent on each other in a patchwork of repair and extension; the structures were opportunistic like the people on the streets. Elrin avoided the drunkards begging favours and promising friendship, blushed past the barely draped welcome girls, and made haste to the dockyards.

Elrin knew the border towns were under Jandan control, but there was no sign of it through Rum Hill. There were no lawmen or town guards, unless they were in the pubs and pleasure houses. Elrin's mother had likened the border towns to poor orphans abandoned by Jando. His father said they had the best and the worst of everything in equal measure. Honest folk with character and spirit worked to feed their families and shady malefactors schemed and skimmed from the unwary. Border towns were places to right wrongs and sing songs; heroes could rise and make things right.

The main road curved around the base of Rum Hill and descended upon the docks. The bay bloomed into a vast ocean, more expansive than he ever imagined possible. As a boy running about Calimska, he thought the Lake

41

of Tears was the sea. His father's stories of the open ocean were incomprehensible until now.

The morning sun skimmed across a horizon without end. The cool kiss of the ocean breeze tasted of salt and filled his mind with the romance of what he could be. He hadn't lost everything; he had his father's dagger and a quest. There was a life of adventure ahead where he could be a hero and save his father. It was as clear as the summer sky.

He walked on in the sunshine and convinced himself that the dead letter against him was just part of the adventure. It was another verse for the bards to sing. There was no better tale to tell than one of adversity overcome.

The bounce in his step petered out; a niggling doubt lodged in his mind like a stone stuck in his boot. The bounty hunters who chased him into the forest were just a taste of the sorts that would spill his blood, and they were so well-equipped. Elrin began to question how a dagger alone would serve as an adequate defence in all situations. He would have to get awfully close to an enemy to strike. If only he had a sword ... if only he knew how to use a sword. Elrin polished the shine in the situation, picking up his step again; his father started out with a dagger and his wits, he could too.

Elrin rested his palm on the dagger's black jewelled pommel. The bedtime tales of his father's adventures were all he really knew of battle. Fighting off goblins and giants to take their ill-gotten treasure. Saving villagers from raiding orcs and recovering the plunder to give to the poor. Something within the dagger reached out to him with comfort, making the tales of his father possible for him too. He was destined for adventure and could learn on his travels; he didn't need to waste his years polishing someone else's steel, he'd sharpen his own.

"Watch where you're goin' son!" A wiry man grabbed Elrin's arm and pulled him back. A stack of planks glanced past Elrin's head as a gantry crane moved to load a cart nearby.

"Sorry." Elrin held his hands up in apology. "Do you know where I can find the head dockman?"

"The what?" shouted the skinny docker.

Elrin waved him off in apology, his voice would only be drowned out by the racket. Dockers hollered and whistled at each other positioning heavy lifts on the gantries while draft horses clattered about pulling cargo. Gulls squabbled around the fishing boats and the ships groaned and jostled in their moorings. It was impossible to have a clear conversation. Dockers used hand signals or whistled to organise loads. Elrin often had made deliveries to the docks on the Lake of Tears and recalled yelling there hadn't been very effective either.

Rather than ask around, Elrin decided to look around. The head docker usually stood out as the most frustrated; some burly, barrel-chested, potbellied hulk, pointing and yelling abuse. He jumped up on a stack of unloaded crates to get a better view. Sharing the docks with a few trade galleys and fishing skiffs was an intimidating Jandan frigate, its three masts towering higher than any other. It was at least twice the length of the biggest merchant ship in the harbour.

The immensity of the frigate and the number of crew that worked its decks impressed upon Elrin the muscle Jando flexed to control Rum Hill. With the Navy holding the port, they secured trade and tax revenues for Jando without having to fortify an outpost on land. It was a simple minded strategy, with merit for expanding Jandan control along the coast, but did nothing to improve life for the locals. One of the books he had snuck from the merchant guild's library articulated a treatise on the failings of these ham-fisted approaches to rent seeking. Elrin thought it was obvious enough without the lengthy explanation; if the people suffer your revenue base suffers.

A shrill whistle from the centre of the shipyard caught Elrin's attention. A man sat on a chair so tall there was a ladder to reach the top. He was like a brusque canary on its perch, whistling commands through a loudhorn. Piercing notes rose and fell, alternating between broken pulses and long calls. His shirt was bright yellow and he had a matching hat with a piece of cloth hanging over his neck and ears. The peak at the front shaded his eyes. He wore loose trousers that extended to his knees, exposing his leather brown legs below.

Elrin jumped down from the stack of crates and walked to the high chair. From below he couldn't see the man, just a pair of hairy brown calloused feet dangling over the chair.

"Hello."

The little man kept on whistling, ignoring Elrin below.

He yelled louder. "Excuse me!"

The lead docker leaned forward, staring down between his feet with a dark look.

"What? This is no safe place for a shiner. Go home."

"No, I think you misunderstand, I wa—"

"There's no throne down here, lad. Head back to town or muck in the bushes, then bugger off!"

"No. That's not what I mean—"

A loud explosion sounded from the central pier where the Jandan frigate was moored. Smoke drifted above a stack of crates and barrels, flames licking at the timber.

The little yellow man put the cone to his mouth and shouted down at Elrin. "Get out of here boy. Now!"

In a moment of brilliance, Elrin knew exactly how to earn his way to Jando. He ran to the smoking crates while the canary went berserk atop his perch. Men raced about in all directions. Elrin got to the fire and realised that he had no pail of water and an empty bladder.

More crates were lighting up and workers nearby leapt into the water, swimming to safety. Elrin stood alone on the pier, unaided by the marines on the frigate who only stared at the barrels in terror. The officers were shouting orders to raise anchor while sailors jumped overboard.

The barrels bore the stamp of a cannon and a flame. Elrin's stomach dropped; black powder. He was going to be pierced with splinters and fried for the fool he was.

The frigate captain's face begged for a miracle, but Elrin was no sorcerer. The heat from the crates intensified. He gripped the hilt of his dagger and imagined what his father might do.

He kicked out at the flaming crates in the hope it might prevent the volatile barrels bringing his quest to an abrupt end. Sparks leapt into the air and the flames licked out, singeing his leg hair. The crates rocked forward in their stack, but then rocked back towards him. He kicked again and several flaming crates fell into the water, sizzling as they were smothered out. Encouraged by that, he struck out once more. Some tumbled back along the pier, but he quickly knocked them off before the decking itself caught alight. Soon all the crates were in the water, even the ones that weren't on fire had accidentally gone in; victims of his enthusiasm. When he stopped he noticed his boot and pants had caught alight.

Elrin was just about to dive off the pier when a gush of water sloshed onto his legs, dousing the flames. The head dockman had rushed to help with a bucket of water, his yellow shirt glaring under the sun. No one else wanted to come near; most of the dockers had taken shelter behind the cargo stacked about the shipyard. Others had run halfway up the road to town, hoping to witness the impending explosion from a safe distance.

"By the root! You're a brave shiner," said the head docker, slapping Elrin's back. Most men I've known don't run towards certain death."

Now that the man was off his perch, Elrin realised his small stature. He only came up to Elrin's elbow, which presented a problem of clarification; was he dwarven or a shankakin? He was leaner than a dwarf, but taller than any shankakin he had met in Calimska. He had no beard, but that was no sure sign he wasn't a dwarf; he had no boots, but that was no sure sign he was a shankakin. Elrin tried not to stare and mumbled a reply. "I suppose death wasn't so certain. You ran here too."

"Don't get me wrong, I saw you doing a stand up job, but I thought I'd lend you a hand. I've found running toward fires with a full bucket of water works out better for me." The canary man pointed to his large feet. They were covered in thick hair and disproportionately large in comparison with his short, compact frame; he had to be a shankakin.

"Didn't want to cause a bushfire on your hoofers huh?" Elrin laughed.

"Thanks for saving mine."

"Not at all, lad. You saved me rebuilding the pier. The thanks are mine. You're a bloody idiot though." He beckoned Elrin closer and lowered his voice. "Next time kick these barrels of hellfire off instead. I know many who'd thank you for that around here."

The officers screamed orders down the chain of command, rallying the men back to their posts. A ramp pushed past the bulwark and dropped onto the pier with a thud. Two Jandan marines escorted an ogre in chains down the gangplank.

One of them, an officer with a brutal grimace, cracked his whip across the ogre's bare back. The ogre shuffled his legs faster in an awkward motion that strained the planks. They bowed and flexed, yet held against the punishment.

Every ogre Elrin heard tell of was covered head to foot in grotesque images of their tribal totems. This one had no ink, only scars, new and old, carving a painful landscape across his brown green skin. Blood caked over the shackles and heavy chains restricted his movement; slavery had reduced the fearsome warrior to a beast of burden.

He grasped a barrel in each hand and lifted them with the ease of two mugs of ale. For a moment his keen blue eyes considered Elrin. The officer behind him dispensed another lash and the ogre winced, dropping his eyes to the ground. His enormous body shambled around and stomped up the gangplank to load the black powder on the ship.

The frigate's commanding officer strode down the gangway. He was a handsome man with an air of insistence that projected from him like a spear. Sunlight spun sharp lines off his polished buttons and buckles. His blue overcoat highlighted his sunburnt cheeks and the crisp white collar of his undershirt.

"What's your name boy? You just saved our dear *Juniper* a week in drydock." His voice carried an expectation of compliance.

Elrin hesitated to answer—he couldn't use his real name.

The head dockman moved between them, his yellow shirt playing in the breeze. He was the blazing sun stealing the horizon from a dark blue sky.

"Keep your mitts off him, Pelegrin. He's not interested."

Pelegrin stretched a difficult smile, refusing to look at the shankakin. "I'm sure the boy is interested in a reward for his bravery. Aren't you boy?"

Elrin was about to answer, but was cut off.

"Bravery! Ha! Stupidity more like, should have pushed your hellfire off before risking his life."

Pelegrin's attention snapped away from Elrin and thrust upon his antagoniser. "I'll have you for conspiracy against the Council for that. Who by divine redemption are you?"

"Delik. Name ring any bells in your hollow head? Or are you still

45

listening to the sound of your own divine trumpet?" Delik's big feet were set firmly in place. Like the frigate to the galley, Pelegrin towered head and shoulders over him.

"Recant, grub!" Pelegrin spat onto the deck and reached for his sabre.

Delik kept his voice even, his demeanour pleasant. "If I'd known it was you up here in this murdering hulk you call a ship, I'd have come to welcome you sooner. I heard you had a promotion after wiping out Tillydale, or did you dress up some other cowardice as glory for your bloodthirsty Lord?"

The shankakin held his ground, daring Pelegrin to draw his weapon. Delik had nerve; positioning his body close enough to strike before Pelegrin could draw his sabre. The smaller man had to be betting he'd be fast enough in close quarters to have a chance against a military officer.

Elrin took a step back; he didn't want to get caught by a swinging blade. None of Pelegrin's men noticed the unfolding conflict and the pier was empty save the barrels of black powder nearby and some noisy gulls. Pelegrin had no support, but was unwilling to show any weakness and call for assistance.

"I am a Commodore, you filthy grub. You'd best remember that. I command this frigate and the four galleons birthed in the cove. If a runt like you is running these docks then I've good reason to suspect you had something to do with this fire." Pelegrin's frustration disappeared as something dawned on him and a cruel grin creased his precise features. "Oh, I see ... This is another pathetic rebellion attack isn't it? Are you sure you want to test me? Didn't work out so well for Tillydale. Come to think of it, Pumpkinvale and Crooked Creek won't be giving us any trouble now either. All you shankakin whelps should be back in chains. If you ask me, the Council should never have let your lot out."

Delik seethed, his face red and trembling, lips curled in bit-back fury. Elrin took another step back. The ogre appeared again on the main deck, making his way back to load more of the black powder barrels.

"Give the grubs a stitch and they'll ruin the seam," Pelegrin sneered. "My father had it right. Let a few out of chains and off they run to scheme against their betters. That's how your lot reward kindness. Thought you could win against the Lord's chosen, but you're pathetic backwards insects, all of you."

"Speaking of fathers," said Delik, hatred sparking off each word. "You're going to help me find mine."

Pelegrin laughed "Of course! I'll be sure to take you straight to the prison. What is daddy's name? The gaoler has such a long list."

"Jaspa Scrambletoe."

Pelegrin lost his smirk. His eyes flicked to the side, searching for aid. He pulled at his sabre and yelled. "Seize the—"

Delik lanced forward, grabbing Pelegrin's sword arm at the wrist before his blade could escape. The shankakin's hand was a blur, striking at Pelegrin's elbow with furious precision. Crunching bones paired with a strangled yelp as Delik twisted the crippled arm downwards and kicked his foot high into Pelegrin's groin. Pelegrin doubled over, allowing Delik to smash his fist square into the Jandan's handsome face. Pelegrin reeled backwards in a stumbling retreat.

Elrin was astonished at the speed and strength of the shankakin. Pelegrin groaned, half hunched over, not sure whether to hold his groin or his maimed sword arm.

A shout went up on the frigate and a whistle blew, summoning a blur of blue uniforms to action. Marines lined the gunwale, training their crossbows at Elrin and Delik. A unit charged down the gangplank to the pier, swords drawn. Delik held his hands high, turning his back to the rush of sabres.

"Put your clappers up, lad. Don't try and run."

Elrin did as Delik said, there was no other option; they were surrounded.

"Don't kill them! These two will have our special treatment. I want them myself. Throw them in the cells." Pelegrin's voice shook with anger and obvious pain, blood fell from his broken nose. "Make them ... comfortable."

Elrin and Delik were escorted up the gangplank onto the war ship, swords at their backs. Joyless crewmen worked *Juniper*'s pristine decks; whether indentured or enslaved, they were in need of a decent meal. Given the marines guarding them, some must have traded the slow rot of a prison sentence for trial by sea. Or, perhaps, they were captured from pirate attacks and given a choice; serve or die.

The crew kept their heads down and out of trouble, wary of the blue uniforms on patrol. Elrin hoped he would have the same option. He needed a convincing story or the dead letter would have him put in a box to Calimska.

Just before the marines escorted them down the hatch into the bowels of the frigate a scrawny bronze boy swabbing the deck tripped over his bucket and knocked into Delik. They went down in a heap.

Delik tried to wriggle out of the boy's tangle of arms and legs. "Get him off me!"

The marines tossed the boy to the side and hauled Delik to his feet, forcing him through the hatch. They were in no mind to delay, though one had enough time to swing a brutal kick at the boy, knocking him in the teeth before heading below. The boy got to his knees, flashing a wink and a ragged smile.

Elrin stepped down through the hatch, rethinking trial by sea as a preferred option.

BELOW DECK

It took a moment for Elrin's eyes to adjust to the sea of activity inside the ship. Officers shouted orders to uniformed sailors and they, in turn, barked at the crew. The crew rushed about accomplishing their jobs as fast as possible. Those who disappointed the overseers were struck with a thick knotted rope then shoved back to task.

Their escort handed Delik and Elrin over to a junior officer who had his men bind their hands behind their backs. The rope was coarse and chafed Elrin's wrists. Comfort was a subjective experience and he was in no mind to complain, lest they clamp him in irons as an alternative. They were taken below another deck and past rows of barrels, many marked with the same seal as those that nearly exploded on the docks.

Elrin was the reason the ship was still afloat, he was the hero not the criminal. Being an adventurer was a tricky business, the pitfalls of doing good deeds were not apparent in the tales of his father's exploits. The bardic interpretation of adventure had glossed over the injustice of punishment by association.

It was all just a simple misunderstanding. Surely if he explained his story to Commodore Pelegrin, he would be let off. After all, Elrin hadn't attacked any Jandans, let alone their commanding officer and he had nothing to do with Delik or this rebellion business. There would be one chance to show his innocence when the Commodore came to interrogate them, Elrin just hoped he didn't ask too many questions about why he wasn't back in Calimska.

Elrin and Delik were prodded further down into *Juniper*'s dark interior. When they arrived in the ship's prison hold, Elrin was surprised at how large it was. He thought it would be a small temporary cell for a few prisoners.

"Big enough for a small village isn't it," said Delik.

48

"Shut it grub!" The junior officer smacked Delik on the back of the head with the flat of his blade, knocking the shankakin to his knees.

Delik staggered to his feet. "Why don't you untie me and give it another try?"

The officer ignored the remark. "Throw 'em in this one," he said, pointing to the first empty cell. "They'll have some company soon."

Delik and Elrin were shoved in, stumbling onto the filthy sand covered deck. The thin layer of sand may have been fresh and white once, but now it told of grim journeys, patches were stained brown from blood and worse—the lone bucket in the corner of the cell reeked. The marines locked the cage door and left, leaving them to relax alone in the disgusting prison.

Delik found himself a relatively clean spot and sat down, leaning against the iron bars that carved up the hold. "You've been mighty quiet for someone who's just got locked up for doing nothing."

"I haven't had the best of luck these past few days. I guess I'm all out of protest." Elrin attempted to sit up without rolling in a patch of dried excrement; bile rose in his throat.

"Nasty in here isn't it?"

"Have you been in here before?"

"Not this ship, but one just like it. That one was packed to the gills. Believe me, an empty prison hold is a real treat."

Elrin was growing tired of these little mysteries. "A decent answer would be a real treat. Why did you provoke him like that? Look where it got us!"

"That's fair I suppose. You heard of Tillydale?"

"No. Where is that?" Elrin found a somewhat comfortable position away from the worst of the smell. "Is that where you're from?"

"Where *was* that? That's what you should be asking. You're not from the coast are you?"

"Is it that obvious?"

"You got the looks of a shiner from over the range, but your Jandan's too perfect for there and too proper for these border towns. Where you from then?"

Delik's interest was disconcerting and Elrin still had no lie ready to tell. The truth came too quick to his lips. "I'm from Calimska."

"Hells, why'd you leave? I'd love to go to the City of Gold, but I've never had the shine to pay the toll."

"I'm an adventurer. I left home a month ago seeking my fortune. One day I hope to be famous like the great hero of the coast, Arbajkha." Elrin decided fitting the lies amongst the truth would be more believable.

"Hero? When was this?" Delik chuckled. "It's a long time since I've heard of heroes gracing the coast. Plenty of bounty hunters though, plenty of thieves and thugs too."

"Surely you know him. He once battled a great wyrm to save a small village from certain destruction." Elrin's eyes brightened.

"Really, a wyrm eh?" Delik shook his head. "Him and the hells' five armies maybe. Where is he now? We need a few like that on our side."

"Mother says he's dead, but I don't believe it."

"Why not trust your own mother?"

"A dragon came to her in a dream and said he wouldn't return again."

"I see," said Delik, trying to be delicate. "Is she, um, addled?"

"Of course not! She knows all the sagas off by heart and can play any song on any instrument. She used to be head of the Bard's Guild."

"Why not now?"

Elrin hung his head. "Father just up and disappeared on us. Everything went to dust. They say she went mad, but she just gets a touch confused sometimes. She just misses him."

"Are you saying that this Arbajkha fella is your father?"

"I was hoping not to say that, actually. Not the best liar, am I?"

"Might it be, he came from somewhere else? The West Coast? Tashiska?"

"No. He was a great hero. He protected the coast. This coast. He even went to the Hoard Islands and took back stolen treasures hoarded by the dragons. He helped the villagers."

"You sure?"

"Yes!" Why didn't they know about his father on the coast? "Even in Calimska they've heard of his adventures. Mother sang his song all the time."

"Your mother, eh?" Delik rubbed the stubble on his chin. "What if she wa—"

"Look, I should be the one asking the questions." Elrin's face flushed. "What's the story with you and the Captain?"

"I'm sure he'd prefer you call him Commodore." Delik gave a bitter grin. "He attacked my homeland. He led the attacks on Tillydale, killed most of us and enslaved the rest."

"Why?"

"That's a long bloody story." Delik thought for a moment. "Jandans believe everything belongs to their god; the living, the dead, the soil, the sea. They come across the ocean spilling tales of their almighty Lord. They tell us they are the Lord's chosen and that they are the keepers of his dominion. So they lay claim to everything."

"Even the dead?"

"O'course the dead! Has all that shine blinded you lot? Or is the air to thin up there in your golden nest? Never mind the dead, they're bound to find their way to the dirt; Ona takes all back to her bosom in time. It's the living that feel the injustice."

"Are you talking about their poaching priests? What they do is vile."

"That's just part of it. It's the whole way they think that's backwards. They claim my people are the property of the Council of Jando because we occupy the Lord's sacred territory; which as far as I can tell is any spot on Oranica the Council takes a fancy too. They seized our towns and placed them under Jandan administration. Our lands were taken, but we were forced to keep working them. Our produce was sent to Jando and we had to buy our food back at higher prices. We were given protection in exchange for a tithe; our children."

"How could you do that? Give away your own children?"

"What? Don't be daft! It's not so simple as that. First off, they stole them. Then they took control of our villages and under the sword of the administrators we were starving and desperate. They harvested us as we did our orchards. Our elders were bribed, tortured or replaced until they signed our lives away. They took the strong or the troublesome so we would never rebel and if one family hid their child another family would report them so their own might have a better chance. You couldn't trust anyone. Some even stole children from neighbouring villages to pass off as their own for tithe. It was a terrible time."

Elrin was struck by the pain Jando had caused. "I knew Jandans owned slaves, but I never really understood what went on down there. Why did they attack Tillydale and your other towns if they were already under Jandan control?"

"Patience lad; you've got to know the roots of the story before you'll understand why the crops got the rot. Over time some of our people, who were slaves to high serving councillors and the rich and influential in Jando, persuaded the Council to allow us more rights. See, first they had us as equal to wild game on the Jandan estates. Shankakin were no more to them than produce for trade; we had less rights than any slaves. Once the laws changed we could own property and have a decent standard of living. We were not to be shackled or caged unless proven of crimes or misconduct through the courts. Owners breaching this would face fines. We also had the right to win our freedom through pardon or purchase."

Elrin was fascinated. Kleith had done his best to teach him, but there was so much history that he didn't know, particularly the history of the Coast. "Then what about tithing your children and the Jandan administrators?"

"Our children were still the property of Jando, but the military was stood down. We had shankakin overmen installed to govern each village. They were Jandan stooges, but conditions relaxed and our crop yields increased, so the Jandans were happy. They still had their slaves and were getting a bigger profit from them."

"How is that any better?" Elrin was shocked that their kin enforced the slavery. It was outlawed in Calimska, though anti-guilders said apprentices were no different to slaves for the guilds. At least an apprentice had a wage and lodgings. This was too awful to understand. "Surely, you couldn't have gone on like that."

"We had no other choice, until my father formed an underground movement to end the Jandan hold on our lands. Many years past before the rebellion was ready to seize our towns back. Shankakin are little people, but we have a lot of patience. We succeeded; the shankakin outside of Jando were free and not a drop of our blood was spilt."

Elrin could never have been so patient, endured those conditions under the corrupted overmen. He nodded for Delik to continue.

"We knew it wouldn't be long before they would send the military to take the towns back by force. My father led the defence of Tillydale. I fought there as well. Each town repelled the forces sent against it. Jando didn't think it would take much. They calculated that we would be under resourced, but we had been stockpiling food and weapons for years. We harried the troops as they moved towards the towns and cut off their supply lines. Without our villagers supplying food to Jando, their city and their soldiers starved.

"That's when Jando proposed a truce. We negotiated territorial borders and trade with Jando. Our children were ours again."

"So you did it, you won your freedom," said Elrin, his eyes bright.

"Not quite; the slaves in Jando were still not free. A splinter group of rebels wouldn't be satisfied until every single soul had their liberation. They would steal slaves from Jando and release them.

"Many joined that group, led by my father. I disagreed with him. I thought it would provoke Jando, and it did. They attacked without warning; waves of soldiers and redeemers claimed us. Our towns were levelled; soil and soul defiled. Pelegrin was in charge of deporting our survivors by ship to Jando for slavery, but that bastard couldn't help himself. He wanted blood and sailed his ship up river following the marching army, blasting shot into any who fled to the water's edge. First Tillydale, then Crooked Creek, all the way up to Pumpkinvale. It was a massacre.

"Rewarded for his bravery too, can you believe it? He was sinking unarmed boats laden with women and children. He's a commodore now, for that. I remembered him when he took me, swore I'd kill him if I ever saw him again. In Jando, I was worse than a slave. My people blamed me for it all."

"But, wasn't it your father's fault?"

"Of course they blamed him, but he was out in the wilds on the run. I was a reminder of their crushed hope. Eventually the old man's rebels sprung me from my chains. I went into hiding for a while then got this job in Rum Hill. Far enough from the City of Bones and close enough to keep tabs on Jandan naval movements."

"Why are you interested in the navy? Why not take your fight to the Jandan leaders, aren't they the problem?"

"Black powder is Jando's strength, not their leaders. If we crippled their navy, they'd be impotent in the border towns. They'd have less reach to hinder the rebellion."

"If you say so."

"I do indeed say so."

"You think black powder is more powerful than magic? Redeemers might just be poachers, but they—"

"I never said that! I've been at these dogs for longer than you've been off the teat. Don't you imagine I'd have given all the angles a measure of thought?"

"Fine." Elrin was not convinced. Delik might be certain, but that didn't make him right.

From the far corner of the prison deck, a shadow moved.

Elrin tapped Delik on the shoulder and pointed. "Did you see that? Something's in that cell over there."

Shadows clung to a mysterious figure, masking their features as they emerged from a recess.

"I guess they have another prisoner on board," said Delik, unsurprised.

"Such a touching story." The shadow's voice, feminine and familiar, was slick with sarcasm. "There really should be a nice fire pit down here. It might help the inmates open up a little. Prisons are so cathartic, don't you think? Perhaps this one was a little too cathartic for some, considering the smell."

"Delik," whispered Elrin. "I've heard that voice before. I think I know who it is." Elrin raised his eyebrows and tilted his head to show he had the situation under control.

Delik took his arm. "Be careful what you say boy. That voice sounds like trouble. Honey's sweet, but sticky."

"Oh, lay it on thick, Delik," said the woman.

"What?" Delik was taken aback.

"Is that you Minni?" Elrin was sure it was.

"Who in the hells?" Delik hollered into the darkness. "How do you know my name?"

"Delik. You don't have to pretend you don't know me. Elrin's harmless in all respects. I'm sure he won't attack you if you tell him the bits you missed from your sentimental recruitment spiel."

"Shut it, Minni." Delik burst out.

"He's very paranoid, Elrin," said Minni still half hidden by shadow. "Not so trusting, though I'm sure it's not personal."

"Minni, enough!" Delik was on his feet pressing his body against the bars.

"How does she know you?" Elrin began to question everything Delik had said, each doubt fanned a rising flame of resentment; he had been far too quick to believe this stranger's tragic tale.

"Yes, a fine question to start," said Minni. Her voice dripped with dark pleasure.

"She is a ..." Delik repositioned his shoulders and lifted his chin. "She's a friend of my father's."

"Come now, Delik. The boy isn't an agent. You heard my report this morning; he's been watched since Calimska."

"So you say. So why did he follow you to the docks? Why didn't he mention his dead letter to me?"

"He's on the run, of course he's going to head for the nearest ship," Minni laughed. "Look at him. He'll fit right in, so why keep him in the dark?"

"He knows enough. He knows what Jando has done to us. He knows about Pelegrin. He heard it spill from the coward's own lips."

"Yes, it was a lovely performance; much better than the fireworks we planned. Bravo for your improvised contingency. Are you happy now that you've got that off your chest?"

"I wouldn't have needed a contingency if you'd kept your shiner off the damn docks!"

"I'm right here. Don't speak of me as though I'm some game piece!" Elrin rose to his feet, frustrated and confused. He must have lost something in the translation, none of this made sense. "Did you say I've been watched? You knew about me? But, how?"

"Oh, you play the innocent so well. I bet you had our man marked from the start. Calling his bluff at the docks so he'd pull you out of harm's way; you don't fool me. What gave him up then? Did you pick out our signals?"

"Signals? I don't understand. What are you up to?"

"Just shut it would you. You'll get us all killed if you don't come clean." Delik kept his voice low, but his frustration was clear.

Elrin edged closer to Delik and with immense control considering his rising fury, bottled his anger behind clenched teeth. "Why should I shut it? Either you tell me what is going on, or I'll tell Pelegrin about you and Minni. I don't know what you have planned, but I'll make sure I'm just as creative as you two."

"Are you an agent?" Delik eased his tone, studying Elrin's face.

"He'd have squawked already, Delik. Don't be a fool," said Minni. "Save the drama for me."

"I'm nobody's agent."

The boards above them creaked and groaned with heavy footfalls.

"Swear it," said Delik.

"On my father's name, Arbajkha."

"By all the gods lad, if we get through this I'll tell you more. For now, just hold your tongue. Pretend you don't know anything."

"That's not going to be difficult," said Elrin.

INTERROGATION

Elrin's throat tightened as the monstrous footfalls stopped outside the door to the prison hold. The lock rattled and the door opened, revealing the ogre at the threshold. With an awkward contraction and twist, he squeezed through the doorframe, scraping fresh lash wounds against the timber. A low whimper escaped his lips. With such a mighty body, rippling with muscle, he had the power to tear a man apart; yet here, under the lash and clamped in irons, his spirit was broken.

Behind the ogre was the officer with the whip and following him were two guards who took positions by the door. Pelegrin came in last; his nose was a mess, crooked and swollen and a cruel grin pressed across his face. He gingerly stepped down into the chamber with his sword arm strapped to a splint, hanging lame by his side. His eyes were crazed, pupils full like a blaze addict hitting sky before the slump.

Minni had returned to the shadows, leaving Elrin without a clue of what they had planned or what he should do about it. Delik was calm; his chin held high, a defiant cockerel stuck in a coop. Elrin admired his confidence. Such a diminutive man, bound and restricted, yet still aloof from his captor.

Delik strutted to the locked cell door, pressing his face through the bars, tempting the Jandans closer. "Ha! You're a sorry sight. Thought you'd be all patched up. Did you leave your bone-sucking priests at home? Oh, poor dear has no one to pray for your sorry soul."

The officer with the whip cracked it forward, lashing the bars where Delik's head had been. The whip was fast, but Delik knew it was coming. "Away from the door, maggot!" The whip cracked again.

The ogre flinched with each crack of the whip. He shuffled nervously and moaned as if he were struck.

"Get in your cage, beast." The officer with the whip gave the ogre a shove. The ogre hurried toward the cage opposite the shadowed one, which

Minni had occupied. He sniffed the air and turned about, searching the dim corners, groaning.

"In!" The officer cracked the whip across the creature's raw back. The ogre opened the cell and moved in. The Jandan rolled up the whip and closed the door, locking it with a key hooked to his belt.

Delik moved to the cell door again, as close as he could to Pelegrin. "Are you fresh out of sinners to feed your hungry Lord? You can have me if you come and take me yourself."

The officer turned quick on his heels and cast the whip between the cell bars, thrashing Delik across the chest. "Away from the door, grub."

Delik sucked in a sharp breath through his teeth. "Coward!"

Pelegrin fumed, having no adequate retort against Delik's belligerent goading.

"I imagine you came here to hurt me, Commodore, but I can't for the life of me figure out how you'll beat me well enough without a decent arm to swing. Or do you plan to keep glaring at me with that mess of a face, hoping I'll swoon?"

"Shut it!" Pelegrin spat at Delik, keeping out of his reach. "I should have put you in shackles."

"I was worried about that big boy you had stomping about, then you went and locked him up. He'd have given me a decent fight. So, how do you plan to question me? You won't like it in here I suppose; these accommodations lack the comforts you might expect. Shall we pop up to your cabin for a spot of tea?"

"Silence!" Pelegrin gave his officer a nod.

The whip swung forward. Delik stepped to the side, the whip cracked and missed. The ogre keened a low moan from his cell.

"Why let your underlings have all the fun, come and get me yourself. Or are you too smacked out?"

Pelegrin would not be lured into another fight with Delik. He stewed from a safe distance with eyes for revenge and a body incapable of dealing the brutality he hungered for.

"You two, take the shiner." Pelegrin motioned for the marines guarding the door.

"The lad's got nothing to do with this, he's just a stupid adventure-hungry boy," said Delik.

"If he isn't especially important, you won't mind if I ask what he knows. Nothing like a keelhauling in the morning to freshen the Lord's spirit. Brightens the day for sailing." Pelegrin straightened with confidence; he was in control now.

Elrin wasn't sure what a keelhauling was, but it didn't sound all that pleasant.

"Fine, take him," Delik shrugged his shoulders. "I don't know him.

What do I care?"

"You don't fool me, Scrambletoe," Pelegrin smiled then waved his good hand at the guards. "Come on then, make it happen! Grab the lad. Just watch the grub doesn't bite."

Elrin backed into the corner of the cell while the Jandan with the whip unlocked the door. The two marines marched into the cell. Delik rushed the door, but the officer had it shut before he could escape.

The marines skirted Delik and advanced on Elrin.

Minni stalked out of the shadows behind Pelegrin and grabbed his good arm by the wrist, twisting it high behind his back. Her knee arced up and slammed into his kidneys, doubling the Jandan over.

She shoved forward, using Pelegrin's body to wedge the officer with the whip against the cell door. Her dagger struck out and blood coursed from the wretched officer's neck, spurting onto Pelegrin's blue jacket. The whip dropped from the officer's dead hands and the ogre wailed, thumping his fist on the deck.

Delik backed up to the bars so Minni could cut his bonds.

The two marines inside the cage were panicked by the speed at which things were going against them. One grabbed Elrin while Delik took Minnie's blade and advanced.

Minni had another dagger on Pelegrin and spoke to the two Jandans stuck in the cell with Elrin and Delik. "Hand over your steel, boys, or the Commodore's dead. And if you don't like him all that much, you can take your chances with us."

Neither man surrendered their weapons.

Delik kept edging forward, closing the distance between him and the guards. "Elrin, walk to me."

Elrin didn't want a blade in his back from a desperate guard. Instead of following Delik's instruction, he shoved all his weight to the right, knocking over one of the men. Delik charged forward and pierced the remaining guard in the gut, grabbing the man's short sword as he slumped forward holding his abdomen. Elrin rolled away from the marine he knocked aside and Delik moved in, slashing at the marine's legs with dagger and short sword. The marine screamed in agony and crumpled back to the deck, grasping at his wounds to try and stem the flow of blood.

Delik cut Elrin's bindings and together they stripped the guards of their weapons and locked them in the cell. Pelegrin withered on the floor in limp defeat while Minni tied his wrists. He watched the prison hold door; his last hope, but no reinforcements came to the rescue.

"Always keep your guards at the door," Minni chided. "What were you thinking, Commodore?"

Elrin rubbed his wrists, encouraging the circulation. "Can either of you explain what is going on?" This mess was spiralling out of control.

"We are going to commandeer dear Pelegrin's ship," said Delik. "What do you think Minni? Better we have *Juniper* for ourselves than leave her to the fish. Can we have it so and still make the original plan work?"

"It only serves in our favour. As long as we get the codes, we can still free all the slaves," Minni flashed Elrin a wicked grin. "Want to go sailing?"

Which hell had this woman come from? He hadn't got Minni mixed up in his troubles; she was trouble enough on her own.

"What slaves?" Elrin flung his arms around in exasperation. "The hold is empty save the Jandans and the ogre."

"They're not on this ship, that's why I was trying to blow a hole in it before you came along with your hero pants on," Minni pouted. "Would have been a lot easier."

Elrin shook his head in confusion. "I don't understand."

Delik grabbed his arm. "This is serious, boy. We are going to pilfer the pride of the Jandan armada and cripple their slave trade. If you're in, we've got room. If you're out, then the safest place is back in that cell."

"How can we take over the ship alone?"

"We're not alone, lad." Delik clapped him on the back. "We're never alone."

"You'll not free a single soul without my authority," snarled Pelegrin.

"That's why I treated you so nicely on the docks," Delik grabbed Pelegrin's injured elbow, making the commodore wince. "I figured if I was polite, you'd help us out. I know how much you deplore slavery, and I assumed you wouldn't mind if I gave all of your crew a free pass too. You don't mind do you?"

"You'll never get a re–" Pelegrin's arm was twisted and he cried out in agony. "Argh! I'll do it; I'll sign a release. Damn vermin!"

"Right then, let's begin." Delik handed Minni's dagger back. "Minni, give the order."

Delik gagged Pelegrin and hauled him into the cell opposite the ogre.

Minni handed Elrin a short sword taken from one of the marines. "You got my back?"

"Of course."

"Then get ready for the five hells to break loose."

MUTINY

Minni eased open the door from the prison hold and snuck up the stairs to the gun deck. A pair of marines passed by on patrol, their backs to her position. The deck was busy with indentured crew cleaning cannons and stockpiling ammunition.

Pulling her mind inwards, she imagined herself as a cat, sure-footed and quiet. She was lithe; sharp death cloaked in silence. The meagre sweepings of daylight from the half-cocked gun ports left rich pickings for stealth. Crouching low, she slunk down into the shadowed belly of the frigate.

She pressed close against the starboard bulkhead, sneaking past industrious men working no more than strides away. They were hard at their chores, looking out for the marines on patrol and none would be concerned by the flick of a shadow in the corner of their eye.

Minni tucked in behind the first cannon she came to and the crewman tending it tripped over her in the darkness. With an awkward fumble and a push, she helped him back onto his feet.

"Gods!" The crewman rubbed the back of his neck, eye's wide at the fright. "Where did you come from?"

"Never you mind. Are you ready?"

"Aye, we're ready." He squinted down the line of cannon looking for the patrol. "Still no signal though, what's happened?"

"You're our new signal. Get a powder boy and ready this cannon. Make some noise, I'll keep the uniforms busy."

"Aye, Miss."

Minni moved further along in the shadows making room for the crewmen to prepare the weapon. She counted six marines guarding the gun deck, enforcing their authority in pairs, marching up and down. Their swords and uniform were enough to assure dominance over a crew that outnumbered them.

Sliding two stilettos from her vest, she crept up behind the closest patrol and pounced, driving a needlepoint into each guard's neck. The poison coating the blades travelled to their brains and they went limp. Before they even hit the deck, Minni was close behind the next patrol. She focused her will on speed, pushing her legs to close the distance as fast as possible.

By the time the first two guards clattered to the deck and alerted their comrades, Minni attacked. They had no time to draw their weapons before she jabbed up with her poisoned stilettos, piercing each guard under the chin. If the poison didn't kill them, the hole in the brain did.

Minni spent no time inspecting her kills. She moved to the last pair of guards. They had witnessed her attack and had their swords already drawn. One edged forward while his partner charged at Minni. She relaxed her body and waited for him to close in. The marine slashed his blade forward in a downward arc and Minni easily stepped to the side, letting the marine's momentum carry him off balance, his sword arm over extended. Minni lunged, piercing through his vulnerable axilla, across into his chest. Her other stiletto struck down between his spine and scapula, piercing through to his heart. His death laden body dropped, pulling the stilettos from her grip.

With practiced ease she slipped her twin daggers from their sheaths and advanced on the remaining marine. He slashed out and she jumped back, just out of range. He slashed again, moving closer to connect. Minni stepped into his swing, her left dagger parried the sword and her body penetrated his attack. Her right dagger moved in, slicing up his arm, across his throat and then ripping back across and down. Blood poured out across his blue uniform while he grasped at her. Minni slid her foot behind and dropped him on his back. He lay there bleeding out, eyes wide in shock.

A gun crew assembled to fire the cannon. The great cast iron weapon was run out, its barrel bursting through the gun port. Minni's contact stood back, lit the linstock and put it to the touchhole.

"Mutiny!" he cried.

The cannon exploded and kicked back against its thick tethers, shaking *Juniper's* bones like a whip from the hells. A roar of voices rose up in unison; like a wave crashing upon the shore after a long journey across the sea, it broke with an irrepressible force.

The crewmen on all decks were ready; they would fight for their freedom, each knew what needed to be done. The uniformed sailors were taken by surprise with a barrage of fists and mop handles. The crew grabbed what they could to overcome their masters, the pent up aggression of being beaten down and ordered about, poured forth like a storm surge battering the shore.

Some of the crew were criminals and some were captured pirates, but others were innocent men, whose only crime was stupidity. Vagrants, drunks and addicts were often taken from the streets of Jando and pressed into labouring on the Jandan fleet. They were rounded up in the early hours of the morning to top up the crew after a skirmish at sea. Minni smiled at how easy it was to get her rebel sleeper agents on board to foment and organise.

The crewmen on the gun deck pushed through to the upper deck, knocking over and trampling the marines blocking the exit. Minni rushed back to meet Elrin and Delik as they came out of the prison hold.

"Come on boys, I don't want to miss out." Minni hurried them up the stairs, eager to take control of the mutiny before an opportunistic junior officer did.

"Don't wait around for us, we won't keep you from your fun," said Delik, moving up the stairs.

Minni didn't wait; she slipped away into the shadows and chaos.

❧☙❦

Delik got to the top of the stairs and shook his head; she'd disappeared again. That woman would be the end of him. Her wicked, self-bloody-satisfied smile would be the last thing he saw before death. She was too damn sure of everything for her age. The truth is she didn't know the half of it and was ignorant of the rest.

This mutiny had to be controlled before it fell into the hands of some petty officer wanting to jump rank. Bet she hadn't planned that—or the lad. What was she thinking, getting him all mixed up in this? The fool had to run into the fire. Typical human; racing into every stupid impulse without any measure of the way ahead.

"Come on then, lad," urged Delik. "Here's the adventure you were looking for."

Elrin's smile was weak with nerves and he held his sword like a limp fish.

"First off, hold it like this." Delik grabbed Elrin's hand and moved it on the grip. "These blades are hangers, you've got no reach against an officer's sabre. You've got to slip inside their reach. Cut and thrust, in close quarters." Delik demonstrated. "Cut. Thrust. Got it?"

"I think so."

"Right then, let's get you some practice."

Delik charged forward, hoping Elrin was following behind. There was no time to baby him; he'd have to sink or swim. Sure enough he kept close—a little too close though—hugging Delik's shadow like a cautious toddler chasing his mother's skirts. There was something about the lad, something larger than his awkward naivety allowed. He doubted Elrin was what Minni hoped for, but he might prove useful nonetheless. Either way,

Ona was busy enough with the bodies of those already fallen to the butchers. So many had died against the Jandan scum, she didn't need any richer soil today.

Up on the main deck the mutinous crew had pinned down a unit of marines. The Jandans were in disarray with mixed commands from conflicting junior officers. Without Commodore Pelegrin's authority behind them, the officers couldn't rally their men.

It was a deadlock. The marines and officers were better armed, but the crew outnumbered them and pressed their flank so neither could advance. Delik shoved his way to the front line, taking stock of the situation. Elrin followed, though he had considerably more trouble squeezing through the agitated crew. The lad needed to grow a stem; he was too damn polite.

Above them on the quarterdeck, the battle raged on, steel clashed and men cried in a cacophony of agony or victory. Delik had to break the deadlock to weigh the scales in their favour; every moment wasted counted the Jandans an opportunity to regroup.

"Your captain is captured. Stand down!" Delik's voice demanded attention, commanding an authority that towered above his mere stature.

"Hold the line!" The officer in command screamed, his face stained with blood from a cut above his eye.

"You have one chance for surrender, you are outnumbered. I have fifty armed and trained men advancing from the docks."

The sailors holding the front line shifted their posture. They were listening now.

"All surrendering troops will be offered clemency. Officers will be interrogated and detained."

Delik waited.

The sailors shifted again and some of them muttered to each other.

"Deserters will be killed! By lord's will, hold the line!" The young officer raised a sabre above his head, fury flashing his eyes wide.

That was no way to command. Morale grew in warm soil, not cold steel; those men needed hope and trust, not threats. Delik sucked in a breath for courage and turned his back on the marines to address the ragtag mutineers. It wasn't as dangerous as it seemed; the mutineers' faces would tell him if an attack was imminent. "Protect those who surrender, disarm or kill those who resist."

Two marines from the front line broke ranks, dropping their weapons and running to the mutinous crew. The crew cheered for the defection and Delik let them through.

"Hold the line!" The officer screamed in a futile rage.

"Prepare to advance. Men with weapons to the front." Delik faced the sailors holding the line, staring down his opponents. The crew behind him rallied their spirits by stomping on the deck in rumbling unison and hollering abuse at the enemy. Delik knew he could not hold them much longer.

Four more soldiers broke the line, filling the mutineer's ranks. Another cheer went up. The commanding officer shoved men forward to fill the gaps, shouting abuse, frantic as his control slipped away.

Delik led the charge. "Attack!"

The crew launched forward in a bluster of screams, blades and blows. The front line of sailors wavered then collapsed; some dropped their weapons and others fell back to a defended corner of the quarterdeck.

Delik made for the commanding officer, breaking through the ranks, deflecting blades, ducking and weaving, slicing a wedge to the officer's position. The officer slashed low with his sabre, trying to keep Delik at a distance. Delik parried and Elrin burst into the fray with a clumsy thrust. The officer stepped to the side and countered, slashing at Elrin's back as he careened off balance. The attack exposed the officer's flank and Delik took the opportunity to move in, cutting through the Jandan's hamstring, collapsing him like a trestle. He kicked the officer's sabre out of reach and advanced on the remaining sailors fighting on the quarterdeck.

Elrin recovered his balance and charged ahead, lucky to fight on with only a scrape across his back. What he lacked in skill, he compensated with daring, pressing an attack on a panicked sailor who slashed a sabre around, trying to swat Elrin away.

The remaining sailors stood at around fifteen men. They were backed against the bulwark without any officer to rally them. Not that an officer would have offered a great advantage to the cornered men; the crew were hungry for the fight, whilst the sailors were just trying to stay alive.

Delik yelled out to the remaining sailors. "Surrender you bastards! I can't control this crew otherwise."

Some of the crew were out for blood, despite Delik's offer of mercy on surrender. Most didn't want to risk their own lives by going easy on the sailors and hoping they would drop their weapons. Delik couldn't hold them back from the passions of battle once they took hold.

The sailor fighting Elrin dropped his blade and held his hands forward, begging for mercy. A mutineer came up from behind, raising his sword for the kill, but Elrin knocked it out of his hands before it could come down on the sailor. The mutineer wheeled around and grabbed Elrin, breaking on berserk, wide-eyed and red with rage. Elrin took a fist full of the madman's hair and brought the hilt of his sword crashing into his crazed skull, knocking him out. The surrendering Jandan fell to his knees, desperate for the melee to be over.

Delik kept an eye on Elrin. He handled himself well enough when the odds were against the enemy, but if the tide of battle were against them, he'd be blood on the deck. Delik pressed on at the front of the fray, Elrin close beside him, disarming vigilante crew intent on killing Jandans who surrendered. The lad might just fit in with his freedom fighters—if he survived long enough.

In the last moments, pressed by mutineers on all sides, there was no opportunity for surrender. The final marine standing was disarmed, only to be struck down from behind by a raging mutineer. Cold blooded murder was all too often cloaked in the heat of battle. Delik's blood boiled in a fight like any other; many of the uniforms deserved everything they got, but he wished there was more honour in it. The disparity of justice afforded his people fuelled a furnace of enmity he wrestled to dampen.

He bottled it down against every raw impulse to paint their blue uniforms red. "Take their weapons and round them up on the main deck. Get the rest of the ship secure and separate the officers."

Delik had expected more resistance; the fight could have been more difficult. He took a breath to survey the decks, tallying the number of blue jackets being rounded up. There were less than he reckoned on and while the rebels had control of Juniper, the true battle had not yet begun.

As planned, his dockers had joined with a unit of rebel elite and pressed in, supporting the mutineers and containing the fight on the frigate. Though they came to battle in motley armour, these men and women fought with formidable precision and discipline. They held the pier and guarded each door and stair on the deck. There was no way past them to escape; now Delik knew they stood a real chance for what was to come. The warrior in charge of the force ran over to update Delik.

The drakkin was a welcome sight.

SIGNAL

Elrin felt soft and vulnerable standing before the burly drakkin warrior. The reptilian was covered in brown and bronze scales with a sinister blade curving from hip level, slung low and dangerous. The weapon was less a sword and more a monstrous cleaver, keen and ready to butcher anyone fool enough to make a challenge. A turtle shell pauldron and a pair of cowry-studded vambraces were the only armour the battle hardy brute required. While displaying a hulking chest with naked pride, the drakkin was civilised enough to keep his dignity covered with loose fitting hemp trousers that also made room for a muscular tail, and were held up by a wide utility belt crowded with pouches and flasks.

Delik showed no apprehension whatsoever, beaming up at the reptilian and grasping his clawed hand in a vigorous shake. "Bloody glad you could make it, Tikis."

"This job is not done yet. There are many dogs still hiding in the officers' quarters and great cabin because Min–" Tikis was interrupted by Minni who snuck up behind the drakkin and slapped his tail. Tikis jumped a little and swung his tail away; the momentum snapped his body around to face her.

"Locked them in." Minni chuckled. "Beat you to it Tik Tik."

Tikis leant over, putting his face level with Minni's. "Tikis wants this job done right, Min Min." He chuckled; a sound mixed between a frog croaking and a cricket chirping. "These ones are locked in, yes. They say they have ten boltmen aiming at this door. This one and us cannot advance without deaths."

"Let them wait Tikky Bik. There's no rush." Minni went to wrap her arm up in his, but Tikis swatted her away.

"Is rush. Very rush. Lookout man on headland sees sails advance."

66

"What! Already?" Delik called down to a thickset man on the main deck. "Coalman! Get me an eyeglass up here."

Tikis pulled his top lip back exposing hundreds of short sharp teeth to Minni. "These dogs are barking. We and us have not replied. This headland beacon repeats the signal. We and us saw this, yet do not know these flashing light words."

Minni poked her tongue out at Tikis. "You don't have to go on about it, Delik doesn't play favourites."

"Where's the codebook, Minni?" Delik let the one-upmanship slide. He took the spyglass from Coalman's runner and put it to his eye, sweeping it over Rum Hill and the headland protecting the harbour. "We've got to reply or we'll be under fire once those galleons round the headland."

"It's in the great cabin," Minni crossed her arms.

"What?" Delik collapsed the spyglass with a curt snap.

"I would have had it, if you'd let me blow a hole in the ship like we planned. Remember the plan, Delik? I would have been in and out before she sunk. Seems to me your gripe with Pelegrin got in the way."

Delik ignored her dig. "What about the ship's signal seal?"

"The first mate didn't want to let it go, so I had to persuade it from him." Minni pulled forth an elaborately sculpted ivory dragon carved from a very large tooth. It perched on a brass tube with a crystal seal mounted on the base. "The blood wiped right off, so it should still work fine."

Elrin had never seen such a magnificent piece. "Is it from a real dragon?" He reached out to touch it.

"Whoa there!" Minni pulled it back and cradled it close to her bosom. "You should ask a lady before you reach for her treasures."

Elrin blushed.

Minni laughed and Tikis swivelled his head around focussing on Elrin with a movement so swift and smooth it was unsettling. Tikis flicked his tongue out, tasting the air. Elrin was nothing but drakkin food, a soft snack after a quick battle.

"Is this one known?" A clear membrane blinked horizontally across each of his staring eyes. He flicked out his tongue again. "He tastes like—"

Delik cut in with a shrill whistle. "Come on you two! Quit it. We have to get those codes."

Elrin was glad for Delik's intervention; Tikis put him on edge. This drakkin warrior had a palpable intensity, a primal, brutal certainty. All of which gave Elrin an idea.

"I know how to get us through the door," Elrin blurted, his thoughts rushed forward. It would be easy.

"How?" asked Delik.

"Release the ogre."

"This one jokes," Tikis bared his teeth and aspirated a choked confusion somewhat resembling laughter.

Elrin readied himself for some jibe from Minni. What was he thinking, saying that out loud? The ogre would raise chaos if he went berserk on deck.

"What then, lad?" Delik asked, in sincere consideration.

"Return his honour," said Elrin, surprised to be taken seriously. "Ask him to fight the Jandans who enslaved him."

Tikis erupted in more fits of strange laughter. "This Ogre? Honour?"

"Honour or not," said Minni. "The beast would be a perfect shield."

Elrin was shocked. "He isn't yours to sacrifice. I thought you were here to free slaves. Give him his own shield, why have him sent to slaughter? It's senseless!"

"Of course, that's what I meant." Minni shook her head with a grin. "Listen to this one boys; half a day with the rebels and he's a zealot."

He'd been baited. Damn this woman, she was impossible!

Delik called to several of his dockers. "Bring the ogre to us and make it quick." The men hesitated a moment before heading down through the hatchway below decks as instructed.

Tikis quit laughing once he saw Delik was serious and instructed his men to unhinge the heavy door below the forecastle for a makeshift shield. Some of the crew protested that their quarters would be open to the weather, but once Tikis made his presence felt, their complaints evaporated.

The deck vibrated as the ogre came up from below, his immense form rising through the hatch, shackles rattling with each shambling step. He kept his eyes to the deck as he was brought before them. Elrin wondered if the ogre noticed his captors were no longer in charge of *Juniper*.

"Ogre, do you want your freedom?" asked Delik

The ogre shifted his weight, but did not raise his head.

"Do you speak?"

The ogre stood still.

"He's too scared to speak. Or, maybe he doesn't speak Jandan." Elrin walked forward, but Delik held him back, out of range of the ogre's muscular arms.

Elrin called to the ogre. "Speak to us, you are free."

"Free is not free." The ogre's voice was like a storm rumbling, a deep rolling power on the horizon. His lightning blue eyes struck Elrin.

Elrin stood tall, though inside he was a lone leaf clinging to a limb in a storm. "We need your help to break down that door and subdue the Jandans."

The ogre swung his arms apart with a low grunt. The chains between his iron cuffs snapped taught then broke under the sudden strain. He flexed his huge arms and rotated his shoulders.

Everyone backed away, hands on their weapons, except Elrin. He stood in shock with a leaden stomach, watching the ogre's hands open and close. He was about to be crushed by keg-sized fists. The young man drew his arm up in a pathetic attempt to block the inevitable blow.

It didn't happen. Elrin dropped his arm, feeling both relieved and foolish.

With a controlled thud, the ogre sat down and grasped the chains on his leg irons. He rolled onto his back and heaved with his arms and pushed with his legs. Thickset muscles bulged and after much grunting and straining, a link in the chain gave way.

The ogre slowly knelt before Elrin and the others. "Hurn Ga Kogh will help now."

Elrin didn't know what to say. Why hadn't the Ogre broken his bonds earlier?

Delik called to Tikis. "Right then, give the big fella that shield and let's get these bone baggers out of bed."

Tikis assisted a burly docker to lift the shield made from the door and carried it to the ogre. The ogre took it with ease; sliding his arm through the rope straps and gripping the improvised handle.

"There's a bunch of Jandans with crossbows in there, Hurn was it? ... Can I call you Hurn?"

The ogre towered over Delik in stony silence.

"Anyway, give that door a tap and keep behind your shield. Just stay put."

"Tikis, get that foul brew ready." Delik called to the rest of the rebels. "Spread out, everyone. Let's take these bastards alive!"

Hurn lifted his foot and crashed it into the door. It shuddered, but held. The second kick knocked the door off its hinges with a splintering crash into the cabin. The ogre ducked behind his makeshift shield as a volley of bolts took flight.

The wall of missiles bit into the shield, and fanned out across the deck. Tikis took cover against the bulkhead beside the open door and uncorked two terracotta flasks, lobbing them into the cabin where they smashed apart, spilling vile smoke. The men trapped inside yelled and spluttered, beginning to choke on the gas. The fumes leached out onto the deck, thick with the smell of putrefied eggs.

Another volley of bolts thudded into Hurn's shield. He grimaced and gave a snort, but held his position. At such close range the bolts were just breaking through, the sharp tips protruding like the spines of an angry manticore. After the second volley, Minni dashed into the room with her face covered in a strange black mask. Tikis retreated away from the door and signalled Hurn to do the same.

Hurn backed away while officers came tumbling out. One brave Jandan ran out holding a handkerchief to his face, sword at the ready. Once he took stock of Hurn looming over him and the rebels that surrounded him, he threw his sabre to the deck and surrendered. Most staggered or crawled out, retching as they went, gasping for untainted air. They were easy to disarm and restrain.

Delik's men lined up the captured Jandans.

"Tikis," called Delik. "Get your men to separate out the officers. We'll need to get as much information as possible. Make them understand we are serious."

"Strange battle," rumbled Hurn. "That all?"

"We need a solid guard in the prison hold," said Delik. "It will be full soon. Can you keep them in line down there?"

Hurn grunted and stomped down through the hatch to the lower decks.

"What about Minni?" Elrin pointed to the dissipating smoke and the bodies on the deck inside the cabin. "She hasn't come out yet."

"Plenty of tricks to keep her busy. She's probably stuffing her pockets while she's in there. Don't fret, she can hold more than her own, lad."

Elrin wasn't convinced; the putrid gas would have overwhelmed her by now. How could they be so calm? Elrin fought the urge to run in to find her. He wouldn't last long if he did. Even outside in the open he was near retching with the lull of the ship on the water and the residual gas hanging in the air. He resigned himself to trust Delik.

Delik shouted into his loudhorn. "Hear this! If you serve the Council of Jando under duress or penalty, if you have no commission or office of merit, then you are free."

The captured sailors and marines weren't sure if it was a trick or not. One man walked towards the gangplank.

Delik presented his offer. "All those who wish to leave will be escorted from the ship to wait in a safe house until we have an understanding of your intent.

"If you can't bear the yoke of your Jandan masters, join us. If you're sick of the Temple taking your flesh for sin; join us. If you want to see the Council bare their own bones instead of taking ours; join us. If you want a Jando that is just, a Jando that is free; join us."

An officer spat on the deck. "The Good Lord will burn you, body and soul!"

"Ha! I'll be earth for Ona before your 'good' lord gets his arse off that throne of bones." Delik turned away from the officer, addressing the marines alone. "Make your choice now."

Half of them chose to leave. Before they were escorted from the ship onto the docks, the volunteers pointed out the officers hiding amongst them. Some of the veteran officers had removed their rank insignia during the fray. Some had cast off their entire uniform. Two officers had replaced their own uniforms with those taken from lower ranked sailors killed in the melee; bloodstains and all.

Tikis pulled these two from the group, one hand wrapped around each neck. He dropped one of the officers to the deck and pinned him with a clawed foot, pushing the air from his chest. The other man was thrust into a headlock.

With a twitching tail, Tikis cast his eyes over the Jandans lined up before him. "Officers will be questioned, one by one. Answers will be checked with others and us." Tikis flexed his bulging bronze arms. The officer in the headlock squirmed, his face bright red with panic and exertion. "Clemency, if ones cooperate. If ones refuse to cooperate or ones deceive us, then ones die."

The drakkin brought his fist down upon the officer in the headlock, shattering his skull like an egg. The sickening wet impact splattered blood and brain matter upon the deck and on the man pinned below. It was too much for the other Jandans. One of them vomited, which prompted another to do the same, as Tikis pummelled the officer's head again. He thrust his clawed hand through the broken shell of the man's skull and drew out a fist full of brain. He threw his head back and swallowed it like an oyster.

"Delicious." Tikis reached in and drew forth another handful and slurped it into his maw before dropping the body to the deck with a limp thud. The officer stuck underfoot passed out while Tikis sucked the remnants of brain from his fingers.

"This is how deceiver ones die." Tikis stared at the officers, then over his rebel unit. The officers looked away, but his unit held their heads up unwavering.

The lizardman lay the same intense examination on Elrin. The young Calimskan lifted his chin and held firm, though his instinct disagreed with that course of action. Tikis licked his mouth clean. Elrin had no idea how to read those hard eyes or his lizard face. Heat flushed his cheeks. Why was Tikis staring at him? He'd done nothing but help the rebels, probably to his own detriment.

Tikis flicked his tongue out and Elrin blinked. The drakkin's stone cold eyes squinted and he burst into chittering croaking laughter, releasing the young man from the standoff. Being humiliated by the drakkin was marginally better than being eaten. Elrin could accommodate the embarrassment.

The Jandans who took the clemency were handed rations and shell as they were escorted off the ship. Once on the docks, they were loaded into wagons and carted away.

The new volunteers were each coupled with a rebel crewman, as were the mutineer crew. They had no desire to return to Jando and end up in prison, or worse still, end up as poached parts for the redeemers. Jando would see them no mercy.

The same applied to Elrin; he was an outlaw to both Calimska and Jando now. The rebels were all he had, unless he cleared his name.

Minni emerged from the broken doorway carrying what appeared to be a large tome under her arm. She removed her mask with her free hand and stuffed it into her belt. Elrin wanted to hug her, though he couldn't of course. She would embarrass him somehow. Besides; it wasn't the proper thing to do. She wasn't his wife or sister, he barely knew her.

"What are you staring at me like that for?" Minni grinned. "Have the boys finished sorting their toys ou—"

"Signal!" called down the spotter from the nest.

An osprey perched on his arm, flapping its wings to balance against a fresh wind kicking up. He pulled a rolled up parchment from the sea eagle's message container and relayed it down.

"Two galleons approaching, at arms. Two galleons remain at sea. Request orders."

CODE

"Minni! Hurry up and open the damn codebook. There's not much time left." Delik clapped his hands as though that would speed her up. It didn't of course; Minni being Minni slowed her inspection more, no doubt just to irk him. "Don't bother looking for traps on the thing. Just get it open."

"Forgive me if I ignore that advice. I'm not so partial to death by poison." Minni placed the book on the deck and knelt beside it. Delik and Elrin hung over her shoulder as she pulled out the seal and examined the tome, figuring out where to place the seal.

"What is it exactly?" Elrin asked Delik.

"It's what the Council agents use to communicate. If you don't know the code, you can't understand what they are saying or how to return communications. We'll use it to figure out what they are saying with those flashes of light."

"Are you sure it's a codebook?" asked Elrin.

The last thing Delik needed now was a nosy know-it-all Calimskan. "The codes are inside. Now shush and let her open the damn thing."

At first glance the book appeared like a large tome, perhaps a spell book or Jandan holy text. On closer inspection though, it was just a fancy wooden box. There were three tones of timber. One side was bone white with an embellished border in ebony and mahogany flowers. The other side was all ebony bordered with mahogany and white stars. Flaming rays beamed across the surface.

"There is no place for the seal. Nothing matches." Minni rubbed her hand softly over all of the surfaces and edges. "It's smooth, one piece by feel."

"It can't be, look at it." Delik poked at it. "There are different colours and grains. Try pushing on the designs in the borders."

Without a reply signal, those two galleons would come round the

73

headland and open fire. Delik knew this was where his plan could sink. Minni's sabotage would have been less risky, but taking Pelegrin and *Juniper* was too good an opportunity to let pass. What a catch to ransom; Pelegrin's father, the Lord's High Admiral, would free four score rebels to get him back alive. The old bastard sat on the Council and had half of Jando in his pocket.

While Minni did her best to access the codes, Delik's mind raced toward the consequences of failure. If the Jandans thought Pelegrin was captured and the ship had mutinied, they wouldn't hesitate to sink *Juniper* and level Rum Hill at the same time. They'd chop a leg at the knee to banish the rot from a toe, such was the Jandan cure for most things. Rum Hill couldn't be sacrificed, they were not to be blamed for his strategy, it wasn't an option.

Without the codes the rest of his plan would be too difficult to pull off. Minni needed to work faster, but saying so wouldn't help. She knew what was at stake and worked her fingers like adders, striking out all over the wood, even tracing the seal over top and bottom hoping something would trigger it to open.

"Why are you doing that?" Elrin asked them.

"Making sure Delik doesn't catch a splinter." Minni joked, but her eyes betrayed growing frustration. She wrapped her knuckles on the wood then shook it, listening for a rattle.

"Open it Minni! You said you knew how!"

"Oh no I didn't, Scrambletoe. You said the seal would open it. You said I would have plenty of time. A lot of bollocks is what you said!"

Elrin picked it up to examine the markings. "It doesn't open."

Ignoring Elrin, Delik was determined to set Minni in line. "It was your contact that said the seal would open it. You dragged the Jandan scum to me!"

"Who said you should trust him? Hell, I didn't. Why do you think I killed him?"

"This isn't actually a book you know." Elrin tried to get their attention.

Delik gave him an incredulous look; annoyed by the persistent intrusions into things he knew nothing about. With Minni's admission of murder Delik's irritation grew all the more and he threw his hat to the deck. "You killed him? Why the hell did you do that? He was our best informant!"

"Well, obviously not very accurate," Minni casually turned her eyes to the headland. "In more ways than one."

Was she worried, or keen for more sport? Cool as ice that woman—and never to blame. Damn her to ash if anyone could figure out her game. "What is your bloody problem?" Delik raged.

"With you or with the dead informant? He had a certain peccadillo that wasn't to my taste. And you? To be honest, you've got more than a few traits I thi—"

"It doesn't open!" Elrin yelled at them.

"We know!" Delik turned on Elrin in his frustration. "I thought you Calimskans were all brains. Haven't you been listening?"

"No, no. You misunderstand me. It doesn't have to. Open, I mean. It doesn't work like a book or a box. It's a magical tablet. The seal doesn't open anything. It just, sort of, unlocks the messages."

This was all too convenient for Delik's liking. How did the boy figure that out so fast? Just when you start to trust a lad, he pulls a trick like this. If he wasn't a Jandan agent, how did he know about this device?

"Hand me the seal, Minni. I think I know how to work it." Elrin put his hand out for the dragon seal.

"Delik?" Minni made a curious face.

Was that a splash of doubt in her eyes? A rare thing, that. Though, it was typical of her to leave off making the tough call herself. Delik knew he would have to let Elrin use the device. With the Jandan galleons on their way they didn't have another option; Elrin was their only chance.

Damn the informant for feeding them half-arsed information and damn the Jandans with their secret bloody messages.

"Go on then, give it to him," said Delik. "Show us what you can do, but if you screw us lad, by Ona, I'll drop you where you stand." He stood back and waited, his face red and arms crossed.

Elrin set to work, speaking half to himself as he went. "One side of the tablet is for sending a message and the other is for receiving them. I think father called it the transcriber; it was so long ago since I played with one. Both it and the seal are needed; together they turn light into words and words into light. What do you want to say to the ships? Exactly."

Shaking his head in wonder, Delik was taken by the easy confidence Elrin had with the object the rebels had coveted for so long. Suspicion stole his words for a moment, running his thoughts on a tangent. The Calimskan was sharp; too sharp. If the lad was an agent for Jando or Calimska he was good, but he'd not be good enough for long enough. Time had a way of revealing the truth of things, the lad ought to be careful not to trip on a lie and take off his toes.

Gathering his thoughts to the immediate task, Delik dictated a false message. "Request Assistance. Commodore Pelegrin injured. Critical. Black powder explosion. Taking water."

Elrin worked his finger upon the dark side of the tablet with the suns embellished around the borders. As he traced invisible words, they then appeared, trailing behind like the script was rising from oily water. The floral Calimskan text grew in confusing swirls and kicks, spreading its creeping tendrils of who knew what sinister plot across the magical device.

"I can't read that!" said Delik. "How do I know you've written what I said?"

"You don't, Delik," said Minni. "Now is the time to trust him."

"It's on your head then, just keep an eye on what he's writing."

Elrin continued to write the message with Delik hovering over his shoulder.

"How the hell do you know they can read your script?" Delik wasn't ready to let this go. There was something suspicious going on; it made no sense.

"The magic of the transcriber and seal interpret the intent of the words not the words themselves."

The young Calimskan traced the golden seal over the words and the dragon carving writhed about. The words lifted from the wooden blackness and were sucked into the miniature beast's mouth. Elrin walked to the gunwale, twisted the seal and flipped the gilded dragon around, setting it within the tube shaped body of the device. Now that the seal was inside out, it revealed a series of lenses.

"I hope you're taking note of this, Minni." Delik had no idea what the boy was doing.

Directing the lenses to the headland, Elrin pressed the back of the seal and a buzz of magical energy coursed through it. The device clacked out a series of flashes, paused, then repeated the series twice more.

High atop the Rum Hill cliffs the Jandan beacon pulsed the same pattern in all directions.

Delik paced the deck watching the beacon, waiting for a response. The sea sloshed against the ship's side. A fish jumped in the distance. A cormorant dried its wings in the sun.

Nothing.

With more patience than Delik thought the situation deserved, Elrin kept the device aimed at the beacon on the headland.

"What's gone wrong?" Delik stormed over to Elrin. "Why haven't they responded?"

"Give it time," said Minni.

Elrin kept his position, trying to ignore Delik's complaints, tension knotting his dark brows.

A cool breeze played across the harbour.

Then the beacon sparked to life.

The flashes were recognised by the seal and it buzzed with another magical charge. Elrin let it finish then twisted the seal and refitted it as before. He passed the golden dragonhead across the bone white side with the carved border of flowers.

A message appeared in Calimskan.

"What does it say?" asked Delik.

Elrin read it without hesitation. "*Templestone* and *Fearless* on approach.

Redeemers aboard. *Deliverance* and *Lord's Flame* holding."

"Signal!" The spotter called as the osprey lighted on his arm.

He called down. "Guns stowed. Approaching at speed. Full sail."

Minni gave Elrin a hug and kissed him on the cheek. "You've saved our skin."

"Don't think I'm done with you lad." Delik slapped Elrin on the back and dashed a reluctant smile. "I'm expecting a good explanation on how the hell you knew what you were doing with that bloody contraption."

"I played with a set when I was a boy."

"I twiddled my thumbs when I was a boy." Delik wasn't going to be convinced by such a convenient intervention. He had a plan to test the lad's steel. "I've got a special job for you, Elrin. Minni, he needs a promotion. Find a nice Jandan uniform. We have a new acting captain."

Delik left Elrin and Minni to work out their costumes in the great cabin. He walked to the wheel on the quarterdeck and put his whistle to his lips. With shrill precision and a worn voice, he directed his dockers. They hauled supplies from the docks up onto the starboard side hidden from the view of the approaching ships. They soon had *Juniper* leaning like a drunk, shifting all the cargo off centre.

Uniforms of the captured Jandans were redistributed to those on the upper decks. All of the men in the open who couldn't find a uniform were directed below deck and out of view. Delik had the men on the upper decks set to their normal duties and set uniformed guards to patrol as normal.

Tikis bounded up to the quarterdeck and reported to Delik. "This and other ones are ready for work."

"Just as we planned, Tikis. It has to be quick and precise." The first ship was peeking its bow around the headland, headed into the harbour. "Right then, disappear. They'll have their spyglasses out."

Tikis ran across the deck and vaulted over the gunwale into the sea. That drakkin was a bloody good soldier. He'd never found a more versatile warrior since the rebellion began. He hoped more like him would rally to the cause; an army of drakkin would be a fine sight. If only all the tribes would stop fighting each other and see the real enemy.

Delik ducked into the officers' quarters to get out of view. Elrin would need a word or two of encouragement to carry this off. It was a fine way to decide what his caper was without jeopardising the mission.

Elrin walked out of the great cabin into the officers' quarters wearing a fresh uniform.

"You stink like the bloody swamp," said Delik

"But he looks the part," Minni picked a pill of lint off Elrin's blue coat. "They aren't going to smell him across the water."

"Why do I have to wear it?" Elrin asked Delik.

"Not sure if you noticed, I'm a slip too short for the thing."

"Surely there is someone else in your, er, group that could wear it."

"Yes, but you've made yourself our only option since you know how to work the magical light-message contraption." Delik sat on a bench with smug satisfaction.

"It's not a contraption! Together, the seal and transcribing tablet are brilliantly designed. It's called a solargraph," said Elrin, trying to educate them.

"See! Delik's right, you're perfect for the task. You even know what it's called." Minni repositioned Elrin's cravat a little and straightened his white waistcoat.

Elrin gave her a curious look. "I think I'm dressed fine now. Thanks."

"You'll be doing the talking, lad." Delik handed Elrin the spyglass, the magical seal and the tablet. "Just stay at the helm and do as I say. When they get within earshot you'll be on your own for a whisker. We want to keep them on the far side of the ship, so get them to double up and dock over there." Delik jabbed his finger in the direction of the neighbouring pier. "You ready?"

"No."

"Good. Head up to the wheel and follow my directions. Can't be simpler."

The reluctant young Calimskan left the cabin and made his way up onto the quarterdeck. Delik followed, sneaking behind barrels and crates as he went. Both ships were in full view now, tacking into the harbour together at a steady pace.

Pulling an oilskin over his head and hunkering down behind a barrel, Delik dictated another message to Elrin. "All haste to south pier. North pier under repair. All troops to disembark and secure dock perimeter. Vulnerable to rebel attack. Reserve units to disembark and proceed with haste to *Juniper*'s bilge. Redeemers to board and proceed to great cabin. Healing required immediately."

With quivering hands, Elrin sent the missive and held the seal aloft, ready to receive a return communication. After a moment, flashes beamed across the water from the leading ship and he translated the signal, calling it back to Delik. "Proceeding as directed."

Even from his sheltered position, Delik could see Elrin looked nervous, and so he should be. This was going to be quick and bloody if things went their way. But, if the rebels failed, a slow agonising death was the best Jando would offer. He hoped the lad handled the pressure if the fight came to him. If he really was green with a blade he'd need help, and if it was an act, then Delik would keep an eye on the lad anyway.

Either way, he'd not be left alone. May as well keep the lad alive and see what he was really after. If Elrin was an agent of Calimska, a dead letter was the perfect cover to get in bed with the rebellion. That humble, innocent runaway act had to be all bluff, Delik saw right through it. No matter, he would play along for now.

Delik wondered if the Jandans were playing along with his own grand bluff. Would they get in close and spring out their cannons? Or were they so self-assured by their military strength that they didn't even question Elrin's communication? Delik knew the ignorance of Jandans. They thought themselves superior to all—the Lord's chosen ones. The Council were so high and mighty they couldn't grasp the roots of the rebellion. They only cut the shoots back, and with every cut the roots grew stronger, deeper. Spring would come and there would not be enough blades under the sun to keep the rebellion from blooming.

TO SEA

Elrin stood squarely behind the wheel, trying his best to look like he was in charge of the situation. The two galleons headed to the north pier as they had been directed. First came *Templestone*, her figurehead a dour cleric holding a holy book under one arm and a corner stone under the other. *Templestone* navigated downwind before coming in to stand off the pier. The crew dropped all of the sails and the captain wheeled her around into the wind. *Templestone* slowed and slid in, docking snug with the pier.

Back home in Calimska, Elrin had been impressed when he saw this manoeuvre at the docks on the Lake of Tears, but the ships that traded up the River Tash to the Lake were half the size of this. The precision was a marvel to behold. While *Templestone* had her lines secured, *Fearless* came around and docked in the same way. Her figurehead was a knight in full plate, carved to attention and layered with enough silver paint to reflect the morning light like polished steel. She gave a gentle nudge to the pier, her forward momentum diminished by the drag of the water and wind.

Both ships were bigger than *Juniper* and to Elrin's relief they kept their gun ports closed. They appeared to have every intention of following the orders Elrin sent on the solargraph. If the Jandans had other plans, the rebels would be slaughtered.

A tall white robed figure stood on the main deck of *Templestone*, shadowed by another shorter figure in red. Both wore identical white cowls, emblazoned black with the holy star of Jando's foreign god. These were the redeemers come to heal the Commodore, nothing but sly poachers stealing essence to fuel their corrupted magics. Barbarous practices like that were outlawed in Calimska long ago, only true sorcery was allowed. Elrin caught himself in his own naivety. What did it matter that the Guildmaster was the greatest sorcerer since Calim himself? It didn't stay his power against an innocent. Elrin had to be wary of man and magic.

The Jandans had arrived with both in force. Five units of marines stood armed and ready on each deck. Elrin tried to grasp their numbers estimating three Jandans for every rebel. Delik and Minni must be insane to try and fight this many men. There was no hope against a force of these proportions, even with the extra men who had volunteered to help the rebels.

About thirty marines and crew had formed bucket brigades. One in each brigade cradled a timber hand pump and the rest carried pails, ready to relieve the bilge.

While the dockers assisted in securing the ships to the pier, the Jandans poured down the gangplanks in pairs, surging along the pier onto the main storage area of the docks. They formed a tertiary perimeter then pushed forward again, extending the defensive line to prevent anyone getting into the area. Access from Rum Hill and the headland was cordoned off and units took positions watching over the swamp and wilderness to the south.

As the soldiers secured the docks, the so-called redeemers were escorted by a small troop of elite marines carrying longswords and dressed in chainmail. Their shields carried the Jandan crest; a black star on a sea of blue. Pulling behind them, the bucket brigades jogged down the southern dock and around to board the listing *Juniper*.

The Jandans left a small unit of marines on *Templestone* and *Fearless*, patrolling the decks and ensuring the crew continued to follow orders of the commanding officers. Elrin fancied the crew on board the galleons were waiting for something. The rebels had dosed *Juniper*'s crew with their own men to execute the mutiny, so it made sense for them to have done so for *Templestone* and *Fearless* too. They would need to have a surprise to overcome this formidable enemy.

Elrin hailed the captain of *Templestone*, which had docked closest to *Juniper*. "About time. He's close to death! So's the damn ship!"

"Who are you?" The captain was perplexed. He paused scanning the decks for someone. "Is Trentin out of action too?"

This was a test; the captain was trying to catch him out. He only had half a chance of guessing. If he gave the wrong answer it would send the whole plan to the bottom of the bay.

"What?" Elrin feigned being unable to hear the man.

"Trentin? Is he injured? He's engaged to my sister, you see."

"Sorry! I didn't get the last bit. Trentin what?"

The captain frowned and reassessed *Juniper*, squinting up at leaning masts. High in the nest the osprey landed on the spotter's arm with a cheerful call.

"What is going on? That bird is not regulation."

"Ah, well, of course it isn't. It's a gift."

"A gift? For who?"

"The High Priest if you have to know. Commodore Pelegrin wishes to keep it a surprise."

The captain crossed his arms. "That doesn't sound like him."

Elrin was stuck. "He has an ivory cage ready too. Very generous is our Commodore." Nathis help him out of this one.

A gust of wind picked up, lifting Elrin's hat off. He grabbed for it and pulled it down over his black hair, but it was too late, the ruse was over.

"You're a damned shiner! What ha—" An arrow shot through the air and lodged in the captain's neck. He keeled overboard and into the sea, grasping at the shaft, choking on his own blood.

There was no time for Elrin to contemplate shock. As soon as the captain's body hit the sea, a volley of hooks launched from the water and lodged on the rails of *Templestone* and *Fearless*. Drakkin hauled out of the water and overpowered the marines patrolling the decks.

A platoon of shankakin sprung from below the southern docks. They emerged from the water brandishing blades and ran up the gangplanks to assist the drakkin. The embedded crew on both galleons took their chance as Elrin had guessed, pitching in with the shankakin and drakkin, using makeshift weapons to subdue the marines and officers that remained to guard each ship.

Each rebel platoon moved with silent death. They didn't scream battle cries and declare their intent. They moved fast and spoke with their blades, disarming and subduing those they could and ending the lives of those that hindered the assault.

The healers' elite guard had already boarded *Juniper* and were marching towards the officers' quarters when they noticed the attack on the *Templestone* and *Fearless*. They went for their swords too late; rebel blades were at their necks, leaving the healers prone to attack.

The poacher priests received special treatment, for the rebels must have dreaded what magic they might wield. Six crossbowmen covered them while they were bound, gagged and forced to their knees. The men binding them moved with haste born of fear, backing away as soon as their task was complete. None wanted to be sapped to a husk by sacrificial magic.

The bucket brigade had already descended through the hatch, headed for the bilge. They would have been weaving through the bowels of the ship before they realised *Juniper*'s crew were the enemy. Just as Delik had said, the prisons would be brimming with Jandans. The tide had turned for Hurn; he'd be enjoying his time as jailor.

While Elrin could only guess what was happening to the bucket brigade below decks, his position at the wheel on the quarterdeck gave him a perfect survey of the wider battle from all directions. Rebels attacked with swift cohesion, working so efficiently together they must have rehearsed. Each fighter knew their task and if one fell another was there to follow through. Drakkin warriors broke the Jandan resistance with blunt force while shankakin fighters overwhelmed them with furious speed. The mutinous crew of *Templestone* and *Fearless* were not as precise or battle hardy as the rebels, but they made up for it with enthusiasm.

The crew's treatment under the Jandan authority must have been poor. They issued forth with conspicuous delight, serving revenge on particular officers and marines. It made Elrin uneasy that men could justify all kinds of cruelty. Revenge was not a good reason, though he doubted any reason would end up being good enough.

The captain of *Fearless* suffered a painful death when the crew swarmed him, pummelling his body with boot and fist. The brutality ceased only when Tikis boarded the ship and separated the bloodthirsty crew, setting them to prepare the sails. If Tikis had not intervened the captain would have been nothing but a bag of meat. The crew would have kept on striking the dead body until they were spent.

Templestone and *Fearless* cast off while the muffled racket from the battle still issued from inside the ships. Each crewman worked with a motivation they had lacked when they docked, setting the ships to sea before the rebels had seized full control.

Without blood smearing Juniper's deck, the Jandan rescue contingent had been put down. The ship was secure and the crew looked to their new command.

"Bosun! Weigh Anchor!" Delik called from the quarterdeck. "Stabilise this ship and set sail!"

Elrin was relieved when a crewman approached the wheel.

"Old Selmet here will navigate," said Delik. "You can release the wheel from that death grip, lad."

Elrin hadn't realised he was clasping the wheel as though it would fly away. He let go and stepped aside for Selmet, a spry old sailor with a weathered grimace and awkward squint. He tipped his threadbare cap to Elrin and took the wheel.

On each deck, every spare hand set to shifting the cargo back while *Juniper* eased away from the pier at an awkward angle.

The marines on the docks were slow to realise the mutiny and theft of their vessels. The officers in command had their attention set on securing the docks from a threat on land. There was a harsh call to about-face, which was countermanded, and an argument erupted between two officers in the middle of the docks.

In the confusion, many of the marines hesitated to charge their own ships. The line of command was in disarray and couldn't coordinate an effective response. The more disciplined squads charged back across the docks. A score of marines reached the southern pier just in time to get aboard *Templestone* and *Fearless*, but in short measure they were repelled and flung overboard. The water darkened with the blood of the dead; laden with armour they sunk into the deep.

With the element of surprise spent, rebel archers on each ship shot at the Jandans. Minni raced up to Juniper's poop deck, leading a squad of marksmen. They first targeted the officers on the docks, then sent volleys of arrows and bolts into the marines. Minni commanded her bow with a sure, fluid motion, picking through the Jandans with such calm calculation, Elrin wondered if any of her shots missed.

The marines broke ranks and retreated behind crate stacks, carts and loading bays. The officers from the outer perimeter rallied their men as it dawned on them they were losing their ships. They organised a second charge of marines to attack with crossbows, but released just two volleys before *Templestone* and *Fearless* had pulled out of range.

Several drakkin dove over the side of *Templestone*, arrows protruding from their scaled hide; with such large bodies they were an easy target without cover. The rebels continued to shoot back, enjoying the advantage of better range and elevation, the archers decimated the Jandan crossbowmen, halving their number and painting the southern pier red.

When *Juniper* approached an even keel, Delik gave the command to come about and prepare the cannons. *Templestone* and *Fearless* kept behind the headland, out of the view of the other two Jandan ships anchored at sea beyond the bay.

Meanwhile, the fringes of the swamp south of the docks came alive. Drakkin rose from the mangroves and reeds, covered in mud, pelting the marines' unprotected flank with stones. Jandans crumpled to the ground clutching their heads and nursing their battered arms and legs; the slings of the drakkin were primitive but lethal.

Again the Jandan officers were taken by surprise as the perimeter they had just held secure was assaulted by an organised enemy. Commands lashed across the Jandan ranks, ordering the troops to protect the southern flank against the drakkin. The marines were doing their best to hold behind any kind of cover, sheltering against stacks of crates and pressing around warehouse corners while the barrage of stones stormed down without relief.

Elrin didn't know if the drakkin had been laying in wait at the edge of the mangroves all this time, or if they had crept up on the Jandans in camouflage; their scaled hide blended perfectly with the surrounding environment. The drakkin slings were in range of the whole dock area, lobbing missiles in high arcs that struck at those stuck behind meagre barriers and those on the northern side of the docks. The troops from the northern flank rallied to engage the slingers from the south.

Marines holding their position at the south of the docks broke cover and charged the drakkin in the swamp. The charge failed, their thin line of attack ripped apart by a volley of drakkin javelins. The Jandan defence could not retaliate with ranged weapons of their own because all of the surviving crossbowmen were pinned on the north and south pier without officers to pull them in to counter the drakkin's constant onslaught.

The ragged southern line broke just as the fresh marines pressed in from the north. A second volley of javelins swept into the confusion and the Jandan forces panicked, tripping over each other to get away. The officers lost all control of their men.

Routed, the marines knocked each other over and trampled the injured to get to safety, all discipline lost, all morale to dust. Zealous officers refused to call a retreat. They rallied a squad on the North Road, cutting down any marines who attempted to flee to Rum Hill.

Marines dived into the bay, taking shelter under the northern pier, desperate to escape the hail of stones. Others tried to fight their way through the drakkin to escape. They were ill prepared to fight in the swamp and were given no mercy; drakkin warriors clubbed and chopped, ending those who faltered in the mire with brutal effect. Elrin watched on from *Juniper* with a deep hollow in his gut, as the ambush fell into a slaughter.

"Wheel her around Selmet," Delik's eyes were grave, his mood as grey as death.

"What are you doing, Delik?" Elrin was uncomfortable in the Jandan uniform. The blue overcoat was oppressive in the heat and itched.

Delik pushed past and leant over the quarterdeck rail, yelling to his man on the main deck below. "Load the grape shot! Broadside the docks!"

"No, you can't. Delik what are you thinking? We're away there's no—"

"Are they your Jandan brothers?"

"No. It's just—"

"Hot lead will sear through their damned souls."

Juniper lined up her starboard guns with the docks. Elrin had a sick churning in his stomach from all of the killing. They had taken measures to preserve the life of the soldiers on the ships, but the battle on the docks was tainted; thick with revenge and darkly disproportionate to the Jandan threat.

"Don't do it, Delik," Elrin pleaded. "You're better than Pelegrin."

"This plan is long in the making lad. The docks have to go and those Jandans are just in the way." Delik watched the battle with empty eyes.

"Then your plan is flawed," Elrin removed the blue Jacket; it was too oppressive in the heat.

"Destroying the docks will weaken the Jandan hold on Rum Hill! It'll cut supply lines to North Eye."

"No, you're wrong. It will strengthen the Jandan hold. When trade grinds to a halt, the people of Rum Hill will turn against you. They will lose their livelihoods. When the Jandans repair the docks the rebels will have gained nothing."

Delik's cheeks flushed, his eyes were damp.

"They defiled her! They murdered her!" Delik slammed his fist down on the rail. "They all deserve to die!"

"If you fire the cannons, the two ships out to sea will hear. You will lose any chance of surprise."

Delik gripped the rail with both his hands, knuckles white.

"Hold fire!" Delik yelled, slamming his fist on the rail again. "Coalman! Hold fire!"

Coalman bellowed the order from the main deck, down the hatch, to the gun deck.

Delik wiped his face with his yellow cloth hat. He gave Elrin a grim sneer and shook his head before casting the hat into the sea. It bobbed in the wake of the ship for a moment before sinking into the blue of the bay.

Elrin stood with Delik in silence. They watched the battle on the docks run its course and stewed on their words.

Drakkin charged from the mangroves, bearing down on the marines with their superior size and strength. The remaining Jandan lines were torn to strips, buckling in a mess of blood and panic. Unruly shouts of victory punctuated the screams of the dying, burgeoning into a rowdy chorus that thrummed across the bay in a great wave.

A cheer went up on the captured ships, matching the vigour of their allies on shore. The rebel crew hollered and clasped each other's arms, showing grins as big as their relief that the battle was won. Delik refused to entertain any such celebration, his gaze drifted on the sea, his brow knit in thought.

Elrin had no joy for the blood spilt; scores of lives were lost and he had been part of it. He worried about what the rebels planned to do with the three prize ships. Jando would want them back.

His quest was burning to ash.

Delik called to his man on the main deck. "Coalman! I want these ships to sail out in formation. Get a message on wing to the others as well."

"The others?" Elrin squirmed. This adventure had him strapped to a demon dog and he had no idea to which of the five hells he was being taken. "How big is this, Delik?"

"Why? You scared lad?"

"Of course, I'm scared! I just wanted passage on a ship. Now, I'm part of this rebellion you're taking against Jando."

"Quit your complaining! You've got passage on our ship," said Minni, walking down the stairs to the quarterdeck. "Won't be free though."

Minni was unshaken by the battle. Her quiver was empty, but her dark eyes were full of mischief. She stood beside Delik and leant her bow against the rail, appraising them both.

"Look here lad. This is big, but the *how* of the big is a little murky." Delik became distant for a moment, as though he were remembering something.

"What does that mean?" Elrin was determined to extract some sense from them.

Delik ignored Elrin's question and called to Selmet at the wheel. "Once we clear that headland, set course to engage the two remaining Jandan vessels anchored beyond the bay."

"What Delik means is; he needs you in his crew," said Minni, giving Delik a nudge. "We've got a big adventure ahead of us. There'll be treasure. Glory too I imagine; if you like a bit of that. Won't be easy, but you seem to handle your head in a pinch."

Delik crossed his arms. "Hold your bloody horses. He's too fresh. He'll just get in the way."

"Didn't I just get you out of a pickle back there," Elrin fumed, the quick defence boiling over before he considered better diplomacy. "If I was so green, how did I know what to do with the solargraph? If I was in the way, how did I take down ten men?"

"Eight actually, but that's not bad if you're weak-wristed," said Minni. "I helped with two. Just keeping an eye on you."

Elrin balked then blushed. Was she really watching out for him or just having another dig? "Thanks Minni, but that doesn't help right now."

"Well," said Minni. "I don't want to appear contrary, but one of them was close to taking your head off its hinge. So, I think it does help right now."

"Damn it, Minni! You know what I mean." Elrin rounded on Delik. "Listen to me. I deserve to know what is going on, you thankless, stubborn, old—"

Delik drew Elrin's blade, stealing it from the sheath so fast, he didn't have time think of his weapon, let alone draw it to defend himself. The blade pressed to the young man's abdomen, the sharp point establishing an uncomfortable clarity of thought. Remarkably explicit images of his intestines spilling onto the deck kept Elrin's body still while carefully raising his hands in surrender; he didn't stand a chance against Delik.

"You listen to me, pup. Hear me sweetly. Because next time, I'll not pause to parley with your mewling. I need a man who'll think for himself. I grant you this, you've a head for thinking, but I sure as shite don't need a boy who cries about what is and whinges about what might be, or once was." Delik pulled the blade away from Elrin's abdomen, flipped it over and presented the hilt for Elrin to take. "Now make up your own mind, lad. You stay, or you go."

The young man considered his dwindling options. These two were trouble, but they fought for freedom and that was something his father would have done. Maybe if he helped them, they would help him. Minni was on his side; she'd helped him out of trouble more than once. She wasn't like any of the girls he knew back in Calimska. Her beauty carried a shadow of death that left him abashed and cautious, harassed with an awkward nervousness that struck him when she smiled. Delik confused him in a very different way. The man was a touchy, cagey little bastard, thrusting Elrin into mortal danger while feeding him half-truths for who knew what reasons.

They both had a plan. Elrin had nothing. Delik was right; he was green and had no real training with a blade. How ironic that he might be safer with these two rebels than by himself, even if it meant fighting the might of Jando.

Elrin took his blade and returned it to his sheath. "I'll stay, for now. Just in case you need me to save your hide again."

Delik scoffed. "Smart arse, eh. Like I need another one of those."

"Then you're in luck, I can't stay with you for long. I need to get to the Hoard Islands, there's something there that will help my father. Will you be going that way?"

Delik laughed. "Very funny, Minni. Did you put him up to this?"

Minni held up her hands to show her innocence. "I've not said a word."

Delik scowled. "Are you tuggin' my chain, lad?"

"No, I ..." Elrin gathered his thoughts. "Am I missing something here?"

"Tell us why you need to get there, Elrin," said Minni.

"I was told by a friend that something called the Dragon Choir would aid my father. I was told to go to the Hoard Islands and seek it out. If you're not going there, I'll still help, but only until you get to another port. I'll ask there."

Minni flaunted her smug smile. Delik was not impressed.

"What's going on?" asked Elrin.

"Never you mind, lad. Minni here is ploughing her own field a little too deep."

"Piss off, Delik," Minni cut back. "And change that damn shirt. You smell like fish and look like a butchers block."

Delik scowled and sniffed at his bloodstained yellow shirt. "Bah! My shirt's fine." The shankakin turned to Elrin. "Pay her no mind. Send a message to the ships at sea and make some good of yourself."

Elrin remained at the helm beside Delik and followed his direction. He wrote the message and sent it to the beacon on the headland to relay on. "Commodore Pelegrin secure. Ship damaged, but seaworthy. Escorting back to fleet. Hold position."

BEANS

The rebel ships rounded the headland, leaving the calm waters of the bay for the windswept chop, roiling across the Salroc Sea. While the fresh gusts buffeted the ships, Coalman and Selmet called and whistled to each other, directing the crew with ease. Delik was glad to have them, he knew his way around a fishing skiff, but sailing a tall ship like *Juniper* required experienced sailors.

The two Jandan galleons were at anchor, awaiting them out to sea. Delik squinted through the ocean glare and noticed more ships farther off. Faster than a curse could form on his lips, the spyglass was out, revealing their ruin approaching.

The spotter called down from the crow's nest affirming his fears. "Five sails pressing from the north. Jandans manoeuvring."

"Ash it!" Delik cursed to the wind. "Impatient bastard!"

Delik could tell Elrin was ready to pester him with another question. The lad was too curious, he never knew when to keep his nose out of it.

"What is it, lad? You look set to burst if you hold it in."

"Shall I send another message?" asked Elrin.

"No, but wait for one. They'll be sure to send something if they are going to engage." Delik eased his expression. The lad wasn't so bad; he didn't whinge all the time.

Elrin held the dragon seal to the north and was ready when the Jandan ships pulsed a series of flashes across the sea. He twisted the seal and allowed the enchanted dragonhead to vent. Magical ink tumbled onto the transcriber and Elrin read as the words coalesced. "Pirates on course to engage. Three caravels. One carrack. One fluyt. Request *Templestone* and *Fearless* to assist."

Delik fumed. "Why couldn't Kobb wait for the signal? What is his bloody caper?"

"Has he ever made things easy?" said Minni. "It doesn't change a thing. We must press on."

At Delik's command *Templestone*, *Fearless* and *Juniper* sailed forth to intercept the remaining Jandan ships with the rebel captains under order to board and subdue. They sailed as fast as the head wind would allow, tacking starboard away from the coast, but without a weather witch they were at the mercy of the belligerent wind, blowing favour into the pirate's sails and against their own.

Delik slammed his hand on the rail, growling at the slow pace of their approach. "The ship may as well have a hole in her side for all the speed we have beating against this damn wind."

"I have an idea," said Elrin.

"Oh, another one is it?" said Delik throwing his hands in the air. "It's not like we are short on time. I'll hear anything you've got. Actually, we've time for a spot of tea and a hand of cards too."

"What have you in mind?" Minni asked, her eyes toying with Elrin. "Don't mind old grumpy lumps, he's not versed in sarcasm."

Delik sneered. Taking sides; she'd chew that poor lad up and spit him out. The woman was too bloody smart for her own good, playing all the angles from the shadows then shining in all her glory when she took the stage. She was the darling of the rebellion and a necessary curse.

"Look at that face. The image of his father," Minni put her arm around Delik and gave his shoulder a squeeze.

"Bugger off, Minni!" Delik shrugged her arm away.

"Doesn't know how to deal with his anger either," Minni mocked Delik's expression with a dour face of her own then burst into laughter. "Just like his father."

Delik found himself smiling despite his every effort to hold it back and give Minni a serve. This bloody woman was impossible.

"My idea?" asked Elrin.

"Go on then," said Delik. "Ignore her if you can."

"We have those two redeemers who came to heal Pelegrin. They're not much use in prison below decks. Maybe they can help speed things up."

"What, to patch up our arses with a cushion so we don't get splinters from sitting around waiting?"

Elrin ignored Delik's sarcasm. "Surely redeemers are more versatile with magic than just killing and healing. One of them might be an elementalist. Who knows until we ask?"

"Could be the last queen of the sea people for all I care. Unless we get a team of dolphins to pull us along, those galleons and their cargo are in the wrong man's hands." Delik crossed his arms, thinking it over. He gave in, it was worth a try. "Alright then, go and get them. Make sure you ask Coalman for an escort, keep them bound and gagged no matter what."

"I will," said Elrin. "And make sure you save some of that tea for me."

Elrin grinned and hurried away. Delik let a smile cross his face after Elrin had gone below decks and turned to talk with Minni. "You might be right about him. He could be just what we need if he knows about the Dragon Choir."

"If the Muden of Gren say it is so, then it is so. They weren't wrong about you. Though you denied it long enough. They weren't wrong about Tikis, nor me." Minni was serious for a change. "He's the Key, I'm sure of it."

"Be as sure as you like," Delik refused to fall into Minni's trap. "That is not what I was saying and you know it. I'm not going to be convinced until I see it happen."

"Why not? All the signs are there. You know the prophecy as well as I do."

"Now you're mixing me up with my old Pa again. He'll have memorised every word they've said since he was a sprout. Not me."

"The Key to free us shall fall in your hand, holding a note, but no name. Sounding the Choir—"

"I've not seen a note," interrupted Delik. "Have you? And I believe he has a bloody name; Elrin. So don't go on spouting their fluff till it makes some sense."

Minni unrolled the dead letter and faced it to Delik. "Like I already showed you, it reads plain as day. *Elrin No Name*. Are you blind or daft?"

"I'd not call a dead letter a note. Don't go pinning your hopes just to have them dashed."

"That's fine advice from you."

"All I'm saying is, the Muden know some things better than others. Sure, they might be able to see it all, but the gibberish that comes out only makes light of some of it. And I wager they don't tell us all of the little they know."

"Listen to yourself would you? You go on about gibberish while your own mutterings are a right confusion."

"Clean the rot out of your ears then."

"Just give Elrin the chance he needs and we will find out. No harm in an extra hand on the way; his heart is in the right place. His sword arm needs a lot of work, though, if he sticks to one of us he won't be such a soft target..."

Delik let Minni prattle on about her new pet. He recalled his father coming home from Gren so many seasons past. He had blathered endlessly about the Muden; their riddles set him wild with hope. Pa was the Fist, they said. Pa would lead them to freedom. They never said freedom would require such blooded knuckles.

"Delik, are you listening to me?"

91

"Yes, Minni. Yes, yes. We must keep him safe. I agree."

Coalman ran up the stair to the quarterdeck and interrupted them. Close behind followed a scrawny youth, black smears on his hands and cheeks.

Coalman presented the boy. "This powder monkey found something strange in the ship's magazine. Thought you'd be interested."

"What is it, boy?" Delik waved him forward. The boy was hesitant to talk. "Spit it out, son. I won't bite."

"Powder's cursed, won't set to flame." The boy hefted a powder horn into Delik's hands.

"By Ona!" Delik tested the weight of the horn. "It's as heavy as a bag of shot." He opened the stopper and emptied a sum into his palm. "It's not even black!"

"Like I said, sir. It's cursed, see. Me and Toppa opened a fresh barrel. Ready for the battle like we was told. Straight away we knew it was cursed, blood red and sparklin'. Knew it wasn't right and came up to me gun boss and showed it."

"And you tried to light it, eh?" asked Delik.

"S'right, sir. Didn't even fizz a spot."

"You've done well, son," said Delik, shaking the boys powder stained hand. "I need you to go back to that magazine and check the other barrels. Separate the ones that are, ah, cursed. Make sure it isn't used in the cannon."

"Me and Toppa tried to shift that one we's opened, sir. Couldn't budge it."

"Hurn," said Delik, half to himself. That's why they had the ogre loading the barrels.

"Sorry, sir?"

"Go and ask the ogre to help you," said Minni. "His name is Hurn."

That didn't sit well with the boy at all.

"Off you go then," said Coalman, without a scrap of sympathy. "You've got your orders."

The boy ran off, likely imagining a gruesome death-by-ogre awaited.

"Anything else whiles I'm close enough you don't have to shout?" asked Coalman, taking off his wool knit cap and scratching his bald head.

"Get the ears of all the lads. Remind them to stay their blades if a Jandan surrenders. I want a cleaner fight this time. If any of the crew don't like the idea, take their weapons and put them in the cells. Those bastards just make the Jandans fight to the death. They'll yield if they know they are outnumbered; less blood the better."

Coalman nodded and descended the stairs as Elrin came up.

Four guards followed, escorting the redeemers. They were filthy from sitting in the cells below deck. With hands bound and mouths gagged, neither struggled with their escort. In the bright mid-morning light their cowls glared white, burning the black star into Delik's eyes. A white afterimage of the star blocked his focus wherever he looked. He rubbed his eyes trying to remove the white glow.

"Get those cowls off!" Delik rubbed his eyes to remove the white glow fouling his vision. "Throw them to the sea."

A guard obliged, stripping off both cowls with rough handed pleasure. Delik's vision cleared, revealing a cruel faced man in white robes and a cowering youth in red. The middle-aged man's severe eyes appraised them while the boy hung his shaven head, keeping his eyes on the deck.

"Why so calm?" asked Delik.

The older man stepped forward jutting his bearded chin out, straining at the gag. His dark hair, olive skin and sharp nose gave him away for a shiner. He'd strayed a long way from home. Probably another poacher banished from Calimska and taken in by Jando. A convert no doubt, redeeming the sins of the masses, whether they liked it or not. With a white silk robe, this man was not just any redeemer. He would have the ear of the high priest, the head of the Council.

The boy kept still, his dark brown skin glistening with sweat. He wasn't Jandan, nor Calimskan; Delik had no idea where he was from, up north perhaps. His hazel eyes were nervous, submissive. The rust red linen tunic he wore reflected a lack of authority; he was an acolyte, or a personal slave. Given the absence of weapons and armour he was likely a magic user of some sort. Being attached to a redeemer in any way made him a dangerous prospect. Either of these men could spawn chaos with an arcane whisper, but one might be willing to cooperate.

"If either of you mutter a spell or so much as wiggle your fingers we'll lop your damn heads off. Right lads, ready your blades and let the boy speak first." Delik motioned for the younger man's gag to be removed.

The boy flicked a fearful glance at his superior and the older man shook his head, yelling into the cloth that stifled his mouth shut. A rebel guard pressed a sword against the priest's neck and he quietened, staring death at the acolyte while the petrified youth's mouth was unbound.

Remaining silent, the boy in red took a step back and bowed to Delik.

"Listen here lad, we're not pirates. We took these vessels to free the people on those galleons out to sea. We're part of the rebellion against the tyrants of Jando." Delik paused to let it sink in.

The gagged redeemer tried to speak again, but a guard clipped his muffled concern short, swatting the back of his head.

"Did you enjoy your imprisonment below? I bet not." Delik pointed out across the sea to the Jandan ships. "Those ships are full of men, woman and children, packed into cells like those you were in."

The boy dropped his eyes from Delik. His mouth was free of the gag but he wouldn't speak, cowering with his shoulders slumped like he was expecting a beating.

"If you help them," said Elrin, walking forward and touching the scared boy's shoulder. "You will be free too."

The elder redeemer rushed at Elrin, but was held back by the guards. He strained in his bindings, shaking his head and biting the gag. Three guards wrestled him to the deck, but his eyes, wild with rage, made the boy cower and tremble with a helpless whimper.

Delik understood the situation at once. Minni had her bow trained on the redeemer. She'd end him soon if Delik didn't intervene. The Reik woman never had much to say to these dogs; nothing a sharp point couldn't express with more meaning.

"Take the old man away," ordered Elrin. "He's terrifying the boy."

The guards didn't budge at Elrin's say so. Delik gave a nod and the old dog was dragged away.

Elrin offered a hand to get the boy to his feet. "Those Jandan ships out there are about to be taken by pirates. We want to save them, but the pirates are going to get there first. Do you know a spell that would help?"

The boy hesitated, casting fearful eyes over his shoulder.

"We'll keep you safe from the old man in white," Elrin put his arm around the boy, who tensed, bracing for punishment. "And don't mind that grumpy old shankakin. He lost his dolly overboard."

Elrin leant away and pulled a funny face at the accolyte. He returned a bright smile, which broke into a gurgle of laughter. The youth had no teeth and only a stub of a tongue.

Delik uncrossed his arms. What had those bastards done to him? The boy noticed them staring and stopped laughing, sealing his lips in a pout to hide his shame.

"Bring food and water," said Minni to the remaining rebel guard. "Now!"

Delik cut through the rope binding the boy's arms behind his back. "What's your name lad?"

The boy wouldn't speak; couldn't speak. He covered his mouth with his hand, his sad eyes unsure where to look.

"Do you have a name?" asked Minni.

The boy shook his head then pointed to a pail of water near Minni. She brought it to him and he gave her a tight-lipped smile in thanks. He cupped his hands in the water and raised his voice in a long high note that carried into the wind. The water rippled like it was alive with excited fish. He splashed it onto the deck where it beaded together forming Jandan words on the timber.

I have no name.

Delik nudged Minni. She punched his arm in return. Now they had two keys; this just proved the prophecy was a load of bollocks.

"What did that man call you?" asked Elrin.

Boy.

"We can't call you that," said Elrin.

Minni knelt down beside him. "Did that name make you feel good?"

No.

I'm a girl.

Minni didn't flinch. "He was a silly old man then wasn't he?"

The young girl shook her head. Without a sob or a whimper, tears streaked through the grime on her tender face, falling into the puddle on the deck.

"We won't talk about him anymore," said Minni, putting her arm around the girl. "Let's talk about a nice name for you. One that you like. What is your most favourite thing in all of Oranica?"

The girl thought for a moment, wiping her quiet tears away. Like a fresh breeze, her sad face was swept aside. She waved her hand across the puddle of water.

Beans.

"Well, that won't do for a name, will it?"

The girl covered her mouth and giggled, eyes warm with honey delight. Minni giggled with her, holding her gentle hands.

"You have beautiful eyes you know. I think they are the most beautiful colour I have ever seen. Your eyes remind me of something my mother gave me when I was a little girl."

Minni undid a charm around her neck and placed it in the girl's hand. The girl examined the polished gemstone on end of the leather thong. Her eyes gleamed with fascination.

"I want you to have it," said Minni.

The girl grinned her toothless smile and altered the water droplets on the deck.

Amber.

Delik cleared his throat. "So, ah, Amber then, is it?"

She affirmed with a sincere nod.

Delik knew this scene all too well; here was yet another daughter to the rebellion, orphaned by the damned almighty. For every pious Jandan there was a wagonload of souls enduring injustice. "Right then, Amber, we need to free the innocent people aboard those ships. Is that something you want to do? Do you want to help us?" Delik didn't like the idea of the poor child doing anything she didn't want to do. She'd suffered enough at the hand of that redeemer.

Yes.

"You're a brave lass. Can you get us to those ships before the pirates do? I don't know how you work your magic, but we need speed. Change the wind or summon a great sea lummox to tow us along, anything. We'll give you what ever you need."

SHOT & SPLINTER

Minni returned from the Captain's quarters carrying the belts, pouches and satchels confiscated from Amber and the redeemer when they were captured. Amber knelt on the deck, playfully swirling her finger above the puddle, creating liquid fish that wriggled through the water. She was still a child, such a dear thing. Minni wanted more than anything to bundle her up and take her away somewhere safe. A ridiculous thought; she knew it. The prophecy had to come first. It had to be followed or all was lost. The Muden knew the Key would free everyone. She had been certain the Key was Elrin, until they discovered Amber right under their noses. It had to be one of them, but which one? Until she knew for certain, both had to be kept safe.

"These are all I could find," said Minni, placing the equipment in front of Amber. "Time to show us what you can do. Are you ready?"

Amber rummaged through her small belt pouches, but wasn't happy with what she found. A sly look gathered upon her face. She pulled a bigger set of belt pouches toward her, stealing a glance down to the main deck, ensuring the old master was not there. She busied through the contents until she found a black silken purse.

Kneeling and spinning her hand around the pail, Amber created a whirlpool. She hummed with such long low notes they were swallowed by the noise of waves pummelling the hull. Her humming layered upon itself, growing in volume. She spun the water with one hand and tipped the black purse over the pail. Fine sand cascaded from the pouch, dissolving into the whirlpool with a vibrant effervescent glow.

The pace of her unnatural baritone hum sped on. She withdrew her hand and the whirlpool dominating the bucket split into two. Her hands shone sea green and wind whipped around her red robes. The whirlpools in the pail continued to duplicate with Amber's low rapid humming, until the pail was a honeycomb of glowing spirals.

Somehow the very air split apart, rending Amber's voice in two. The wind whirled around her, seeding a high note from the low, both pulsing in tandem, warping water and air. The whirlwind around her split in two, each half anchoring upon her sandalled feet. They twisted and danced around each other; writhing snakes under Amber's control. Her voice became impossibly loud, so deep and so high, like the ocean and sky would collide.

The young elementalist flung her arms out wide, propelling the whirlwinds across the quarterdeck, port and starboard. Each moment they grew, gathering speed. The sails filled tight like the skin on a drum. Clouds of sea spray misted the deck.

"Selmet!" cried Delik, holding the pilot's arm to get his attention. "Bring us straight on to those galleons!"

Selmet's face wrinkled with simple joy. The wind and spray whipped his thin white hair across his whiskered cheeks as he wheeled the ship to a direct heading.

Minni laughed and screamed into the lashing wind. Never before had she seen such a weaver, someone so in touch with the magical essence of the world. Elrin whooped and hollered through the sheets of spray, gripping the rail with one hand and waving the other around like a fool trying to rope a wild horse.

Amber was lost in concentration, her arms straighter than a ship's yard and her robes a red sail in the middle of a magical tempest.

The ship crashed through the sea towards two whirlpools forming a torment in the ocean. Selmet kept the ship on course steering between them. The current tugged at the ship, creaking timbers and shifting the deck under their feet. *Juniper* shot ahead, propelled by the twin whirlpools pulling the ship and the whirlwinds filling the sails.

Templestone and *Fearless* pulled in to line behind *Juniper,* catching meagre elemental echoes rippling through the air and sea in her wake. It was not enough to keep up. *Juniper* sailed on, carving through the ocean, Amber's magical vortices of wind and water twisting for her alone. The ship travelled so fast, they arrived beside the two Jandan galleons just before the pirates intercepted them.

Amber drove *Juniper* as a wedge between the two galleons. The whirlwinds hovered over the Jandan ships, tearing sails and snapping the rigging, sending their crew reeling across the decks. A crack split the air and a mast fell, broken in two by the concentrated force of the wind. It tipped back upon the ship, ripping through the lines, crashing to the deck. The collapsed sails and mast blocked off the main access to the marines quarters, inhibiting their force mounting a counterattack.

The sound of the mast splitting jolted Amber from her trance and she lost control of the two whirlwinds. They spun off across the sea, one meandered away from the ships, but the other moved toward the pirate vessels that were almost upon them. The ships altered their course in time to avoid being directly hit, but one of the caravels was knocked about as the whirlwind changed course across its deck, sending pirates into the sea and tearing through its sails.

Amber collapsed, crumpling in a limp heap upon the deck. Minni rushed to her side, rolled her over and put an ear to her lips. She still had breath. Elrin grabbed the pail of water, which had lost its glow, and splashed a little across Amber's face. Amber opened her eyes and blinked, dazed and vacant. Her eyes dipped and her head tilted back into unconsciousness again.

A gaudy carrack, painted brighter than a rainbow over a spring fair, danced through the sea towards the galleon with the broken mast.

"You must keep her safe," Minni touched Elrin's hand.

A hint of red flushed Elrin's cheeks. "Of course I will." Confusion flicked through his innocent brown eyes. "But, where are you going?"

Chaos broke out around them and Minni ran.

⇛⇚

A thunderous salvo blasted into the galleon with the broken mast, pounding through the hull, filling the air with white smoke and splinters. One, then two of the galleon's cannons answered back, but the shots fell short of the carrack, peppering the sea. A caravel sailed in, following the colourful carrack's heading, preparing to broadside the galleon with a second dose.

The indentured crew on both Jandan galleons mutinied, lead by the rebel agents planted aboard.

"All blades board portside! Crew hold firm!" Delik directed his men to seize the undamaged galleon—splitting the rebels between two ships would stretch them too far. *Juniper's* crew were left to defend her decks while the rebel warriors followed Delik's orders, swinging across the water on ropes and using hooks to pull the galleon tight against *Juniper*.

Two pirate caravels also grappled onto the portside galleon and a wave of fighters broke upon its decks, battering back the Jandans and aiding the rebels—for now at least. The pirates were fearless, clashing into the melee with reckless enjoyment, brandishing smiles as wide as the cuts they made. They outnumbered his rebels two to one and Delik knew once the Jandans were under control, the pirates would see their chance to take everything. These men weren't the type to hesitate.

Marines were already swinging onto *Juniper*, attempting to dislodge the ships and enable their escape. *Templestone* and *Fearless* still sailed against the wind and wouldn't make it in time to storm the starboard galleon with the broken mast. The rebels would soon be outnumbered on the *Juniper* unless Kobb's pirates took the fight to that damaged galleon first.

"Take cover!" Delik screamed to his crew holding *Juniper*. The starboard caravel followed the carrack's lead, rolling out its cannons to take aim.

Delik ducked behind the mizzenmast. Selmet hit the deck, prompting Elrin to do the same. The caravel broadsided the damaged galleon; shrapnel scoured the deck and tore into the rigging. Stray shot careened across *Juniper*, burning hot through the air. Screams of friend and foe congealed with gun smoke drifting over the battle.

"Kobb! There's shankakin in there! Cease fire!"

It was useless, Kobb couldn't hear him shouting over sea and the clamour of battle. The lead carrack sailed a lazy turn, followed by the eager caravel, both coming around for another attack.

"Send a bird. Cease fire!" Delik couldn't tell if the spotter in the nest was dead or alive. The osprey had flown, along with their chances of negotiation.

Minni was gone. Right when he needed her, she had disappeared in the thick of it. He caught sight of a shadow slinking across the deck of the broken-masted galleon; that had to be her. The figure jumped down through the hatch just as more shot screamed across the galleon's ravaged deck. She'd not free them alone; Delik had to help.

The shankakin grabbed Elrin's arm. "Listen lad! We've got to free the prisoners on that ship. Kobb's doing his damnedest to sink it. You and Amber both need to stay here and stay alive, or everything is lost. If it all goes to ash you'll get your passage on that harlequin carrack. Keep your head down and work hard. You'll be fine."

❧❦

Amber was out cold on the deck, she wouldn't wake up no matter how much Elrin tried. She was no poacher; that elemental magic was woven from the source, no wonder she was drained. How could she muster so much power, so young? The Order of Calim would know what to do for her. Sorcerers would help their own. Elrin cradled her head, fearing for her life while he watched his companions risk theirs.

Delik had leapt across to the galleon with the broken mast and ran towards the hatch, not even stopping when attacked by a marine. He stepped to the side and lashed out with his short sword. The marine crumpled to the deck, incapacitated by the slash to his hamstring. Delik sped on, disappearing below the deck of the damaged galleon.

Jandans boarded *Juniper*, some fleeing the mutineers on their own ship, others driven by their officers to abandon the damaged galleon. An officer raced up the stairs to the quarterdeck with his sword drawn. He took one look at Amber lying on the deck in her red robes and charged at Elrin. Elrin dove to the side avoiding the sabre as it arced around with the full force of the muscular Jandan. Elrin swung his sword, hoping to catch the officer's exposed back, but the hanger was too short and the attack went wide.

The officer turned in a fervour, lunging and slashing. Cannon blasts exploded, shaking Elrin's nerve and dulling his ears. He retreated from the blows until the small of his back pressed against the rail. The officer lunged. Elrin dodged to the side, but the officer had expected it, turning the sabre out and slashing around with a killing blow to Elrin's neck.

Elrin saw his own death in the polished steel. The sabre quivered just under his chin, stopped by a huge olive-green hand. Hurn Ga Kogh loomed over them. He grabbed the officer's head like an apple, and dashed his body against the mast. The man crumpled in an unfortunate heap.

"My thanks, Hurn," said Elrin, his heart racing. "You saved my life."

"That death not for you," said Hurn in his deep rumble. He knelt beside Amber, laying unconscious on the deck. "Little Bell stopped ringing?"

"No, she's ok, just exhausted from weaving more than her body could handle. Do you know her?"

"Sang tiny bells in head, help sleep."

Elrin raised his sword. "Look out, Hurn!"

Three marines came swinging across to take the quarterdeck. The pirate ships fired again, ripping through flesh and rigging. The rope holding one of the marines snapped and he fell hard against the gunwale then slipped into the sea. Elrin grabbed the pail of water and swung it at one of the others. It flew through the air and slammed into his target. The marine let go in midswing and crashed onto the deck at an awkward angle, clutching at his crooked leg. The remaining marine landed hard on the deck, tumbling into Amber. The impact roused the magical prodigy, who groaned and sat up, grasping her head. She scrambled behind Hurn, frightened by the black star on blue of the marine's surcoat. Elrin circled around while Hurn swung his tremendous arms, swatting and grasping for the Jandan fighter.

Elrin pressed an attack from behind, slapping the flat of his blade against the side of the man's head. "Yield!"

The Jandan counterattacked, swinging his blade around in a wild arc. Elrin stepped back, dodging the blow while Hurn brought his fist about, knocking the marine to the deck.

"We've got to help Delik and Minni free the slaves from that galleon," insisted Elrin. "Stay together and follow me." He jumped across from the gunwale onto the galleon's main deck.

Amber gathered up her satchel and pouches then froze at the gunwale, unable to make the jump across to the galleon. Hurn lifted her like a doll under his arm and leapt across, his large feet splitting several boards on the deck where he landed. The girl slapped his arm and giggled in nervous excitement.

Men ran from below decks in a panic, scrambling across the fallen rigging and collapsed sails to climb onto Juniper. Mutineers filled with bloodlust raged at anyone in a uniform, beating them down with fists or slashing at them with stolen blades. Amber pulled Elrin out of the way of a berserk Jandan swinging a fire stoker at all who came near him. Blood oozed from a gash on the man's forehead, caking congealed gore over his eyes.

Hurn stepped in front of Amber and Elrin and cleared a path to the hatch, batting any foolish aggressor out of their way with a heavy hand. On the gun deck below, cannon smoke hung in the air greased with the smell of burnt flesh and thick with curses. Spot fires licked the bloodstained deck, crackling along with the cries of the wounded and battle hungry.

Amber pulled out a jar from her satchel and gave it a rattle while clicking the stump of her tongue and popping her lips in a tune of fire licking spring tinder. The room flared an eerie blue-white, lit from the jar full of twigs.

"I can hear people calling out further down," said Elrin.

"Follow," said Hurn, stooping as he moved off into the depths of the ship.

Elrin took Amber's free hand and pressed on after the ogre. She rattled her jar of twigs as they went, the cold blue light falling on a grim scene of carnage. They passed body after body. Most were dead, or soon would be. They littered the deck, groaning with wooden debris lodged in their flesh and gashes across their skin. Hurn guided them deeper still, past more of the dead. The design of the galleon was similar to *Juniper*, but far bigger. The shouts and screams were clearer now, the prison hold had to be close.

Cannon fire pounded the galleon with such force it lurched and groaned, knocking Elrin off his feet. Hurn helped him up and pointed down the nearby stairs. The young Calimskan hoped it was safer from the cannon and hurried on, descending into knee high water and a sea of panicked faces imprisoned behind bars.

Minni was tackling the locks in the dim, her face tight with worry. She had only managed to open one cell and the prisoners' panic had risen with the infiltrating water. Delik was trying to keep the calm, but his face was grim. If the pirates kept up the endless barrage, water would flood the whole deck before Minni could pick every lock.

The ceiling leaked, heavy drips falling upon Elrin's head. Stepping to the side he wiped his face and his hand came away slick with blood.

The prisoners wailed and cursed, jostling to get to the cell doors. Amber took the jar of light to Minni, holding it steady beside the lock. Minni brightened, rolling her shoulders and flexing her fingers before trying the lock again.

Elrin helped Delik settle the prisoners. "You must calm down. We are here to set you free. We will have you out soon. Our ship is waiting for you. You will all be safe. Preserve your strength." Elrin and Delik repeated themselves over, helping some, but others were too lost in their craze, banging on the bars and screaming. Elrin had never heard such distress.

As soon as Minni got another cell open she moved to the next, determined to beat the rising water. The prisoners rushed from the cell with Elrin and Delik pointing to the stairs. It would be useless trying to guide them out; they would have trampled anyone in their way. The prisoners panicked in the other cells, grabbing at Minni and Amber. They pleaded, they cursed and the water kept rising.

Cannon fire rocked the ship again and the prisoners screamed. Minni lost her composure. Her hands shook, dropping a pick into the water.

"There's too many," she said, fumbling with another pick from her kit. "They're all different! I can't get to them all in time."

Elrin went to her side and put his hand on her shoulder. Her dark eyes were brimming with tears. "You're doing fine, Minni," said Elrin. "I'll keep their hands off you. Just imagine it's the door to the Calimskan treasury. You do what you do best."

The young man gave her a reassuring smile, but he knew Minni was right. There were too many cells in the room and not enough time. Minni didn't say anything more. She wiped her eyes and returned to the lock. She had light and friends at her back. Her fingers eased through a series of manipulations with renewed confidence. The lock released and the door burst open, knocking Minni and Amber into the water. The prisoners poured out in a desperate rush to escape, trampling over any who stumbled.

"Stop!" Elrin reached into the water and grabbed for Minni. He looped his arms under hers and heaved her up and out of danger. She was warm, pressed close, water dripping from her hair down her cheeks, over her lips. She was soaked through to her skin, but her chest rose and fell; she was alive.

Hurn was not so delicate. He plunged his arm into the crowd of prisoners wading to their escape and swept them back. He scooped his hand into the water and plucked Amber out, placing her back on her feet.

"Elrin?" said Minni, placing her hands on his shoulders. "You can let me go now, I'm fine."

"Yes, of course, I ..." Elrin blushed, releasing Minni from his embrace.

"You were meant to keep those hands off me, weren't you?" Minni gave Elrin her wicked smile, then moved straight to the next cell lock.

Another attack blasted the side of the ship, lurching it to the side and tilting the deck, knocking Hurn hard against the bars. The ogre regained his footing, pushing himself away from the cell, now misshapen from his impact.

"Hurn!" called Elrin, wading over to the ogre. "Quickly. You have to break them all out. Bend those bars!"

"Should ask sooner," said Hurn, furrowing his brow. "Leave late."

Hurn sloshed through the water to the next cell. He grabbed the barred door and heaved, his muscled arms rippling. The door buckled, he heaved again and the door bent open. The prisoners pushed their way out, some managing to call their thanks as they passed. Hurn moved to each of the remaining cells and broke the doors open. The prisoners soon calmed when they saw the ogre's work, standing back and giving him room to bend the metal.

The last of the prisoners waded out as a barrage of cannon fire rocked the ship again. The galleon tipped and wrenched, its wooden bones splitting with an awful groan and crack.

"Follow me," said Minni, leading the way out.

Elrin grabbed Amber's hand and helped her out of the prison hold. Hurn came after them with a face full of worry, his eyes stark. They climbed out of the flooded room and up through the decks. Delik followed behind Hurn, urging the ogre to press on through the chaos.

Sunlight and water spilled through jagged holes piercing the hull. The galleon leaned and rolled in the sea like a drunkard. The incline of the deck made a straight run impossible, forcing them to scramble over cannons tied down with block and tackle, dodging fallen debris and the dead, and slipping on the blood-slick deck. Finally they made it out through the hatch, only to see that the brutalised galleon had rolled too far for them to jump back to the safety of *Juniper*.

The crippled vessel was sinking fast. Bubbles boiled from the tortured hull, churning the water into a lather. Kobb's pirate ships loitered in the haze of smoke with cannons out like eager dragons, protruding through the bulwark ready to spit the five hells upon them.

The freed prisoners balanced on the ship's sloping hull, as close to Juniper as they could manage without falling in the sea, grasping for the rope ladders hurled down to rescue them. Hurn moved into the crowd with careful steps and grabbed a woman, lifting her above his head. Men shouted and one punched at the ogre's back, though he was too busy helping the woman to notice.

"Calm down!" hollered Elrin. "Can't you see he's saving your skins?"

Hurn lifted the woman high enough to climb through a cannon port. Once the prisoners understood, they clamoured to be the next one to be rescued. As he passed up the last child, the sinking ship lurched onto its side, tipping everyone off their feet. The remaining masts and their tattered sails slapped against the frothing sea.

Delik and Minni fell into the water. Hurn caught hold of a rail as he slid and grabbed Elrin's belt, saving him from going overboard as well. Amber was nowhere to be seen. Hurn hoisted Elrin up to the rail, then onto the exposed hull. When the ogre pulled himself up, he was pale with fear. Elrin thought to ask what was wrong, but was distracted by muffled shouts and thumping on the hull. The young man scrambled to where the sound was the loudest and kicked his heel onto the timber. The shouts and thumping became more frantic. Hurn followed Elrin's lead and jumped with all his weight onto the hull. It creaked a little, but held strong.

Amber appeared floating on the water, ferrying people to *Juniper*. Her legs were like a little raft, magically buoyant, shunting flotsam to those who couldn't swim and pushing them to safety. Minni and Delik treaded water beside *Juniper*, helping people up onto to the ladders after Amber dropped them off.

"Amber! We need your help!" Elrin waved his arms to show where they were.

Amber dropped her legs into the water then rose to the surface like a cork. She ran over the water and up the hull to them, making a strange swishing noise with her mouth like a quart trying to escape a wineskin. Hurn continued to stamp on the hull. An arrow sped past his head and landed in the sea. Another two followed, thunking into the hull.

Elrin couldn't understand why the pirates were taking shots at them. When would it end? He crouched down on the hull and tugged on Hurn's arm, getting him to do the same. A smaller target would slow them down.

"Amber, can you freeze water?"

Amber nodded. And made her dripping hand freeze over. Elrin shivered.

"Freeze the hull right here."

Amber placed her hand on the hull and whispered. The wet wood bulged and crackled, freezing a small radius around her hand.

"Bash that, Hurn," said Elrin.

He hesitated at first, staring at Amber's frozen hand.

The screams and thumps from below grew louder, more frantic. Hurn clenched his fists like great mallets and clasped his eyes shut. With monstrous force he brought them down, shattering through the hull. Inside, men gulped for fresh air, floating amongst lacquered black stars, kegs and refuse. Amber iced another section of the hull and Hurn battered through, revealing more trapped marines. From water murky with blood and thick with the dead they pulled the living, one section at a time, until no more cries for help could be heard.

Arrows fell around them and Elrin was glad for the wind and swell, which hampered their precision. The archers on the brightly coloured carrack laughed as they shot, joking with each other. An arrow lodged in Hurn's shoulder while he lifted a marine to safety and a roar of laughter and cheers went up from the carrack. Hurn pulled at the arrow shaft jutting from his muscular arm, tearing it out with a grunt. Blood slid from the wound.

"We've done all we can for these Jandans," said Elrin. "The ship wont float much longer. Even if it did, those idiots will hit one of us again."

Amber pointed to *Juniper*.

"You're right. We should get Hurn to a ladder before all this blood attracts sharks or a clan of koprani.

Elrin and Amber prepared to dive in, but stopped when Hurn rumbled.

"Hurn Ga Kogh not swim, Hurn Ga Kogh sink like ship."

Amber shook her head then reached around the ogre's waist. She swished a liquid rhythm from puffed pulsing cheeks and her arms glowed sea green, creating a radiant ring around Hurn's waist. His complexion drained of colour in fear of what was to come.

"It's safe, Hurn." Elrin dove in to demonstrate how easy it was. "Don't be afraid. Amber's magic won't let you sink."

Hurn wasn't convinced.

Amber wrapped her hand around his thumb and waited as though there was no hurry. Her honey coloured eyes warmed the ice blue panic in his. Her gentle smile and understanding melted his fear. They dove in together, making a great splash. His body bobbed out of the water like an awkward duck, thrashing around.

Once he realised he couldn't sink, he calmed, allowing Amber to ferry him across to a rope ladder. It snapped under his weight, dropping him back into the sea. Elrin waved them over to a thick, knotted rope and Hurn hauled himself up hand over hand. Elrin scaled a ladder and swung over the gunwale to safety.

"That's the one," said Coalman, his voice shaking. "He can operate the signals." Coalman's eye was black and swollen shut. A gash on his cheek and a busted lip bled down his face. Beside him, brandishing a hooked blade, stood a man decorated face to foot with black swirls of ink.

Two men in motley colours seized Elrin. They took his sword and scabbard and marched him past the gathering mass of rescued prisoners on the main deck. He resisted at first, but the men just twisted his arm until the pain stopped him. They pushed him up the stair onto the quarterdeck. Minni and Delik were waiting, each with their own escort holding them in check.

The pirates had forgotten to take Elrin's dagger. If he got his hands free, he might have a chance. The young man gave Delik a wink and prepared himself.

Delik warned him off the idea. "Kobb's taken the lot, lad. Save your fight now. Plenty of time for that yet."

"How did they take all the ships? What about Tikis?"

"We had to surrender," said Delik. "That fluyt was full of men. It would have been a slaughter."

"What do we do now?"

"We give Kobb whatever he wants," said Minni, her neck scraped and bleeding onto her blouse.

Elrin hung his head.

They'd freed the slaves only to imprison themselves.

KING KOBB

The ships rolled with the swell, congregating on the ocean like seaweed. Gulls flocked, pecking and squabbling over the floating dead. The sunken galleon delivered a fine feast for the creatures of the sea. High above, the sun peaked noon, drying Elrin's skin salty and hot while he waited. The fresh breeze was a comfort, cooling his anger as he stewed on the quarterdeck, wondering if he would ever find the Dragon Choir, or his father.

The bright glaring day was thick with an air of quiet tension. The rebels had given a reluctant surrender and Delik's order to cooperate with Kobb's men didn't sit easy with them. Hurn had raged, knocking four men overboard. Amber was the only one who could calm him. She sat beside the ogre, a pebble beside a mountain, soothing him with a calm wordless melody.

Minni's hair had dried in the heat, curling in a tangled, beautiful mess. She brushed a recalcitrant ringlet from her eye and tucked it behind her ear. It obeyed for a while, then sprung back. The wind made it dance about while she stared across the sea, her brows knitted and lips tight.

Was she upset, or perhaps just lost in a pensive mood? More likely she was plotting an escape, but Elrin could only guess. A woman's thoughts had ever been a mystery to the young man, though he had never cared to wonder what they were until Minni came along. She caught him watching and her face relaxed, dark eyes enquiring. Elrin didn't know what to say and she didn't speak, just smiled. The cut on her neck bothered him, making him angry. He wanted to punch one of Kobb's men in the mouth, he didn't care which, any would do.

Rough hands dragged Elrin to his feet. Thoughts of revenge withered as the tattooed man came up to the quarterdeck, two hooked blades slung on his hips. He was built solid like a barbican and dressed in loose cotton for the heat. A comb carved of bone held his thick black hair, gathered into a topknot.

"Kobb would like to thank you in person for getting here so soon." The tattooed man spoke Jandan with an accent foreign to Elrin. His face was impassive, one half covered in an intricate embroider of ink. His conversational tone was hollow, empty of the smile it required. "Follow me, the captain's gig is waiting."

"Where's Tikis?" asked Minni.

"The gig is waiting," repeated the tattooed man.

"Kobb's had us waiting on our arses for more than a twist," said Delik. "He can bloody well hold his horses while you answer the question!"

The tattoos rippled on his face, his eyes clouded black. "The drakkin chief is safe. He awaits Kobb's reception." His eyes cleared. "You waste time."

"Ash on that! You could've picked us out of the water to start with."

The tattooed man ignored Delik's protest and led them to the main deck, ordering them to descend a rope ladder into a large boat with oarsmen at the ready. Hurn shinned down a thick mooring line, lest he break the ladder, and took a place in the centre of the boat, which dipped low in the water and quivered as he adjusted his weight. Amber chimed her song to calm Hurn's nerves, making a ringing melody that baffled Elrin. He watched her mouth, the incongruous movement of her lips dancing before the tune. It had to be magic, it made no sense.

The oars plunged into the sea and stroked in time to Amber's tune. Elrin closed his eyes and listened to her song, remembering his mother's voice, like honey on silver, lulling him to sleep when he was a child. He wondered if she was standing by the shutters as she always did, staring down Flint Street to the Cog and Wheel, waiting for Father. A wave broke over the gunwale, sloshing cold water across Elrin's lap and rousing him from his daydream.

"Why's the bloody Ogre have to come along?" whined Delik.

Hurn shifted, tilting the boat to snort at Delik.

"He is of value to Kobb," said the tattooed man. "Kobb has requested him and that is enough."

Hurn sneezed, rocking the boat again. Delik huffed to himself and stifled any further objections.

The oarsmen cut their way through the swell to Kobb's ship; *Bone Dancer*. It was the largest of the pirate's ships, bristling with cannons, colourful and ungainly. The ship's high forecastle and poop deck stood proud, rounding down to her trim waist, while her sails were an outlandish spectacle of colour; *Bone Dancer* was a giant floating peacock.

჻

Once aboard *Bone Dancer*, they were escorted to the captain's quarters. It was a large room adorned in finery. Silverware rested on a central dining table with platters of fruit, biscuits and cut meats. A great bed, draped in red velvet curtains, indulged the far corner in luxury. Beside it stood a tall mirror. Decadent paintings of barely dressed men and women hung in golden frames.

Tikis was already seated at the long table. Opposite him was Commodore Pelegrin, healed, but foul faced by their presence. The bearded redeemer sneered at them and oiled a predatory smile for Amber. She tucked herself behind Hurn out of her master's view.

"He'll not harm you here," Minni placed her hands on the fearful girl's shoulders and straightened them out of their slump. "Not with all of us to protect you."

Tikis was uncomfortable. What was worse for the drakkin; sitting on a chair or sitting down with his enemies? Kobb hadn't thought through the seating arrangements. Or, perhaps he had. Perhaps it amused him to have a drakkin sit at the edge of his seat, so his tail wouldn't kink. Either way, Elrin wondered how long the meal would last before someone was stabbed with the silver.

Behind each chair a man stood guard. Tattoos covered their muscular bodies like the ones on the companions' escort, but their faces were bare. The guard beside Tikis offered Minni her seat first, though Minni ignored the suggested chair, sauntering her way around the table to take the one beside the redeemer. Two of the guards grabbed her and guided her back to sit where she was first invited. Elrin was ushered beside the redeemer while Amber sat between Minni and Delik. Hurn was invited to sit last, on a chair beside Elrin. The ogre stooped over his seat scratching his chin, then pushed the seat aside and dropped his weight onto the floor, bumping the table as he bent his broad legs to kneel. He gave Elrin a gentle nudge, grinning at the food spread out on the table. Elrin's stomach growled in agreement.

Only one seat remained at the head of the table, carved of tooth and bone. The scrimshaw elaborated intricate swirling patterns, like the ink on the men who stood guard. The tattoo-faced man gave a curt nod and his warriors straightened to attention, ready for the pirate leader's grand entrance.

Elrin expected Kobb to be an imposing battle-hardened buccaneer, but the manicured, well-cut pirate who gambolled through the door was far from it. He was a diminutive shankakin, shorter than Delik and wearing a glaring clash of bright silks, puffing him out with frills like feathers. Leather boots with thick heels and polished buckles gave just enough extra height to make him seem at once vain and unstable. Elrin had never seen a shankakin cover their feet; Kleith had taught him it severed their connection with Ona, their favoured Goddess.

Kobb's sword swayed as he swaggered to his seat, the jewelled pommel and filigree basket guard catching the light, shining like his toothy grin. A tight leather vest girdled his round belly, accentuating the flamboyance of the silken sleeves that burst out in colourful ruffles. Both vest and blouse plunged with a low neck, revealing Kobb's thick black, tightly curled chest hair. Something moved on his shoulder. At first glance Elrin missed it, his eyes diverted by the pirate's attire. Then it moved again, something wriggling in the ruffles of Kobb's garish blouse, lurking over his neck and shoulders.

"Please remain seated!" Kobb announced. "Don't get up on my account."

Minni rolled her eyes; no one had made any effort to stand in the first place.

With the utmost dignity, Kobb took his seat at the head of the table. The creature he carried on his shoulder spread its wings and fluttered onto a golden perch hanging from the ceiling. It was a tiny dragon, the size of a parrot and skinny like a skink. In every way it appeared just like the dragons Elrin had read about, just like the shadows that flew over Calimska when the season began, but smaller—much smaller. Its long tail wrapped around the gilded perch and ended in a barbed stinger. It preened, chittering to itself.

"So I trust you all know each other by now, hmm?" Kobb leant back and delivered a cheerful smile to his guests. For good or ill, Elrin had met everyone, but certainly didn't know them. Before he had time to consider asking, Kobb swung into his speech.

"I'd like to welcome you all to stay as my honoured guests this evening. I'm sure it has been some time since you all had a good meal." The pirate swept his arms wide showing the feast before them. "Others, such as my good man Fjhor, eat with me every night. He even eats before I do!" Kobb paused for a moment scanning the room, hoping someone found his joke amusing. After a brief moment of awkward silence, their host continued with the speech unperturbed by his humourless guests. "Many thanks to these two fine Jandans; well, one fine Jandan and a Calimskan outcast. Sorry Brother Uighara, you won't live that down I'm afraid—redemption or not, infamy is a sticky business. Now, where was I ..." Kobb squinted at a sheet of paper on the table. "Ah yes, my thanks to you both for taking the time to drag yourselves away from the conference below decks. How are the troops, Commodore? Morale must be high now that you've all got the day off." Kobb searched their faces with an eager grin, desperate for a laugh.

He flung his hands up, exasperated by the silence.

"Enough of your pompous prancing about, grub!" Pelegrin stood up and snatched the carving knife from the meat platter. The guard behind had Pelegrin's hair in a fist and a dagger at his throat before he moved to attack anyone. The Commodore stilled himself and dropped the knife. Though his arm had been healed, his reflexes were no match for the mercenary behind him. Pelegrin was forced back into his chair before the mercenary's blade was removed from his throat.

"Manners please, Commodore!" Kobb feigned shock, rising from his chair, his cheeks quivering. Kobb leant over, reaching across to the finely polished dinner setting in front of Pelegrin. He lifted the knife from the outside of the set and held it in front of the man's eye.

"You should know better, Pelegrin," Kobb winked to the others. "This one is for your appetiser."

Even though Kobb's dramatics put him on edge, Elrin couldn't resist a smirk. Hurn slapped his hand on the deck and rumbled. The outburst gave everyone a fright until they realised Hurn was only chuckling. Amber burst into giggles, then Kobb laughed, clapping his hands.

"Wonderful, wonderful. Let's start shall we? Fjhor, bring in the first course."

The tattoo-faced warrior walked across the room to let in a line of servants, each displaying the etiquette of domestic help entrusted to wait on elite families in their great houses. One carried a large pot, steaming its way to the side table. With poise and grace, bowls of fragrant soup were ladled and placed in front of everyone.

"Don't worry, Commodore," said Kobb. "You won't need that knife just yet."

A servant followed the soup service with a pitcher, filling their silver goblets with wine. Pelegrin downed his and held his goblet up for more, sneering at Kobb. Kobb was served last before the servants retreated out the door. Fjhor walked to Kobb's side and sampled his soup and wine. He swished each taste around in his mouth then nodded to the pirate, taking a step back to stand guard.

"Please, enjoy," said Kobb.

Elrin took his spoon from the outside and sipped the broth. It was delicious; the sweet spiced seafood with pepper and lime sent his taste buds in a whirl. He hadn't had such fine food since he was a boy; not since his mother was the Pride of the Bard's Guild, waited on by servants. Hurn lifted the bowl to his mouth and slurped his soup down in one great gulp. The ogre must have found utensils rather foolish. Elrin wouldn't hurry his; every spoonful was a delight.

Tikis also refused to use a spoon, using his long tongue to lap at the liquid instead. After a few flicks of his tongue his scaled snout wrinkled in distaste. Pushing the bowl to the side, the drakkin reached for his goblet and emptied the wine into his maw, closing his eyes in pleasure. With a satisfied clicking sound from his throat, he opened his eyes to catch Elrin and Hurn staring. The warrior darted his tongue out at them, tasting the air.

"Why this ogre not scared?" asked Tikis. "These whips and chains so easy to forget?"

Hurn narrowed his ice blue eyes and snorted. "Hurn Ga Kogh does not forget. Free is not free. Chained is not chained."

"Oh, very profound indeed," Kobb dabbed his mouth with a white silk napkin, eager to join the conversation. "And from the mouth of an ogre no less. You must tell us your story, Hurn-Ka-Gop. Ogres with brains are in short supply around here."

Hurn snorted at Kobb and repositioned his legs, bumping the table again.

"Is this going somewhere, Kobb?" Delik dropped his spoon in his soup bowl, making a clatter on the porcelain.

"Yes, yes, be patient. I always begin with a soup; it is nice, isn't it. Hungry hmm? You can have the scaler's too if you like, he won't mind."

Tikis hissed at Kobb and rose from his chair, but Delik grabbed his shoulder, urging him to keep calm. The pseudodragon batted the air with its wings and swung on its perch with a hiss of its own. Kobb feigned misunderstanding, acting shocked by Tikis's reaction. With a knife at everyone's back, they would all have to be patient and endure the performance.

Amber hadn't touched her soup. Uighara stared over the table at her while he ate. Amber kept her eyes down, shoulders slumped under the weight of the redeemer's eyes. There was a thump under the table and Uighara flinched, screwing up his face in pain, eyes darting between Delik and Minni.

Minni pointed her finger at the redeemer. "Leave the child alone, dog."

Uighara sneered and returned his foul gaze to Amber.

Elrin grabbed his fork. He'd pin the poaching bastard's hand to the table; that would break his hold on the poor girl. Uighara sensed the intent and turned on Elrin, binding his hand with magic. Crushing pain seized him as if the redeemer's own heel was standing on the young man's wrist.

Minni kicked under the table again, diverting Uighara's attention and releasing the magical grip. Elrin took the chance to drop the fork, rubbing his wrist in pain. The redeemer's strange magic left him racked by guilt for his offence, festering with a sense of not amounting to expectation. Just a scraping of the foul priest's oppression had made him wilt in mere moments. What poor Amber had suffered as Uighara's acolyte was beyond him.

Kobb tapped his bowl with the spoon. "Now, now, children! No fighting at the table! Commodore, get a leash on your hound. Or I'll tie him up my own way." The flamboyant pirate stood, snapping his fingers at Uighara. "Hoy! Over here! Eyes on me, poacher."

Uighara shot his gaze upon Kobb; vile pride smearing his lips into a smile. Kobb grasped at his throat, wheezing. The tiny dragon flew to Kobb's shoulder and hissed at Uighara, whipping its long tail. A guard pressed a blade into Uighara's neck, piercing the flesh, spilling a line of blood onto the white silk collar of his robe.

Gasping for air, Kobb fell back into his ornate seat. The face of Uighara's guard rippled like a bucket full of eels, morphing the guard's face into Fjhor's. Fjhor's body had not moved, but his face was alive with moving black ink. He was both here and there. Elrin had seen sorcerers teleport themselves around Calimska. He'd even heard of invisibility spells, but how was this possible?

With a final hiss at Uighara, the pseudodragon encircled its serpentine tail around Kobb's arm and nestled its body in to the ruffles of his shirt, satisfied it had nullified the hostile magic. Breathing easier, Kobb scratched the little creature's chin. "My dear, Prisella. What would I do without you?" Prisella nuzzled up to Kobb's cheek, appreciating the gratitude. Bolstered with confidence in his pet, Kobb waved off Uighara's guard. The warrior withdrew his blade and the tattoos on his face rippled away, dissolving into the black pools of his eyes, his original features restored.

Kobb leapt onto his chair and rising as high as a human might stand, he thrust a quivering finger at Uighara. "That was your last chance. Use your ill-gotten magic on my ship again and I'll have you flogged till the Lord's black star shines white." The poacher priest maintained his greasy self-satisfied smile, tilting his head in mock acquiescence to Kobb's scolding.

Standing down from his chair, Kobb called the servants to clear the first course and serve the second. While the food was delightful and filling, the mood at the grand table was oppressive; dense with undigested conflict. Their pirate host sulked at the head of the table, no longer the entertainer. He ate, filling his mouth through each course, drawing out the long gluttonous silence. The room condensed the unsaid. A thick expectation of argument clouded the air, brewing like a thundercloud that would not break.

Only after dessert was served did the shankakin pirate regain his cheerful resolve, stabbing cubes of mango with joyful appetite, smiling to himself and relaxing into his chair. He fidgeted, waiting for his guests to finish, like a child brimming with a new secret he had to tell.

Once the table was cleared, Kobb rose from his chair. "I just can't think straight without a meal under my belt. Now that we're all full and in good spirits, it's time for a little game."

Pelegrin and Delik stood at the same time.

"I will not be part of this charade any longer!" bellowed Pelegrin, slapping his palm on the table. Delik yelled something in Shankan that Elrin didn't understand. Minni smirked.

The tattooed guards deflated their bluster, quietening all protest with a sharp blade pressing into each man's back.

"Aha! I can see you are excited to play. Let me tell you the rules. Each of you think of something you want, and I will to give it to you. Sounds good doesn't it, but in return you give something to me. I help you. You help me. We all get what we want. Are you ready to play?"

"Do we have a choice?" asked Elrin.

"It would certainly be impolite to refuse. You've just filled your bellies with my generosity, what's the harm in a little after-dinner game? Goodness, gracious me."

Hurn held up eight of his meaty fingers, with hands strong enough to pluck Kobb's head from his shoulders. "This many gifts you take, we take one. Hurn Ga Kogh knows not equal."

"Well, you ate more than everyone else. That's not equal is it? One gift is better than none. Think yourself lucky to get anything. When was the last time you got a present, eh?" The pirate grinned and his gold teeth caught the glare of afternoon sun shining through the stern gallery.

"Got free, got shield, got battle, got little bell song, got swim. Hurn Ga Kogh much got. You much take. Give little."

"My glory! If I knew the cogs in that noggin had so much grease, I would have thought twice about saving you." Kobb crossed his arms like a petulant child, unhappy with a toy.

"You no save. Pirate's little spears bite." Hurn slapped the weeping wound on his shoulder.

"You fired on the ship!" said Elrin, incensed. "How does that save anyone?"

"Why didn't you board the ship like we agreed?" asked Delik.

"Enough!" yelled Kobb. "Can we please just get along? Can't you understand, I'm trying to help you?"

Delik pressed on. "Why sink that one and not the others? Why risk *Juniper* at the same time? You said you would board, not fire. That's why I got you for the job."

"Enough!" Kobb climbed back on his chair, standing over Delik.

"You knew the cargo, Kobb," said Minni. "How could you?"

"Your new toy churned through the sea like some great sea monster! How was I to know it was the work of this fine young boy, rushing you all to aid my attack?" Kobb threw his arms up, innocence personified with a splash of colour. "I panicked! I wrongly guessed the two others were chasing you. How was I to know that young Scrambletoe would do so well in his first big cut up?"

"That one lies," said Tikis. "These ones sent messages flying. That one has long eye. That one knows drakkin sailing Jando ships."

"Yes, yes, perhaps I did stretch the truth a little," Kobb sat back down in his chair, deflated. "If you wish the truth dear friends; I do feel I should be totally honest now that we've got to know one another over a meal."

Pelegrin crossed his arms and leaned back into his chair. "Truth from a pirate grub, this will be a riot."

"I was to sink both ships, though I'm not proud of it," said Kobb. It was hard to know if his shame was true or just an act.

"But our deal was that you got your pick of three of the ships anyway," said Delik.

"Yes, I admit it was fair at the time. Which is precisely why I had a problem with it. Dear boy, I can't let you go sailing about, armed to the teeth. Moral crusaders like you are bad for business; fighting for a cause is dangerous for those without one. Doing it this way saved my crew getting too bloodied up, yours as well I might add, and I still got my ships. Four now; I must thank you again for your speedy arrival. It did make my job a little easier."

"And what would you have done with us?" asked Elrin.

"I would have thanked you very much and said ta ta, but Delik here brought so many lovely gifts with him, I had to invite you all to dinner. I hear it was you who turned it all around. My quarry was nervous, she upped her anchor and made for Rum Hill to investigate. I never would have caught them in time. But you out did this lot, so I hear, and mastered the Council's secret gadgets. Magnificent work!"

"But I ..." Elrin didn't know what to say; thanks from a pirate made him wary.

"So you were prepared to sacrifice the lives of hundreds of innocents to save a few of your freebooters?" Delik shook his head.

"No, no, to tell you the truth, I just didn't want you to have the ships. Two shankakin at sea, I don't think so. I don't want the competition."

"Braggart!" spat Delik. "All for your damned ego!"

"And how is it, that you find yourself in the rebellion? Is it not your own ego? Couldn't you stand the whispers behind your back about your father? Is this not an effort to clear your family's name from your shame at Tillydale? There is no gain without loss, dear boy."

"Don't preach to me, Kobb. You're no holy man."

"Indeed not, they're no fun at all. So let us begin our game before the day is through, eh? Commodore Pelegrin, we will start with you. What gift would you like?"

"I tire of your game and it has only begun," Pelegrin sneered at his guard. "Yet, I have no choice. I want my ships, my men, my sword and my return to Jando."

"Well, well, that is quite a list. And as a Jandan you should know about what is whose and whose is what. All which was yours, dear Pelegrin, now is not so. How can I give you your ship if it simply isn't? I'm not some djinn. I have to work by the law of the sea. Now remember everyone; only one wish each. Because Pelegrin had to go first, I will give him two of his wishes, but only for him because he is such a good friend and has helped me in the past. I'll give you a sword and your passage home. In return you tell me all about your black powder."

"It comes from Calimska. That is all I know."

"Come now, that's common knowledge. I could have asked the scaler that."

Tikis jumped forward without warning. Kobb tumbled off his chair, rolling out of the way of the drakkin's claws. Three guards leapt on Tikis, forcing him to the floor. They bound his hands behind his back and sat him on the chair again, then tied his feet to the legs of the chair.

Kobb dusted himself off. "Touchy, eh. You scalers are all so sensitive."

The drakkin snarled and lashed his tongue. His muscles strained as he tested his bonds, making the chair creak. The guard pressed the point of a blade against the back of his neck.

"Now wait your turn. Uighara is next and I haven't even got my answer from Pelegrin yet. Patience, scaler, patience."

"Come on, Pelegrin. Don't keep us all waiting. Out with it." Kobb nodded to Fjhor, but it was Pelegrin's guard who moved forward as if the nod were to him. Heavy hands twisted the Commodore's freshly healed arm into an awkward position, extracting a grimace as the newly fused tendons stretched more than comfort allowed.

Pelegrin gasped. "Calimska supplies us in exchange for trade and treaty."

"Where do they get it from?" pressed Kobb.

"We don't know," Pelegrin gritted his teeth in pain.

"I doubt that." Kobb gave another nod.

The guard's face rippled with ink; Fjhor was in control. The fist came down like a hammer, snapping Pelegrin's elbow backwards. The Commodore issued an involuntary shriek before fainting. His head thumped on the table, disturbing the cutlery.

Amber rocked from side to side and an intense pulse of nausea caught Elrin. This torture was unnecessary and abhorrent.

Kobb slapped Pelegrin across the face. "Wakey, Wakey."

Fjhor pulled the Commodore's other arm, stretching it up behind his back.

"Tell me, Pelegrin, or that sword will be useless to you."

"We know it comes from Calimska. They make it." Pelegrin gasped.

"Where do they make it, and how?" asked Kobb.

"Our agent was compromised before we found out."

Kobb nodded again.

"No! Please! He managed to get to an alchemist's apprentice. He said it comes from dragons."

"That can't be true," said Elrin.

"Why not?" asked Kobb. "Calimska had a dragon patron before. Another might have turned up with the knowledge of black powder."

"Daniakesh left us before I was born. The Guildmaster's great golden shield has kept us safe every season since. We only see their shadows pass nowadays; none even bother to attack. There aren't any near Calimska."

"Damn it, I want one!" said Kobb. His pet beat its wings in annoyance and chittered in Kobb's ear. "Prisella! Come now, you're no dragon, dear."

Prisella launched from Kobb's shoulder in a huff, chittering and clicking, making a raucous flight around the room before landing on her golden perch, her back to Kobb.

"Last chance, Commodore. Tell me what it's got to do with dragons."

Pelegrin shook his head, desperate for mercy. "I don't know. I thought it nothing more than some fancy of a bored apprentice."

Kobb nodded to Fjhor. Pelegrin screamed as his second arm was drawn up at a painful angle, dislocating his shoulder. His face streamed with tears of pain. "I don't know. I don't know," he sobbed.

"Well, that doesn't help anyone does it? Now, Brother Uighara, what do you want?"

"Give me my acolyte." Uighara's voice was gravel under the wheel, unmoved by the torture his comrade had endured.

"He is not mine to give," said Kobb. "But, let's just say I will not keep him from you."

"That is more than satisfactory. What do you wish of me?"

"You will return our dear Commodore back to the Council of Jando, revived and in tip top condition. Do let my dear friend the High Priest know the Buccaneer King Kobb—use those exact words please—has their ships and is happy to have any more they might send my way."

"But, my acolyte, how can I—"

"That isn't my problem," interjected Kobb. "You figure it out. Someone has to row, remember, and the poor Commodore isn't fit for such strenuous activity in his current state."

Uighara grimaced, which wasn't so different from his brutal bristled smile. The air shifted around him, an exasperation of energy, clawing for traction.

The pirate ignored the impotent threat, turning toward Elrin with an alluring offer and a hearty smile. "Now what would you like son? Treasure? Glory? A night of passion with a lass?"

Elrin thought through his options. Treasure and glory were fine things, a woman's touch finer still. Once those things would have been all he wanted, but since hearing his father's name, all he wanted was to help him. All he had done was run. And now, after meeting Delik and Minni, after freeing Amber and Hurn, learning Calimska was behind the black powder trade, he was filled with guilt.

How could he wish only for his father, when there were so many more lives at risk? If he asked for their freedom, or a ship, Kobb would give it only to take it away again. He couldn't trust Kobb to give him any wish he asked, it had to be something the pirate didn't really care to lose.

"I want you to free us on the Hoard Islands with a small boat and supplies."

"So be it," Kobb laughed. "Your wish is my wish. Now, mine must be yours. You will teach me how to operate these Jandan gadgets that flash their secrets about. I have quite a collection from all these prize ships."

Elrin didn't know what to say. Kobb was too eager to let them sail to Hoard Island, but Elrin had to get there somehow. There was no way to win his game. If he refused to help he would end up with his arms in knots like Pelegrin. If he didn't tell Kobb how to work the devices, surely someone else would.

Elrin looked to the rebel generals, Minni shrugged, Tikis just stared back, but Delik gave a gentle nod of approval. That was enough for Elrin. "Alright, do you have one here?"

"Good lad. It can wait. Let's finish our game first. What do you want ogre?"

"Hurn Ga Kogh keep Little Bell safe, no more screams for her."

"Such a popular commodity! What ever can I do to keep my promises to everyone?" Kobb appealed to Amber. "What say you lad? Do you want this big oaf to follow you around and keep you safe?"

Amber nodded, shrinking from the redeemer's intense gaze, grasping across the table, probing with a hollow, hungry need.

"Done and done! Two fish on one hook. I won't stand in the way of a rolling mountain. Now, I need you to do some heavy lifting for me, so don't wear out your arms before we get to port."

"Hurn Ga Kogh will lift for you."

Uighara's fist slammed into the table and the whole room shook, rattling the table, and vibrating through the chairs. A guard pushed his blade to the base of Uighara's skull, and the tremors eased, accompanied by a tightness in the air.

"You said you would not keep my acolyte from me."

"Indeed I did. I'm an honest man, Uighara ... well I keep my promises at least. I believe I said, I would not keep him from you. I never said, I wouldn't keep you from him."

Uighara spat on the floor. "You will suffer the wrath of the Lord Almighty! I'll see to it you are skinned for my boots."

"Oh my, make sure you give me a nice rub and polish if you wear me in front of the High Priest. I'd want him to see me at my best."

Stewing in a white-hot rage, Uighara pursed his lips, making white knuckled fists upon the table. The guard kept his knife on the redeemer, the fine point was all that kept the Jandan priest in check.

Amber wilted into Minni for comfort, for fear Uighara's anger would ignite.

"There now deary, don't you worry about him. Once that sour old dog without a bone is on his way, I'll introduce you to Granny Shan. She can juggle and knit at the same time." Kobb leant across the table and whispered, "She's got a bit of wind, like you."

The pirate made a silly face and Amber hid a creeping grin, tucking down into Minni's shoulder.

"Now then, Delik, my dear boy, what can I do for you?"

"I want you to honour our original agreement, but I know that's as likely as milk from a dragon."

"Indeed, things change. So how do you want them to change now? What do you want?"

"Take me to my father, we've been told you know where he is."

Kobb's ruffles shook with his laughter. "Granted! I told you this game would be good. Your old man was such a prize! Don't fret, I have him well fed and kept quite secure. You'll see him soon enough."

Pelegrin focused on the conversation, lifting his pain-creased face from the table. "You've got Jaspa Scrambletoe? Where the hell are you keeping him? Listen Kobb; I'll make sure you are richly rewarded—above the going sum. We can work out a fine price for you."

"Let's just say that old man Jaspa is more valuable to me than anything your lot will offer. He's not for sale." Kobb grinned at Pelegrin and Delik. "You both look so surprised."

"What do you want of me, Kobb?" asked Delik, determined to maintain his composure.

"I want you and your men to follow me to the Hoard Islands; the scalers too."

"You'll take us either way," said Minni. "What's the point?"

"You're of more use to me out of chains than in them."

"My rebels will follow," conceded Delik. "But, I do not speak for Tikis and his drakkin brethren."

"Well then, what do you say, scaler? In chains or out?"

"These ones will walk free and Kobb must name these; *drakkin*. Say *scalers* no more."

Kobb contended with the idea. He paced along the stern gallery then pivoted on his heel, his face grim. "Untie the drakkin," he ordered. "Mind you play fair."

Tikis rubbed his wrists and adjusted his position on the seat. Once Kobb was satisfied the drakkin warrior would not launch another attack, he continued with his game.

"Now, my ravishingly magnificent Minella, finally we get to dessert, hmm?"

"Oh, Kobb," she said, flushing a coy smile. "I'm so glad you finally got round to me."

"I'm told ladies enjoy gentle anticipation." The pirate topped his slick smirk off with a wink.

Minni dropped her coquettish facade like the headsman's axe, replacing it with sharp eyes and a scowl. "I'm no lady, as you well appreciate, and my tolerance for your drivel is near expired."

"What do you want then?" asked Kobb, caught off guard by her change in mood.

"Just free all of the captured slaves at a safe port. Don't sell them on again, they'll end up in the same place they began."

"Certainly so. They're simply far too much bother for me at the moment. Now, my dear, I have a delicate situation that requires your utmost confidence and those talented fingers."

She laughed. "I'll give you one of those things, but not both."

LORD'S BLESSING

Each tiny movement disturbed a flock of flaming hooks, which tore up his arms and attacked his brain. Pelegrin did all he could to stay conscious. He focused on *Bone Dancer* sailing away while their small rowboat idly rocked in the sea. The ship eased away to the north, its tawdry, flagrant defacement an offence to its long years in the Lord's armada.

He would make them suffer. The Scrambletoes, Kobb and all the half pint grubs infesting the chosen land would feel his pain multiplied by the four points of the black star. They had brought this agony on him and he would return it with the Lord's brand, marking their sin to eternal damnation.

"Does it pain you?" asked Uighara, fastening his bandolier of spell components. His less than subtle lack of empathy was greased with pleasure.

"Of course it does, you sadistic bastard!"

"Yes, surely it must. Tell me though, is it more or less painful than the injuries you received from the young Scrambletoe?"

"What's it matter? Heal it!"

"The Lord's gift is great and powerful indeed, yet its full potential will only be revealed through study."

"Uighara, so help me, heal these arms, or I'll ..."

"What will you do Commodore? I assure you I can mend your body, but I cannot mend your soul if you forgo your faith. What do you seek?"

"Blast it, Uighara. Absolve my sins. Black star burn them. Just make it stop!"

"Good child, good. The Lord hears you. Now, take my hand."

"I can't ... the pain."

"You must have faith, give me a hand. The pain will purify."

Pelegrin clenched his teeth and swung his maimed sword arm to the redeemer. Uighara caught it and held it firm. The pain intensified with the angle and the tension lanced a burning rod through his shoulder. Pelegrin screamed and twisted his body, kneeling with his head over the gunwale. Uighara dipped his free hand into the water and chanted, his rough voice grating the holy prayer into incomprehensibility.

Nonetheless, the Lord's power bridged across Uighara's hand to the Commodore's. At first, the excruciating pain in each arm increased, then it receded to an ice like numbness. That too faded, leaving a pleasant tingling over his skin. Pelegrin sat up in the boat and tested his arms, rotating his shoulders and flexing his grip.

"Thanks be to the Lord! I feel so good, filled with ... a strength, it's hard to describe. What did you do?"

"You have been blessed in many ways Commodore. The Lord has infused your body with the spiritual fortitude to see us home. Now take my hands."

Pelegrin smiled and took Uighara's hands in his.

"Jando must be told," said Uighara, staring into his eyes.

"Yes, Jando must be told."

"The rebels and the pirates are working together, plotting Jando's destruction from the Hoard Islands. They must be eliminated."

"They must be eliminated."

"We will rally the Armada to our cause. You must persuade your father."

"I will persuade my father."

"Thanks be. Now Commodore, navigate us to shore. We must get to Rum Hill"

"Of course! We must get to Rum Hill."

Uighara released Pelegrin's hands and the Lord's blessing lingered like a balm on his fingers.

Dipping the oars to water, the Commodore turned the boat to shore. Everything was as it should be. The Lord had chosen these trials to make him strong. The proof was plain as the bright blue sky. The sun was glorious, shining on them in all its splendour. Uighara in his holy white robes was the vision of a saint and Pelegrin was his champion. Together they were the Lord's men.

An oar bumped into a shark floating dead on the surface. All around the boat dead fish floated belly up. The Lord must have his sacrifices. Nothing given, nothing gained.

Pelegrin pitched the oars in deep strokes and marvelled at the strength in his arms and back. The boat charged through the water, its bow cutting an easy path to the distant shore. Uighara rested at the stern, dipping his hand in the water as they went, praying with a rhythm that spurred Pelegrin on. A swathe of silver scales bobbed in their wake.

By the time the boat pulled in to the docks of Rum Hill, dusk crept upon the sky. They disembarked while the western sky burned with the dying glow of the setting sun, shedding enough light to witness the ruins of his finest marines strewn across the docks. The rebel forces and the drakkin were no longer present. The survivors dragged bodies into neat rows where the day's heat had already ripened the dead enough for summer flies to take upon them.

Pelegrin's strength faded; this defeat was avoidable. Complacency had determined the outcome, not numbers, skill, weaponry, or any other factor. He might have let the rats into the hold, but he would sink every last ship they took before they had a chance to ambush him again. Determination lit a fire in his belly, melting away the leaden cloak of his failure. The Commodore hooked on his sabre and scabbard, bolstered by its weight at his side once again. Iron in hand, he'd cast the rebels to all the hells. They'd feel the full wrath of the Lord's armada.

Pelegrin adjusted his uniform; it was in a sad state with buttons missing and bloodstains. He neatened it and rolled back his shoulders, lifting his chin. With a purpose in his stride he approached a marine kneeling beside a fallen comrade in the assembly of bodies. His uniform was ragged and a long cut had torn through his padded jack leaving a weeping open gash.

"Who is in command?" asked Pelegrin.

"Sir!" The marine rose to attention, after a moment of recognition. "Nobody, sir!"

"Nobody?"

"The rebels took all our officers, sir. Left us alone if we gave up our weapons and surrendered."

"Is this all that remain?"

"Some have left with the enemy, sir. Most of us who can walk are trying to lay the dead ready for the Priest's words this evenin'."

"Brother Demnirin?" asked Uighara.

"Yeah, that's him."

Uighara dug into one of his pouches, paying more attention to the line of dead bodies than the marine. "Is he at the temple?"

"Think so, he's been tending the wounded."

Uighara marked the four points of the black star in the air. "Go with the Lord's blessings, my child."

The marine bowed to Uighara. "Thank you, Brother." He saluted Pelegrin, stretching his chest wound in the process, wincing with pain.

Uighara led the way to the temple, the streets a hazard of filth and sin. The Good Lord's children made their way to the temple while the lost and damned gathered to drink and gamble, likely accomplishing worse debauchery as the dark night took the town.

Folk of both faith and sin made way, for their mission was blessed by the Lord. No one would stand in their path. Pelegrin saw it in the wide eyes of the people staring at them. The Lord was calling. He would deliver them to certain victory.

The temple was a humble stone structure at the top of a small rise. It faced the ramshackle town of Rum Hill with a stoic, gumption. The gable roof pointed to the heavens like an arrowhead, reminding the town that the Lord was watching. Heavy studded timber doors hung open for the evening service, welcoming townsfolk to pray.

Pelegrin took the temple steps in long strides past the faithful, lining up to cleanse their grubby hands and dirty faces. Pelegrin's own hands were filthy with the mistakes of the long day. Uighara motioned to an acolyte who brought them black glazed bowls filled with blessed water. As they knelt and cleansed their hands then faces, they prayed together, Uighara's dark accent and rough tones abrasive against Pelegrin's refined, precise voice. "Wash the sins of the day, O'Lord, take my hands. See the face of my faith, O'Lord, take my love."

The acolyte removed the cleansing bowls and emptied the tainted water down a sluice where it drained into a fishpond, teeming with silver perch and lilies, closing their petals for the night. With a bow to Uighara, the acolyte ushered them through the arch and into the temple.

In front of the altar knelt a man, his head dipped in prayer. Uighara strode down the aisle, past odd looks and sharp whispers. Pelegrin was uncomfortable in temples at the best of time and as he followed Uighara through the nave, he sensed the eyes of the congregation like they were the Lord's jury, critiquing his very soul. This was not the best day to receive such a review. Everyone in town would know by now. All hells knew, word of his defeat would be half way to Jando. The bright new Commodore lost his fleet to the rebels. There was a light tittering in the wings, he was a laughing stock. They wouldn't be laughing when he paraded the Scrambletoes to the chopping block; he'd be the pride of the Lord's chosen.

The priest finished his prayer with hands to the heavens and rose before the altar, turning just as Uighara and Pelegrin came to the crossing.

"Brother Uighara! Commodore! The Lord has blessed us."

"Brother Demnirin," Uighara ever so slightly inclined his head.

Demnirin came to Uighara and kissed his outstretched hand before marking the sign of the black star. "I was just praying for your souls and the Good Lord sends you here. I was told they took all of the officers, how did you escape? Do you require healing?"

"Calm yourself, Brother, we have little time and need to return to the High Temple."

"We have only a mule, though there are two rounseys for sale with old man Carter. I'll send fo—"

"Take me to your temple stone," interrupted Uighara.

"Of course, but shouldn't I send for the horses first?"

"They won't be needed," Uighara's harsh tone rasped at Demnirin's good intentions.

"Follow me then," Demnirin took them up a step and behind the pulpit. A circular tile mosaic, rich in detail, covered the stone floor. Black, blue and purple tiles marked out the points of the black star. At one point stood the altar, the opposite point the pulpit. The two remaining points led to stairs on either side for the congregation's procession each service. A sea of green and yellow tiles surrounded the star and the temple stone lay in the very centre, polished by an age of hands seeking blessings of the Lord. The idea of that very stone once gracing the most hallowed temple in his ancestral homeland filled the Commodore with awe. Saint Jan took the temple stones in the great exodus, carrying them across raging oceans, battling demons and tempests, guided by the black star and his faith in the Lord. The stones were a foundation that connected the faithful to their roots and from each stone the chosen would build a new temple for the Lord.

Kneeling to the temple stone, Uighara emptied the meagre contents of a pouch into his palm and closed his hand into a fist, muttering in a low voice. Demnirin's welcome faded as he watched Uighara dwell on the stone, sorting through the ritual components.

"Brother Uighara, we must go now," Pelegrin gave Demnirin an apologetic shrug. "We waste time here and the good priest needs to begin the evening prayers."

"I will lead the congregation this evening," said Uighara, rising to his feet, returning something to a pouch. "I will redeem their sins for the Lord."

"If that is your wish," Demnirin's joy at their arrival diminished with each word from Uighara. "Though if you are in a hurry to get to Jando, it would be easier if I led the—"

"Gather your congregation, Brother Demnirin."

Demnirin hesitated, watching Uighara untying another pouch. "What are you planning? These are good people."

"Then there is nothing to worry about, Brother." Uighara's greased smile polluted his face. "Now make haste, the dark star is risen."

Demnirin hurried off to help the acolytes cleanse the last of the congregation before the service. Uighara emptied reddish glittering sand from his pouch, making a circle around the temple stone. He deftly made an arcane symbol at each point of the black star and muttered to himself while he checked over his work.

"Stand on the temple stone, Commodore. One foot on it and one foot off, but not outside the circle."

"Why are we wasting our time here for an elaborate blessing?"

"Because the Lord wants you to command the armada," Uighara licked his thumb and dipped it into his pouch. It came out glimmering red and he dabbed it on Pelegrin's forehead, his chin and each cheek, muttering as he did so. He swapped hands and repeated the pattern on his own face. "Do you want to command the armada, Commodore? Do you want to avenge the souls of your men?"

"Yes, but how—"

"Do as I say,"

Pelegrin did so, careful not to step on any of the powder. He didn't want to foul the blessing. The armada, under his command! By the Lord if he convinced his father of the threat it might just be possible. He might have lost a few ships, but that was a small price to pay for finding the Scrambletoes and crushing the rebellion. "Admiral," said Pelegrin, enjoying the sound as it rolled off his tongue.

Uighara took a tiny white component from a pouch, a tooth perhaps, and bent his head in prayer. He brought his hands together, elbows on the pulpit, forehead resting on his interlocked fingers. A warm glow emanated from his praying hands and grew to encompass him in a golden aura.

Pelegrin waited in position to receive the redeemer's blessing. He'd been warned by his father not to trust him; though the same was said about all converts. Pelegrin trusted the High Priest and he said that any poacher outcast from Calimska was the Lord's gift to Jando. That sat fine with him. Uighara might be an arse of a man sometimes, but he was raised in Calimska. What more could be expected? Uighara had found his faith; devout to the Lord and loyal to the High Priest, so devout that Pelegrin's own faith was pale in comparison.

Leaving that young acolyte behind was a good thing too. Now, Uighara was focused on the task at hand. Pelegrin knew redeemers had strange secret rituals to train acolytes in the ways of the Lord's gift, but there was something unusual with that one. The boy never said a word and shadowed Uighara everywhere. There was a determination in Uighara's eye since their capture, a fresh drive. Things were falling together. Soon, Jando would have another victory. They had faith, they had the armada, and they had the location of the outlaws that plagued the chosen.

Uighara finished his prayer and rang a small bell on the pulpit. His aura radiated warmth around his white robes. He was the sun breaching the clouds. As he spoke, the congregation hushed their amazed whispers and listened to his reassuring voice. His usual voice of gravel and tar was reborn in velvet, deep and consuming.

"The Lord welcomes you! Gather unto our Lord!"

"We hear the word of the Lord," responded the congregation in unison.

"Brother Demnirin, your good priest, prayed for me this eve. He also prayed for the son of the Lord's High Admiral, Commodore Pelegrin. The power of his prayer so great, so endowed with faith, it summoned us here this night. Here we stand blessed by the Lord, alive, ready to preach the word, to redeem the sins of the land, to cast the blight off with blade and faith."

The congregation sounded its agreement, calling out 'blessed be' and 'preach the word'.

"The Lord has blessed me with a gift, the gift of redemption in his almighty name. I was born of sin and he raised me up. He showed me truth: Nothing for nothing, dear folk of faith; sin for salvation. I sacrificed my sins and he bore me up with a commanding faith, a sanctified purpose and a deep and pure urgency for his love. Do you feel that love? Do you have that purpose, that faith?"

The congregation called their assent. Pelegrin knew his love for the Lord and called with them, his heart pounding with faith. "I feel it!"

"Good! The Lord knows your love and he has brought us here together today to witness a miracle. An angel of the Lord has spoken to me! He gave me a message and a mission. The Lord is coming. He will return and grant his faithful life eternal. Let the black star swallow our sin and purify our soul!"

"Praise be!" called the congregation.

"Do you have sins in your hearts you want gone?"

"Yes!"

"Do you have doubts you want to cast aside?"

"Yes!"

"Then you must give of yourself unto the Lord!"

The aura around Uighara pulsed with the energy of the congregation. The white of his robes shone upon the joyful faces of the congregation, raising their hands to heaven, asking for their sins to be redeemed and replaced with the Lord's love. Demnirin stood at the back of the pews, his face dour, unengaged by the blessed energy that buzzed in the air. He was a black rock and Uighara a diamond. Pelegrin forgave Brother Demnirin his jealousy. Joy wrapped its splendour around him and nothing else mattered.

"Take each other's hands, unburden your hearts, give yourself to the Lord. Let him have your naked souls, goodness and evil."

The congregation took the hands of their neighbour and beamed their joy to Uighara, elated by every word, ecstatic by his presence.

"I feel your faith this day, you feel it too, rising up to heaven's blessed halls, the seat of our Lord on high. Your faith knows heaven, but I know sin clings on, weighs you down, holds you back from life eternal. It mires your immortal souls in filth, dragging you under. The demons of the five hells whisper through the earth, lead you into temptation. Charlatans and shamans crush your faith until you are dead and nothing but dirt in the gardens of the false gods. Sorcerous powers dwell at your doorstep, speaking in tongues of demons, rejecting the Lord's gift of redemption."

"It is time to root out that sin. Reach deep inside your souls and dig that sin out, feel it rise up, surrender it to the Lord. Redemption is yours!"

Uighara crossed to the aisle between the pews and took the outstretched hands offered on each side of the front row. They cried out in ecstasy. Honey light spread from Uighara to each man and woman, hand to hand, trickling to the end of each pew. Their faces raised to the rafters, mouths open, gasping in thrall. Uighara's own light grew around him with each soul he connected.

He withdrew his hand from the first row and they collapsed forward onto the floor, rag dolls left for a newer toy. Moving forward Uighara took the hands of the second row; they arched their backs, lips shuddering as the honey light oozed across them. Uighara's light swelled, pulsating with the beat of many hearts.

Pelegrin called out. "There's something wrong!" But, Uighara did not hear. The euphoric calls from the congregation drowned him out. He had to get the fervent priest's attention, the exhortation was going horribly wrong. If he left the temple stone, his blessing might break. He had to have faith; Uighara knew what he was doing. The fallen congregation were just exhausted from their glimpse of the Lord's power—that was all.

Demnirin was not standing at the back any longer. He strode towards Uighara touching the outstretched hands of his congregation. His black robes deepening to a rift of darkness compared to the blazing glory of Uighara. Another row fell with Uighara's redemption, slumping across each other, their heads lolling, faces devoid of expression.

Demnirin's voice boomed down the aisle. "By the grace of our Lord, cease this madness!"

Uighara's laughter rumbled and fell like an avalanche, shaking the temple. "I will not cease until the Lord's return has cleansed this land."

"Leave my people! Take no more for your schemes!"

Uighara laughed again, plaster and dust fell from the ceiling as he took the hands of the next row. "The pure of faith never need fear the hand of redemption. The Lord be their judge this day. Not you, Brother."

"Nor you!" cried Demnirin, grasping his hands forward, then thrusting them apart. The pews skittered to the edge of the temple, taking Demnirin's congregation out of Uighara's reach. The townsfolk not yet touched by Uighara panicked, fallen men and women lay still on the temple floor.

Pelegrin was at a loss. What could he do? He had to act, but if he moved he'd ruin the blessing and hinder the Lord's holy work.

Uighara flicked his palm like he was swatting a fly. Demnirin flew across the temple, crashing into the stone wall and falling to the floor. Uighara chuckled, and walked back to Pelegrin, each step filling Pelegrin with doubt. This was no blessing, how could the Lord abide his chosen fighting each other?

Uighara stepped into the circle, placing one foot on the temple stone and the other to the side. The redeemer's aura enveloped him and glaring white robes obliterated all doubt. Here was the Lord's blessed servant. Demnirin was just another corruption, another border town priest strayed from the true path.

"Take my hand," said Uighara, his voice smooth and warm like dark rum.

Pelegrin took it.

Uighara spoke a word of power and everything folded upon itself.

SUNSET

Dusk eased upon the sea. Minni leaned on the gunwale of the forecastle, watching the sun's fire set to the west. The Great Dividing Range painted a black fence against a golden horizon and peach lit clouds drifted over the wild coast. Jando had no hold this far north, the wilderness wrestled with its own demons, untamed by men, alive with primal magic.

"I got us the last of that soup. Here take this." Elrin handed Minni a warm tankard. "I was talking with Kobb's cook, he's Calimskan. Of all things, he apprenticed with the chef that served the Order of Calim."

"He must have shown talent," said Minni, glad for Elrin's company.

"The chef kept him down, never let him make journeyman. After two years being held back he takes off in the night with his master's recipes. Kobb found him in Jando working the docks."

"And now we reap the benefits." Minni sipped at the seafood soup, enjoying the hit of pepper, cushioned with cinnamon and spiked with citrus tang.

"The crew love him, don't they."

"Won your heart too, has he? Don't trust him, Elrin. Kobb only granted us what we asked because he was already going to do it. You saw what he gave Pelegrin and Uighara."

"But, he did let them free," said Elrin, frowning. "Would you have done that?"

"It served Kobb's purpose to do so. If it served ours we would have done the same."

Elrin was quiet, the sunset glow warming his intelligent eyes. How could she explain he was caught in something dangerous, more dangerous than a dead letter? No fool would trust the word of someone they just met. Not about this. She had enough trouble herself.

With raven hair kicking up in the wind, he broke the silence. "The mountains are so high above the sea. I can't tell where the road to Calimska would be."

"You'll not see it now, we've sailed too far north. Stoneheart's pass is way back to the south now. Are you missing home?"

"No, but I miss my mother. That sounds like I'm, you know, I don't really miss her, I'm just worried about her."

"I miss mine too."

"Where is she?"

Minni noted the waxing moon glowing through the dusk. "All the Reik will be gathering. Our camp will be on the roll by now."

"I was saving my shine. You know, to get out. I would have loved to see a gathering. I heard Reik can play down the stars with music so loud all the gods come and join in."

"Ha! What a story. An outright lie, of course. There's no Reik who can play a tune to please Jandan's Lord high and mighty. No song would tempt that old bastard to so much as tap his toes, let alone set to with a jig!"

Elrin laughed. Minni was glad for the moment to rest her eyes on his. She caught herself letting down her guard. She hardly knew the shiner and was thinking of him like some stupid girl, lost in a dream. It bothered her; he was too kind, too accepting, too ready to help, too damn easy to like. She needed to take her own advice. She couldn't trust him, not yet anyway. Damn her heart melting under a single sunset. She had to know more before she made her choice.

"Elrin, you need to tell me what happened in Calimska, why you stowed away in those wagons."

"I was fleeing the city guard. I already told you; they tried to kill me."

"Why the wagons I was with?"

"I overheard those Jandans arguing in the tent. They were leaving Calimska, but I didn't know you were with them. I would have asked otherwise."

Minni smiled, adding 'too polite' to her list of things that bothered her. "Not a good idea for a stowaway to ask permission. Ruins the whole idea of stealing yourself away."

"You make a good point," Elrin shook his head. "Remember, I'm new to all this. You seem to be, ah, quite an accomplished woman. Is that the right word for your line of work?"

"My line of work?" Minni mocked her concern. "What exactly are you implying?"

"Oh no, I didn't mean that, my Jandan isn't so good. I just meant that I noticed your—"

"Noticed my what?"

Elrin flushed red.

"What were you looking at?" pressed Minni.

"No, no, I didn't, well, not deliberately—"

Minni laughed and punched his shoulder. "Come on Elrin! You're far too easy."

Elrin took it in good humour. "You'll keep."

Sailors came down the rigging and gathered on the decks. The night crew took to their stations with the final light of the day fading from the sky. A sailor came up to the forecastle with a glowing taper in hand and gave them both a knowing look while he lit the lantern on the fore mast.

"Smokin' lamps a'lit!" he called to the milling sailors below. He gave Elrin a sly wink. "The lads'll be takin' a breath or two. Wants ta git a bit rowdy up ere for a spit. Might's ya lay the lass aft for a spell."

Elrin's face wrinkled with confusion then flushed red as he processed an inadequate translation of the sailor's words. "What did he just say I should do?"

Minni stifled her laughter, grabbed Elrin's hand and led him past the sailors lining up for their smoke. They relocated to a couple of barrels beside the stair to the quarterdeck and watched the stars glittering across the night sky. The sailors off their shift cursed and called, with rowdy laughter.

"What did Kobb have from you?" asked Elrin.

"Is that of concern now is it?"

"Just asking after you, that's all, to make sure he didn't ... you know."

"What if he did?"

"If he did then I'd, I'd stick him while he sleeps."

"I'm sure he'd enjoy that, coming from a strapping lad like you. Are you in the habit of sticking idle men unawares? I never guessed that was your thing."

"No, I didn't mean ... Oh I see, go on then, have your fun with me."

"You just walk yourself into trouble don't you." Minni couldn't keep a straight face. "Fall right in it every time."

Elrin didn't laugh with her, his face was sombre as he stared at the moon. "You're right, I couldn't even deliver a note to the Guildmaster without landing a bounty on my head. Everything I've done since then dropped me in deeper water, like I'm the punchline of a grand joke; a plaything for the god's petty amusement."

"What if you were?" Minni wanted him to know the truth.

"I guess it wouldn't be so bad if the joke was funny, but I'm no fool. You and Delik dodge my questions and tell me half of nothing. You know something about the Dragon Choir and you know I need to find it."

"What makes you say that?" Minni couldn't tell him, she had to be sure.

"You both made it quite obvious when I told you I was seeking passage to the Hoard Islands. Why don't you just tell me?"

"Delik's not convinced you are ... He wasn't sure if you were ready to be told."

"That's just what I mean; damn secrets and lies. What do I have to do to be trusted?"

"I don't know. I trust you, but prophecy is a murky business."

"What prophecy?"

"It's a secret. You are right; damn secrets and lies."

"Why is it a secret? If it's a prophecy of what will come to pass then it will happen no matter what, whether I know or not."

"Not so. It is our guide to a future of hope, a map that tells us how to free the coast from slavery. If I get it wrong, if I stray from the markers then ... I don't know. I don't know if I can decide." Minni slumped her chin onto her knees and hugged her legs.

"Who told you the prophecy?"

"That is the secret. If you betrayed our source, if the Jandans knew ..."

"So don't tell me who gave the prophecy. I don't need to know. I do need to know if your prophecy means you won't let me find the Dragon Choir."

Minni sat silently, berating herself for letting so much out, chastising herself for needing help, wanting Elrin to be the one and fearing that he was no more than another tool she would need to use. She hugged her knees tight.

"Minni, you're crying. I'm sorry." Elrin reached out and put a tentative hand on her shoulder. "I shouldn't have pressed you."

Minni sniffed and wiped the back of her hand across her eyes. "Yes, you should." Minni smiled, liking Elrin's hand reassuring her, enjoying the tender contact. She put her hand on his. Damn the secrets and lies.

"Elrin, I need your help to find a key."

"Of course, what does it look like? Did you leave it on *Juniper*?"

"The key to free us shall fall in your hand,

holding a note, but no name.

Sounding the choir to your aid,

shifting the balance, sinking the stars.

Darkened threads will stain the weave,

summoning the blood monsoon."

There, it was out. Minni studied Elrin, tried to gauge him, measure his fit and weigh his response. Elrin was confused at first then thoughtful. He removed his reassuring hand and rubbed his neck, squinting his left eye.

"Amber!" he said, excited, grabbing her shoulder again. Realising his outburst, he quietened his voice. "Amber is the Key. It has to be her, she had no name, she weaved that magic with her voice and those notes she was holding made such potent elemental magic. Her power would rival sorcerers in the Order of Calim."

Minni just listened, smiling with him, loving his exuberance.

"You said, 'sounding the choir,' it has to be her. Perhaps she sings and the Dragon Choir is activated. What is the Dragon Choir anyway?"

"We aren't sure; some kind of device to summon dragons."

Elrin's hope dropped, touched by doubt. "I suppose we shall soon find out. Once she has it, do you think she would let me use it to help my father?"

"She doesn't know about this. Elrin, you mustn't say anything yet."

"Why ever not? She might already know about the Dragon Choir. Have you asked her?"

"I did. She has overheard Uighara speak about it more than once. He must seek it too."

"How did he know Amber was the key?"

"He is a powerful redeemer, close to the High Priest of Jando. Those dogs have their ways."

"At least she's safe with us now, out of the hands of that cruel monster. It explains why Uighara was so upset when Kobb refused to give her back."

Minni agreed, Amber must be the Key; everything Elrin said made perfect sense. So why did she still think it was him? Why didn't he even have an inkling that he might be the Key? She had secretly hoped that the prophecy would have sparked something for him, something to light a beacon of truth to make the path clear, but telling him made no difference. She still had two keys and couldn't decide which one fit. Some 'Lock' she turned out to be.

Minni pressed on, looking for a sign. "What about the rest of the prophecy? What do you make of that?"

"Your mysterious prophet must like teasing you with riddles. I didn't understand much, though it didn't sound pleasant at the end. A blood monsoon, that can't be good. And what about the stars sinking, do you think that means the Jandan armada?"

"That is what we hoped," said Minni, desperate for Elrin to find himself in the prophecy. "You were told to seek the aid of the choir, weren't you?"

"That's what Herder Kleith said. Though, I didn't have time to ask why or how before the guards came for me and I had to run."

"How did he know about the Dragon Choir or to go looking on the Hoard Islands?"

"How did you know?" Elrin shot back.

"We were told in the Prophecy of the Fist."

"Another prophecy, how many are there?"

"Many."

"Fine," said Elrin, holding his hands up in surrender. "I get the hint. I don't need to know."

"No, you don't," Minni chided gently. "Not now."

"So there's hope for me, then?" Elrin's mischievous grin was a gem in the night.

"Maybe," Minni returned the smile, expecting Elrin's lips to take her own.

Elrin just held her eyes for a moment longer, his smile warmed her heart, but his lips never approached. He adjusted his position against the barrel, shuffling a touch nearer.

They sat together quietly. Elrin chuckled then looked around to make sure no one was near.

"What are you doing?" she asked. He'd kiss her now. How could he not?

He brought his face closer to hers and whispered. "I'd bet my pants you both planned for Kobb to capture us and take us to his hideout. You did, didn't you!"

"Careful what you bet, Elrin."

"No, you don't fool me. Why else would Delik say that *Bone Dancer* was my passage? He knew. You knew."

She leaned her face close to his, caught in his know-it-all grin. "Keep your pants then, and keep that smart mouth shut too. If Kobb finds out we'll be overboard before you figure what you've missed."

"What did I miss?" whispered Elrin, his grin fading.

"Wouldn't you like to know!"

RALLY THE FAITHFUL

Pelegrin was compressed to dust, then stretched to the stars. A heartbeat felt a day, and then in a blink he was himself again. Every organ rebelled against the contortion. His mind spun and he collapsed to the floor in the grip of nausea. With a heave his stomach emptied upon polished black tiles.

Uighara was on his knees, panting. Even with bloodshot eyes and blood dripping from his nose, the strain of the blessing was not enough to weaken the Priest's severe manner. "You'll be cleaning that up."

At that thought, Pelegrin wretched again, his vision blurring with tears.

Leaving the circle, Uighara opened a drawer and tossed Pelegrin a rag. "Quick now, before it spreads to that sigil! Disturb an active net and you'll know about it."

He did as he was told, mopping up the mess with care not to rub out any of the red luminescent powder.

They had been delivered onto another temple stone, surrounded by neatly cut black tiles, which formed the four points of the black star. It reminded him of the mosaic in the high temple, though this was much smaller. At each point of the star was a bowl with a green flame burning above a thick red substance.

What was wrong with his head? He was thinking through a fog. He took care as he rose to his feet, fighting to control his senses. The air was damp, smothered in a pungent mix of urine, burnt hair and manure.

"Where are we?"

The redeemer snorted, but didn't answer. He busied himself, writing something upon a table in the corner. Pelegrin stepped out of the glowing circle, tossing the soiled rag beside a large wooden crate. The crate shook and a rooster crowed from inside. Startled, Pelegrin took a quick step backwards, bumping into a cabinet and rattling the jars and bottles on its shelves. Beside him came the short wail of a baby. He reeled in shock, not

137

knowing how he could have trusted Uighara. A child in a place like this? It was abhorrent to think of such a thing. Pelegrin pulled back a dark cloth covering the large cage.

Inside was a monstrous rat covered in feathers. It pressed its fanged snout through the bars, licking and mewling like a babe. Pelegrin covered the drape over the cage again.

"What demons do you keep?"

Uighara's face screwed up at the distraction from his writing. "Would a demon keep in a cage like that? Leave the colo colo be! Unless you want to feed it?"

"What does it eat? Human flesh?"

"Spittle!" The priest close to spat the word himself, his annoyance growing. "It's a colo colo, imbecile. If you want to feed your flesh to something, open up the cockatrice crate and stuff your nose in there!"

The small room crowded in around Pelegrin. He had to get some air. The only shutters were above Uighara's writing desk. There was no door. Pelegrin strode over to the desk. He pulled on the shutters, but they were nailed closed.

"Do you mind?" Uighara shoved him away. "You'll ruin the script."

"How do we get out of here?"

"Oh, calm yourself, for mercy's sake."

"What are you doing?"

"Nothing at the moment, you keep interrupting."

Pelegrin retreated, confused by his memories. How did they get here? Wherever here was, he didn't like it. He found a stool by the wall and sat, trying to navigate the fog of his memory. He remembered being set free and Uighara healing his arms. He remembered the strength he had, rowing so fast, the sea shining silver and then the dead bodies of his men on the docks. They went to the temple and Uighara delivered a sermon. He remembered that much, Uighara was amazing, the Lord shone upon him. Something went wrong though, what was it?

"There," said Uighara, sprinkling sand over the paper. "All done. Patience pays its own rewards."

Pelegrin shook his head full of cotton and rubbed his brow.

"What happened? We were in Rum Hill a moment ago, a day ago, how long? Why can't I remember?"

"The Lord's power is difficult to fathom without his gift. Don't worry yourself, you are home, Commodore. We are in Jando."

"That's ... that's impossible."

"I agree and yet we are here. The Lord's blessings are many. Come now, we mus—"

"The blessing! You were to give me a blessing."

"And I did," said Uighara, twisting his mouth around a smile. He walked toward Pelegrin and took his hands. "You will convince your father to rally the armada."

Pelegrin's head cleared. "Yes, I will convince him," he said, confident in his task.

"You have proof the rebel leaders and the pirates are hiding out on the Hoard Islands. He will be grateful. You will be rewarded."

It was true. "I have the proof. I will be rewarded."

Uighara let go of Pelegrin's hands and walked over to an empty bookcase against the wall.

Pelegrin straightened his shoulders; everything made perfect sense. The Lord was great and mighty. The Lord was with him, guiding his hand. He was blessed with righteous power and would see the Lord's will accomplished, or die trying.

The redeemer leant his shoulder against the bookcase and it slid to the side. Behind was a door with strange symbols scratched into the timber. He incanted a coarse unintelligible phrase, tracing over four of the symbols. They glowed after his touch and with a soft click the door opened into a dim corridor.

They strode through a mess of silent halls and small connecting chambers, passing furniture draped in linen and caked with years of dust. Webs hung in the corners, the spiders absent, given up on catching anything. Uighara opened a door into a stairwell where reverent choral voices drifted down with the specs of dust, filtered and faint like the moonlight from a skylight high above.

The singing invigorated his spirit. Pelegrin sung along with the hymn in his head as he climbed the stairs. The Seas of Faith. It was the very song that had played for his graduation from the academy. Every step up brought him closer to crowning that small glory. This would please his father and be an end to the Scrambletoes. An end to them would end the rebellion and the glory of Jando would bring peace to the chosen land. The grubs and wanderers, the scalers and frogs, every corrupted soul would yield, or serve under the yoke.

Uighara took him through a door and into a back room behind the choir, just as the hymn came to a close. An acolyte was peeping through some curtains, a lookout for two others who were taking swigs from a carafe of wine as red as their robes. They lost all colour in their cheeks when confronted by Uighara. The boy with the carafe returned it to the table and dropped to his knees. The other two followed his lead.

"Forgive us! Don't tell Brother Brennan."

Uighara snorted. "I need not forgive anything here, seek it from the Lord, or Brother Brennan if you prefer. I need one of you to take this message to the Lord's High Admiral."

The boys were shocked; none made a move to take the message. Each waited for the other to do something. Pelegrin remembered being caught in a similar situation. He also remembered the thrashing Brennan gave him.

"You there," Pelegrin selected the lookout, he'd less likely smell like wine. "Come on then, take it, quick and quiet. You know what he looks like?"

The boy nodded, he took the note from Uighara and left through the drapery. The Lord's High Admiral had never missed the evening service in his life. Pelegrin knew he would be seated in the front row with perfect posture, his fresh pressed blue uniform, adorned with medals of iron and bronze, his rigid attention on the sermon.

Uighara guided Pelegrin out of the choir's recess past several guards into the High Priest's receiving room where they found Brother Brennan tasting the wine from a small table of refreshments.

He swallowed the wine with an awkward smile. "Brother Uighara! Does the High Priest know you have returned? I have not had notice on his appointment list."

"Be at ease Brother, no notice was given."

"Would you like to make an appointment then, I'll get the book and see if he can fit you in. He is so very busy, as you know."

Brennan removed himself from the room. Pelegrin chuckled as he made himself comfortable on a red velvet seat by the wall. He picked several grapes from a fruit bowl and enjoyed the juicy crunch, cleansing the aftertaste of bile from his palate. Uighara did not sit. He was motionless save his whispering lips, his hands held together, praying for an appointment or praying Brother Brennan didn't return. Perhaps, praying that the Lord's High Admiral would rally the armada to end the rebels once and for all.

Pelegrin waited and Uighara prayed. The seats grew uncomfortable; too soft for Pelegrin's liking. He was used to life at sea with the constant movement of wind and wave shifting the deck under his feet. He paced, listening to another hymn finish and the even tones of the High Priest leading a prayer.

"Is this the same night, or have I slept a day, or four? When did we leave Rum Hill?"

"This very night," said Uighara, his hands still clasped in prayer, eyes unmoved from the door.

"But, how?"

"A miracle of the Lord's power. Let that be enough."

Pelegrin found himself staring at the door as well, wondering about the events of the day. The impossible distance travelled in a moment. No steed could match that pace. It was faster than a ship with an air savant feeding the sails, faster even than a dragon.

"We must find a way to use this power! Can you imagine what we could do?"

"Indeed, I can."

The pipe organ played a joyous tune, leading the congregation and choir in the final hymn for the service, *The Chosen's Return*.

There was movement in the other room and a heated voice rose in a berating tone. The voice continued in a rant with no opposition for several minutes then went quiet and a moment later the door opened. Brother Brennan entered first his head lowered and face red.

"The Lord's most Holy, High Priest of Jando."

Pelegrin and Uighara dropped to their knees and bowed.

"Rise Brother Uighara, Commodore Pelegrin, take my blessing."

Uighara kissed the High Priest's proffered hand, then rose to his feet. Pelegrin also kissed the outstretched hand, but could not rise, his legs overcome by weakness. He had never received an audience with the High Priest and never expected to find the old man so daunting. His sacramental vestments radiated power like it was the Lord himself standing before them. The silken robes of white were woven with a thousand black stars and each one stared at him, judging his soul. A black stole scarfed his neck, hanging on either side of a thick iron chain, the last link on each end bent open. This was the chain of Saint Jan, the very one that the Lord broke to set him free.

"Rise child."

Touched by awe and nervousness in equal measure, the Commodore snapped his gapping mouth shut. He tested his legs and found them strong again, rising with aplomb to stand before the holiest of the chosen.

"Is this your proof, Brother Uighara?"

"He will affirm my testimony, Your Grace."

"Brother Brennan, invite the Lord's High Admiral in, would you."

"Your Grace," Brennan bowed his head. "Shall I bring more refreshments?"

The High Priest furrowed his brow and shooed him away, "Did I ask for that? Stop trying to think for me. Go!"

Brennan hurried away and the High Priest huffed, raising a hand to the heavens in a plea for help. He took a bunch of the plump red grapes in hand and sat on the elegant bone seat at the back of the room. It was a humble model of the grand Lord's Throne, which resided in the temple proper. This one was raised on a small dais, just enough to set it above the other seats in the room, lending the High Priest the authority of any conversation. The legs were stout femurs and the arms were indeed arms. A humerus, radius and ulna ending neatly with a full hand of varnished white fingers.

The High Priest inspected each grape before eating. "Nice to have you here in the flesh again, Uighara. This project has been diverting you from your obligations to the Temple."

"Respectfully, Your Grace, my work will serve the Lord's interests far more than sipping wine and listening to the Council's trivial debates."

"Bah! You left me with Brennan. Brennan! That fool doesn't know his carpals from his tarsals."

"Is there something from the Council meeting I missed that you wish to discuss before the Lord's High Admiral arrives?"

"Don't get glib with me. You know very well the agenda was devoid of interest. Why else would you leave me?"

Uighara refrained from reply.

"You there," the High Priest thrust a skinny finger. "Firstborn Pelegrin, eh?"

"No, Your Grace, my elder died in—"

"Tragedy, yes it was. I remember, he thought he had the little ones cornered too, eh. As sure as sin, he was."

Brennan burst through the door, saving Pelegrin from a response.

"The Lord's High Admiral," he announced.

"Well, of course it is! Now, shut the door as you go."

"Are you sure you don't need any refresh—"

"GO!"

A flash of energy burst from the High Priest's hand, encircling Brother Brennan and ejecting him from the room. The door slammed shut.

Pelegrin's father wore a face of cool reserve and dutifully dropped to his knee before the High Priest. "Your Grace, I thank you for this audience. I hope the Commodore has not imposed."

"Rise, let's not pretend you have anything presently to thank me for."

The Lord's High Admiral abstained from greeting Uighara and stood before his son. The Commodore saluted the chief military commander, who returned the salute with crisp authority.

"I have reports that you lost the fleet in your command, can you account for this?"

Pelegrin swallowed, sunk by a wave of pride to see his father and torn by a tempest of guilt for the loss of his men.

"*Juniper* was docked at Rum Hill on resupply. We were ambushed in dock by rebel forces. They lured *Templestone* and *Fearless* to dock and seized our ships with heavy losses to Jandan forces. Five pirate vessels intercepted *Deliverance* and *Lord's Flame,* assisted by rebels on our hijacked vessels."

"Kobb?"

"Yes, sir."

"Jaspa?"

"No, sir, this was Delik; the son we thought had fled. Kobb has Jaspa at his hideout on the Hoard Islands."

"You know this, how?"

"Kobb was gloating, sir, he gave away that he and the rebel command were plotting together."

"I presume they let you two go to pass on this information."

"Yes, sir."

The Lord's High Admiral withdrew a message from his inside breast pocket. "And this?" He waved it around. "Do you corroborate this?"

"Sir, I have not read it."

"Then you had better do so and explain yourself."

Pelegrin read Uighara's detailed message. It outlined the same information he gave his father with the addition of the miraculous transport home to Jando. Further, it included a recommendation to approve the use of specially armed and warded barges to capture a dragon to sacrifice.

"Sir, I don't know about the capture of any dragon."

"No, you don't. What of the … How does he call it? 'Blessed transportation'. What say you?"

"It is true, sir. Though I don't understand it. In one moment we were in Rum Hill, the next here in the Lord's High Temple. Uighara is very … adept with the gift. He—"

"The Lord himself will be the judge of Uighara. So, you say it works for us then, the chosen?"

"I stand before you as proof, though I do not know how it is possible."

The Lord's High Admiral considered them in silence.

The High Priest leant forward. "Share your mind. Does this satisfy your earlier reservations?"

"Somewhat, Your Grace."

Uighara clutched his hands in fists "What could possibly remain an impediment to you understanding? Everything is for the benefit of the Lord's work in this land. We have a chance to crush the rebellion that gnaws at our heels, destroy the pirates that harry us at sea, and smoke out the nest of evil dragons. Do you not see? The grand new dawn of the Lord is upon us!"

"I see risk, I see a trap, and I see your grasping insidious schemes coming to naught but grief."

"Father, this is our chance to end it. We outnumber them. What trap could hold the armada?"

"What trap could ambush five of our finest ships? Your command outnumbered the rebels at Rum Hill. Yet you and this scheming Calimskan outcast stand as the only survivors."

"Many more survive, they—"

The Lord's High Admiral barked his son down. "Enough!"

"Yes, sir."

The High Priest finished the last of his grapes and rose from his chair. "Tell me, Admiral, do we have the superior force for the engagement?"

"Yes, of course, Your Grace."

"Would the death or capture of the rebel leaders, rid us of their insurgency?"

"It would mark their decline, Your Grace."

"Would Jando benefit without dragon's harassing the coast every year?"

"Yes, but how can you trust him? How do we know he isn't in cahoots with the Golden Shield of Calimska?"

"I trust no man, I trust their deeds. Brother Uighara's work with the infidels has borne us black powder and cannon, silk and steel. He has delivered your own son to safety. What has your tenure as Lord's High Admiral built for our nation, eh? The rebellion has grown stronger. Merchant ships avoid our ports for fear of piracy. What of that, eh?"

The Lord's High Admiral was not to be defeated, even as his arguments crumbled around him. "Your Grace, every trade we make favours Calimska. We suckle at their teat till seasons come, then they leave us to the dragons, hiding behind their sorcerous corruptions."

Uighara sneered. "And that truth will remain as long as the dragons do. They stole the Lord's treasures and divided it among themselves. He won't rule this orb from a throne of bones. His chosen will gather unto him all Oranica's treasure, and they will build him a seat of gold, silver and platinum, studded with precious gems, enough to envy the stars. And he will rule again."

"This is preposterous! I will not be sermonised by you!"

"Father, please listen."

The Lord's High Admiral turned on his son. "You listen! And fall in line, Commodore. You'd choose the ravings of an exiled shiner over your commanding officer? Uighara has no military experience and this entire strategy is flawed."

The High Priest rapped his knuckles on the bony arm of his chair. "Then you must improve the strategy."

"Your Grace, I cannot advi—"

The High Priest cut off the Lord's High Admiral. "I have heard enough. You called for more proof and rightly so. Such has been provided. I will summon the Council and make my proclamation. You can abide by my authority or resign your post. What is your choice?"

"I abide your authority, of course. Your Grace, I wish to install Commodore Pelegrin to Admiral of the fleet, and recommend we reserve a fifth of the armada as a contingency."

"Agreed. Now then; let us rally the faithful."

SANCTUARY

The delicate blush of dawn kissed the rolling sea. Elrin stretched his back, thinking of his bed in Calimska, hoping the next night's sleep would involve something other than a barrel. Minni rested against a crate beside him and Amber lay on the deck, her head cradled in Minni's lap. Minni had a protective arm draped over the girl while Hurn lay across the deck, a barricade of muscle fencing them off to sleep in safety.

They had talked into the night, sharing stories and telling jokes, forgetting the blood and battle of the day past. Delik and Tikis had spent the night in Kobb's quarters, Minni wouldn't say why. Elrin guessed they were smoothing out their differences for what was to come. They could have their secrets as long as they let him find the Dragon Choir. With Amber safe, they had the key. Even if the prophecy was a cartload of rot, having Amber on their side had to be a good thing.

With dawn came the change of shift. Crew from below decks emerged to trade their hammock for a day of sweat. They were in high spirits, whistling and singing bawdy tunes as they took to work. Elrin navigated past the arms and legs of his new friends, careful not to tread on anyone. Minni woke, alerted by the movement. She relaxed, seeing it was just him and raised her arms up in a deep stretch, arching her back and yawning.

Bone Dancer led the column of ships, *Juniper* behind her, sleek and powerful. The three larger Jandan galleons trailed behind with the rest of Kobb's ships holding the rear of the line. Flashes beamed back and forth along the convoy as Kobb's captains practised with the solargraphs, most likely exchanging crude jokes rather than important strategic information.

Elrin took a trip down to the mess and returned with pickled eggs and salted fish, rousing Hurn and Amber from their slumber to eat. Over the simple breakfast they watched the convoy wind through a warren of turquoise channels like a great serpent of sails. They past islands with luxurious golden beaches encircling patches of rich green forest, some long and narrow, others no more than the size of a single ship. The islands grew in size and the water calmed, shielded from the swell of the open ocean.

"Quick!" Elrin waved them over to the side of *Bone Dancer.*

Minni went to find out what the fuss was for. "What's wrong?"

Elrin pointed down through the water. "Look!"

The reef on one side of the ship was shimmering under a blanket of coins. Treasure littered the shoreline and smothered the beaches in gold from distant lands. How many ancient kings with empty vaults would have mourned for this fortune, snatched up by greedy dragons through the ages?

They were actually here. They'd come to the Hoard Islands.

Elrin ran to the other side of the ship, eyes wide with amazement. Minni followed, waving over Amber and Hurn to see. Great mounds piled across another island, its mantle of riches so thick, trees had no room to grow. It was barren save the precious treasures.

Erin shook his head in disbelief. "There is so much here. How would a dragon possibly miss any of it?"

Minni gave him a nudge. "It looks nice to a Calimskan maybe, but there is a good reason we rid ourselves of precious metals for the Surrender Moon. That's the last moon before the dragons descend to collect. Here on the coast it's gold to the grave."

"Even a little bit?"

"Sure, take a piece and see if you make it through the season."

"Why would a mighty dragon bother me for one little gold coin?"

"A mighty dragon wouldn't, it's the young ones that sniff out the small stuff."

"I could defend myself from a small dragon, couldn't I?"

Delik walked up beside them with a chuckle. "You might survive one, but what about the next, and the next? What about a pack of the bastards, each with an aching to please their sweetheart? What then?"

"I would bury it."

"Sure beats holding it in your pocket," said Minni.

Delik shook his head. "It'd be gone by seasons end. Fools still try though."

"So how does Kobb get away with keeping all his silverware?"

"That's not his," said Minni.

Delik chuckled. "Prisella rules the roost, Kobb just polishes her collection."

"Then I'd take it to Calimska, before the season began. I'd be rich and safe there."

"Not with that dead letter you wouldn't," said Minni. "Your escort on the other hand. They'd do just fine after your delivery."

"Maybe so," said Delik, scratching his stubble. "But even without his bounty he'd have Stoneheart's toll."

"And the carry laws," added Minni.

"Alright, alright, I yield." Elrin dipped his head to Minni and Delik in mock defeat. "The rebellion's finest have obviously considered doing the same."

Delik gripped Elrin's shoulder, enjoying the banter. "Considered and applied without success. Minni can tell you the story."

Minni darkened, punching Delik in the arm.

Delik took the jab in good humour. "Perhaps another time then, I forgot how sensitive she was about it."

"Hells, you did," said Minni.

The light-hearted ribbing continued through the morning. Delik and Minni bickered like an old couple, digging at each other's sore points and goading one another on. Tikis joined in and was just as bad with both of them. They recounted fragments of times past, enough for them to have a laugh together, but not enough for Elrin to decipher the meaning. He found himself laughing along with the camaraderie, though he didn't feel it himself. He wanted in, but there was so much history he couldn't penetrate. He was just a shiner from the wrong side of the range.

The heat of the day took hold early. The cloudless sky scorched and the cool breeze of the morning burned up, draining the wind from the sails. The crew worked the rigging to catch what they could, easing *Bone Dancer* through the shallow channels.

The channel opened up into deep water and the ship changed tack, heading for a wall of rock, a mountain range growing out of the ocean dappled with greenery. It stretched across the sea, rising higher as they approached. Closer they came and Kobb made no move or call to correct *Bone Dancer*'s course.

Elrin held onto the rail, bracing himself for the ship to run aground. Instead they passed right into the mountain. There was an enormous unseen hole in the rock, wide enough for three ships to sail through side by side. It must have been a trick of the eye, for the hidden entrance was no magical force; solid rock arched high above them in a winding cavern. Kobb wheeled *Bone Dancer* starboard, through a kink in the tunnel. Ahead lay the tunnel exit, opening into a wide natural harbour. At the centre, huddled in a busy mess, an entire village of ships were at anchor.

Kobb called down from the quarterdeck, his bright clothes glaring in the sun like the treasures that surrounded them. "Welcome to Kobbton!"

പ്രൈ

Smoke from cook fires snaked into the sky through a forest of masts.

Fresh baked bread made Delik's stomach growl. Kobb's pirate town thrived on the rich hauls he stole and traded. The outer edge of the village where the ships came to dock echoed with the cacophonous hammering of coopers and carpenters, breaking down barrels and building them, repairing damaged ships and modifying them.

The buoyant village teemed with humans and shankakin, though other races were speckled amongst them. A team of dwarves smithed around a well-insulated forge and an elf rowed by the pier with a boat full of crab pots. An old orc sat out of place with a group of sailmakers, his needle in hand, hard at work. Ona only knew what would happen if the dwarves, elves and orcs bumped each other's drinks. Perhaps here in Kobbton they had escaped the ancient feuds. More likely they just avoided each other; the slights of dynastic snobbery weighed heavy and crimes of war heavier still.

The rescued slaves disembarked, free to walk amongst those who traversed the boardwalks and bridges, those who made their home and livelihoods upon the modified hulls of Kobbton. There were vessels of all shapes and sizes, a shamble of interlinking ships, stitched by plank and line, floating in the shell of some long dead volcano.

Blue-green water lapped against the steep rock, shielding the hideout from the open sea. The high cliffs were occupied by opportunistic trees and shrubs, collecting the strewn treasures with windswept limbs and grasping roots. Scores of boats and ships were berthed at piers that wheeled out like spokes around the hub of the pirate village. At the ready to sail were war galleys with sharp rams at the bow and ballista upon the decks. Docked nearby were Jandan caravels with their lateen sails and carracks like *Bone Dancer*, fitted with cannon. Drakkin longboats floated low beside merchant fluyts.

The pirate fleet was expansive and varied, yet Kobb's most recent prize ships, sailing in such a grand procession, would be his new pride. *Juniper* and the galleons were the finest examples of Jandan naval might. They surpassed the carracks and caravels the Jandans brought with them when they had first made landfall on the coast, laying claim to everything in the name of their greedy Lord. The Jandan armada had multiplied its ranks with these war machines, galleons and frigates bristling with cannon, sturdy and fast.

Using these ships as bait for Kobb and themselves as bait for Jando was a gamble that didn't sit well with Delik. He wasn't the gambling type and here he was playing his hand of cards against a table full of chancers. He made it this far into the game and only had a few cards left. The trouble was which cards should he play next? Kobb had played his hand as Delik expected; the pirate didn't have a good card face. If Jando didn't play their armada, they had room to breathe, but if Jando did lay the armada on the table, Minni had best pluck the right card from her sleeve, or they were sunk.

Kobb swaggered across the deck and cut in front of Hurn as he approached the gangplank; a dangerous move considering the ogre was five times his size. "I'll be calling in that favour now. Shouldn't take you too long, given your extraordinary proportions."

Hurn leant down and snorted his reluctant consent. Kobb flinched under the sudden rush of air from the ogre's nostrils, streaming over his face.

"Hurn Ga Kogh lift what?"

Kobb motioned over one of Fjhor's warriors. "Get the brute to move the cannon and shot. When he's done with those, all the ballista need to be mounted. Report back when the jobs are finished."

Amber took Hurn's hand, ready to follow.

Minni grabbed her other hand. "Stay with me, love. Hurn will be finished soon."

Amber produced the saddest eyes Delik had ever witnessed, her bottom lip slung in a pout, her spirit shattered.

"Little Bell safe with Hurn Ga Kogh. Little village sink if small man hurt—"

"No, no! None of that sort of talk, thank you." Kobb jabbed his thumb over his shoulder. "I'll get Granny Shan to keep an eye on them, they got along fine last night after dinner. Isn't that right, deary?"

Amber nodded her vigorous approval. Granny Shan had become a fast favourite with both Hurn and Amber, spoiling them with lollies and delighting them with stories of dragons and magic. Minni was confronted by the pleading eyes of all three, Kobb, Hurn and Amber.

Minni broke. "Oh, fine then. Just look out for each other and not so many treats. If they come back with a scratch, it'll be your head, Kobb."

Delik made his way down the gangplank, wondering if Minni had just handed Kobb the wild card they needed. If Amber was the Key to the Dragon Choir they must keep her close. Elrin too. What if it was the lad? He could chase the meanings of the prophecies to the five hells and still not know what they were about. He had to put it from his mind.

Delik followed Fjhor along criss-crossing walkways between the village ships. "How is it that Jandan scouts don't spot the rising smoke and find your hideout?"

Fjhor's face remained deadpan, though his broad shoulders straightened with pride. "They see the smoke, but they don't see their way back to tell anyone."

Kobb must have placed ships on guard throughout the maze of islands, perhaps hidden fortifications and fixed batteries of cannon. He had to have some weather witches tucked away somewhere. Perhaps they had a role to play. Kobb's modified caravels would catch any ship with a witch at the sails. Whatever his strategy, Kobb would need something better to face off the armada he was goading into battle.

Passing through a crowded market square, Delik calculated how many in the village would take up arms. There were many children about, elderly too. Some would have to remain to care for them. At least a third of the population here would not be fighting fit. That still left hundreds of capable hands. There were also the rescued slaves, the rebels under his command and however many other ships Kobb had ready at sea.

They had a chance, but there was no way that Kobb had as many guns as the Jandans. He would win by boarding, overpowering the marines in melee. Like the market square, with the decks of several barges tied together, they would incapacitate the Jandans, grapple them together and swarm the decks.

The market was a clamour of trade. Shell was exchanged for all manner or goods from lands near and far. The irony of being surrounded with gold and silver and trading in shell gave Delik a chuckle. These people would know the taboos more keenly than any other. Making their sanctuary in the dragon hoards was both brilliant and extremely dangerous. He wondered how long it took to dismantle the village and float it somewhere safe when dragon season came.

They arrived in the guesthouse, away from the noise and bustle of the market. Atop the wide deck of a modified drakkin war galley a bungalow rested. The two blue shuttered windows, red door and thatched roof made it appear like a giant's disembodied head, floating in the bay. Across the deck, all manner of plants grew from pails and pots. There were miniature fruit trees and thick bunches of herbs. Tikis took one look at the hull, turned his back and folded his arms tight across his broad scaled chest.

"Don't take it personally, Tikis. It just shows our hosts poor taste. Only Kobb would think to ruin a fine galley like this." Delik chuckled hoping Tikis would find the humour in it. "Come on, I bet she's perfect under the deck. Let's take a peek."

"This one shall remain." Tikis sat cross-legged on the pier.

"It's just for a while, I'll cook you up something."

"You and yours go and rest. This one's shadow will set it aflame. This ship is for death and this home is for life. Drakkin cannot mix sacred places."

It was a lost battle to urge Tikis any further. He had known him too long. "I understand," said Delik, resting his hand on the drakkin's shoulder. "This will be behind us soon."

Delik led Minni and Elrin into the cottage, opening the shutters and enjoying the cool breeze that blew in off the water. Fjhor showed them the pantry and the fresh water barrel, the privy, and the loft sleeping space. His expression was impossible to read as he described the amenities. The warrior was hospitable, but preoccupied; his attention split.

Delik lit the fire in a small cast iron stove and put the kettle on to heat. "Would you like to stay for a tea?"

Fjhor shook his head, absent eyes tunnelled through the walls of the cottage into the distance. "Thank you, no. I will remain on the pier, should you need me." He walked out and stood beside Tikis, the two warriors content with the mutual silence.

Delik found a pot and some tea, relaxing into the simple ritual. "Anyone going to join me for a cup?"

Elrin rubbed his eyes. "I'm heading up to catch some rest while I can. I was up far too late last night, considering the day we had. Don't think me rude."

"Go on lad, get some sleep, we'll manage," Delik waved him off, feeling lethargic himself. "Minni?"

She snatched the bag of tea leaves from Delik and inhaled. "Oh, that's so nice! Pour for me too."

Delik spooned the aromatic black leaves into the pot and sorted through the pantry. By the time the kettle had come to the boil he had a plate of cut cheese, torn bread and pickled onions on a plate for them both. He poured the steaming water into the teapot and let it steep before serving.

"Here we are then," Minni kept her voice low. "Just as planned."

"Except for all the hiccups, I suppose." Dealing with Kobb was necessary, though it was never going to be easy.

Minni stacked a small tower of cheese, pickle and rye. "Don't be so down on how it turned out. We're here. That's better than dead. We can pull this off, I know it."

"Do you now? We've lost too many men back there. He sank a galleon. By Ona, his brains are in his trousers."

"Count your shells. The Jandans fared worse than us. We saved most of the slaves and now they are safe here."

"Here is not safe. It's just a floating prison until we can take them home."

"And home is just a prison until we find the choir."

Delik sipped his tea, bitter and dark. He wished for some milk, though settled for sugar. "I lost it back there, at Rum Hill." The shankakin offered some to Minni who shook her head, unable to speak with a mouthful. He stirred a lump into his own cup then took another sip, warming his hands. "Pelegrin got to me, everything got to me. I just wanted them all to suffer, whether it helped us or not. That lad of yours had me pegged. Sure as knots, he braved my stupor and stayed my hand. If it weren't for him, I'd be planting the same bloody field as Pelegrin."

Minni touched his hand, finishing her mouthful. "Don't be so hard on yourself. Even if we spared every Jandan, the Council would have denounced it. They'd make up what ever they liked because we took their ships and their slaves. You know how the print will read. They'd call it an atrocity against the Lord's chosen. Jandans live in a hive of lies. Truth matters little to what they say. I'll take my blades to any who care to haul me back there and serve in chains again."

"You sound just like him. We have to be smart about this and control our impulse to slaughter the bastards, the less blood the better. Blood breeds vengeance and hatred. Just look at Pa. He boils with it. And what good has it done us? For every one he's killed, he's set three against us."

"Take it easy on him. You've seen it; he is not as he was. Not since you've come back. Things are better now. He listens to you. He's put every resource we have into this plan of yours. If Jaspa didn't believe in what you do, he would've gone on and done things his own way. We'd be hunkered in a muddy hole, smelling the sweat of each other's pits, waiting for a patrol to pass by. Small fry raids and breakouts weren't working, you're right. You've brought us some hope, Delik. But, you've got to give the old boy a chance. He believes in you."

"Ha! He'll never show it."

"You're both so alike." Minni built another cheese and pickle tower. "You're more your father's son than I'm his daughter."

"What do you mean?"

"You know, not his real daughter," said Minni, searching for the right words. "You said I sound like Jaspa. Well, I'd say you sound more like him than me. Stubborn old grumps who don't trust their own barber with a blade."

Delik chuckled, rubbing his stubble. "All right then, enough talk about the old man when he can't defend himself. We'd best get our heads together and break him out to find this Dragon Choir."

"Kobb said we could see him for ourselves," insisted Minni. "Maybe he's not locked up."

"Yes, of course, Kobb has him staying in a guesthouse down the next pier darning socks. Heck, he's probably lured Granny Shan to tea and made friends with Amber and Hurn already. Such an amicable old coot, always up for a chat."

"If he's locked up out of sight, we have to break him out."

"This guesthouse might be cosy," said Delik, "but Fjhor is our jailor, not our protector. If we behave, or in your case appear to behave, we might be able to get out and gather some information."

"Play to Kobb's plans?"

Delik smiled across his cup. "For now. Provided he continues to serve our own."

"All his flamboyance is a distraction. What if we're playing into his hands? He could have a different angle he's working, one we haven't seen.

Sinking that ship was pointless, but what if it wasn't? Why did he let Uighara and Pelegrin go? He didn't get anything from either of them really. Why didn't he just send one of them as bait and keep the other for surety?"

"It doesn't sit well with me either." Delik sipped his tea, soaking in the warm comfort. "We should wait for another audience with Kobb. Sit tight until then. He's sure to be boasting about his conquest, something will slip. We might find out if his plans extend any further than the Salroc Sea. Then we can make our move."

Minni pointed her last piece of cheese at Delik. "What about the Key?"

"How should I know? You're the expert."

"How often do I bother with a key?"

The shankakin furrowed his brow and scratched his chin, pretending to think. "Having two keys is better than one, though you did let Amber go just now. Kobb must have the drop on us. He'll be off with her on some magical wind, snatching up the choir as we chew upon this prophecy."

"Your poor humour doesn't help."

"Neither does the prophecy. I don't see how it makes a difference. If the Key will fall in your hand, then what can we do wrong? You've got two. Take them both. What is the problem?"

"Part of my prophecy has that only one key will work. A false Key will bring the Choir's wrath. I have to pick the right one."

"Prophecy upon prophecy for a magical trinket no one knows anything about."

"Elrin's priest, Kleith, knew about it. Knew enough to send Elrin here to find it."

"Didn't Amber show you that Uighara knew about it too? He might have had his hooks in Amber because she was the only one to work the damn thing. That'd explain him keeping her close."

"If he knew where it was, why were the Jandan ships preparing to return to Lord's Landing? When I read the Captain's log on *Juniper*, Pelegrin's last entry was clear. They weren't heading for the Hoard Islands. They were just waiting on that last shipment of black powder."

Delik tutted. "The black powder that wasn't black and weighed as much as the shot it wouldn't fire."

"Do you have to speak like that? This is confusing enough."

"Just trying to get all the pieces on the table so we can sort it out. That red powder was what they were waiting on, hidden amongst the black. Why disguise it? What's more valuable to the Jandans than black powder?"

"Whatever it is, it was headed to Lord's Landing."

Delik drummed his fingers on the cup. Lord's Landing was a big town with a temple, second only to the monstrosity in Jando. It was a thriving town of smiths and smelters, eating ore barged down river from the iron mines and chewing up the forest to spit out Jando's finest ships. It was the untouchable linchpin of the armada, heavily guarded and a step away from Jando. "What about the new shipyards? The galleons, the frigates, the—"

"Forget the red powder, you're supposed to be helping."

Delik huffed. "If the prophecy of the Key isn't helping, there must be another prophecy that mentions the Key?"

"Only my own."

"Well, what is the problem? There must be some daft riddle in it that gives you an idea."

Minni was quiet. Saying it over in her head, keeping it to herself. She had the nerve to chastise him about trust. Delik had never heard a peep about the prophecy of the Lock. She kept her mouth shut about her own while she nagged him and Tikis about theirs.

If Ona planted a seed, it would grow; life was simple. The Muden of Gren could not sway the will of the gods with their prophecy. Who were they to think stirring the pot of portent and scooping out winners would alter the outcome of the struggle? The gods would do as they pleased and he would do what was right for his people. He'd fight the Lord himself if it returned Ona's sacred soils back to his kin.

Delik drained the last of his tea. "Bah! Keep it to yourself then. Prophecy is getting us lost in our own importance." He reached for the pot to pour another, offering Minni a refill first. Her cup was full, though her plate was empty. Delik noticed his own plate remained untouched. So he ate, enjoying the sharp cheese and sour pickle.

Minni sipped her tea, leaning back in her chair. "Maybe so, maybe because we are important."

"So we are tools of the gods then. A scythe to reap, a shovel to dig a grave."

"Why not keep those tools oiled and sharp, so that they do a better job?"

"What would the old Muden of Gren say if they heard you call them sacred oily rags of Ona? Fit only to keep rust from our blades, that we better serve her will."

"In your case they'd prefer to be a whetstone and hone out that dull edge."

"You're the one who can't figure out your job. Take a sharpening yourself!"

Elrin walked down the steps of the house, his eyes still clouded with sleep. "What are you sharpening?"

Minni's freckled cheeks hinted red. "How long have you been up?" Her eyes were wide, worried the Calimskan might have caught a whisper of their conversation.

"Just now. I've a splitting headache. Did I sleep long?"

"Not long enough it seems." Delik waved him over. "Pull up a chair, I'll pour you a tea."

Elrin took a seat and thanked Delik for the warm brew. "I was thinking about what Kobb asked Pelegrin at dinner last night. You know, about the black powder."

Minni gave Delik a slight nod. She didn't think Elrin had overheard them, though her winsome eyes for the young man betrayed a bias to that conclusion.

Delik passed Elrin his half eaten plate of food. "What were you thinking?"

"For one thing, you rarely see cannon on ships docked at Calimska, and there are none on our battlements. We don't use them. Yet Pelegrin says the Jandans get their black powder from us. Don't you think that's strange?"

"I guess the Guildmaster thinks a fireball from a sorcerer is better than shot from a cannon," suggested Minni.

"Maybe. But, Calimska doesn't trade in shell like coasters. We trade in precious metals. The Guildmaster's golden shield protects us through dragon season and before him we had Daniakesh; our patron dragon."

Delik liked the way Elrin thought. He had a knack for seeing a problem from a different angle. His Calimskan blood painted him inquisitive, but he hadn't been stained by the arrogant superiority most shiners wore with pride. "So what are you getting at?"

"How is Jando paying for the black powder and cannon? Shell wouldn't make trade, neither would bone. Are they trading in treasure, from here?"

Delik shook his head. "The only gold they'd have would be from the Surrender Moon. That wouldn't balance the trade. No lad, it's slaves and livestock. Jandans see them all the same. Wagons full of my people are sent under heavy guard to Calimska. Separate wagons are loaded full of black powder. They've been doing it for years."

"I've lived in Calimska all my life and the only shankakin I've seen are labourers and traders, never a slave. The hamlets and farms around Calimska have plenty of livestock. Why would we trade something so powerful that we don't use, for something that we don't need? It doesn't make sense."

"They're moved on to inlanders for profit. I've witnessed the inlanders take them myself," said Minni. "Calimska must collect the shine from them."

"We don't have slaves. It's illegal to keep a life."

Delik tapped his finger on the table. "What rot! Calimska still has slaves. If I had the shine I could march to the trading post and buy one right now!"

Elrin wrestled to find the right words, at pains to defend the City of Gold. "It's legal to buy slaves from outside the city walls, like at the trading post, but once bought, they are free. They usually work for their buyer to earn a living and are free to leave as they wish; it's really a market for cheap labourers. I've heard stories where men with cruel intentions have abused the laws, but it's more common for wealthy houses to buy slaves just to free them. They dress them up and parade them around. It improves their standing in society. Shows we are above all that."

Minni crossed her arms. "So, either guild authorities are breaking their own laws and selling Jandan slaves for a profit or they are buying them from Jando and giving them away to inland traders."

Delik wished he had better information about what happened after Calimska received the slaves. Minni had her eyes in the city, but spies were expensive in the golden nest and rarely worth the shine. It was a tough job knowing what to ask if you didn't know what you were looking for. "Calimska is involved nonetheless. It doesn't change anything."

"Doesn't change what?" Elrin's face was an annoying cross of curiosity and expectation.

"The slave trade in Jando is only half the problem. We've tried to stop the convoys sending slaves to Calimska with raids, but they were too well guarded and we suffered heavy losses. For our plan to succeed we have to stem the flow of black powder. It is the only way to weaken the Jandans for the long term. It is their power. It brings them more slaves, and buys them more powder. To free the people we have to stop the powder."

"I want to help you. I know my way around."

"I thank you lad. We could use your help, but that dead letter will be a problem. We'll have to dig a way around it and get you home."

Elrin got out of his seat and wrapped his arms around Delik in an awkward, but brief, back-slapping hug. The young man grinned like a boy flying a kite.

"Bloody shiner's and your customs! A hand shake's fine enough for most." Delik cleared his throat. "Alright then, that's enough of the nonsense. We've got a spot of work to do here first."

A LETTER

Elrin stacked a slice of cheese and a pickle. "What of Amber and Hurn? Shouldn't they know about this? They could help too."

"Not yet," said Delik. "Keep this to yourself for now. They've both just found a moment of freedom. I'll not burden that child with any more than I have to and I'm not sure Hurn would understand the greater plan."

"Hurn's no fool," said Elrin, adamant the ogre was smarter than he appeared. "And Amber is the Key to working the Dragon Choir. You have to let her know what you want it for. It's the right thing to do."

Delik crossed his arms, scalding Minni with a disapproving glare.

"Don't give me that look!" Minni wasn't to be left wearing Delik's objection alone. "I thought Elrin could help me interpret the prophecy from a different angle. He thinks Amber is the key."

Delik huffed, reframing his glare on the young man. "Is that right?"

Elrin squirmed, but didn't back down from his hypothesis. "Who else could it be? She fits the prophecy perfectly. We have to tell her sometime."

"This prophecy business is Minni's charge. She will make that decision."

A deep rumble of Hurn laughing rolled down the pier, interrupting the conversation.

Delik pointed his finger at Elrin. "Not a word."

Elrin chuckled and nodded. "Fine, I'll keep quiet, but you're being far too cautious. She'd help us more if she knew."

"Caution has kept me alive so far." Delik collected the empty plates and stacked them on a side bench. "Only a fool trusts a smile alone."

The cottage lurched, sliding the plates towards the edge. Delik caught them before they fell to the floor while outside, Amber's giggles bubbled though the air, propelled in a fit of hysterics. Hurn's indelicate footfalls hurried to the centre of the deck, levelling the cottage again, but drawing loud protest from each timber that bore his weight.

Elrin ran to the door just as Hurn pounded out a knock that almost shook it off its hinges. A gentle knock from the ogre would wake the dead. He opened the still quivering door and was greeted by a pair of contagious grins.

"Well, look at you two!" Elrin crossed his arms with mock disappointment. "Did Kobb send you off already? Causing a ruckus were you Amber?"

Amber giggled then shook her head, nudging Hurn to say something.

Hurn obliged her. "Kobb says finished lifts for today. Says, go."

"That was quick," said Minni.

"No whips, no chains. Hurn Ga Kogh move fast." Hurn sized up the doorway and frowned. He stooped and twisted his body sideways, half crawling to get through.

Amber was taken by another giggling fit.

Delik hustled over and stood in front of the ogre, their eyes level, preventing him from crawling inside. "Easy lad! You'll get yourself stuck in here. Wait outside, would you."

Amber stopped her giggles and helped Hurn to back out.

Elrin smoothed over Delik's abrasive direction. "Why don't we all sit out on the deck? We don't want you getting stuck outside with two fearsome warriors all by yourselves."

While the rest of them sat down amongst the planters on the deck, Delik set to work. He made a quick circuit picking ripe tomatoes, curly kale and fresh green beans from the little garden. Lastly, he plucked a handful of herbs then busied himself about the kitchen, chopping and boiling and frying.

The air soon filled with delicious aromas of warm spices, frying garlic and onions. Delik knew his way around a kitchen. He called for Elrin to help hand out plates full of steaming vegetables. Spiced potatoes occupied one side and a fry up of kale, tomato and beans, the other. Elrin's stomach groaned even though he had not long had a snack.

Delik handed two overloaded plates to Hurn. "I hope this is better than what the Jandans served."

Hurn sniffed it before he ate. His face lit up.

"That's it lad, tuck in."

Elrin took a plate each for Tikis and Fjhor who still sat on the pier. They both refused the food until Delik intervened and insisted, bringing a wineskin to share amongst them.

Tikis skewered the spiced potatoes on his claws and dropped them into his mouth, slavering the morsels down. "If brood mother found Tikis eats cooked foods, she would bite this head off."

Delik took a swig of the wine and passed the skin around. "So what have you two been nattering about?"

Tikis drank then offered it to Fjhor, bypassing Elrin. "Nattering?"

"Talking," said Fjhor, taking two great draws from the skin.

Tikis blinked twice, clicking a strange chuckle before he went back to his meal.

Elrin watched the tattoos on Fjhor's face rhythmically pulse, as if they had a quiet breath or heartbeat. "You must have some stories to tell, Fjhor? Where did you get those tattoos?"

Fjhor handed the wineskin back to Delik and ate his meal without acknowledging the question. His attention was dispersed, though he had no trouble concentrating on eating. His plate was empty before the wine made it back around for a second swig. He took another long draw before his attention jolted into focus.

The tattoos swirled over his tanned body. "You are all requested to attend a welcoming feast this eve. You are free to explore Kobbton until then. An escort will wait for you here." Fjhor passed the wine to Delik and marched away without a farewell.

Delik shook the wineskin, and replaced the cork. "Strange fellow."

"Don't think I frightened him off asking about those tattoos, do you?"

Tikis chuckled. "That one doesn't taste of fear, tastes of spirit world."

"He smells like wine now." Delik tossed the empty wineskin to Tikis. "Did you make friends?"

"Spoke of blades and the sea. That one is Storm Islander."

"Anything on Kobb?"

Tikis hesitated to answer, flicking his eyes over Elrin. "Wash these dishes now, shiner," he said, pushing his empty plate aside. "Generals talk now."

The young man was relieved to be offered an escape. Tikis made him uneasy, always eyeing him over, assessing him. The drakkin radiated certain violent death. Those teeth and claws, that dominating muscular frame—he was made for battle. In the drakkin's presence, Elrin felt better conditioned for a library, knowing words were a flimsy defence in raw combat. He couldn't shake the image of Tikis eating the brains of that officer. It was a challenge just to look the drakkin in the eye, sitting so close. Elrin sensed Tikis's mistrust, for what; he didn't know. It was unwarranted, yet guilt brewed inside him for no other reason than an uncertainty of his innocence. Perhaps the young man had broken a drakkin greeting custom or needed to prove himself through some tribal ritual.

Delik took the plate away from Elrin and stacked it on his own. "Elrin is one of us now, Tikis. We can trust him."

The drakkin blinked at Delik and then at Elrin, saying nothing for a moment. Elrin sensed a turbulent mix of acceptance and scrutiny.

"Time in the hand beside the Lock does not make this one the Key."

Tikis might be a lethal warrior, but his grasp of the prophecy was loose at best. Elrin found himself correcting the drakkin, his enthusiasm for accuracy overcoming his fear of death by tooth and claw. "This one is not the Key. I think you'll find it is that one." Elrin tipped his head in the direction of Amber sitting with Hurn and Minni, juggling spheres of water.

Tikis curled up his lips, revealing sharp and numerous teeth. Elrin tensed, cursing himself for being a know all, preparing for a blow that would crush his skull. Instead, Tikis slapped Delik's arm, sounding his aspirant choked laughter.

Delik chuckled along with Tikis, so Elrin thought it best to accompany them. His awkward laughter aside, the young Calimskan found himself a little less scared of Tikis. He was making progress up the food chain.

As quick as mirth arrived for Tikis, it vanished, leaving his scaled features impassive once more. He darted his tongue about, tasting the air in all directions. "When do we start?"

"Not yet. We'll attend Kobb's welcome feast first. We need to find out what he is planning for certain. I don't want any surprises."

"What does knowing Kobb's plans matter? Whatever that one wants makes a quiet escape harder. These ones should go now."

"Go where?" asked Delik. "We can't all swim like a bloody drakkin. We need my father for a start. He knows the way. I think Kobb expects us to escape; maybe he wants us to. Why do you think he gave us free rein until tonight?"

"That one is a slow bird. That one thinks there is no escape. Might think these ones are better at sea bottom, out of that one's way."

Delik shook his head. "No, he could have done that long ago. He needs us, like we need him ... We wait."

Tikis rose to his feet, hulking over Delik and Elrin. "Tikis does not wait. These ones should not wait. These ones should walk this place. Scout and hunt for information."

"That is a fine plan, but no escape. Meet back here before dusk. We'll share what we have found."

"Done." Tikis dove off the pier with a quiet splash, disappearing in the shadows under Kobbton.

Delik and Elrin told the others about Kobb's feast. Delik paired them off to scout around Kobbton, Delik with Elrin, Amber with Hurn, and Minni alone with the shadows.

After a few moments walking through the sprawling town, Elrin noticed they were being followed. It wasn't Fjhor or any of his men, nor was it one of Kobb's crew in motley colours. This man was dressed simply, like a fisherman, tanned skin and bare foot, trousers cut at the knees. He remained at a distance as they meandered across the decks and bridges, but when Delik and Elrin arrived at the busy market area, he closed in. Elrin instinctively reached for his dagger; it was there, safe and unseen. Delik pulled Elrin's arm, urging him into a brisk walk, bumping their way through the crowd.

Their pursuer increased his pace, gaining on them thanks to the locals thinning in the wake of Delik and Elrin barging through.

Elrin spotted something in the man's hand. "I think he has a knife."

"Right then, get yourself out of this market. Double back and I'll meet you at the guesthouse. Go as fast as you can." Delik melted into the crowd, dodging behind carts and produce stalls.

Elrin pushed and nudged ahead. It was slow going in the press. He stood taller than most of the crowd, his raven hair became a beacon in a sea of blonde and brown, marking him the easier quarry. Elrin barged his way behind some fruit stalls and tripped into the fish market.

The fish might have been fresh that morning, but the sunny day had ripened them enough to make him gag. He pushed on, trying to escape the stench and the man who followed him. Skirting around the fishmongers, he leapt across a rowboat onto a platform leading away from the markets. The man was not behind him any longer, so Elrin pressed on in a different direction, he didn't want to be flushed into an ambush.

After so many different turns, Elrin was out of breath and lost. He ran up a gangplank and across a wide deck broken by large hatches. The ship had a lonely mast rising above a small timber cabin. The door was painted black with golden wings. Elrin ran in and shut the door, leaning against it to catch his breath. It was dark inside, but his dagger emanated a soft glow, enough to discern a stairwell leading down.

Elrin took the stairs to the bottom. A dry hinge squealed and light flooded in. A shadow moved above and Elrin ran from the stairwell, his footfalls echoing through a dim corridor. The door shut and all was dark again. The dagger lost its glow. Elrin held it in front of his face and tried to will it to life. If anything, the blade appeared to be blacker than the darkness around it.

With slow steps and his hands waving in front of him, Elrin shuffled forward, kicking into some crates and stumbling over a broom. Blood pounded in his ears, covering any sound his pursuer might have made.

The walls of the corridor opened out into a larger chamber. The air was thick with rotting straw and dung. His eyes and nose watered in the stale air. High above was a sliver of light. It had to be the hatches he saw up on the deck. He searched for something that would lead him up to the light, arms swinging in wide arcs, desperate to bump into a stairway and not his quiet pursuer.

Elrin's hands closed around a wooden rung. He scrambled up a ladder and onto a landing, probing around for a door handle, anything to get him out of the festering dark stench. He found a metal bar and twisted. Nothing happened. He pushed and jiggled it, but it didn't yield. He pulled and it gave a little; the scrape of light grew. He heaved down with all his weight and light exploded through the hatch. The young Calimskan shielded his eyes from the sudden glare. It bit down, splitting the darkness to reveal the pursuer, squinting below.

Elrin was trapped up on the platform. "What do you want?"

The man kept walking forward. "You must follow me, I have a message from Jaspa. Come down the ladder."

Elrin edged over the railing getting ready to jump. If he jumped and caught onto the open hatch, he could pull himself out. Delik told him to run, so that's what he would do.

"Don't jump! You wont make it. I'll just put the message down here." He reached into his coat and removed a scroll. "See, I'm walking away."

Something moved in the shadows behind the man as he edged backwards. Minni must have followed them. She would know if the messenger was truly one of Jaspa's allies. Elrin climbed down the ladder. She might need some help restraining him if he turned out foul. The shadow struck out and the man was knocked down and dragged into a dark corner, yelling for help.

Elrin walked to the scroll and picked it up. "Minni, I know you're there. Don't hurt him, he might be one of Jaspa's men."

A wet crunching sound came from the dark corner, something was feeding, something ravenous. The shadows moved again and Elrin caught a glimpse of fur and feathers, a monstrous beast. Its hooked beak tore strips off the man's body then it lifted its eagle head from feeding to inspect Elrin. Intelligent eyes narrowed and it shrieked with such furious intensity, the young man involuntarily screamed back and bolted for the stairwell.

The beast shrieked so loud, Elrin couldn't judge if it had moved or was tight on his heels. He didn't want to check. The Calimskan put everything he had into his legs and pelted up the stairwell and out of the cabin. He doubled over, hands on his knees, lungs heaving. The shriek sounded again, blaring out of the open hatch. Elrin raced over and pulled the lever beside the hatch. The lid slammed shut leaving the monster shrieking alone with its unfortunate meal. Elrin ran from the ship, backtracking through Kobbton with anxious looks behind him, worried the beast may break out and take to the sky to hunt him down.

Delik was waiting for him at the head of the pier where the guesthouse was moored. "What happened to you? You're bone white."

"The man chased me," Elrin gasped for air. "I thought I'd lost him after the fish mongers ... but he followed me into this ship ... It was too dark ... I got lost and I—"

"Easy, lad! Take a touch to breathe. Let's head back, I'll put on a brew."

Elrin recounted his story inside the safety of the guesthouse as soon as his lungs allowed.

Delik slapped the table. "So Kobb's wrangled himself a griffon. What's he up to?"

"It was terrifying, that messenger mustn't have known."

"Let's hope his death was worth the message. Bloody fool could have signalled us some other way."

"Here," Elrin passed the rolled up paper across the table.

Delik spread it flat on the table. Neat black symbols were interspersed with Jandan script.

"What kind of writing is that?" asked Elrin.

"The kind that confuses Jandans," said Delik, running his finger up and down, zigzagging across the page. His lips moved in silent recognition of the coded text, scrutinising the message hidden within.

Elrin leaned over to get a better look at the code himself. It was a jumble without any form he recognised. The cipher to unlock the meaning must be complicated, yet Delik read it without any reference to translate it.

"Well? What does it say?"

Delik slumped back in his chair and blew a puff of air, staring at the message.

"Delik, are you ok?"

"Hmm? Oh, I'm fine, just thinking. We'll have to work fast."

"What did the letter say?"

"My father says we must breakout tonight after dinner."

"Can we do that? Where is he anyway?"

"Kobb is keeping him safe. Pa has a plan, but we should have one ready too. You stay here and wait for the others. Tell them what we know. I'll be back before sunset."

"Where are you going?"

"I'm going to see what the locals have to say about Kobb. Don't worry, I'm not planning on riding away on your griffon."

Elrin waited for the others to return, stewing over the messenger's death. A life wasted because he fled. Paranoia had spooked him; he had to think things though. He had his dagger and next time he would stand his ground.

Minni would be out there, shadowing Amber and Hurn, keeping them out of danger. If Minni had shadowed him instead, Jaspa's man wouldn't have been torn apart. She would have intercepted the messenger before it got to that. Why hadn't she been paired with him?

Jealousy bit him and he regretted it. Amber needed Minni looking out for her. She was powerful, but still a child and Elrin was a man grown. He was responsible for his own fate and had to focus on the quest to see the bigger picture. Amber was the key to working the Dragon Choir and without her he had no chance to help his father.

FAMILY TIFF

Fjhor and six of his tattooed warriors escorted the companions to Kobb's latest extravagance. The festivities spread out through the town, radiating from a hulking ship in the heart of Kobbton. Glowing paper lanterns, vigorous music and well-lubricated cheer relieved the fading day. Boards and trestles were draped in bright silks and laden with a feast of fresh seafood and colourful fruits. Shells of all descriptions decorated the tables, enormous shells Elrin had never thought possible, some with spikes and others, pearlised rainbows. Ribbons and strings of pointed teeth hung overhead, the first stars of night shined high above, twinkling with the rising mood of the party.

Kobb waved to the band up on the poop deck and they bounced into a rickety jam as colourful as Kobb's outfit. The music ended almost as soon as it began, rounding off with a flourish of percussion.

Kobb spun away from the band and called out to all his guests. "Welcome your heroes!"

A rowdy cheer went up, tankards were raised and drained. Freed slaves, desperate to express their gratitude mobbed the companions. Fjhor and his warriors stood back, they made no move to hold back the crowd pressing in. Elrin was overwhelmed by the intensity of emotion. Men and women wept with joy and thanks, placing shells and tokens of luck into their hands, tying plaited string bracelets over their arms and embracing their rescuers.

Elrin blushed with the undue affections of several different women laying kisses upon his cheeks. This is what his father must have experienced when he rescued villages from dragons and monsters. Elrin never had many friends; without a name for himself he had no guild, no fellowship. It was good to be a hero. He felt strong, worthy, ready to march back to Calimska and claim justice.

Kobb was cunning. How easy it was for him to win over the freed slaves with his stolen bounty and welcoming act, gifting the rebel leaders to them as idols of hope. Elrin thought himself a fool, luxuriating in his swelling vanity. Minni and Delik had Kobb pegged. He was manipulating them with fanfare, hoping to make them more pliable by tethering them with guilt or pride. Elrin was ashamed for feeling both.

The companions accepted the welcome with grace, though Amber shrunk behind Hurn, wary of all the attention. The freed slaves resisted pressing around Hurn until a young boy ran out of the crowd and hugged the ogre's tree trunk of a leg, looking up at the towering hulk with excited eyes.

"Can I have a ride?" he asked.

Hurn knelt down for the boy. He scrambled up Hurn's sturdy arms and straddled his neck. Hurn rose to his feet and the boy hollered with joy, seeing the world on high like never before.

The boy's mother edged to the front of the crowd, her face a mix of terror and meek resignation. Hurn knelt in front of her and plucked the boy from his shoulders, placing him in his mother's arms. The child reached out and touched Hurn's nose and laughed, showing his mother and urging her to do the same. Instead she leant forward and placed a kiss upon the ogre's scarred cheek.

Kobb called out to disperse the crowd. "It is time to let our heroes make merry with me at our table of honour." He sat himself down at the head, with his back to the band and his eyes on the festivities. Fjhor and his warriors took the companions to their seats, this time Hurn had a cushion placed for him and Tikis had a strong stool to hold his weight and allow room for his tail.

Fjhor's men left through the cabin door behind Kobb. They appeared again a moment later, an extra pair of legs walking with them, two bare feet standing out against the warriors' sandals. They escorted an older, bearded shankakin to his seat beside Kobb and opposite Delik. The man was the image of Delik—he could only be Jaspa Scrambletoe.

A tense quiet stretched like a drum skin over the celebration. The silence deepened in awe of who had come before them. A spark of whispers coaxed the crowd into a fire of shouts and cheers. The crowd chanted, "Scrambletoe! Scrambletoe! Scrambletoe!"

The freed slaves approached Jaspa, hoping for an audience, reaching out to touch the symbol of the rebellion in the flesh. Fjhor's men formed a tight circle around Jaspa pushing them back.

Kobb stood upon his chair and shouted out into the crowd. "Let the feast begin!" He waved his arms to the band and they took up a bouncing tune.

Jaspa did his best to greet all who pressed against the wall of guards, though after their time in the Jandan prison holds, good food and drink was temptation enough to lure them away. The crowd dispersed to the lower feasting tables with renewed conversation and happy music building their positive mood.

Elrin waited for Delik and Jaspa to embrace, but they didn't. Jaspa took his seat beside Kobb and Minni opposite Delik. They appraised each other, the tension between father and son souring the air of celebration.

Delik broke the silence. "Hail Father, good fortune has found you here. You've become quite an idol again." His voice cracked with emotion, though his face could have been cut from slate for all the feeling it showed.

"I believe the good fortune is with these people. If it weren't for you, they'd be dead or worse. You did well, son," said Jaspa, nodding to Tikis and touching Minni's shoulder, sharing a tender smile. "You all did well. I thank you."

Minni motioned to Fjhor's warriors. "Why all the guards? Have you been attacked?"

Kobb interrupted them, pouring wine into Jaspa's cup, then Delik's and his own. He motioned to the table servers to fill the others then stood upon his chair again, raising his drink high. "To Freedom!"

The crowd raised their drinks and called the same, cheering and banging the tables.

Kobb returned to his seat, his charming smile a hazard for the unwary. "Thank you for your work yesterday; every one of you. I know it wasn't easy, but we do make a potent team don't you think?"

Kobb didn't wait for a reply, enjoying his own voice too much to stop. "As we sit here with a feast before us, the Jandans are setting the armada to hunt us down. Isn't that just superb! This is what we should be celebrating, though the recently freed would be awfully worried if that was tonight's theme. Slaves get terribly jumpy after a breakout. We've all been there, every knock on the door is the guard come to get you."

Tikis drained his wine. "How can this be known?"

Kobb furrowed his brow. "Of course I know, I wouldn't be so happy otherwise. I'd be sipping on vinegar like you lot. Where is your faith? It's heartbreaking."

"This is more of your bluster," accused Elrin. "Pelegrin and Uighara might be in the belly of a serpent for all we know."

Kobb shook his head in dismay at Delik. "See what you've done! Gone and soured the new boy."

Elrin wasn't having it, he had to keep Kobb on the point or he would digress from any real information. "What proof do you have?"

Kobb huffed in defence. "I have it on good authority. Fjhor here has a man in Jando. Told me just before you got here. Pelegrin is going to lead the charge. That's nepotism for you. I thought they'd choose someone with a touch more experience, but alas, I've already sent their best to the bottom of the sea."

"How can Fjhor do that?" Elrin glanced at Fjhor who was staring straight back at him. Fjhor's tattoo rippled and Elrin had to turn away.

"Who knows? Ask him sometime." Kobb shrugged his shoulders and Prisella raised her head from Kobb's shirt, then disappeared again, camouflaged amongst the colourful frills. "Now, I think we should talk about defeating the armada. First, we—"

Delik cut in before Kobb could rattle on. "Does this involve you sinking defenceless ships full of slaves?"

Kobb was about to reply, but Jaspa held up his hand. Kobb was all too happy for Jaspa to handle his son's complaints. "Look, son, we had to sink a ship and Jandan fighters had to die otherwise the citizens of Jando will begin to like us rather than fear us. The Council can only do so much without the people kicking them out. We want the dogs to come after us with all of their might. We don't want them to leave a ship in their harbour. If we are to beat their armada and shut down the slaving lanes at sea, this is our only chance. That galleon was sunk by my order."

Delik took the news like a slap in the face. "There were slaves on board!"

"An unfortunate sacrifice. Kobb must be seen as a ruthless villain who will stop at nothing to damage Jandan property. Son, the powers in Jando don't care about the lives, they care about the economic damage from declining growth in their supply of slaves. Council propaganda will blame the selfish pirate Kobb for stealing their free labour for his own personal gain. They will blame us for killing their men. The people will demand retribution. The council will have no choice but to send the armada. All this works in our favour. Kobb is on our side. Think of the greater picture. We had to bait the trap."

"How can we trust him?" asked Delik, exasperated.

"I'm sure he trusts us even less."

"I couldn't have put it better myself," said Kobb. "I don't trust you a drop, but don't take it to heart. I feel that way about everybody. It's a lifesaver when you're in my trade."

Delik and Jaspa steamed at each other.

Kobb wasn't going to let a little family drama ruin his fanfare. "Come now, we all want the same thing. It just so happens that we are going to do it my way. Jaspa has been so very helpful. He's quite a strategist and his comrades are so loyal. Piracy is a different game to be sure. Though, we are all rebels in our own way."

Minni sucked the flesh from a crushed crab leg and tossed the shell into a basket. "What will you do with us after our great victory over the Jandan armada? What worth are we then?"

"Oh, I know you've got bigger plans than that. Old Kobb isn't going to feed you to the sharks, not when you've still got work to do. Let us all be honest here, shall we. We are all using each other. You want the Jandan fleet gone so the slave trade routes on the sea are no more. I want the fleet gone so I can ply my trade where I please. I have humble ambitions; I'm a merchant really. You, on the other hand, are after something more complicated. Overthrowing the Council of Jando and liberating all the slaves will serve my interests too. It's true; I don't care for these slaves as you do. One way or another we are all slaves. However, if you overthrow the powers in Jando ... that would help me even more. I can just imagine the wealthy Jandan elite, loading up their ships in the middle of the night and taking flight from the city of bones. The seas will be rich pickings, if you get what you want."

Kobb selected an oyster and slurped it down. "So you must see that while I am not as self righteous and morally superior as say, Delik, I am still your only hope of destroying the armada."

Tikis stopped gnawing on a fish head and waved it around in an arc. "These ships are not enough. These folk are not warriors. This battle is lost already."

"A king keeps his treasures hidden, as do I. I have more ships at sea and my associates have more still."

"More than the armada?" asked Minni.

Kobb wiped his brow with a pink silk napkin. "See here, Minella. Do you expect me to have every ship on display for your satisfaction?"

Jaspa intervened, placing his hand on Minni's to quieten her, his voice calm against the rising frustration. "We don't need more than the Armada, we have a better strategy."

Delik pushed his plate away and dusted some crumbs from his lap. "Right then, we're listening."

Jaspa grabbed a whole crab from a platter. "This is the armada, heavy weapons with strong defences. They have the biggest ships, their galleons and frigates are strong, but we have shown they can be overcome by speed and surprise." He picked up a handful of scampi and dropped them beside the crab. "This is us; our fleet is weaker, we are out gunned. Our strength is in our flexibility."

"Really, Jaspa!" Kobb screwed up his nose. "Do you have to use the food?"

"As I said, our strength is our flexibility, we will use our surroundings to our advantage." Jaspa picked up the crab and placed it on Minni's plate. "Jando will mass from the south." He picked up a couple of scampi and confronted the crab. "A third of our fleet, the fastest ships we have will await them just outside the Hoard Islands. We will wait long enough for them to count our number then we will retreat to the island channels. The best option for Pelegrin is to split off a small force to pursue us and scout," Jaspa broke off two of the crab's back legs. "We will lead them into the channels and pin them where they cannot broadside us, letting a ship or two escape to tell the tale."

"What if the whole armada pursues them from the start?" asked Elrin.

Jaspa doused Elrin with a cold stare, worse than any Delik had given. "I would welcome that. If the whole armada entered the channels, they would be split on six or more fronts, snaking their way through in pursuit, sailing into our trap. Pelegrin is no fool. He was caught by surprise and will be wary for a trap. "

"So how will a trap work if he thinks it there?"

"We show him it isn't there. The Jandan ships we let go will signal back to the armada that they were outflanked, not ambushed. Pelegrin will send a force with superior numbers." Jaspa tore off one of the crab's heavily built pincers. "We will retreat further into the archipelago. If he is smart he will send more ships up the east and west side of the archipelago, preventing our escape into the open ocean, and stopping us from doubling back and flanking them again." Jaspa pulled off the two more crab legs.

"Our ships will split up as they retreat, spreading out the Jandan lines. Their communication will be fragmented between the islands; the claw will be attacking without a brain. Pelegrin will have guessed that our ships would continue to retreat, he'll be hoping we lead him to our hideout. He knows, as long as the hideout is still here, Kobb will be replaced or worse still, the rebellion will assume control of the Pirate fleet."

"Not bloody likely," grumbled Delik.

"Indeed," said Kobb, sipping his wine.

"We will continue to retreat through the channels, Pelegrin will have to pursue us, or all is lost. He can't risk the bulk of the armada to an ambush in the channels. He will split his main fleet again in two or three forces."

Kobb drew his sabre, polished steel gleaming in the lamplight. "May I?"

Jaspa gave a nod and Kobb struck the crab's last claw off and split the body neatly in two, exposing the succulent flesh.

"He will send forces along the east and west flank and maybe another into the channels to reinforce the ships in pursuit." Jaspa moved the scampi along the table. "Kobb will lead them all the way back to the open sea just south of the hideout. Here, some will remain to block the channels, the rest will join our fleet and take on the western flanking force. Once they are defeated we will turn and take on the eastern force. It is the best use of our inferior numbers."

"What about the ships in the channels?" asked Delik. "They could just spill out the east and west channels and reinforce either flank. They'll route our fleet."

"That is exactly what they will try to do," emphasised Jaspa. "But we have concealed cannons all through the northern half of the archipelago. Our men and women will defend these positions, we rebels are better suited to combat on land."

Kobb laughed. "What you mean is, you're as good as a barrel of kippers loose on the deck."

"Try us in a fair fight at sea," growled Tikis.

"That's rich, coming from you lot," Kobb retorted. "Since when have any of us started a fair fight? Best to keep you landlopers doing what you're good at."

"Kobb is right, Tikis. We have to play our advantages. We'll open fire, using treasure as shot. We might not sink their ships, but they'll be dead in the water, blocking up every exit."

"What will you do about their poachers?" asked Elrin.

"The dogs won't be a concern." Jaspa's annoyance chilled his stony face again.

Elrin wasn't going to let a cold stare get in the way of a perfectly reasonable question. "What will you do when they cast lightning bolts or fireballs in your direction? They could have more elementalists like Amber, set a strong wind in their sails and catch up with the first retreat. The crippled ships might be moved with their magic."

Kobb puffed out his chest. "I've got the best weather witches this side of the Salroc. We'll keep ahead of anything the bone suckers throw at us."

Elrin had found a blind spot in Jaspa's grand plan. "Amber, how many elementalists do the Jandans have?"

Amber thought about it and shrugged. She put up ten fingers and then tipped her hands up and down like a balance scale.

Jaspa shook his head and screwed up his face, like he was trying to get rid of an irritating insect. "It changes nothing. They're all pinned. They'll waste half their puff rushing the armada to get here before the battle even starts."

Amber nodded in agreement and tipped her hands up and down again. Jaspa was right, more or less.

A crack emerged in Kobb's confidence, an inch of worry crept across the wall of his conviction. "What does she mean by that?"

Jaspa moved fast to reassure him. "How many of these redeemers can weave the elements like you?"

Amber giggled holding up two scrunched fists.

Jaspa poured more wine for Kobb and himself. "See, there's nothing to worry about. We've talked these things over already, Kobb. You know it will work. You know what you will gain. I've not given you my only son and our best generals to play with and let die."

Delik wrapped his knuckles on the table like a hammer. "What do you mean given? Did you set up that meeting with Kobb? Have you been rigging this thing the whole time?"

"I suggested that Kobb should go to Rum Hill for a stop and you did the rest my boy."

"Don't boy me, ya lying old bastard!" Delik threw his seat back and jumped across the table to attack his father. They rolled on the floor, cursing and punching each other. Jaspa pinned Delik then Delik slipped out, landing a punch in Jaspa's stomach.

Minni and Tikis pulled them apart.

"You mongrel! I'm not going to help you! What have you got us? Kobb's got you trapped and you lure us in just to pull your sorry arse out. Kobb'll bite you the first chance he gets. He'll sit himself on the throne of bones in Jando and we'll all be just as buggered. Your plans will kill us all. They killed Ma and Tisha. Who knows where they have Shanda. Ash it! You'll not have me."

Kobb waved his arms to the band to keep playing then sauntered over to the Scrambletoes. "We don't need you Delik. Hells, I don't really want you to help if you are determined to cause this stink. Your father wanted you in on this, but you've played out your use. Tell you the truth, the ogre and the shiner are not much good to me now either. You can sip tea here in Kobbton with the elderly and watch the children while we keep the dogs away." Kobb turned to leave, calling back over his shoulder. "Jaspa, sort out your command. We sail at dawn."

Minni and Tikis released the Scrambletoes. Delik slumped to the floor, his face red with burnt out fury and eyes moist with tears that refused to fall.

Though his shirt was torn, Jaspa kept his composure. Eyes of stone refused to look upon his son. "Minni, Tikis, young man. What's his name? Come along now. You have your mission to study."

Hurn leaned over Jaspa bearing over him like a thunderhead. "Amber."

Jaspa took a few steps back straining his neck to take in the full sum of Hurn's hulking body. "What? Is that your name? You might want—"

Hurn thumped his chest like a great drum. "Hurn Ga Kogh. This is Amber. You should know names of your slaves."

Jaspa reddened with anger and embarrassment while Delik raised his head and laughed, a tragic lost sound, devoid of joy.

"Amber go. Hurn Ga Kogh go."

"That won't be happening. Where ..." Jaspa paused and spoke the name with deliberation. "Where Amber goes, you cannot. Hurn Ga Kogh must stay."

"No!" Hurn beat his chest again, thunder boomed. "Hurn Ga Kogh keep Little Bell safe!"

Jaspa nodded at Minni. She lanced the ogre's inner thigh then supported his arm as he dropped to one knee.

Elrin braced his shoulder against Hurn trying to keep him steady. "What did you do?"

Minni let go of Hurn's arm and took Amber's hand. "He'll be ok."

Elrin couldn't support all of Hurn's weight and the ogre keeled over, hitting the deck in a deep sleep.

Fjhor and his men rounded up Jaspa, Tikis, Minni and Amber, marching them off the ship and into the lamp lit night.

Elrin pulled Delik to his feet. "Was that meant to happen?"

"Not quite like that, no. Didn't think Pa would fight back so readily. Sure as the five hells, I didn't figure on dragging an ogre home."

They grabbed an arm each, trying to slide Hurn across the deck. He wouldn't budge. Delik collapsed beside Hurn, laughing at the futility of their task.

Delik poured wine and passed Elrin a cup. "I guess we wait while he finishes his snooze."

Elrin took a sip, thinking over the heated argument between the shankakin. "Did you lose your family in the fighting?"

"My mother and sister aren't lost. I know exactly where they lie, deep in Ona's embrace. I buried them myself, the old man was holed up somewhere, on the run from the dogs."

"Who's Shanda?"

"My Moon, my dear ..." Delik cleared his throat and wiped his eyes, staring up at the night sky. He downed his cup of wine. "They made me watch, then ... then they took her, I don't know where."

Elrin poured them both a refill and didn't press Delik for more information. The young man just sat quietly with the shankakin and watched the moon drifting over the caldera wall. Delik had suffered enough, he didn't need a stranger picking the stitches from his wounds.

Hurn didn't stir until they had finished their second refill. The ogre sat up groaning and rubbing his enormous head.

"You all right big fella?" asked Delik with more compassion than Elrin had seen from the usually gruff shankakin leader.

"Bug bite and head hurt."

"Can you stand up?" Delik patted Hurn's back. "We can't lift your big bag of bones."

"You have my bone bag?" Hurn lurched to his knees then stood, bumping into the table and breaking a chair. "Where is it?"

"Let me see." Delik took Hurn's hand. "It might be back at our guesthouse. We'd better get a move on and go find it."

THE KEY

Kobb had wiped his hands of them, giving them no escort back to the floating guesthouse, cocksure they weren't a threat. It was an obvious bluff. Kobb would still have eyes on them. Delik hadn't made out anyone following them, but he wasn't taking any chances. Just because he didn't see anyone, didn't mean they weren't looking.

"So, what now?" Elrin leant back against a timber planter on the deck, his arms folded with worry. "Kobb said they sail at first light. We have to break them out now."

"Little Bell be scared. Tiny pirate takes her slave. Need to keep her safe."

"I know, Hurn. Don't worry, Minni is keeping her safe. If Amber is in any danger Minni will get her out of there. Tikis will be right behind Kobb too. No one will let her be harmed."

"What about the Dragon Choir?" Elrin protested. "I can't leave without it."

"That's why we need my Pa."

"And the key," said Elrin. "You need Amber."

Delik chuckled to himself. The lad still had no idea it could be him. Typical Calimskan, stuck so tight in their own skull they can't spot their own shadow. "We'll have to find what fits the lock, I suppose." Delik pulled out a small scroll case from under his belt and removed several curled up pages, flattening them out on the deck.

"Where did you get these?"

"Pa stuffed them down the back of my pants when he had me pinned. Good thing they're in the case!"

"You're a sly bunch like I've never come across."

"Bah! You're young yet; you've not met many. Now, go and bring us some light."

The scrolls contained detailed maps of where his father was being locked up. They showed guard patrols, doors, locks and shift rotations. He had also described various escape scenarios.

Delik rubbed his forehead, preparing for an argument. "You both should be clear that we can't take everyone."

"Hurn Ga Kogh take Little Bell."

"That's right Hurn," said Elrin. "Delik's father too, but the others are going to stay."

Delik wrestled with the best way to explain a prophecy he didn't think mattered. He found himself trapped, letting it determine the fate of two lives. "No, that might not happen. I can't say that Amber will come with us."

Hurn frowned and snorted. "Why?"

"I don't know if Amber is the Key to the Dragon Choir. There is another that fits the prophecy and Minni is the only one who can decide which is the true Key."

"Another Key?"

"Think about it lad, it's you."

Elrin was dumbstruck, his eyes wide, cheeks flushed.

"We'd take you both, but Minni knows that if the wrong Key goes before the Choir, they'll be killed. It must have a magic ward or perhaps the device calls the wrath of the dragons upon us all. We don't know."

"Little Bell die?"

"Hurn, where we need to go, Amber would be safer if she stayed behind. We should only take her if Minni thinks she is the one. And Elrin, if you aren't the key, you will have to stay behind. There is too much risk, a false key is said to trigger the Choir's wrath. What that may be is best not to discover."

Hurn calmed at the thought of Amber having a better chance of living if he followed Delik's plan. Elrin was not so pleased with the options.

"You rescue your own father, but not mine? I have to find the choir, you can't leave me behind."

"We might not have to. That's between Minni and Ona. I think it's all a bunch of rot myself."

"What Choir do?" asked Hurn.

"We don't really know. I'm not convinced it even exists; it's such a long shot. If it is real and not some old myth, it must be a magical device, something that calls the dragons here every season. Pa thought to summon the season early. If the dragons come here and find the armada on their hoard the beasts will put them all to ash."

"What about the people on the Coast?" Elrin shot back. "They won't expect dragons for another half moon. They won't be ready."

"The dragons never arrive all at once, there'll be plenty of time to prepare once the first shadow is spotted. Some may die, but no more than any other season. If it actually works, the dragons will feast on the dogs, not the innocent. We just need a few of the winged devils to see the armada on their hoard and start blazing."

"And what of the rebels and the freed slaves here in Kobbton?"

"See here! I can't guarantee everybody lives. This is war, lad. My men know each day might be their last, but they fight on for a future without shackles. We freed those slaves. Ona help me if they would have preferred to die in chains. They're not babes mewling for a teat, they'll fight to keep the freedom we gave them."

"Hurn Ga Kogh will fight."

"I will too, but if you do find the Choir, I have to know you will let me use it to save my father."

"You have my word. Now douse the lamp, lad. We've got to keep a look out for the signal."

The festivities continued in the centre of Kobbton. Music echoed across the water while the distant glow of the lanterns warmed the night. A gentle breeze meandered through the cove and moonlight cast haphazard shadows, morphing and bending as the floating town swayed to the rhythm of the gentle swell.

There was something, perhaps a man standing alone, half obscured by a beam and a hanging plant. Delik waited for a movement. The form was still. Delik didn't blink. The more he stared, the more he was convinced that someone was staring back.

Two revellers approached; shankakin women, full of wine and chatter. The form moved out of the shadows; it was one of Kobb's pirates. He struck up a conversation, leaning an arm on a post, cutlass flashing in the moonlight. It wasn't long before flirting led them giggling into the shadows. The amorous trio made a quick ruckus. Delik strained his eyes with guilty pleasure, but couldn't make out much more than a leg and arm here and there. All was quiet and then Delik caught sight of the women dragging the man's body. She propped him up against a wall like he had fallen asleep on his watch.

One of the women held aloft a blacked out lantern and flashed it open three times, before walking off with her friend, chatting away without remorse.

This was it. Delik gathered Elrin and Hurn and they took off down the pier. The perimeter of Kobbton was busy with men and women loading and repairing ships by lantern light. Nervous expectation for the coming battle perspired in the air. Fear and excitement, last minute labours and passions; an anxious tension built as dawn approached. The night called blades to whetstones and lovers to tears, mortal hopes wrestling with the gods' machinations.

They followed the route his father had mapped out, making swift progress, avoiding notice even with Hurn, lumbering along behind them as quiet as a bullock pulling a tree stump. Navigating the walkways in the dark was difficult. Without the old man's map they'd be lost at best, if not caught by the guards.

The ship marked on the map was *Bone Dancer*'s refined sister, *Near Song*. She too was a shapely carrack, though her hull was painted black as night, an elegant evening gown draped across dangerous curves and cannons. The figurehead was a woman with bat wings, her hands in prayer, fangs pressing past her plump parted lips.

The companions took cover behind a large pile of empty crates, big enough to hide Hurn crouching down. Guards watched over the workers loading the ship. They spoke with intoxicated volume, sharing crude stories and several bottles between them. The ships crew and the dock labourers worked on through the boisterous laughter.

"Let's try the guards at the other end," whispered Delik.

"Why there?" Elrin screwed his face up. "This lot are plastered."

"They're shankakin."

"What difference does that make? Are you all best friends now?"

That shiner had to argue with everything! Delik held his temper and watched the guards for some proof that his gut feeling was correct. The shankakin guards were not out of place because they were shankakin. Kobb had plenty of shankakin amongst his crew, but these two were different.

"Look, they're over attentive; guarding a gangplank that no one is using. And what do you make of that? Those lamps right beside them are out. They've got to be Pa's men, but we need to be able to get there unseen."

"Swim?" suggested Elrin.

"What? Drip all the way through the ship and leave a nice trail to follow. No, we need a distraction. How good are you at throwing things, Hurn?"

"Good. Hurn can throw Delik on ship. Elrin too big, I get him half way."

Hurn reached for Delik.

"Ash it Hurn! Not me." Delik swatted the ogre's hands. "See those guards up on the forecastle, near the edge? Think you could hit one with something?"

"Will hit." Hurn grunted. "Head might smash."

"Best if it didn't, just go easy, eh."

They searched around the pile of crates for some ammunition. Delik found a basket filled with yellow melons and put one in Hurn's sizable hand. It fit like an apple would in his own.

"Listen carefully, Hurn. You have to wait here. If you hear trouble on board, if you hear us yelling, we'll need your help to get out. Just smash your way through anyone that gets in your way. You understand?"

Hurn grunted and gave Delik a solemn nod. He tested the weight of the melon, gently tossing it from one hand to the other. "Hurn throw melon now?"

"When you're ready, if it goes wide there are plenty mo—"

The melon flew from Hurn's hand in a long arc through the night. It spun through the air and smashed across the back of the guard's head. The force of the blow toppled him over the gunwale. His friend tried to grab him, but only succeeded in dropping his bottle. With a great splash, the guard hit the water. The other drunken guards ran to find out what happened and the crew crowded around, happy for a distraction from their labour.

Delik slapped Hurn's arm. "Who would believe that?"

While everyone crowded over the edge laughing and jeering at the flailing guard in the water, Delik and Elrin took up a crate each and walked by, bearing their load down the pier and up the far ramp. Delik nodded to the guards.

They didn't respond in kind.

⧽∘⧼

Elrin dropped the crate as the first guard seized Delik. He pulled his dagger and lunged.

The shankakin guard dodged to the side. "Easy, son, we're on your side."

Elrin slashed the dagger in front of him, keeping the guards at bay. "Delik?"

Delik chuckled. "Why are you waving your arm about like a fool? Do what they say before we're found out."

Elrin flushed with embarrassment. He had come close to stabbing one of their own men. The dagger was invisible to them, so there was no point arguing to recover his pride. Elrin relaxed his stance and allowed the guards to do their work. A hood went over his head and his hands were loosely bound behind his back. Elrin kept hold of his dagger, just in case things went sour. He hoped it still cut even if it was invisible.

They were taken below decks, weaving through several corridors. Elrin soon became disorientated. They passed through a rowdy room smelling of stale beer and mutton. After a few more turns the drunken revelry faded behind them.

They stopped and a fist banged on something solid, giving Elrin a start. There was a click then a quick metallic scrape.

A phlegmy voice spat at them. "Bugger off!"

Their hoods were removed. Delik stood beside Elrin and a sweaty faced

177

jailer scrutinised them from behind a shutter hole in a heavy studded door.

"This lot tried to escape," said one of the guards. "Kobb wants 'em locked up."

"There's no bloody room! I'm full up with Jaspa's mates. Piss off!" The jailor slid the shutter closed.

The guard banged on the door again.

"Kobb says to put them in Jaspa's cell. There's plenty of room."

The shutter opened. "Tell Kobb he can stick any more in his own cabin!"

The door shook and there was a grunt and a thud. "Lord's balls afire! In and out, in and out. I'll be dead before I sleep." The Jailor muttered on as keys jingled together. A moment later the lock clunked and the door swung open.

Elrin was shoved through. He gripped the hilt of the dagger and tested his bindings. Two guards stood outside Jaspa's cell. It was furnished with a fine upholstered chair and a small table holding a bowl of fruit. Short stacks of books and piles of scrolls accumulated in the corners. Jaspa sat cross-legged, reading a book illuminated by the dying nub of a candle. Tikis and Minni were cramped into the other cell, a quarter the size of Jaspa's. Amber was not there.

The fat greasy jailor shut the door and locked it behind them. With a disturbing grunt, he hefted a timber beam to bar it shut. One of their escort struck up a joking conversation with the jailor while the other forced Elrin ahead to the guards at Jaspa's cell.

One of Jaspa's guards gave their escort a quick wink, half-heartedly patting Delik down. His partner was not so lax. He fingered through Elrin's hair and slipped his palms down to his neck and shoulders.

Elrin's dagger came alive and thrummed in his hand, coaxing his muscles with an insistent hunger. The loose bindings fell away from his wrist and the dagger lashed out, jabbing up into the guard's chest. The man wrapped tight fingers around Elrin's throat, squeezing with strength enough to snap his neck. The enchanted blade jabbed up again, and again, searching for the guard's heart, probing to server anything vital, anything to release the death grip around the young Calimskan's neck. Time slowed, stars swam and his vision dimmed to black. With the last of his breath Elrin pushed and twisted the blade, willing it to end the guard and save his life.

The hands around his throat went limp. Elrin gasped for air, drawing it in a rasping flurry, coughing as it inundated his lungs and brought his vision back. He swung around on the remaining guard, brandishing his blood-drenched blade, his red right hand eager to please the weapon.

The guard threw his arms up in surrender. "No! Not me, I'm with Jaspa!"

Delik eased forward in front of the cowering guard, reaching for Elrin's shoulder. "It's over lad. There now, it's all right." Delik pointed to the fat jailor, slumped in his chair, waiting for Nathis to guide his soul to his maker. The conversational escort stood over the rotund body, wiping his blade clean on the dead man's tunic.

Elrin's blade glowed, drawing in the wet red mess from across his hand, drinking the lifeblood and unfolding a calm, warm comfort that wrapped about him.

Delik touched his arm, easing him out of the red fog. "Lad? Where did you get that?"

"My father." It was all he could think of.

"A strange blade, that one. How about you rest it in your belt for now?"

Elrin sheathed the blade, the warmth faded as he let it go. He rushed to Minni's cell, clasping at the cold iron bars. "Where's Amber? What happened?"

Minni wrapped her hands over his, giving them a gentle squeeze. "Kobb wouldn't have her put in a cell, she's up in a cabin with Granny Shan. I tucked her in myself, before they took us down here. She's got a big day ahead of her."

Delik slid the jailor's key into Jaspa's cell door and with a crisp oiled click the door swung open. Jaspa blew out the candle and shut the book, leaving the ribbon marking the page. Jaspa went to his son with open arms.

Delik embraced his father, his face a joy of teeth and dimpled stubble. "You ready, old man?"

"Old? Ha! I can still beat you in a wrestle."

"I let you get out of that pin. I didn't want to embarrass you in front of all your admirers."

"Oh, that's what it was, eh? Ona's arse!"

Delik clapped his hands. Keen to get moving. "Has the lock figured out which is the key?"

"The time is upon us, Minella," said Jaspa.

Minni was quiet, staring up into Elrin's eyes. Her clammy hands would not let go of his. The young man was lost in her dark eyes, his heart wound up like her wild hair. She reached forward running her caress up his arms, behind his neck. Elrin leant in and their lips met. Dizzy in bliss, he wanted to reach through and pull her close, return her embrace, but his hands continued to grip the iron bars with a nervous assurance, an anchor to ground him.

And then it was over, all too soon. His lips wanted to feel hers again, just to make sure it was real, to taste that delicious soft pleasure.

Minni poked her finger at his chest. "Now, can you work out what you missed?"

Elrin grinned, dumb with heart's blood flooding his thoughts.

"It's you, Elrin," Minni caressed his flushed cheek. "You're the Key."

"How could it be? I'm no sorcerer. I'm nothing."

"The Lock to secure us shall know the Key, eyes at sunset, heart alight.

Death bell song stirs Choir's wrath, false key fails dawn's only hope.

Hand to the Fist, Key to the Lock, captive embrace, dawning glory."

The prophecy was manifesting; the riddles were growing into truth, entwining tendrils around them all.

"It's me?"

"This Key might break in this Lock," grumbled Tikis from the back of the cell. "Smoothskins take strange mates."

Jaspa laughed. "Don't listen to him, lad. Tikis is a little overprotective of our Minella."

"Come on then," said Delik. "We can to and fro once we've got the choir and this bloody battle is won."

Minni pulled Elrin in for a parting kiss, as delicious as the first. "That's for luck. Return safe."

While their escorts wrestled with the bar holding the door shut, Jaspa and Delik stripped the dead guards of their weapons. Delik found a hatchet in the fat jailor's belt. Jaspa took a cutlass from the man Elrin had stabbed to death. They tested the weight of the weapons then swapped with each other.

Jaspa flipped the hatchet, caught it by the handle and made several mock cuts in the air. "Now, this feels more like it."

Delik slung the sword belt around his waist and slid the cutlass through the leather frog. "I think you're happy with your thirsty blade too, eh?"

Elrin touched his father's heirloom. "It's kept me alive this far."

Their escorts waved them out the heavy door and guided them through the ship. They travelled a convoluted way up to the gun deck, avoiding the busy mess hall to climb a stairway at the stern of the ship. There they squeezed through a rear cannon port, down a rope ladder and into a waiting boat. They took the oars and rowed to an unguarded pier near Hurn's hiding place.

Hurn's hulking form backed out of the shadows behind the stack of crates and snuck toward them as best as an ogre could. He managed it well. The groaning timber under the Ogre's weight blended in with the complaining boards of every ship and walkway in the floating village. His lumbering silhouette stood out against the sleeping huts and hulks. He was a child's nightmare, the melon in his hand a victim's skull.

As Hurn got to the boat, a guard on patrol emerged from between two shacks at the end of the short pier. He gave a yell, half in alarm at the monster he had discovered, half in fear of what might become of him if he tried to hinder Hurn's progress.

"Row! Get us away!" rasped Jaspa, his whisper as unnecessary as his command.

Elrin heaved on the oars. "Get in the middle! Sit down, before the boat tips over. Quick!"

Hurn had a different idea. He stepped to the middle of the boat, but instead of sitting down he twisted and threw the melon with grace unbecoming of his bulk. Hurn threw it so hard that the boat rocked and he almost fell out. The melon hurtled through the air and smashed into the guard's head, knocking him to the creaking boards with a grim thud.

FREE

Halfway across the lagoon Elrin was exhausted and his back was cramping up. He wished for a second pair of arms at the oars and grew ever more irritated as Delik prattled on to his father. Since they were clear of Kobbton Delik and Jaspa hadn't shut up, barely dipping their oars in. First they speculated on the logistics of dismantling Kobbton and floating it to a safe harbour each season, then they started on about the advantages of a well manned galley over a cannon-rigged Jandan galleon.

Elrin's fatigued chagrin caught Hurn's attention. "Hurn Ga Kogh row now. Elrin rest."

Elrin pulled the oars in. "Thanks, Hurn. Should be easy for your big arms."

Changing positions was not so easy. Everyone clung on as the boat rocked with Hurn's shifting mass, sloshing water over the side.

Delik lost his balance and tipped from his seat. "What in the hells are you doing? Sit down before we're all in the drink."

Hurn found his seat and the boat stabilised. Elrin couldn't help but laugh at the awkwardness of the seemingly simple task. Jaspa laughed too, giving his son a hand off the bottom of the boat. Delik didn't see the funny side. With Hurn at the oars the boat lurched into motion, leaping ahead with each stroke.

Elrin rubbed the ache out of his arms. "Back there, throwing those melons. Where did you learn to do that?"

Hurn pulled the oars, his face blank. "Slave games."

"Oh," Elrin didn't know what to say.

"Hurn Ga Kogh not run so fast, not lift so much, not fight so good. Pelegrin keep because I throw iron ball, win him games, win him bones."

Delik spat over the side of the boat. "That bastard makes me sick. Why

182

didn't you escape before we got there? You broke your chains easy enough?"

Hurn grunted. "Keeper dropped whip, Minni open his neck. Hurn Ga Kogh think free is not free, slave is not slave. Broken is broke."

Jaspa patted Hurn on the shoulder. "You'll never take a whip from us. You're free now."

Hurn shrugged it off, losing the rhythm of his stroke. "Chains of revenge, stronger than iron. Chains of family, stronger still. None here are free."

They all kept quiet. Hurn was right; they were all slaves to their quest. Elrin was as bound to the rebellion as they were to him. The quest to find his father had entangled him with the fight to end slavery. This band of insurrectionist misfits thought he was some prophetical Key to commanding dragons. He could no less help them than he could his own father.

When the boat hit the shore, they dragged it up onto a small beach of pebbles mingled with treasure. Elrin scooped up a handful of gold and silver coins. They were much nicer than tabs, though Elrin had never enjoyed the fortune of holding a handful of gold tabs to compare. Age-old kings and queens stared at him in the moonlight, imprints from times long past or lands far from home. He let the strangers fall back to the beach. They had no use here.

Jaspa lifted a canvas in the boat and revealed a stash of equipment. He passed out a backpack to each of them. Hurn's had no hope of getting over his wide shoulders, so he strapped it tight over his upper arm before hooping a long coil of rope over his chest. Jaspa attached a pouch full of shot and a sling to his belt. Delik took a sling and ammunition too. Elrin had no idea how to use one and Hurn mocked the flimsy looking missile weapons with a snort. There was nothing that suited Hurn's massive hands; they were deadly enough.

Once all were equipped, Jaspa led them to the forest at the base of the cliff face. It was an awkward walk up the beach of treasure. Coins, cups and other precious paraphernalia shifted under their tread, Elrin feared it would cut through his soles, but most of it was worn smooth by the elements and flattened under the weight of countless dragons. Jaspa pulled out an old folded leather square from his pack.

"Where did you get that old hanky?" asked Delik.

"Found it lying about in the High Temple archives."

Delik snorted. "Just happened across it last time you gave thanks to the Lord, eh?"

Elrin squinted at the soft hide. "Is it a map to the Dragon Choir?"

Jaspa nodded. "This is it. Are you ready? Are you all ready?"

None of them were. How could they be? Jaspa had a map and a

prophecy Delik had no faith in. Hurn had as good an idea of what lay ahead as any of them and he hadn't been told much of anything. Ready or not, Elrin hoped he could work the device when they found it. Minni believed in him. Kleith believed in him. This was what he had to do.

Elrin touched the hilt of his dagger. "Let's go."

Jaspa tucked the map in his belt and drew his hatchet, hacking through the underbrush. Hurn pulled vines from up high, tearing them away and dumping great clumps of vegetation to the side. Soon they stood before the mouth of a cave, smooth on all sides and rounded like a great pipe. Jaspa pulled a torch out of Delik's backpack. With flint, steel and tinder, he had the torch alight and held it into the cave's dark throat.

Hurn walked ahead, squinting and holding his hand over his eyes. "Keep torch from Hurn Ga Kogh. See good in dark."

"Go on then," said Jaspa. "Just keep your back to the light, we're right behind you."

As they walked deeper into the cave, Jaspa directed them past smaller openings branching off either side and above their heads. Hurn stopped, sniffing the air.

Jaspa held the torch aloft, peering down the winding tunnel. "What do you see?"

"See nothing. Smell something."

Elrin sniffed the air too, but smelt nothing. "What is it?" He felt a deep unease standing still in the darkness.

"Don't know."

Jaspa opened his map, examining it in the torchlight. "We just have to stay with the biggest tunnel. Let's take this slow. Ready your weapons; who knows what dark creatures lurk in these caverns. If you pick up the smell again, signal a stop."

Hurn sniffed the air, planting each step with a caution Elrin had never seen in the ogre. They crept in the darkness for a long time with only the sound of their footfalls on the smooth stone floor and the crackling of the torch flame. The tunnel grew higher and wider, weaving and bending like a restless river. Elrin had lost all sense of direction and depth. They could be under the sea for all he knew or somewhere in the great shield wall of the caldera.

The tunnel swelled in size, their movements echoing from distant walls, the torchlight could not reach. A breeze shuddered over Elrin's skin, chilling the sweat from the tunnel hike and tightening his nerves. It carried an acrid metallic scent, like blood and bile.

The ill wind knocked Hurn to his knees, where he cowered on the floor. The odour itself was not alone. Fear hung over them, petrifying the air. Delik and Jaspa tucked into Hurn, all three trembling with an incapacitating panic.

Elrin clutched at his dagger. The fear thickened, but it didn't break him. It flirted with his mind then redirected into worry for his friends. "Don't panic, there's nothing here."

No one would respond. Hurn was the worst affected, burying his head under his hands, face to the cold stone ground. Delik and Jaspa were wide-eyed like spooked horses. Jaspa had dropped the torch when he ran to Hurn. It made their shadows leap about, crazed elongated demons clutching at Hurn, an immovable trembling boulder.

Elrin sat with them, stroked them and tried to ease their terror with reassuring words. In a final effort, Elrin grabbed Delik and shook him, then slapped him across the face.

Delik snapped back, his eyes settled on Elrin, the haze lifted. "What happened?"

"You're all cursed."

Elrin shook and slapped Jaspa next.

Delik pushed Elrin away. "Go easy!"

"I did the same to you, now help me with these two. There was a spell, some magic in the wind."

Once roused from the inexplicable fear, Jaspa decided they should rest. None of them comprehended their actions, their memory marred.

"Can't any of you remember?" asked Elrin. "Hurn, you tucked yourself up like a giant tortoise and you two were scampering about like kobolds on fire."

"There's no wizard come to finish us off," chuckled Delik. "We must have triggered a ward. Does the map have any detail about what might be protecting the choir?"

The fallen torch sputtered and failed, leaving them encased in pitch black.

"Pass me another, Delik," called Jaspa.

There was a ruffling from Delik's direction. "I don't have another."

Jaspa huffed. "Anyone?"

Elrin had none in his pack. "You've already used the one I had."

"Hurn?"

"Mine here."

There was a bump and the clang of a tin falling on the stone floor.

"Ona's arse!"

"Don't tell us that was the tinderbox," said Delik.

"Hang on," said Jaspa. "I've got the steel."

"Let me help," said Delik. "Feel about for the flint. That's what we need."

"Argh! That's my finger!"

"Well then, don't put it under my foot!"

"Shut up you two," said Elrin, his eyes adjusting to the dark. "Can you see those faint lights up ahead?"

"Many, many stars," said Hurn. "Still night."

"The flint could be anywhere," said Elrin. "Let's follow Hurn. He can see better than us even if we got the torch lit."

"Right then, you lead Hurn. Unwind a loop of your rope and we'll hold on. Keep an eye out for a big hole up ahead, we must be close."

Hurn led them toward the stars. The tunnel opened into a great arching cavern roof with stalactites hanging like immense chandeliers. The points of light were not stars; there was no moon, no constellations.

Hurn brought them to a halt, sweeping his arms wide to stop them falling. The cavern dropped away into a deep darkness below them, swallowing the soft light from the multitude of glowing things on the cavern roof.

Elrin gaped. "This place is amazing!"

In the centre of the cavern an enormous stalagmite rose out of the darkness and met a stalactite from above. The column shimmered with blinking points of light, shedding form in the darkness.

"See where the big dripper from the top meets the rising mound from below," said Jaspa. "That's where the choir must be kept."

"How in the hells do we get over there?" asked Delik.

"That's why I got the rope."

"What's Hurn got there? Sixty yards? Where's the rest?"

"There's no scale on the map. How could I know it was so bloody big?"

"Oh, I don't know. Perhaps a scout around first might have nailed it."

"Kobb never availed me of much free time to roam about."

"Would you two quit bickering!" Elrin peered over the edge into the darkness. "Why don't we test the depth of the pit first?"

"That's the spirit, lad," said Jaspa. "No point whinging about what we don't have, let's use what we do."

"Oh, very nice," said Delik. "Takes me back, that does. Any other gems you want to polish on my pocket?"

Elrin had heard enough of their pointless arguments. "Do either of you really know what the choir is? You talk about it like it's something you can stuff in you backpack and toddle off with, but a choir is more than one thing. What if the column is the choir? What if the column is actually a magical resonance device of some sort, like a pipe organ or something?"

Jaspa tied a rope end around one of the used up torches. "The descriptions I have read speak of the choir calling dragons to order and to union, lest they forget, lost in their own importance. The beasts are vein creatures in love with their own company, lusting after knowledge, seeking only power and wealth. Yoni placed the choir here after he defeated Drensel Tath, the evil king of all dragons. I thought it to be an instrument of sorts, a magical harp or a lute. Yoni's always depicted with an instrument, serenading one maiden or another. I thought finding it would tell us for sure."

Elrin knew the legends of Yoni and the Dragon King; every child knew the story. Every bard sung of their epic battles. None of that had anything to do with a choir. "Why call it a choir if somebody plays it? Choirs aren't played, they sing."

"So the wind might sing through the column and call the dragons," said Delik. "Maybe when the season changes. When the trade winds shift, they might funnel through these tunnels and sound the choir. No one needs to play anything. The choir works naturally."

"That must be it," said Elrin. "But how do I get winds to blow through the column early?"

They were quiet, kind in their silence, not saying what Elrin had known all along.

"I'm not the Key am I? Minni was wrong about me. We need to get back and break out Amber."

Elrin hung his head, feeling useless again. Hurn stood with him in the strange phosphorescent glow of the false stars. His massive hand patted Elrin's shoulder, the solid assurance a welcome comfort.

Delik and Jaspa bickered about how best to break Amber out. Elrin drowned in bleak thoughts, his eyes moist with silent bittersweet tears. He didn't need the burden of prophecy to help his father, so why did he feel so low? No one depended on him now. He had his own quest, yet he wanted to be the Key to Minni's. If he wasn't the Key, would Minni still have him in her heart?

A breeze rose up from the dark pit, cooling Elrin's wet cheeks. Next a gust of wind whipped up, buffeting them away from the edge of the precipice. Jaspa and Delik ceased their argument.

From the bottom of the wide shaft something huge was moving. It sounded like boulders dragging across a riverbed. There was a scratching rattle, a great thump of something very large shifting its weight. Then came a deep taught clap of sound like a mainsail catching a solid wind after a dull spell. Blind to what befell them, great gusts battered the companions to the ground as though a fleet of ships coursed overhead with a score of dwarves carving and scraping at the stone walls. The gale howled down through the labyrinth of passageways.

Delik, Jaspa and Hurn were lost in the same terror that caught them before. They crushed their heads down against the rock and tucked their arms over their heads. Elrin was scared, but didn't panic, transfixed by the gargantuan shadows writhing across the walls. They crawled and slithered, twisting around the column in the centre of the cavern, blotting out the shallow glow from above.

A burst of light flashed out from the centre of the column. Elrin shut his eyes, but the light was just as intense. A warm tingle passed over his body and the light faded to a golden haze, emanating from the centre of the column. Delik, Hurn and Jaspa got to their feet as the fear stripped away, mesmerised by six shining figures standing around the column's light.

A voice boomed across the chasm like a wave crashing ashore. It was liquid in his mind, slipping around in his skull. First it rolled around like a pearl in a porcelain dish then it fused in place, solidified in cognizance.

Be silent.

The voice knew no language, it had only meaning and context. There was no room for misunderstanding. There could be no error in the communion. It was like the voice of a god.

Stone bloomed from the central column. A great arm of rock reached across the darkness, bridging the divide.

Approach.

DRAGON CHOIR

They were compelled across the stone bridge, the voice so intense in their minds that the word rooted in an unavoidable reality.

Six figures stood before six thrones; an undanae, an orc, an elf, an akiri, a human and a muden. Such an unlikely council of disparate beings astounded Elrin. Surely they must control the Dragon Choir, but how did they reconcile their enmity. The young Calimskan's readings of history proved the only things shared by all these nations were wars and transgressions, the blood spilt in ancient feuds and territorial disputes. Humans traded while orcs raided. The bird-like akiri guarded wind scoured mountaintop fortresses. The muden patrolled inland rivers and marshes, defending crannogs deep in the wilderness. While elves venerated the sun and knew the secrets of life, undanae claimed the night and manipulated death. Across the many lands of Oranica these nations had breached the borders and beliefs of the other, yet here in the belly of a rock, in the middle of the ocean, they held sway together.

Explain your intent.

The six figures sat down on their thrones. Elrin could not decide which of the figures was the speaker. There was no obvious leader among them, nor did any move their lips. Together they exuded an aura, filling Elrin with both terror and elation. His body felt heavy and his will stretched thin, drawn to them.

Jaspa stepped forward to explain. "We have come to use the Dragon Choir." Jaspa's voice was muted, a distant obscurity against the presence of the voice.

From a throne of smoky pink quartz, inlaid with iron, ivory and shell, the orc spoke. "Who are you to use the choir?" Her charcoal tones echoed through the cavern. Though the orc's voice was not at all pleasant, it was real. Much better than the compelling power of the anonymous voice.

"I am Jaspa Scrambletoe. This is my son Del—"

The undanae tittered, disturbing the air with dark derision, his pale moon blue skin and saucer eyes a shock against the black of his onyx throne. "I do believe my dear sister was attempting sarcasm. We know your name. We know many things. Yet we know not how you propose to use the Dragon Choir? This you must tell us."

Jaspa turned to the others for help.

Delik stepped forward. "We would send a mighty wind and have the choir sing."

The guardians laughed and the chamber shook with their mirth.

"Glorious!" The undanae scarcely contained his glee. "Where might such a wind arise?"

The human stood from a golden throne, his purple robes flew about like a storm and lightning arced around him. He thrust an accusing finger at the undanae. "Enough Zarkas! You waste our time with your petty amusements."

The elf woman peered down her nose at them from her silver throne, green silk and steel scalemail hugging her lithe body. She swept her arms wide in introduction. "We are the Dragon Choir."

They were so naïve; no wonder the derision. The rebellion hoped for an object of great magic to wield against the Jandans, but now Delik and Jaspa could only wield sullen faces. Their mistake would cost them the whole campaign. Elrin wouldn't let fate laugh his own quest into oblivion. There must be a way, if he could just persuade the choir to aid them, all would be well.

Hurn had a different notion, booming his doubt into the faces of the powers before them. "You not choir, choir sings. What you sing?"

Elrin cringed as Hurn stomped across his hope for a diplomatic plea for aid.

The muden, reclining on a throne encrusted in coloured pearls, spoke with a voice like a stream over smooth stones. "There is much here that is beyond you." Amphibious eyes blinked atop her head, then her fleshy, half naked body quivered into motion. With lightning speed, the muden's wet webbed hands levelled a trident at Hurn. "Do not call our words to question. Our songs weave life and death for mortals."

A drip of doubt fell, stirring faint ripples in Elrin's mind. He clutched his dagger's hilt for reassurance. It gave him none, instead granting him eyes that shattered the illusion of the choir.

"Dragons!" Elrin's thought spilled upon his tongue and his voice tolled like the tower bell at season's first shadow.

With that word came a light; the truth. A flash of clarity exposed the company they kept. The heads of six great dragons lurked over them, teeth like racks of swords, eyes like the masters of the five hells. Their size was difficult to comprehend in the flash, most of their bodies were out of view in the darkness of the pit, though they must have been ancient wyrms; larger than any dragon Elrin had ever seen flying over Calimska. Bigger than any story he heard tell from braggart or bard.

In that momentary vision, the image of each monstrous head affirmed Elrin's fragile mortality. Each one was a different death; different colours, spines and plates, feathers, fur and scale. All with claws, fangs and unsettling appetite in their eyes. The instant passed, yet the image was forever seen, seared in his memory.

"How interesting," said the elf in the elegant armour, studying Elrin. Her voice was honey on ice, sweetness hardened by winter.

The orc slammed her fist down and rose from her throne. She was the most imposing of all of the guardians, black iron plate and bone armoured the warrior's frame, the skin of a great brown bear cloaked her shoulders. Her rage flared and she stormed toward the man in the purple robes. "He shows clarity! Here! We should—"

The man in the purple robes cut her off, his voice quiet and cool, yet strong as the sun. "We should do the same."

From the throne of opal the akiri trilled, calling the attention of the Choir. His shrewd eyes flicked between the robed man and the orc, his curved beak clicked together, chastising them like a tutting mother. "Come now, sit down. Let this be done."

They returned to their thrones and the undanae pierced each with a barbed smile.

The akiri sat forward on his throne, adjusting his wings in a splash of blue, orange and violet, flexing the banded leather armour over his barrel chest. His voice lanced out, as sharp as the spear resting across his beanpole legs. "You have come. You are before us as you wished. What would you have us do?"

Jaspa was silent, paralysed by fear, or failure. Delik stood beside him with a hand on his father's shoulder. He would speak for the group. "We ask that you sing for the dragons return."

"Why would we call them before they are due?" asked the undanae, his eyes even wider than usual.

"Why would we alter our vigil on your whim?" sneered the orc.

"We are to battle the Jandan armada. They sail here as we speak. They come with murderous intent. They want this place ... They come for the treasure."

Each of the choir shifted on their thrones, discomforted by Delik's implication.

The akiri twisted his head on an awkward angle, crossing his arms. "You know this? Or you think this?"

"I know they come to this place. I know their leader. He is hungry for power no matter the cost. The magical treasures here would make him very powerful."

The choir was silent, though the silence was thick, heated by the friction of an unheard argument.

The orc jabbed her finger at Delik. "Your words are deceptive. We will not sing."

Delik sank, desperation flooding his words. "Pelegrin must be stopped. He'll sap your hoard and come for you next. You have to destroy the armada."

The undanae fumed. "You do not make demands of us! Why do you care if they come here for our treasure? Do you want it? If any mortal takes from these hoards, they will face our wrath. We don't need your pathetic, self-serving warnings. We shall not sing for you or any other mortal."

The muden stamped the butt of her trident on the ground. "We sing for the weave."

The man in purple robes agreed. "We shall not sing early and disturb the balance."

"No, we shall not sing," said the elf. "However, I would hear more of these Jandans ... more of the truth."

"Human, come forward." The man in purple robes beckoned Elrin closer. "Does this shankakin speak the truth?"

"Does an army approach?" asked the akiri.

"Do they seek our hoard?" asked the muden.

Elrin walked before the choir, summoning all his courage to speak. "They do come and they are many. They have black powder and the biggest ships I have ever seen. We helped another, the pirate Kobb, to face them in battle."

The undanae sneered. "Indeed. Our little parasite uses black powder also, does he not? We've allowed him to float in the sanctuary and prey on those who venture too close to our islands. He knows what not to touch and when to leave, and so he is tolerated."

"Our desire is to end slavery. The Jandans trade slaves for black powder with Calimska. Kobb would do this too if he defeats the Jandan armada. He would be the only power over the sea."

Smooth delight grew across the elven battle maiden's face. "So, you wish them both crushed. If either wins, you lose. What better than the might of dragons to foil your enemies?"

"We thought the choir was a device to use, to call dragons here. We didn't come here to offend you with demands. If we had known ... We should have known." Elrin wondered if he would have been brave enough to seek out the choir, if he had.

"Your words speak true," said the akiri. "And yet, you desire more."

"He covets our hoard!" roared the orc.

"No! I don't."

"Truly?" The undanae produced a sack and tossed it at Elrin's feet. Treasure spilt across stone. "You don't lust after gold and silver? You're Calimskan, yes?"

"Yes, but I—"

The orc slammed her fist on the arm of her throne. "As I say, they come for our hoard. At the end of this battle they will plunder our birthright."

Elrin was insignificant. They twisted his words and ground him down. He gripped at his dagger, searching for strength. "I didn't come here for your treasure! And neither did they."

"You set yourself apart from them." The man in purple bore through him, burrowing in his mind. "Your desire flows from a different stream, yet meets the same river. Why did you come here?"

"I was sent to seek your aid to help my father."

The undanae chuckled. "What is it? Gambling debts? Is Papa locked up in some dungeon ready for the axe?"

"I don't know where he is."

The muden croaked with laughter. "This is ridiculous."

The man in purple ignored his fellows' amusements. "Who is your father?"

"He's a famous adventurer from the coast, he—" Elrin cut himself short when he saw Delik's face wrinkle in disapproval. If the shankakin had never heard of his father then why would these dragons know or care of his exploits.

The Akiri leant forward, probing Elrin's hesitation with avian eyes. "Reveal not what he does, but who he is. Speak his name."

"Arbajkha."

A moment of emptiness engulfed the cavern, a drop of vacant time fell before his father's name exploded into chaos amongst the choir.

ADVANCE THE ARMADA

Uighara wrapped the last of the rations and placed them in his pack, pulling the drawstring tight. He wished for a stronger back to carry more, then thought better of it. Brawn was its own burden. The Good Lord's gifts would supply him with all he needed. They had delivered him thus far and tomorrow they would crown him in the glory he so rightly deserved.

Fatigue weighed on his eyelids. He sat in his hammock, mentally ticking off the day's preparations, rubbing his forehead to relax. His brothers in the Lord knew the ritual and while their part was simple, if a few of them faltered, their sacrifice would only please the Lord more. The clear weather had been a blessing and the pontoons were taking the journey well. All was in order. It was time to rest.

Just as he rose and blew out the flame in his lantern, the familiar rattle of sacrificial bones caught his ear. A faint yellow glow danced with two metacarpals upon the blackstone at his desk.

Uighara placed his hands on the stone. "Almighty Lord, receive this sacrifice and bless this communion."

"I know what you are up to," said his father. The leagues between them were no security against the scolding his tone implied.

Uighara tensed. "You shouldn't be using this."

"You should have contacted me when your feet touched land."

"I've been busy."

"You lied."

"What are you saying?"

"I'm not blind, I have eyes in the High Temple."

"Are mine no longer good enough?"

"Explain yourself!"

"I already have. The plan is unaltered. Their net will fail."

"Why did my agent detect a jump just before you arrived, thumping your pious stick on the wasps nest?"

"The inferior batch was hijacked by rebels, as was I. I got away and jumped back to my ... to a net I had prepared as a contingency. I had to use the untainted powder."

"So the net under the High Temple does work."

"To some extent, yes, but it is flawed."

"Yet, my agent tells me it is not. Did you actually think you could get away with pulling the prize from under my nose? You?"

"Who is your agent to know the difference? Does he have the Lord's gift or is he a charlatan? There are only two who know the process back to front; you and I."

"Don't bring your god into this."

"The Lord is your god too, whether you believe or not. When he returns to his throne, you will bow down before him and ask for redemption."

"By Calim, you really believe that nonsense. Where is the proof of their Lord? Does he even have an arse to sit on his fictitious throne?"

"He will return."

"Why? Because some glorified poachers are praying for it? No wonder the Jandans were banished across the ocean. They're second rate hacks who use religion to justify their inferior magic."

"How then do you justify yours?"

"Don't give me that! I protect Calimska by whatever means are necessary. I had no choice. You did."

Uighara ground his teeth; this argument was without end. Every time it was the same, he couldn't win.

Not yet.

The redeemer held his tongue, and redirected the subject. "So, here we are again, have you got yourself ready yet?"

"I have, no thanks to you. However, the transition will be problematic. Arbajkha won't survive the increased strain."

"A shame, though it won't matter. Just supplement the draw from another source."

"Don't you think I know that!" His father's voice cracked with the retort. It pleased Uighara to know he was so tense.

The redeemer pressed the advantage. "If you're not able to capture your own, I'll have some candidates transported. Did you find the eavesdropper?"

"No. He was last seen at Rum Hill. If he's smart he'll be on his way across the ocean."

"He can't get in the way now." Sleep weighed down Uighara's eyelids. "Is that everything?"

"Don't cross me, Uighara."

"I pay my debts. This will be the last."

The ether retracted from his mind. He didn't bother cleaning the bone dust off the blackstone, just shuffled across the cabin in the dark and dropped into his hammock, letting sleep blanket his weary body.

❧

"Last one in's gotta clean out the bins!"

Uighara's cousins ran through the meadow down to the creek. Tep had the lead while Roel and Klana shouldered each other for second place. Uighara bolted after them, through the squelchy patch, under old Dernin's fence and down through the orchard. He tried to keep up, but they were too fast. He slid down the bank and dove into the cool water. When he came up for air, his cousins were floating face down surrounded by fish floating belly up.

Uighara swam to Klana and turned her over, her blue face stared at the green canopy arching over the creek. He dragged her to the bank then went to get Tep and Roel, but they were gone. The creek was low and stagnant. He was covered in mud.

Zarkas walked through the tea brown sludge, his saucer eyes devoid of his usual aloof cheer. "A deep sleep. Perhaps, too deep, yes?"

Klana had disappeared too, though the memory of her cold limp body still weighed down his arms. His heart twisted with grief; dredged from the past, yet still as painful as the day he buried it.

With great effort, Uighara reined in the emotion and narrowed his focus, morphing into his adult self. "It has been a tiring day, you should be pleased. I bring the armada."

Zarkas shifted the dreamscape to a cliff top.

Uighara flinched, taking a quick step away from the edge. Death came just as swift in dreams as it did when conscious.

"Arbajkha's son is in the sanctuary," announced Zarkas, unloading the fact with a gust of wind that buffeted Uighara back to the edge.

"What? How can that be?"

"He arrived with Kobb and the rebels."

Uighara's stomach dropped. Could it be the same Calimskan who tried to stab him with a fork? He was man grown, not a boy. How long had it been? Thirteen years? Fourteen?

With every question Uighara came to realise the depth of his mistake. How could he have been so close and not known; under his very nose and he never thought to ask a name, to make the connection.

Zarkas's wide eyes narrowed. "You knew?"

"No, how could I? I wouldn't recognise him now."

"He has clarity, he sways them. I will delay the debate as long as I can.

You must make haste." Zarkas pointed to the open water between the islands and the caldera. "Advance with everything you have."

❧

The fresh dawn light greeted Pelegrin's command. Great galleons and frigates, carracks and caravels sailed shoulder to shoulder. Signals flashed between the vessels and the armada fanned out in a battle front thirty ships wide and two deep. Pelegrin ordered twenty more to bolster the centre and flanks. He would not be caught out by an ambush this time.

From the quarterdeck of the flagship Saint Jan, Pelegrin watched the pirate fleet quiver their way out of the island channels and square up to face him. It was a pathetic sight. Kobb's prize ship Bone Dancer pranced to the centre of a single line of scrawny caravels and galleys; twelve in all their bravado. There would be more, they had his Juniper, and the galleons they took as prizes. Kobb would have them protecting their hideout or laying in wait to ambush.

Pelegrin spoke to his solargraph officer. "Advance. Maintain formation."

The armada sailed forward, a pride of sails hungry for the hunt. The pirate ships fled, one by one, deserting Kobb in the face of the invincible might of Jando. Only after all his line had left did Kobb wheel Bone Dancer around and flee. Pelegrin didn't blame him. He would do the same faced with these odds.

If Kobb wanted him to chase then he would wait. "Halt advance. Await instructions." The solargrapher wrote the order and transmitted the message to the armada.

Pelegrin watched the pirates sail into the calm waters between the hoard islands through his spyglass. Just as he had suspected, they slowed and came to rest before losing sight of the armada behind the islands. They weren't fleeing. They were bait.

Uighara strode up to the quarterdeck, patting down his dishevelled hair.

"Ah, Uighara! Glad you could join us. You've missed the first manoeuvres I'm afraid."

"Why wasn't I awoken?"

"I sent for you, but you did not answer your door. The messenger feared you would rather not be disturbed should you be praying for our souls in the coming battle."

Uighara pulled his cowl up to shield his eyes from the new morning's glare. "Yes, that was considerate of him."

"Are you ill? You seem out of sorts."

"No, there is urgent news from Jando. I have received instructions from the High Priest."

"Have you now?"

"We must advance."

"All in good time."

"Now!"

"I am the commanding officer of the armada, not you. I will make that judgement."

"The High Priest conveyed that he had a vision."

"A vision?"

"Yes, from the Lord."

"The Lord spoke to him directly?"

"Do you question our most venerable and holy leader?"

"No, I question you."

Uighara stepped close. "See where you stand. You command the armada. Is that not what I promised the Lord wished for you?"

"Yes, but ..."

"The Lord has great plans for you. This is the beginning or the end; faith or death. Take my hands and choose for yourself."

Pelegrin took Uighara's hands and was pulled into a dream.

He commanded the armada to halt and wait it out, probing the island channels and testing for an ambush. He advanced the armada north with caution and discovered the pirate hideout empty. Monstrous shadows circled. The sky clouded with dragons raining fire upon the entire fleet.

Uighara squeezed his hands, lifting him back to the present. "You must advance with the full force of the armada."

He was right. "I will advance with our full force."

"The Lord protects the bold and faithful. Use everything he has blessed you with to smite his enemies."

"I have faith, I will smite the Good Lord's enemies."

Uighara released Pelegrin's hands and embraced him. "May faith be your armour, the will of the Lord your sword."

The Lord's arms surrounded Pelegrin with strength. He was chosen to wield the Lord's armada. He wasn't going to waste this blessing.

Pelegrin called to the solargrapher. "Advance full speed north in trident formation."

PROTECTION

The ancient dragons wrestled in an intense debate. A strange field had wrapped around the companions, distorting sound and warping light. Elrin's senses were skinned and pulled inside out, altering the landscape of understanding. It was impossible to penetrate any meaning. Only the memories of times past had real substance. The dragons had warped the weave, stitching him into an inescapable, incomprehensible pocket of incapability.

Time bent around them, a moment was at once an age. When an understanding of the present finally emerged in Elrin's consciousness, his legs were weak from standing. Against dry eyes, a parched mouth and a stomach that ached for food, Elrin battled to recover his senses.

Jaspa fell to his knees, exhausted. "What did they do to us?"

Delik helped Jaspa back to his feet, his own legs struggling with the effort. "If they bothered to tell us, it would make no sense."

Hurn rested on his knees and his stomach growled like a tiger. "We here long? Have we missed battle?"

The unified voice of the choir tolled.

Silence. We have chosen the path ahead.

The companions were compelled to cease their questions and bear witness to the choir's decision.

The akiri rose from his throne, clutching his spear in his clawed hands. "I shall remain to defend our sanctuary and the innocents within from the aggressors."

The muden stood and thumped the butt of her trident down. "I shall also remain to guard our sanctuary and protect those who did not choose this battle. When the aggressors have been dealt with, those who remain must depart. Neither have any place here. We have grown lazy, leaving others to defend our hoard."

The elven warrior stood beside the man in purple robes, placing a hand on his shoulder. "We shall join you in battle. Your cause to end slavery is just. We will secure the birthright of our kin and punish the aggressors. We will aid Arbajkha when the sanctuary is secure."

"Now we must go," said the man in purple. "The time is upon us."

"I am Tetula," said the elf warrior. She motioned to the man in purple. "This is Qarim." Next, she motioned to the akiri, stretching his wings. "That is Wyggen." The muden approached, her soft speckled skin shining with moisture. "And this is Obst."

The undanae and the orc left their thrones, throwing foul looks at their fellows before disappearing behind the column.

Elrin listened to the sound of claws scrapping down stone and great wings flapping. "What of the others?"

"Zarkas and Goranuk will keep the vigil," said Obst, dripping water. "They do not see any advantage to helping you. They will hold until it is time to sing the return."

"Each of you will ride into this battle with us," said Tetula, her polished armour catching the light like a sunrise over the sea. "You do not command us like pets to face your enemies. You will suffer this battle just as we do, in a common cause."

Wyggen handed his spear to Hurn. "Take this and defend the innocent with your life."

Obst passed his trident to Jaspa. "Ready yourself to repel any who threaten our sanctuary."

Qarim hung an amulet around Delik's neck. "This will shield you from the storm you summoned."

Tetula unsheathed her sword and held it before Elrin. "Show me the weapon you carry."

Elrin pulled the dagger from his belt and held it next to Tetula's elegantly inscribed, exotic sabre. The same foreign symbols were etched across the gentle curve of both blades, their hilts were of the same design, each pommel held a stone as black as the abyss. The arcane sigils on both weapons pulsed, as if in recognition of each other's presence, two long lost friends united again.

"Is it yours? Did my father take it from you?"

"No." Tetula's face softened, her eyes moist. "It was given."

"You knew my father?"

Obst chuckled. "How could we not?"

Elrin was ready to burst with questions. "Then you'll help me find him?"

"First we must join in mind and battle," said Qarim. "Behold our true forms and stand strong."

Tetula and her sword vanished, as did the other avatars of the choir. They dissolved in a flare of light, extinguishing the illusion from Elrin's mind. Before them were four dragons, their serpentine necks arcing around the column, their intelligent eyes regarding them in cool omnipotence. This was no flash of truth, it was an awful reality; the dragons' power set their fragile mortality into stark relief. Elrin and the others fought against every impulse to crumble before their might.

Elrin was snatched up in a cage of claws and dropped astride the great silver shoulders of Tetula. Her frosted honey voice entered his mind. "Hold tight."

Tetula's muscular body was plated with smooth metallic scales, each as big as a warrior's shield. Thick tufts of hair sprouted down her spine from head to tail. Elrin grasped a handful of her blonde mane and shifted into the dip between two vertebrae. "I'm ready."

Tetula leapt into the air, her powerful wings beat twice, flying them up to the cavern ceiling. Elrin thought he would be impaled by the shafts of rock that jutted out like an army of upside-down pikes, but instead Tetula tucked in her wings and they slipped into a dark tunnel hidden in the side of the cavern. Elrin hugged close to the dragon's back. Her claws scraped along the stone while her body half crawled and half slithered, gaining speed as they careened down the black tunnel. They shot out from the top of the caldera wall into bright daylight. The silver dragon spread her wings and lifted them over the sea.

Elrin screamed into the wind. The thrill of the speed and the height ignited his insides with an ecstatic joy that buzzed through his body; the ultimate wish to fly coupled with the ultimate test of courage, both exposed to the whim of the most formidable being under the gods. He was living the fantasy every child dreamed of and every adult grew to fear.

With several beats, her wings caught a thermal current, circling them up in a grand lazy spiral, borne of the rising warm air. Clutching Tetula's mane and gripping her neck with his thighs, Elrin dared himself to lean over and look straight down.

࿇

Qarim emerged from the sanctuary like a bolt from a crossbow. Delik clung to the spines protruding like giant needles from the dragon's long slim body. As he wedged his ankles and hooked his feet under the spines, his only thought was for the long fall down if Qarim decided to flip over in some daft manoeuvre. Tetula circled in a thermal above with Elrin leaning over her neck, gawking down at them. The shankakin's stomach sank to think of doing the same. Bloody fool, grinning like an idiot. Delik had a fine enough view without hanging out into the empty sky. Qarim beat his mottled purple and gold wings hard, lifting them to catch up and join the same air current. The late morning sun reflected on Qarim's golden scales and the islands of treasure far below.

The armada was a plague of white sails on the blue-green ocean, swarming the advance pirate fleet. Kobb's feint retreat had lured the armada amongst the islands as planned, fanning out in a fragmented chase through the passages, but there was a problem. The sheer number of ships deployed against them was far larger than anything Delik had estimated. His father couldn't have received accurate intelligence on the true size of the Jandan fleet. Or had he known and bet everything on the choir? How else could they win?

The armada pushed along the east and west flank of the archipelago, sealing each passage to open water as they went. They were leaving no chance of escape, confident that they had the numbers and positioning sentries to guard from a surprise attack. The bulk of Kobb's ragtag pirate fleet sailed to the west of the sanctuary, amounting to no more than the Jandan contingent flanking the islands from the same direction.

Treasure glimmered through the patches of dense green forest scattered across the islands. Even from high above the rebels were invisible. What good was he up in the air, riding this beast? He should be down there with his comrades, ready to stitch up the ships in the channels.

Qarim stretched his long neck around and eyeballed Delik, prodding him with his thoughts. "This 'beast' can hear your little mind tripping over itself. Think with some decency, please."

Delik directed his thoughts to Qarim. "Sorry, I didn't think a tough old stick would be so sensitive. What keeps us from the battle?"

"You are brave to goad a dragon, perhaps stupid. I find there is small difference amongst the shortlives."

"Then, we have that in common."

❧

Minni pulled Amber to the deck as another shot from the Jandan bow chaser blasted into *Bone Dancer*, tearing through her mizzen rigging.

Kobb yelled up at them from the quarterdeck. "Cough it ladies! Give us more puff!"

Minni helped Amber to her feet, glaring at Kobb. "Make up your mind. You just told her to slow down."

Kobb ignored her, shouting at his bosun. "Get another lateen up!"

Amber was enjoying herself. Even under fire her magic flowed, directing the wind and water to speed *Bone Dancer* ahead of her pursuers. It was a fine game. She was a child playing with a new toy at season's end. She sung and giggled, weaving the elements to her whim. Ample gusts of wind filled their sails and tiny water creations leapt out of her buckets and into the sea. Once overboard they swam toward the pursuing Jandan ships, growing as they went, magnified in the open water. Dolphins and sharks, monstrous fish and sea serpents made from water and magic harried the Jandans. They leapt onto the ships causing havoc, their life only as long as Amber's own entertainment saw fit. She laughed and played, experimenting with strange and ridiculous shapes. Amber favoured the comic relief of cows leaping onto their decks, though they didn't last very long before she disintegrated into fits of mirth.

The redeemer on board the leading ship showed himself on the forecastle. His white robes billowed around him like angry clouds. His acolyte set down a cage of unsettled doves and the redeemer cast a spell, waving his arms in strange patterns. The cage shimmered and the birds churned in a craze of feathers, their energy funnelling to the redeemer.

Minni nocked an arrow. "Amber! Get down!" The arrow loosed, falling short of the redeemer. Out of range.

A bolt of energy shot from the redeemer's palm. It seared through the air, white and blue lightning twisting around itself in a lance of destruction. Amber dove flat on the deck and the bolt crackled past where she had been standing, tearing through the new lateen sail, setting it aflame and blasting splinters off the mizzenmast.

Kobb yelled orders, a man screamed in pain. Minni sharpened her attention on the redeemer. She knocked another arrow, knowing it would likely miss. It was all she could do. She drew back and aimed high, praying for the Welcome Stranger to bring her luck.

Amber cupped her hand in one of her water pails and ran to Minni. She dripped the water over the broadhead and it hugged the steel like a bubble of glue. Amber pointed to the sea, then at the redeemer, her mouth set firm, an eerie tune curling from the back of her throat. Minni released just as a second bolt of lightning sizzled from the redeemer's hands, careening towards them. The arrow plunged into the water then Amber raised her fist and the enchanted missile emerged faster than when it was shot, surrounded by a vortex of water. She thrust her palm forward and the water arrow streaked into the bolt of lightning absorbing its energy. With a shout the young elementalist cast the deadly missile into the redeemer's chest, blasting him open and knocking him off the forecastle.

બ∘ન

Far beneath Elrin, Obst and Wyggen emerged from the tunnel in the caldera cliff face. Wyggen's enormous wings fanned out, lifting in a thermal without a single beat. His lazy circles above the caldera darkened Kobbton in shadow. Obst had no wings and yet she flew through the air, weaving in and out of the sea. Her long serpent body was an aquamarine ribbon, flowing along the junction of water and air. Her sturdy limbs were needles stitching the elements together. She patrolled the sea around the caldera then retired to the caldera wall, draping herself across the mountainside, guarding the entrance.

Tetula and Qarim banked out of their thermal at a dizzying height and flew toward Kobb's ships fleeing through the channels. White smoke drifted in the wake of the chase. The crash of cannon fire split into the sky, distant and violent, spoiling the peace of the altitude like a smith in a temple.

Elrin shouted into the wind. "We have to protect the last of the fleeing ships!" His words were consumed by the wind and the dragon's wings carving through the air.

Tetula's voice resonated in his head. "Use your thoughts, young one. I am listening, but keep it clear."

Elrin closed his eyes and pronounced his mind, imagining the words radiating through the air. "We have to help those fleeing ships."

"Why help them? They are pirates. I can destroy both."

"No! My friends might be on those ships." Elrin thought of Amber and hoped Minni and Tikis were there to protect her. They were seasoned in battle, but Amber was just a child trapped in this mess. She had to be rescued.

"An innocent?"

"How did you know?"

"Your thoughts are clear, if not concise."

Tetula stretched her long neck to Qarim, flying at her side. They exchanged a euphonious song of high-pitched whistles and clicks. Qarim lifted his long spiny neck and Tetula returned the gesture. A mental flash of Tetula attacking the ships below accompanied her words.

"Ready yourself."

Qarim dipped his graceful neck and tucked in his wings like a falcon. Delik screamed as they dropped from the sky, shooting down like a falling star toward the armada advancing up the western flank. Tetula dove a moment later, her angle so steep, Elrin clutched her body close for fear the wind streaking by would tear him off her back. The wind sang chaos in his ears and whipped at his skin. Elrin held on with white knuckles, sure they would crash into the sea. A rumble grew deep in Tetula's chest as she extended her wings, pulling from the dive at the last moment. Her body dipped, skimming her claws into the sea before rising again and spewing flames over the Jandan ships.

Searing hot air coursed by. The silver dragon beat her wings to gain some altitude then circled back to survey the damage. Two leading ships were floating pyres, those behind wheeled hard, confronted with either running aground in the narrow channel, or colliding with the flaming ships.

A bolt of lightning shot towards Tetula from a frigate sailing up the other side of the island. She banked hard and it sizzled past them. Another bolt followed from a different vessel below and the dragon dove toward the closer enemy, twisting away at the last moment and setting it afire. A volley of arrows arced across from the ship behind and a swivel-mounted cannon blasted. Shot thudded into Tetula's chest. She reared up and roared, buffeting the vessel with a gale that knocked the crew off their feet.

☙❧

Qarim and Delik streamed over the western fleet. The dragon hung his head low and breathed noxious gas over them then pulled up and around, avoiding the volleys of bolts and arrows. Delik's amulet glowed as Qarim cast chaos upon the Jandans. Illusory kraken emerged from the ocean, wrapping their tentacles about the vessels and sending men overboard, fighting each other to get away. Cannons opened fire in a wild effort to blast the sea monsters back into the depths, but the shots went straight through the illusions and into the neighbouring ships, inflicting extensive damage to the fleet.

Qarim circled, bending the magic of the weave to his will. Water beaded on Delik's skin and thick storm clouds built around them. It was cold inside the clouds. The glow from his amulet pulsed and his hair stood on end. A crack of lightning struck down, splitting through a mast and setting the sails aflame. Strike after strike carved through the western fleet. Damaged ships limped south in retreat while others advanced north, trying to escape Qarim's storm. The remainder fought on, battling the monstrous illusions and themselves.

The pirate fleet laying in wait saw its chance and pounced, speeding down from the north to take advantage of the divided Jandan fleet. The Jandans formed up, broadsiding the pirates' advance. Shot tore across the pirate fleet and white smoke swirled from the spitting cannons. The pirates pushed forward even faster, aided by weather witches in a race to beat the second volley. *Juniper* led the charge, beating the guns and boarding the closest galleon.

Qarim blasted lightning into a pirate galley, knocking its mast into the sea. Their mission was to eliminate both pirates and the armada, but guilt gnawed at Delik's bones. He remembered Elrin staying his hand back in Rum Hill, sparing the Jandan marines from the ungodly black powder and shot. How was this any different?

Qarim penetrated his mind. "I feel your doubts condense."

"It doesn't seem fair. You could obliterate them all."

"Yes."

"They have families waiting in the Caldera."

"And the others, do they not have families too? What difference is there?"

"They come to kill ... They would have us all dead or enslaved, the rebels, the pirates, you. The pirates are thieves and opportunists. They're a mixed bag, but they don't want us dead, they don't want you dead. They're defending their home."

"What would you have us do?"

"Help the pirates, they have shown you no harm and left your hoard untouched. I cannot condemn them for a promise Kobb has not yet broken."

"I am glad you have come to that conclusion. Yet again we find something in common."

Down in the island channels Tetula sent a thunderous roar bleeding into the sky.

↪↩

Bone Dancer's crew whooped and whistled, watching the silver dragon breathe death upon their pursuers. Minni watched on in awe. It had to be the biggest silver ever spotted, swooping and diving with a grace and power unbelievable for its size. As the ancient wyrm dodged a redeemer's lightning bolt, it twisted around revealing a human rider.

Minni gasped and the pit of her stomach sank in a tumble of elation and fear.

Amber grabbed Minni's arm and pointed, eyes wide with excitement.

"I saw too! It's Elrin. He did it!"

Kobb seized the crew's boost in morale to press ahead. "Right boys! Let's see the *Dancer* clear. It's time for the rebels to take some heat."

Amber summoned a steady wind with her magical song and the crew set to work making the most of it. The Jandan ships kept coming, faster than before, motivated more by fear of the dragon than the thrill of the chase.

Menacing storm clouds gathered to the west and the silhouette of another dragon appeared in the clouds while lightning struck out with unnatural abandon. Elrin and his dragon swooped through a barrage of arrows and vehement bursts of magic, flying over the islands to engage the ships sailing the other channels.

Minni lost sight of them for a moment. A cannon fired, followed by a roar loud enough to curdle the clouds. Silver wings appeared over the island and a second cannon blasted. The dragon ripped the air with a terrible scream. A bright flash scalded the daylight white. The dragon lifted above the island and swooped away beating hard through the sky.

Minni ran to the rail squinting through the sun, trying to see if Elrin was still safe atop the dragon. She couldn't spot him through the glare of the silver scales. The dragon flew in a wide circle and came straight at them.

The Jandan ships that followed *Bone Dancer* shot arrows up at the dragon as it passed overhead. Several green bolts of energy shot out and hit. The dragon ignored them, staying on course. Minni grabbed Amber and pulled her to the side. The dragon landed on the stern, its enormous claws digging into the aft castle, its tail dragging in the water. The impact lifted the bow high, knocking the pirates off their feet. The dragon brought its violently regal head level with Minni, inspecting her with eyes as silver as her scales. Amber clung to Minni's side.

Elrin extended his hand. "Climb up. She won't hurt you."

"Are you sure?"

"Quick, take my hand."

Minni helped Amber up behind Elrin before climbing on herself. The dragon leapt into the air, rocking *Bone Dancer* with a violent heave. The ship's mangled stern was left like a giant dog had gnawed on it.

"Where's Tikis?" called Elrin.

"On the big island just to the north," she shouted back. "Did the others make it?"

"Jaspa and Hurn are guarding the sanctuary." Elrin pointed to the storm. "Delik's in there."

"Daft bastard!"

They were supposed to summon them not ride them. Give her a horse any day. Something you could control. Not something that would eat the rider if it got hungry. At least she had a nice view; there were worse places to be killed. Minni resigned herself to the short flight, making the most of her vantage point to survey the battle below.

With no opposition, the armada's eastern flank had sped through the open sea, advancing ahead of the pirate ships in the channels. The fleet escorted four barges, each armed with ballista. The armada was set to rout Kobb's retreat; those barges would barricade them in. *Bone Dancer* wouldn't make it out without Amber. Minni had a soft spot for the long shot and harboured a secret hope the pirates might have destroyed the armada on their own. She knew the pirates had to be restrained though. Kobb couldn't be trusted to govern the sea. Even if he could, his power over the other pirate captains was limited. They'd be trading slaves again and preying on merchant traders unchecked.

The dragon landed on a mountain of treasure, her chest heaving.

Minni swung down and helped Amber off.

"Get her to safety," said Elrin.

"What? You're not coming?"

"We battle together."

Could he hear himself? "Don't be a hero, Elrin. You're no warrior."

Elrin flinched, stung by her thoughtless words. "What am I then?" My key, my heart alight. "I don't know." I don't want you to die. "I don't know either. I won't know until I find my father." "You're not going to find him up there." "They know him. They're going to help me. So I will help them." "What use are you up there? You'll just get yourself killed." "I have my honour, I have to do this." Honour be damned.

❧❦

Elrin couldn't leave Tetula to battle alone and expect her to help find his father after. Besides, how could he pass up the opportunity to take to battle riding on a dragon? Minni should be happy for him, but she was angry. One minute she stole a kiss and the next she knocked him down. How could he lose her favour so fast?

Tetula reached into his mind. "Love is complicated. It has no place in battle."

"I've disappointed her."

"Then let us impress her."

Tetula leapt from the mountain of treasure and beat her way into the sky. She circled back over the archipelago to harry the Jandan ships pursuing the pirate retreat. The weave tingled over his skin as Tetula incanted a long verse. An orb of frosty blue energy formed between her claws and shot bolts of ice upon the Jandans, ripping through sails, piercing hulls and tearing through soldier and sailor alike.

Ships from the unhindered eastern fleet branched off into the channels to intercept Kobb's retreat. The hidden cannon batteries there opened fire, splitting the air with hellish blasts and clouding their positions in gun smoke. The bulk of the eastern fleet slowed and formed up in the open sea near the caldera. The site of Wyggen circling overhead and Obst guarding the sanctuary gave the Jandans enough pause for Kobb's retreat to emerge from the channels and turn on their pursuers.

The eastern fleet advanced to break the attack, but it was too late.

In a deafening rage the rebel positions opened fire from the islands, ripping through the Jandans with treasure shot in blast after blast. The pursuing ships were already stretched thin in the pursuit and worn down by Tetula's fire and ice.

The Jandans fought back with every cannon they had. Gun smoke hung a shroud over them, the rebel ambush was inescapable, but they did not give in. They fired with disciplined rhythm while the rebels peppered them from the cover of the islands. The standoff would only last as long as the black powder did.

Tetula rested her assault, arcing around in an easy circle. She watched Qarim attacking remnants of the armada's western force and Elrin sensed the edges of Tetula's thoughts, flowing with a heady mix of tender warmth and simmering excitement. She called out a vigorous song of trills and rising notes, so enamoured of her mate she didn't notice the two dragons flying toward them from the sanctuary.

Elrin called with his mind. "Tetula! The others have left their vigil. They've come to help."

Tetula cut short her song and strove to gain altitude.

Zarkas and Goranuk flew low over the armada's eastern force. Elrin was expecting them to attack, but they didn't. A cone of energy snaked up from one of the barges and the black shadow and red hulk rode the shimmering pulse in a tight spiral.

Tetula laboured on, breathing hard, while Zarkas and Goranuk were buoyed on the magical thermal. As they rose higher and higher, Tetula's fear sunk into his mind. She couldn't match them in height or speed and shrieked her frustration.

Qarim heard her call and sped towards them to help.

It was not fast enough. The two dragons dove from the sky. Zarkas was a jet black bolt, screaming toward Tetula. He phased in and out of view as he dove, appearing in a different position with each blink. Goranuk was rust-red fury, bleeding through the sky to intercept Qarim.

Tetula cast bolts of blue lightning searing through the weave toward Zarkas, but the black dragon blinked in and out of sight, dodging each one.

Tetula's mind screamed. "Why?"

Zarkas closed in, belching a jet of acid at them. Tetula reared up shielding Elrin from the worst of the attack, taking the brunt across her exposed chest. The caustic splash licked at the soles of his feet and he screamed in agony. Then Zarkas was upon them, crashing into Tetula with his hind legs extended, raking her belly. The impact sent both dragons tumbling off balance.

Elrin lost his seating as they spun through the air, his legs trailed behind him, but he kept his grip on Tetula's bristly mane. Tetula regained her balance and Elrin slammed into her neck. Blocking the pain of the impact, he slung his legs around her again and gripped with his knees, determined not to lose his seat again.

Tetula headed for the sanctuary, beating her wings with a ferocious drive. Zarkas followed, herding them toward the armada.

The barges had come alongside each other, making a giant platform. Eight ballistae loaded with cruel harpoons lined the sides and a large red circle dominated the centre of the expanded deck.

Elrin tugged on Tetula's mane. "It's a trap. Don't go near that fleet."

Tetula screamed for help. Qarim was locked in battle with Goranuk, her relentless attacks holding him back. Wyggen and Obst broke their positions to intervene. Wyggen flew to the aid of Tetula and Obst dipped and weaved toward Qarim.

Tetula screamed again, reaching her mind out to warn Wyggen. The soaring feathered giant dipped his wing and altered course, but it was too late. Harpoons shot through the air like stingers on a jellyfish, rope trailing behind them. Two lanced into Wyggen and pulled taught. He struggled, straining against the line, shrieking. More harpoons connected and he plummeted from the sky, coursing fire and torching three ships before he hit the water, thrashing against his captors.

Tetula veered away from the barges. It was all that Zarkas needed to catch up with her. He clamped his jaw around her tail and pulled. Elrin clung on while the two dragons clawed and bit at each other, spinning down in their death grip. Elrin drew his dagger and stabbed Zarkas's grip around Tetula's throat.

Qarim flew towards them, limping through the air. Behind him Obst wrestled in the sea with Goranuk, keeping her back.

Elrin's ears split with Tetula's last scream. Her body tensed in an explosion of arcane power.

And with that the young man was thrown from her back and into a void of darkness.

DISCORD

The vile corruption was hauled onto the barge and into the red circle, limp and leadened by the blessed serum coating the harpoons. Gone was its glory, its challenge in the face of the creator. The dragon was a pathetic mess of blood and scale with broken wings and slack maw. Their kind would no longer terrorise the Lord's chosen. They would no longer wield his power as gods themselves. They would remember their place and pledge fealty to the Lord.

Uighara pulled a feather from the dragon's shoulder and a vial from his backpack. He circled the dragon, dipping the feather in the vial and flicking the potion on the unconscious terror as he went. Four redeemers took their positions on the sigils marked around the perimeter and sung a redemption in unison. The holy song thrummed with power stronger than any redeemer alone could muster. The deck vibrated with the force of the sins being extracted from the slaves below. Screams and moans of pleasure and pain intermingled, a hundred sinners and a thousand sins purged before the might of the Good Lord.

Uighara stood upon the monstrous head of the dragon. He marked the four points of the black star on himself and sung the song of blessed redemption, syncopated to his Brothers' harmony.

Energy surged from the four redeemers and flowed into Uighara, filling his soul with holy bliss. The redeemers diligently maintained their song of redemption, writhing in the contortions of their own sins stripped bare before the light of the Lord.

Uighara channelled the energy into his spell, warping the physical laws to the will of the almighty. The Lord's hand raised the dragon as he balanced on its head. Together they floated up like a feather in the breeze; redeemed souls to the heavens.

The Good Lord would have his throne returned.

⤞⤝

Pelegrin didn't cheer with his crew as the great beast was brought down and hauled in. He was occupied enough counting the cost to the armada. Uighara's plan had worked perfectly, the High Priest would doubtless be pleased, as would the Lord, but his father would not. His central force was trapped in the channels, under siege from the islands. Pelegrin had sent nine of his best frigates to break the pirates strangle hold on the northern channels, keeping the rest of the eastern fleet on guard until the redeemers finished the Lord's work on the captured dragon. The central force could hold out as long as they rationed their magazines.

The brawny red dragon and the agile black were making short work of the evil ones protecting the outlaws. He'd heard stories of benevolent dragons of course, but had never believed them to be more than children's tales, until now. After an ear-splitting explosion of magic, the valiant jet-black fury brought the frightful silver wyrm crashing down amongst the islands then fought a courageous retreat from the thorny purple and gold monster loping across the sky. The glossy red wrestled an immense serpent, churning the sea to a boiling soup, hot with dragon flames and thrashing violence.

While Uighara believed these benevolent dragons were guardians of the Lord, and Pelegrin was grateful for their aid, he observed their presence in the battle with a lingering nervousness, an anxious brew of natural fear and awe. The sooner he had Kobb and the Scrambletoes in chains the better.

"Any signal from the western contingent?"

The solargrapher watched the redeemers taking their positions around the fallen dragon on the barge, oblivious to Pelegrin's question.

Pelegrin clipped his ear. "Pay attention! Anyone would think you've never seen a dragon."

"Not like these, sir."

"Signal the western force again, as before."

"Yes, sir."

There was no need.

The lookout called down from the nest. "Sails!"

Pelegrin held his spyglass to the west. The ships might have raised false flags, but he knew those figureheads. The pirate fleet sailed toward them, led by *Juniper, Templestone* and *Fearless*.

"Bastards!"

He couldn't mount an attack and leave the redeemers vulnerable now they had started their rites. The holy chanting charged the air with power. The barges wailed and groaned like an old ship in a tempest. Uighara radiated power, floating the massive dragon into the air as if it was weightless. Pelegrin squinted, preparing for a magical flash or a clap of power, something that would zap them away, back to the High Temple. Then he would be free to press the attack.

There was no magical climax. Uighara and the dragon remained. The screams from the slaves died down and the four redeemers fell to their knees. The spell must have failed. The Lord had retracted his blessing.

The great black dragon swooped in, blistering the Saint Jan from stern to bow with an acidic torrent of destruction. Pelegrin rolled aside, dodging the noxious attack. He tore off his blue jacket as a spatter of green liquid sizzled and smoked toward his skin. The beast swept back over and attacked again; ships all around burned in a caustic panic.

"Man the ballista!"

None of his men were listening. His solargrapher was a wet bubbling mess on the deck. Chaos ruled his command. Some men screamed, half melted, others stood in puddles of their own fear, but most were jumping overboard.

The black came about in a tight circle and scooped up the levitating dragon and Uighara, stealing off to the southwest. The red dragon beat its way out of the sea like a giant water fowl and flew after the black, scorching a flaming path through any ships in its way.

The armada had no more than fifteen ships that could sail. Most of his force was dead in the water, including *Saint Jan*. Pelegrin gripped the rail, watching his defeat approach. He had been so sure. He was the Lord's chosen, glory bound to follow his will. Was this the Lord's will? Was he cursed to failure at the hands of these reprobates?

Pelegrin had shamed his father. He was warned, but Uighara had seduced him with false promises. How long had he been led on? He was just a pawn in the Council's politics, the High Priest and his father wrestling for power. Uighara was always the High Priest's man. Together they had orchestrated his failure and in turn his father's, stripping the Lord's High Admiral of his power over the Council, reducing his armada to a pittance.

At the same time they had taken an ancient dragon as sacrifice and secured two more to defend Jando like the Calimska of old. The High Priest was a cunning bastard. He would be a saint before the new moon rose. His father would be on the street begging bone, Lord's High Admiral no longer.

Pelegrin was not going to let that happen. This battle could not be won, but the next would be different. He would expose the High Priest and Uighara for what they were; conspirators against the Lord's will, treasonous filth to be purged from Jando.

He pried the solargraph from the officer's dead hand and savouring the thought of revenge, he signalled a full retreat.

❧❧

Embedded in trenches of treasure while cannon balls screamed overhead, Minni called a squad of rebels to account. "Ease it back! Don't match them shot for shot."

A lump of a man with a crooked eye chuckled, coating his retort with blood hungry arrogance. "We've enough treasure shot here to fire till next season. What's your gripe? Leave off and let us men take care of it." This was no man she knew, a fresh recruit; no doubt unaware of how close he was to a busted lip. The squad leader was quick to smack him upside his bald head.

Minni gave the leader a scowl. "Keep your team in line. There's no more powder to go around. Ration back your fire; count three of theirs to one of ours. We still need a reserve if they take to the shore."

"Aye, commander," replied the squad leader, prodding the man who spoke out of turn.

"Aye, apologies, ma'am…I didn't realise you were…"

"Well, now you do. Seeing you have such a way with words, run my message down the line."

The nugget of a man gulped. "How far?"

"Till you reach the last cannon. Make sure you speak kindly to the drakkin now, won't you."

With a crouching run, Minni returned to her own elite squad of archers. Amber had used her powers to manipulate and fuse the mounds of treasure into a rough crenelated fort, allowing the marksmen to harry at the trapped Jandan ships in relative safety. The out of place structure had become a favoured target, though with every shot that pounded the glittering fort, Amber was quick to plaster on another layer of precious metals to repair the damage.

Plumes of white smoke blew across the field of battle, rising from the trenches like undead mist and wafting around the war ships like steam from hot springs, bubbling up from the underworld. Neither side had a perfect view of the enemy, but by now the Jandans knew the positions of the rebel cannons and their own ships were dead in the water, sails shredded and hanging like unkempt weeds on tombstones.

The death-drum beat of rebel cannons slowed as her order made its way down the length of the island. The rigidly timed Jandan broadsides didn't falter until high above the clouds of smoke came a warping clap of power that put lightning to shame, shaking the very treasure under their feet. A broken star plummeted through the white, a silver giant torn from the sky. The once thunderous dragon ploughed into the enemy, splitting a galleon in two with its tail and sending up a great wave that washed the Jandan ships upon the golden shore.

Minni's stomach rose up and battered her heart like the surge that broke against the bejewelled fort. "Elrin!" she screamed, vaulting over the battlements and landing hard. Again she screamed as she ran to the limp silver behemoth, chasing the receding wave. She called Elrin's name until there was no breath left for it.

The silver dragon was a knotted twist of mangled wings and buckled limbs; her hindquarters lolling in the water while the rest of her body lay upon the hoard. Elrin was not astride her back or by her side. He must have landed in the water and swam to safety. Determined to find him, Minni turned to scour the shore, but found herself stuck in the middle of the battlefield, crowded with combatants.

Her screaming charge across the battlefield had inspired the rebels to follow. They hurtled down the golden dunes, brandishing weapons like beacons of freedom, war cries swirling up into the heavens. The Jandan forces poured out of their washed up ships to meet the stampede in a final stand. Their cannons were of no use now, only crooked black fingers pointing at the beach with impotent accusation.

Arrows flew from her archers in the fort, glowing arcs charged with Amber's creative magic. They burst above the Jandan units with deafening pops and screamed with shrill intensity where they landed, eroding the soldiers' discipline to maintain formation. Minni took up with a team of rebels in a maddened boil, throwing herself into the killing, her twin daggers painting red riot across each opponent.

A bare-chested man emerged from the shattered corpse of the sinking galleon, levitating to shore with a cleaver in hand and hundreds of bones piercing his flesh like a horned demon. A reaper; a brutal redeemer conditioned for fighting the Lord's wars. He hacked down one of his own men from behind and poached the ripe soul, wrenching it from the dying soldier's lips. The gold coins around the sacrifice rattled at the violent extraction and scattered like ripples on a pond as the reaper cast a fireball at Amber's fortress. The young elementalist intercepted the spell with a small ball of treasure, but the collision exploded molten metal across the field, searing unfortunate combatants on both sides and curdling the air with screams. The reaper claimed another sacrifice, then another, casting and killing, carving a path up the shore to the fort, wanting only Amber.

Minni retreated from the front line, drawing her bow and taking several shots at the determined poacher. The archers in fort concentrated their fire on him too, but each arrow burned to cinders as it reached the target. With every victim he claimed, the reaper grew in strength and the treasure at his feet became more agitated. He had to be stopped and she would be his assassin.

Casting her bow aside, Minni sprung into a full sprint, her stilettos nestling into her hungry grip. She came around and attacked from behind, intent on the death of the vile leech. A single stride was all that stood between them when her momentum vanished. Gold and silver tentacles, a fusion of coins and jewellery entwined with magic, wrapped around her, tying her arms to her side and rooting her legs in place.

The reaper turned on her, his face shimmering and warping with stolen power, bristling with bones and claws that stitched a graveyard over his pale skin. "Such a treat that comes rushing to be redeemed." The reaper's hot hand came upon her cheek. She recoiled, but he grabbed her jaw, forcing her to face him while the battle raged. "Your eyes are familiar … those lips, just so."

He leaned in, pulling a callous kiss that hurled barbs to the pit of her stomach. Minni spat in his face, furious tears brimming over. "Coward! Free me and die like the dog you are."

An elongated tongue probed the spittle on his face. "Mmm, yes. Just so. My sweet little Miss Ajharra. You've grown sweeter. Sweeter even than your delicious mother."

Minni spat at him again. It was all she could do.

The reaper wiped his leering face while arrows flamed out harmlessly around them. "Do you not recognise me? I brought you candies."

She didn't. Why would she want any of their faces as keepsakes? They'd weigh her to the bottom of the Salroc Sea. Minni wanted to goad the reaper, but knew once her life was taken, such a man would go on for Amber. She had to stall him long enough for the girl to get to safety. "You all brought sweets," she said, in mock interest. "Which ones did you bring?"

The man's eyes lit up with the change in his captive's attitude. "The triple stripe drops. They were your favourite."

Behind the reaper a grand boulder of treasure rolled toward them, gathering speed and layering a fortune upon itself. Amber ran behind it, her hands outstretched, controlling the monolithic orb. Minni averted her gaze to the left, not wanting to give away the twisted perversion's approaching doom, but there came Tikis and a band of drakkin, carving their way through the enemy to her aid. The reaper noted a change in her expression and followed her stare to the warriors.

A smile ossified around the bones penetrating his cheeks and he swelled with magical power, drawing it up from the dead and dying. "I'll keep you safe, Little Miss. I'll take you home to Jando." The surface of the hoard underfoot quivered in anticipation, spreading outwards with anxious fervour, snagging the essence of combatants and sapping their strength, dropping them to their knees. The reaper was intoxicated with the power, arms wide, delirious appetite demanding ever more. The treasure channelled his desire, arcing pulses of energy into his swelling, radiant body from a battlefield of sacrifice. "Such power! I see the Lord's throne anew!" The reaper pointed to the sky with a maniacal laugh and bolts of lightning struck down, jolting around his body and setting the bone piercings aflame.

The drakkin unit hesitated, but Tikis muscled forth. The reaper levelled his charred finger at Tikis and cast a blistering crackle of energy. The drakkin warrior dove to the side and rolled as the spell sizzled past him, electrifying a chain of combatants before dissipating.

Amber's rolling mass of treasure sped toward Minni and the reaper. The young elementalist no longer ran, but skimmed across the hoard on a cushion of air. Tikis kept on barrelling forward, pumping his legs like a bull. The reaper raised his finger and sneered. The drakkin would not dodge another bolt at such close range.

The rolling ball of treasure loomed into the reaper's line of sight, rousing a moment's confusion. He loosed the next bolt of energy at the ball and treasure exploded where it hit, but the ball swallowed the magical force and kept coming. The distraction was all Tikis needed to close the gap and leap through the air. The reaper turned to attack the drakkin too late. Tikis ploughed into Minni, bending the bonds of gold and silver as he tackled her to the ground, swamping her beneath his huge frame.

With a sickening crush, the ball consumed the reaper. His hands poured forth energy to slow it, to repel it, but Amber's creation absorbed the magic like a sponge and rolled on, mashing the Jandan to death with no regard to slow its journey to the water. There it steamed and churned the sea before collapsing upon itself.

Minni squirmed under the drakkin. "All right, you've had your fun. Off!"

Huffing like a pair of bellows, Tikis got up and inspected his tail, his lips retracted, baring razor teeth in pain. The tip was crushed in a kink. "A happy memory," he shucked a tight breath and helped Minni up.

Amber ran to them and embraced Minni in the biggest bear hug her scrawny arms could manage. The battle in the channels was all but over with only a few pockets of fighting to the south. The rebels had the enemy boxed up and when the Jandan horns of retreat blew across the sea, they knew they had won the day. A roar of voices shook the sky and the remaining Jandans yielded.

It was no victory Minni could celebrate. She busied herself along the shoreline, looking for any sign of Elrin. The horizon was a ragged stage with jagged masts and tattered sails. Ships listed and flotsam swayed with cold bodies in the sea's slow dance. Waves lapped the shore in a gentle rhythm while gulls gorged on war's fortune, singing their joy with sharp clarion calls. All Minni found was the silent knowing of the dead and the jubilant victory of the living.

Neither gave her comfort.

THE PLAN

Minni hated the prophecies.

They always bloomed. Their truth was at once abstract and precise. Unbelievable and unfathomable when told, confusing and contradictory as events came to pass, and for her, their fruit was ever more bitter than sweet.

For the others, things were not so bad. The dragon they called Wyggen had left Hurn atop the Caldera wall before flying to his doom. Obst had done the same before battling the muscle bound red savage, saving Jaspa from a lung full of water. They had watched the whole battle from the safest seats in the theatre. She had put her life on the line in the final battle and recklessly endangered Amber and Tikis with her impulsive charge. Even then, they all survived.

All but Elrin.

He had fallen in her hand; a gift of fate, the key to their victory, the key to the choir. He had trusted her as she led him to his death. He would never find his father, because she had let him fall. He had fallen into the rebellion, into her heart, and into the sea.

For all the ships and all the eyes on the water, no one had found his body. She had looked in the dead eyes of hundreds of bodies on the beach, even sailed out in a skiff with Delik, searching the channels and the open water in case he had drifted.

Nothing.

She begged Qarim to help by searching from the sky, but the great gold dragon would not budge from his love's side. Tetula was dead. Minni had been overcome with the mourning dragon's pain. Tears had poured down her cheeks and fallen on the beach of gold and silver. She should never have left Elrin's side.

Obst was no help. She claimed the sea did not speak his name. Minni had laughed at that; the gods enjoyed such heartless irony. Delik told her not to blame herself. Jaspa told her she would feel better in time. Time would heal. They both knew the pain of love lost and while their words may have been true, Kobb was the only one who gave her true comfort. He told her time might dry the tears and time might scar the wound, but the hurt would forever remain beneath the surface. She would never heal.

Kobb had proved more than fair to his word after the battle was won. He could have turned on the rebels, slaved them off or marched them into the sea. After all, he had the numbers and the means. Instead, he and Jaspa divided between them an equal share of prize ships and cargo then opened up their ranks for any man or woman who wished a new life at sea or on land. Kobb released every former slave and Jandan prisoner, and offered them the same.

Minni considered crewing with Kobb aboard *Bone Dancer*. She would have a better chance of forgetting Elrin at sea, but there were too many counting on her and too many other debts to pay. So Minni found herself on *Juniper* with her companions, leaving the Hoard Islands and her heart behind.

The rag tag convoy of ships limped through the Salroc Sea heading for the coast and safe harbour. Jaspa called his generals into the captain's quarters. There was much to arrange. They had taken charge of many hungry bellies and the season was almost upon them. Obst warned it would be dire with the Choir broken.

Jaspa popped the top off a large cylinder and removed a scroll, spreading it across the table. A Jandan map depicted the coast with precise red and black ink.

"Right then," said Delik, tapping his finger on the city of Calimska. "Here's the plan ..."

Minni shrunk away, holding in the swelling sob that rose in her throat. Her weakness made her angry. She walked to the dresser, where Elrin had changed into the Jandan officer's uniform. He had been so shy; she had laughed, turning away while he got changed. The awkward Calimskan had taken so long she had peeked just to satisfy her curiosity. He was so out of place, a handsome shiner blushing in the blue. She'd helped him with his hat, tucking in the restless raven hair to hide his obvious heritage. He had smelled of sandalwood and cloves.

Opening the drawer, Minni found Elrin's satchel and inside, folded in a neat square, was his vest. She lifted it to her face and inhaled. A note dropped out, falling on the dresser. It was wrapped in string with a black wax seal, devoid of any initial or insignia. Desperate for answers, she broke the wax and read.

Herik,

The shankakin do not fare well. The increased schedule you have set is taking an awful toll. The workers delivered last moon started strong and healthy. Now they are half in number and half again are already afflicted by the lung blight. The shankakin take worse to it than the others. They are not suitable for work underground.

Have you considered the measures I outlined in our last meeting? Improving the conditions of work has the twin benefits of improved production and decreasing input costs.

Surely this is a good thing for all concerned.

Yours,

Kleith

Minni read it over again, finding it hard to believe what Elrin had carried all along. This was the note the prophecy spoke of, not the dead letter. It held the truth of what was going on between the City of Gold and the City of Bones. She was sure of it. What were the Calimskan's doing with shankakin underground? Mining? Why not employ dwarves to do it? Calimska had the wealth to pay them and they would do a better job than any shankakin. Surely that was a better arrangement than trading with their rival, Jando.

The message was from Kleith. This had to be the same Herder Kleith that Elrin had spoken of, but he was Elrin's mentor who had dressed the fleeing Calimskan as a collector and sent him to find the Dragon Choir. Kleith had known about the Choir and thought they would help. Why would he be involved with this awful business, drafting Elrin to ferry the clandestine messages? And who was Herik? The Guildmaster? Why would the great Golden Shield be using shankakin slaves? What had any of this to do with Elrin's father? Was all of this for black powder? It made no sense.

With slow strides, Minni returned to the table, watching her companions argue about the politics of Calimskan guild hierarchy. Seeing her return, they quietened, pity diluting their passionate discussion. Where once they looked upon her with respect, now flaccid condolence overshadowed every conversation. No one dared say Elrin was dead, but every expression was a silent eulogy. This had to end.

She read the secret missive aloud, translating every neatly written word with a cold coherence that froze her grief. Once finished, she slapped Elrin's note onto the map, knocking the markers they had placed around Calimska.

"When I find this, Herik, I'm going to see him stripped to ash."

ABOUT THE AUTHOR

Benjamin Descovich is the founder of ethicalwriter.com and works everyday writing the seeds to grow a better future. He is a passionate environmentalist, social justice advocate and holds a degree in Political Science. As an Australian living and working in Scotland, he has been spoilt with inspiration for his fiction. Dramatic landscapes, political intrigue and epic battles will keep you turning the pages while the dragons and magic take your breath away.

The adventure continues in . . .

Blood Monsoon

Gold to the grave, for the season has come.
Buckle your bandoliers and bracers;
Prepare for the Blood Monsoon.

Available 2015

Until then…
Sign up for my free newsletter
& get a free ebook!

Come on in and discover the secrets of the Dragon Choir.

Visit my website:
www.benjamindescovich.com

Follow the Dragon Choir fan page:
www.facebook.com/dragonchoir

Hire me to write for you:
www.ethicalwriter.com

Drop me a line:
info@benjamindescovich.com

10271351R00137

Printed in Great Britain
by Amazon.co.uk, Ltd.,
Marston Gate.